ACCLAIM FOR Arturo Pérez-Reverte's
The Club Dumas

"Pérez-Reverte has . . . improved on the detective story, taking the often predictable formula and convoluting it with delicious material about eclectic aspects of the literary world." —*Los Angeles Times*

"The action parallels the design of 19th-century serial-adventures such as *The Three Musketeers*, in which crisis after crisis explodes like a string of firecrackers. *The Club Dumas* rises above the level of the formulaic thriller." —*Boston Globe*

"Mystery addicts who believe that the genre has certain rules of fair play will be infuriated by Mr. Pérez-Reverte's gothic eccentricities. Readers with a taste for Dumas and demonology will enjoy his devious inventions." —*Atlantic Monthly*

"Among the pleasures of *The Club Dumas* is the intimate sense it conveys of this highly specialized type of commerce. . . . An intelligent and delightful novel." —Margot Livesey, *The New York Times Book Review*

"Suspense-filled and ingenious . . . a witty meditation on the relationship between book lovers and the texts they adore." —*Publishers Weekly*

Arturo Pérez-Reverte

The Club Dumas

Arturo Pérez-Reverte was born in 1951 in
Cartagena. He is a television journalist who
has reported on some of the world's most
dangerous crises. He is the author of two
previous books, *The Fencing Master* and
The Flanders Panel.

VINTAGE

INTERNATIONAL

The Club Dumas

The Club Dumas

A Novel

Arturo Pérez-Reverte

Translated from the Spanish by
Sonia Soto

Vintage International
Vintage Books
A Division of Random House, Inc.
New York

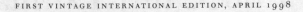

FIRST VINTAGE INTERNATIONAL EDITION, APRIL 1998

English translation copyright © 1996 by Sonia Soto

Pérez-Reverte, Arturo.

[Club Dumas. English]

The Club Dumas / Arturo Pérez-Reverte ; translated from the Spanish by Sonia Soto.

p.   cm.

ISBN 0-679-77754-7

I. Soto, Sonia. II. Title.

PQ6666.E765C5813   1998

863'.64—dc21   97-50179

CIP

Author photograph © Jerry Bauer

Random House Web address: www.randomhouse.com

Printed in the United States of America

9B

CONTENTS

The Club Dumas

The flash projected the outline of the hanged man onto the wall. He hung motionless from a light fixture in the center of the room, and as the photographer moved around him, taking pictures, the flashes threw the silhouette onto a succession of paintings, glass cabinets full of porcelain, shelves of books, open curtains framing great windows beyond which the rain was falling.

The examining magistrate was a young man. His thinning hair was untidy and still damp, as was the raincoat he wore while he dictated to a clerk who sat on a sofa as he typed, his typewriter on a chair. The tapping punctuated the monotonous voice of the magistrate and the whispered comments of the policemen who were moving about the room.

"... wearing pajamas and a robe. The cord of the robe was the cause of death by hanging. The deceased has his hands bound in front of him with a tie. On his left foot he is still wearing one of his slippers, the other foot is bare...."

The magistrate touched the slippered foot of the dead man, and the body turned slightly, slowly, at the end of the taut silk cord that ran from its neck to the light fixture on the ceiling. The body moved from left to right, then back again, until it came gradually to a stop in its original position, like the needle of a compass reverting to north. As the magistrate moved away, he turned sideways to avoid a uniformed policeman who was searching for fingerprints beneath the corpse. There was a broken vase on the floor and a book open at a page covered with red pencil marks. The book was an old copy of The Vicomte de Bragelonne, a cheap edition bound in cloth. Leaning over the policeman's shoulder, the magistrate glanced at the underlined sentences:

"They have betrayed me," he murmured. "All is known!"
"All is known at last," answered Porthos, who knew nothing.

He made the clerk write this down and ordered that the book be included in the report. Then he went to join a tall man who stood smoking by one of the open windows.
"What do you think?" he asked.
The tall man wore his police badge fastened to a pocket of his leather jacket. Before answering, he took time to finish his cigarette, then threw it over his shoulder and out the window without looking.
"If it's white and in a bottle, it tends to be milk," he answered, cryptically, at last, but not so cryptically that the magistrate didn't smile slightly.
Unlike the policeman, he was looking out into the street, where it was still raining hard. Somebody opened a door on the other side of the room, and a gust of air splashed drops of water into his face.
"Shut the door," he ordered without turning around. Then he spoke to the policeman. "Sometimes homicide disguises itself as suicide."
"And vice versa," the other man pointed out calmly.
"What do you think of the hands and tie?"
"Sometimes they're afraid they'll change their minds at the

last minute... If it was homicide, he'd have had them tied behind him."

"It makes no difference," objected the magistrate. "It's a strong, thin cord. Once he lost his footing, he wouldn't have a chance, even with his hands free."

"Anything's possible. The autopsy will tell us more."

The magistrate glanced once more at the corpse. The policeman searching for fingerprints stood up with the book.

"Strange, that business of the page," said the magistrate.

The tall policeman shrugged.

"I don't read much," he said, "but Porthos, wasn't he one of those... Athos, Porthos, Aramis, and d'Artagnan." He was counting with his thumb on the fingers of the same hand. He stopped, looking thoughtful. "Funny. I've always wondered why they were called the three musketeers when there were really four of them."

I. "THE ANJOU WINE"

The reader must be prepared to witness the most sinister scenes.
—E. Sue, THE MYSTERIES OF PARIS

My name is Boris Balkan and I once translated *The Charterhouse of Parma*. Apart from that, I've edited a few books on the nineteenth-century popular novel, my reviews and articles appear in supplements and journals throughout Europe, and I organize summer-school courses on contemporary writers. Nothing spectacular, I'm afraid. Particularly these days, when suicide disguises itself as homicide, novels are written by Roger Ackroyd's doctor, and far too many people insist on publishing two hundred pages on the fascinating emotions they experience when they look in the mirror.

But let's stick to the story.

I first met Lucas Corso when he came to see me; he was carrying "The Anjou Wine" under his arm. Corso was a mercenary of the book world, hunting down books for other people. That meant talking fast and getting his hands dirty. He needed good reflexes, patience, and a lot of luck—and a prodigious memory to recall the exact dusty corner of an old man's shop where a book now worth a fortune lay forgotten. His clientele was small and select: a couple of dozen book dealers in Milan, Paris, London, Barcelona, and Lausanne, the kind that sell through catalogues, make only safe investments, and never handle more than fifty or so titles at any one time. High-class dealers in early printed books, for whom thousands of dollars depend on whether something is parchment or vellum or three centimeters wider in the margin. Jackals on the scent of the Gutenberg Bible, antique-fair sharks, auction-room leeches, they would sell their grandmothers for a first edition. But they receive their clients in rooms with leather sofas, views of the Duomo or Lake Constance, and they never get their hands— or their consciences—dirty. That's what men like Corso are for.

He took his canvas bag off his shoulder and put it on the floor by his scuffed oxfords. He stared at the framed portrait of Rafael Sabatini that stands on my desk next to the fountain pen I use for correcting articles and proofs. I was pleased, because most visitors paid Sabatini little attention, taking him for an aged relative. I waited for Corso's reaction. He was half smiling as he sat down—a youthful expression, like that of a cartoon rabbit in a dead-end street. The kind of look that wins over the audience straightaway. In time I found out he could also smile like a cruel, hungry wolf, and that he chose his smiles to suit the circumstances. But that was much later. Now he seemed trustworthy, so I decided to risk a password.

"He was born with the gift of laughter," I quoted, pointing at the portrait. *"... and with a feeling that the world was mad..."*

Corso nodded slowly and deliberately. I felt a friendly complicity with him, which, in spite of all that happened later, I still feel. From a hidden packet he brought out an unfiltered cigarette that was as crumpled as his old overcoat and corduroy trousers. He turned it over in his fingers, watching me through steel-rimmed glasses set crookedly on his nose under an untidy fringe of slightly graying hair. As if holding a hidden gun, he kept his other hand in one of his pockets, a pocket huge and deformed by books, catalogues, papers, and, as I also found out later, a hip flask full of Bols gin.

"*...and this was his entire inheritance.*" He completed the quotation effortlessly, then settled himself in the armchair and smiled again. "But to be honest, I prefer *Captain Blood.*"

With a stern expression I lifted my fountain pen. "You're mistaken. *Scaramouche* is to Sabatini what *The Three Musketeers* is to Dumas." I bowed briefly to the portrait. " '*He was born with the gift of laughter....*' In the entire history of the adventure serial no two opening lines can compare."

"That may be true," Corso conceded after a moment's reflection. Then he laid the manuscript on the table, in a protective folder with plastic pockets, one for each page. "It's a coincidence you should mention Dumas."

He pushed the folder toward me, turning it around so I could read its contents. The text was in French, written on one side of the page only. There were two types of paper, both discolored by age: one white, the other pale blue with light squares. The handwriting on each was different—on the white pages it was smaller and more spiky. The handwriting of the blue paper, in black ink, also appeared on the white pages but as annotations only. There were fifteen pages in all, eleven of them blue.

"Interesting." I looked up at Corso. He was watching me, his calm gaze moving from the folder to me, then back again. "Where did you find it?"

He scratched an eyebrow, no doubt calculating whether he needed to provide such details in exchange for the information he wanted. The result was a third facial expression, this time an innocent rabbit. Corso was a professional.

"Around. Through a client of a client."

"I see."

He paused briefly, cautious. Caution is a sign of prudence and reserve, but also of shrewdness. And we both knew it.

"Of course," he added, "I'll give you names if you request them."

I answered that it wouldn't be necessary, which seemed to

7

reassure him. He adjusted his glasses before asking my opinion of the manuscript. Not answering immediately, I turned to the first page. The title was written in capital letters, in thicker strokes: LE VIN D'ANJOU.

I read aloud the first few lines: "*Après de nouvelles presque désespérées du roi, le bruit de sa convalescence commençait à se répandre dans le camp....*" I couldn't help smiling.

Corso indicated his approval, inviting me to comment.

"Without the slightest doubt," I said, "this is by Alexandre Dumas père. 'The Anjou Wine': chapter forty-something, I seem to remember, of *The Three Musketeers.*"

"Forty-two," confirmed Corso. "Chapter forty-two."

"Is it authentic? Dumas's original manuscript?"

"That's why I'm here. I want you to tell me."

I shrugged slightly, reluctant to assume such a responsibility. "Why me?"

It was a stupid question, the kind that only serves to gain time. It must have seemed like false modesty, because he suppressed a look of impatience.

"You're an expert," he retorted, somewhat dryly. "As well as being Spain's most influential literary critic, you know all there is to know about the nineteenth-century popular novel."

"You're forgetting Stendhal."

"Not at all. I read your translation of *The Charterhouse of Parma.*"

"Indeed. I am honored."

"Don't be. I preferred Consuelo Berges's version."

We both smiled. I continued to find him likable, and I was beginning to form an idea of his style.

"Do you know any of my books?" I asked.

"Some. *Lupin, Raffles, Rocambole, Holmes,* for instance. And your studies of Valle-Inclan, Baroja, and Galdos. Also *Dumas: the Shadow of a Giant.* And your essay on *The Count of Monte Cristo.*"

"Have you read all those?"

"No. I work with books, but that doesn't mean I have to read them."

He was lying. Or at least exaggerating. The man was conscientious: before coming to see me, he'd looked at everything about me he could lay his hands on. He was one of those compulsive readers who have devoured anything in print from a most tender age—although it was highly unlikely that Corso's childhood ever merited the term "tender."

"I understand," I answered, just to say something.

He frowned for a moment, wondering whether he'd forgotten anything. He took off his glasses, breathed on the lenses, and set about cleaning them with a very crumpled handkerchief, which he pulled from one of the bottomless pockets of his coat. However fragile the oversized coat made him appear, with his rodentlike incisors and calm expression Corso was as solid as a concrete block. His features were sharp and precise, full of angles. They framed alert eyes always ready to express an innocence dangerous for anyone who was taken in by it. At times, particularly when still, he seemed slower and clumsier than he really was. He looked vulnerable and defenseless: barmen gave him an extra drink on the house, men offered him cigarettes, and women wanted to adopt him on the spot. Later, when you realized what had happened, it was too late to catch him. He was running off in the distance, having scored another victory.

Corso gestured with his glasses at the manuscript. "To return to Dumas. Surely a man who's written five hundred pages about him ought to sense something familiar when faced with one of his original manuscripts."

With the reverence of a priest handling holy vestments I put a hand on the pages protected by plastic.

"I fear I'm going to disappoint you, but I don't sense anything."

We both laughed, Corso in a peculiar way, almost under his breath, like someone who is not sure whether he and his companion are laughing at the same thing. An oblique, distant laugh, with a hint of insolence, the kind of laugh that lingers in the air after it stops. Even after its owner has been gone for a while.

"Let's take this a step at a time," I went on. "Does the manuscript belong to you?"

"I've already told you that it doesn't. A client of mine has just acquired it, and he finds it strange that no one should have heard of this complete, original chapter of *The Three Musketeers* until now.... He wants it authenticated by an expert, so that's what I'm working on."

"I'm surprised at your dealing with such a minor matter." This was true. I'd heard of Corso before this meeting. "I mean, after all, nowadays Dumas..."

I let the sentence hang and smiled with the appropriate expression of bitter complicity. But Corso didn't take up my invitation and stayed on the defensive. "The client's a friend of mine," he said evenly. "It's a personal favor."

"I see, but I'm not sure that I can be of any help to you. I have seen some of the original manuscripts, and this one could be authentic. However, certifying it is another matter. For that you'd need a good graphologist... I know an excellent one in Paris, Achille Replinger. He owns a shop that specializes in autographs and historical documents, near Saint Germain des Prés. He's an expert on nineteenth-century French writers, a charming man and a good friend of mine." I pointed to one of the frames on the wall. "He sold me that Balzac letter many years ago. For a very high price."

I took out my datebook and copied the address for Corso on a card. He put the card in an old worn wallet full of notes and papers. Then he brought out a notepad and pencil from one of his coat pockets. The pencil had a chewed eraser at one end, like a schoolboy's pencil.

"Could I ask you a few questions?" he said.

"Yes, of course."

"Did you know of any complete handwritten chapter of *The Three Musketeers?*"

I shook my head and replaced the cap on my Mont Blanc.

"No. The novel came out in installments in *Le Siècle* between March and July 1844 ... Once the text was typeset by a compositor, the original manuscript was discarded. A few fragments remained, however. You can see them in an appendix to the 1968 Garnier edition."

"Four months isn't very long." Corso chewed the end of his pencil thoughtfully. "Dumas wrote quickly."

"They all did in those days. Stendhal wrote *The Charterhouse of Parma* in seven weeks. And in any case Dumas used collaborators, ghostwriters. The one for *The Three Musketeers* was called Auguste Maquet. They worked together on the sequel, *Twenty Years After*, and on *The Vicomte de Bragelonne*, which completes the cycle. And on *The Count of Monte Cristo* and a few other novels. You have read those, I suppose."

"Of course. Everybody has."

"Everybody in the old days, you mean." I leafed respectfully through the manuscript. "The times are long gone when Dumas's name increased print runs and made publishers rich. Almost all his novels came out in installments that ended with 'to be continued. ...' The readers would be on tenterhooks until the next episode. But of course you know all that."

"Don't worry. Go on."

"What more can I tell you? In the classic serial, the recipe for success is simple: the hero and heroine have qualities or features that make the reader identify with them. If that happens nowadays in TV soaps, imagine the effect in those days, when there was no television or radio, on a middle class hungry for surprise and entertainment, and undiscriminating when it came to formal quality or taste. ... Dumas was a genius, and he understood this. Like an alchemist in his laboratory, he added a dash of this, a dash of that, and with his talent combined it all to create a drug that had many addicts." I tapped my chest, not without pride. "That has them still."

Corso was taking notes. Precise, unscrupulous, and deadly as a black mamba was how one of his acquaintances described him later when Corso's name came up in conversation. He had a singular way of facing people, peering through his crooked glasses and slowly nodding in agreement, with a reasonable, well-meaning, but doubtful expression, like a whore tolerantly listening to a romantic sonnet. As if he was giving you a chance to correct yourself before it was too late.

After a moment he stopped and looked up. "But your work doesn't only deal with the popular novel. You're a well-known literary critic of other, more ..." He hesitated, searching for a word. "More serious works. Dumas himself described his novels as easy literature. Sounds rather patronizing toward his readers."

This device was typical of him. It was one of his trademarks, like Rocambole's leaving a playing card instead of a calling card. Corso would say something casually, as if he himself had no opinion on the matter, slyly goading you to react. If you put forward arguments and justifications when you are annoyed, you give out more information to your opponent. I was no fool and knew what Corso was doing, but even so, or maybe because of it, I felt irritated.

"Don't talk in clichés," I said. "The serial genre produced a lot of disposable stuff, but Dumas was way above all that. In literature, time is like a shipwreck in which God looks after His own. I challenge you to name any fictional heroes who have survived in as good health as d'Artagnan and his friends. Sherlock Holmes is a possible exception. Yes, *The Three Musketeers* was a swashbuckling novel full of melodrama and all the sins of the genre. But it's also a distinguished example of the serial, and of a standard well above the norm. A tale of friendship and adventure that has stayed fresh even though tastes have changed and there is an now an idiotic tendency to despise action in novels. It would seem that since Joyce we have had to make do with Molly Bloom and give up Nausicaa on the beach after the shipwreck.... Have you read my essay 'Friday, or the Ship's Compass'? Give me Homer's *Ulysses* any day."

I sharpened my tone at that point, waiting for Corso's reaction. He smiled slightly and remained silent, but, remembering his expression when I had quoted from *Scaramouche,* I felt sure I was on the right track.

"I know what you're referring to," he said at last. "Your views are well known and controversial, Mr. Balkan."

"My views are well known because I've seen to that. And as for patronizing his readers, as you claimed a moment ago, perhaps you didn't know that the author of *The Three Musketeers* fought in the streets during the revolutions of 1830 and 1848. And he supplied arms, paying for them out of his own pocket, to Garibaldi. Don't forget that Dumas's father was a well-known republican general.... The man was full of love for the people and liberty."

"Although his respect for the truth was only relative."

"That's not important. Do you know how he answered those who accused him of raping History? 'True, I have raped History, but it has produced some beautiful offspring.' "

I put my pen down and went to the glass cabinets full of books. They covered the walls of my study. I opened one and took out a volume bound in dark leather.

"Like all great writers of fables," I went on, "Dumas was a liar. Countess Dash, who knew him well, says in her memoirs that any apocryphal anecdote he told was received as the historical truth. Take Cardinal Richelieu: he was the greatest man of his time, but once the treacherous Dumas had finished with him, the image left to us was that of a sinister villain...." I turned to Corso, holding the book. "Do you know this? It was written by Gatien de Courtilz de Sandras, a musketeer who lived in the late seventeenth century. They're the memoirs of the real d'Artagnan, Charles de Batz-Castelmore, Comte d'Artagnan. He was a Gascon, born in 1615, and was indeed a musketeer. Although he lived in Mazarin's time, not Richelieu's. He died in 1673 during the siege of Maastricht, when, like his fictional namesake, he was about to be awarded the marshal's staff. . . . So you see, Dumas's raping did indeed produce beautiful offspring. An obscure flesh-and-blood Gascon, forgotten by History, transformed into a legendary giant by the novelist's genius."

Corso sat and listened. When I handed him the book, he leafed through it carefully, with great interest. He turned the pages slowly, barely brushing them with his fingertips, only touching the very edge. From time to time he paused over a name or a chapter heading. Behind his spectacles his eyes worked sure and fast. He stopped once to write in his notebook: "*Memoires de M. d'Artagnan*, G. de Courtilz, 1704, P. Rouge, 4 volumes in 12mo, 4th edition." Then he shut the notebook and looked up at me.

"You said it: he was a trickster."

"Yes," I agreed, sitting down again. "But a genius. While some would simply have plagiarized, he created a fictional world that still endures today . . . 'Man does not steal, he conquers,' he often said. 'Every province he seizes becomes an annex of his empire: he imposes laws, peoples it with themes and characters, casting his shadow over it.' What else is literary creation? For Dumas, the history of France was a rich source of material. His was an extraordinary trick: he'd leave the frame alone but alter the picture, mercilessly plundering the treasure that was offered to him. He turned central characters into minor ones, humble secondary characters became protagonists, and he wrote pages about events that took up only two lines in the historical chronicles. The pact of friendship between d'Artagnan and his companions never existed, one of the reasons being that half of them didn't even know each other. Nor was there a

Comte de la Fère. Or, rather, there were several of them, though none called Athos. But Athos did exist. He was Armand de Sillegue, Lord of Athos, and he was killed in a duel before d'Artagnan ever joined the king's musketeers. Aramis was Henri d'Aramitz, a squire and lay priest in the seneschalship of Oloron, who enrolled in the musketeers under his uncle's command in 1640. He ended his days on his estate, with a wife and four children. As for Porthos . . ."

"Don't tell me there was a Porthos too."

"Yes. His name was Isaac de Portau and he must have known Aramis, because he joined the musketeers just three years after him, in 1643. According to the chronicles, he died prematurely, from a disease, at war, or in a duel like Athos."

Corso drummed his fingers on d'Artagnan's *Memoirs* and shook his head, smiling. "Any minute now you'll tell me there was a Milady."

"Correct. But her name wasn't Anne de Breuil, and she wasn't the Duchess de Winter. Nor did she have a fleur-de-lis tattooed on her shoulder. But she *was* one of Richelieu's secret agents. Her name was the Countess of Carlisle and she stole two diamond tags from the Duke of Buckingham . . . Don't look at me like that. It's all in La Rochefoucauld's memoirs. And La Rochefoucauld was a very reliable man."

Corso was staring at me intently. He wasn't the type to be easily surprised, particularly when it came to books, but he seemed impressed. Later, when I came to know him better, I wondered whether his admiration was sincere or just another of his professional wiles. Now that it's all over, I think I know: I was one more source of information, and Corso was trying to get as much out of me as possible.

"This is all very interesting," he said.

"If you go to Paris, Replinger can tell you much more than I can." I looked at the manuscript on the table. "Though I'm not sure it's worth the price of a trip . . . What would this chapter fetch on the market?"

He started chewing his pencil again and looked doubtful. "Not much. I'm really after something else."

I gave a sad conspiratorial smile. Among my few possessions I have an Ibarra edition of *Don Quixote* and a Volkswagen. Of course the car cost more than the book.

"I know what you mean," I said warmly.

Corso made a resigned gesture. He bared his rodent teeth in a bitter smile. "Unless the Japanese get fed up with Van Gogh and Picasso," he suggested, "and start investing in rare books."

I shuddered. "God help us if that ever happens."

"Speak for yourself." He looked at me sardonically through his crooked glasses. "I plan to make a fortune."

He put his notebook away and stood up, the strap of his canvas bag over his shoulder. I couldn't help wondering about his falsely placid appearance, with his steel-rimmed glasses sitting unsteadily on his nose. I found out later that he lived alone, surrounded by books, both his own and other people's, and that as well as being a hired hunter of books he was an expert on Napoleon's battles. He could set out on a board, from memory, the exact positions of troops on the eve of Waterloo. A detail from his family, slightly strange, and I found out about it only much later. I have to admit that from this description Corso doesn't sound very appealing. And yet, if I keep to the strict accuracy with which I am narrating this story, I must add that his awkward appearance, the very clumsiness that seemed— and I don't know how he managed it—vulnerable and caustic, ingenuous and aggressive at the same time, made him both attractive to women and sympathetic to men. But the positive feeling was quickly dispelled, as when you touch your pocket and realize that your wallet has just been stolen.

Corso picked up his manuscript, and I saw him to the door. He shook my hand in the hallway, where portraits of Stendhal, Conrad, and Valle-Inclan looked out severely at an atrocious print that the building's residents' association had decided to hang on the landing a few months earlier, much against my wishes.

Only then did I dare ask him: "I confess I'm intrigued as to where you found it."

He hesitated before answering, weighing the pros and cons. I had received him in a friendly manner, so he was in my debt. Also he might need my help again.

"Maybe you know him," he answered at last. "My client bought the manuscript from a certain Taillefer."

I allowed myself a look of moderate surprise. "Enrique Taillefer? The publisher?"

He was gazing absently around the hallway. At last he nodded. "The same."

We both fell silent. Corso shrugged, and I knew why. The reason could be found in the pages of any newspaper: Enrique Taillefer had been dead a week. He had been found hanged in his house, the cord of his silk robe around his neck, his feet dangling in empty space over an open book and a porcelain vase smashed to pieces.

Some time later, when it was all over, Corso agreed to tell me the rest of the story. So I can now give a fairly accurate picture of a chain of events that I didn't witness, events that led to the fatal dénouement and the solution to the mystery surrounding the Club Dumas. Thanks to what Corso told me I can now tell you, like Doctor Watson, that the following scene took place in Makarova's bar an hour after our meeting:

Flavio La Ponte came in shaking off the rain, leaned on the bar next to Corso, and ordered a beer while he caught his breath. Then he looked back at the street, aggressive but triumphant, as if he had just come through sniper fire. It was raining with biblical force.

"The firm of Armengol & Sons, Antiquarian Books and Bibliographical Curiosities, intends to sue you," he said. He had a ring of froth on his curly blond beard, around his mouth. "Their solicitor just telephoned."

"What are they accusing me of?" asked Corso.

"Cheating a little old lady and plundering her library. They swear the deal was theirs."

"Well, they should have got up early, as I did."

"That's what I said, but they're still furious. When they went to pick up the books, the *Persiles* and the *Royal Charter of Castille* had disappeared. And you gave a valuation for the rest that was more than expected. So now the owner won't sell. She wants double what they're prepared to pay." He drank some beer and winked conspiratorially. "That neat maneuver is known as nailing a library."

"I know what it's called." Corso smiled malevolently. "And Armengol & Sons know it too."

"You're being unnecessarily cruel," said La Ponte impartially. "But what they're most sore about is the *Royal Charter*. They say that your taking it was a low blow."

"How could I leave it there? Latin glossary by Diaz de Montalvo, no typographical details but printed in Seville by Alonso Del Puerto, possibly 1482..." He adjusted his glasses and looked at his friend. "What do you think?"

"Sounds good to me. But they're a bit jumpy."

"They should take a Valium."

It was early evening. There was very little room at the bar, and they were pressed shoulder to shoulder, surrounded by cigarette smoke and the murmur of conversation, trying not to get their elbows in the puddles of beer on the counter.

"Apparently," continued La Ponte, "the *Persiles* is a first edition. The binding's signed by Trautz-Bauzonnet."

Corso shook his head. "By Hardy. Morocco leather."

"Even better. Anyway I swore I had nothing to do with it. You know I have an aversion to lawsuits."

"But not to your thirty percent."

La Ponte raised his hand with dignity. "Stop right there. Don't confuse business with pleasure, Corso. Our beautiful friendship is one thing, food for my children is quite another."

"You don't have any children."

La Ponte looked at him mischievously. "Give me time. I'm still young."

He was short, good-looking, neat, and something of a dandy. His hair was thinning on top. He smoothed it down with his hand, checking to see how it looked in the bar's mirror. Then he cast a practiced eye around the room, checking out the ladies. He was always on the lookout, and always liked to use short sentences in conversation. His father, a very cultured bookseller, had taught him to write by dictating to him texts by Azorin. Hardly anyone reads Azorin anymore, but La Ponte still constructed his sentences like Azorin. With lots of full stops. It gave him a certain aplomb when it came to seducing female customers in the back room of his bookshop in the Calle Mayor, where he kept his erotic classics.

"Anyway," he added, "I have some unfinished business with Armengol & Sons. Rather delicate, but I could make a quick profit."

"You have business with me too," said Corso over his beer. "You're the only poor bookseller I work with. And you're going to be the one who sells those books."

"All right, all right," said La Ponte equably. "You know I'm a practical man. A despicable pragmatist."

"Yes."

"Imagine this was a Western. As your friend, I'd take a bullet for you, but only in the shoulder."

"At the very most," said Corso.

"Anyway, it doesn't matter." La Ponte was looking around distractedly. "I already have a buyer for the *Persiles*."

"Then get me another beer. An advance on your commission."

They were old friends. They both loved frothy beer and, in its glazed earthenware bottle, Bols gin. But above all they loved antiquarian books and the auctions held in old Madrid auction rooms. They had met many years earlier, when Corso was rooting around in bookshops that specialized in Spanish authors. A client of his was looking for a bogus copy of *Celestina* that was supposed to predate the known 1499 edition. La Ponte didn't have the book and hadn't even heard of it, but he did have an edition of Julio Ollero's *Dictionary of Rare and Improbable Books* in which it was mentioned. They chatted about books and realized that they had a lot in common. La Ponte closed his shop, and they sealed their friendship by drinking all there was to drink in Makarova's bar while swapping anecdotes about Melville. La Ponte had been brought up on tales of the *Pequod* and the escapades of Azorin. "Call me Ishmael," he said as he drained his third Bols in one swallow. And Corso called him Ishmael, quoting from memory and in his honor the episode of the forging of Ahab's harpoon: "*Three punctures were made in the heathen flesh, and the White Whale's barbs were then tempered.*"

They duly drank a toast. By then La Ponte was no longer watching the girls coming in and out of the bar. He swore eternal friendship to Corso. Despite his militant cynicism and his occupation as a rapacious seller of old books, underneath he was a naive man. So he was unaware that his new friend with the crooked glasses was discreetly outflanking him: Corso had glanced over his shelves and spotted a few books he planned to make an offer for. But La Ponte, with his pale, curly beard, the gentle look of seaman Billy Budd with daydreams of a frustrated whale hunter, had awakened Corso's sympathy. La Ponte could even recite the names of all the crew of the *Pequod:* Ahab, Stubb, Starbuck, Flask, Perth, Parsee, Queequeg, Tasthego, Daggoo . . . Or the names of all the ships mentioned in *Moby-Dick*: the *Goney,* the *Town-Ho,* the *Jeroboam,* the *Jungfrau,* the *Rose-bud,* the *Batchelor,* the *Delight,* the *Rachel* . . . And, proof of proof, he even knew what ambergris was. They talked of books and whales. And so that night the Brotherhood of Nantucket Harpooneers was founded, with Flavio La Ponte as chairman, Lucas Corso as treasurer. They were the only two members and had Makarova's tolerant patronage. She gave them their last round on the house and ended up sharing another bottle of gin with them.

"I'm going to Paris," said Corso, watching the reflection of a fat woman putting coin after coin in a slot machine. It seemed as if the silly little tune and the colors, fruits, and bells would keep her there for all eternity, hypnotized and motionless but for her hand pushing the buttons. "To see about your 'Anjou Wine.' "

His friend wrinkled his nose and gave him a sideways glance. Paris meant more expense, complications. La Ponte was a stingy, small-time bookseller.

"You know I can't afford it."

Corso slowly emptied his glass. "Yes, you can." He took out a few coins and paid his round. "I'm going about something else."

"Oh yes?" said La Ponte, intrigued.

Makarova put two more beers on the counter. She was large, blond, in her forties, and had short hair and a ring in one ear, a souvenir of her time on a Russian trawler. She wore narrow trousers and a shirt with the sleeves rolled up to her shoulders. Her overdeveloped biceps weren't the only masculine thing about her. She always had a lighted cigarette smoldering in the corner of her mouth. With her Baltic look and her way of moving, she looked like a fitter from a ball-bearing factory in Leningrad.

"I read that book," she told Corso, rolling her *r*'s. As she spoke, ash from her cigarette dropped onto her damp shirt. "That tart Bovary. Poor little fool."

"I'm so glad you grasped the heart of the matter."

Makarova wiped down the counter with a cloth. At the other end of the bar Zizi was watching as she worked the till. She was the complete opposite of Makarova: much younger, slight, and terribly jealous. Sometimes, just before closing time, they would quarrel drunkenly and come to blows, the last few regulars watching. Once, with a black eye after one of these rows, Zizi upped and left, furious and vindictive. Makarova wept copiously into the beer until Zizi returned three days later. That night they closed early and left with their arms around each other's waist, kissing in doorways like two teenagers in love.

"He's off to Paris," La Ponte said, nodding in Corso's direction. "To see what he can pull out of the hat."

Makarova collected the empty glasses and looked at Corso through the smoke of her cigarette. "He's always up to something," she said in her flat, guttural tone.

Then she put the glasses in the sink and went to serve some other customers, swinging her broad shoulders. Corso was the only member of the opposite sex who escaped her contempt, and she would proclaim this when she didn't charge him for a drink. Even Zizi looked upon him with a certain neutrality. Once, when Makarova was arrested for punching a policeman in the face during a gay rights march, Zizi had waited all night on a bench in the police station. Corso called all his contacts in the police, stayed with her, and supplied sandwiches and a bottle of gin. It all made La Ponte absurdly jealous.

"Why Paris?" he asked, though his mind was on other things. His left elbow had just prodded something deliciously soft. He was delighted to find that his neighbor at the bar was a young blonde with enormous breasts.

Corso took another gulp of beer. "I'm also going to Sintra, in Portugal." He was still watching the fat woman at the slot machine. She'd run out of coins and was now getting change from Zizi. "On some business for Varo Borja."

His friend made a whistling sound. Varo Borja, Spain's leading book dealer. His catalogue was small and select. He was also well known as a book lover to whom money was no object. Impressed, La Ponte asked for more beer and more information, with that greedy look that automatically clicked on when he heard the word *book*. Although he admitted to being a miser and a coward, he wasn't an envious man, except when it came to pretty, harpoonable women. In professional matters, he was always glad to get hold of good pieces with little risk, but he also had real respect for his friend's work and clientele.

"Have you ever heard of *The Nine Doors?*"

The bookseller was searching slowly through his pockets, hoping that Corso would pay for this round too. He was also just about to turn and take a closer look at his voluptuous neighbor, but Corso's words caused him to forget her instantly. He was openmouthed.

"Don't tell me Varo Borja's after that book. . . ."

Corso put his last few coins on the counter. Makarova brought another two beers. "He's had it for some time. He paid a fortune for it."

"I'll bet he did. There are only three or four known copies."

"Three," specified Corso. "One in Sintra, in the Fargas collection. Another at the Ungern Foundation in Paris. The third, from the sale of the Terral-Coy Library in Madrid, was bought by Varo Borja."

Fascinated, La Ponte stroked his curly beard. Of course he had heard of Fargas, the Portuguese book collector. As for Baroness Ungern, she was a potty old woman who'd become a millionairess from writing books about demonology and the occult. Her recent book, *Naked Isis*, was a runaway bestseller in all the stores.

"What I don't understand," said La Ponte, "is what you have to do with any of it."

"Do you know the book's history?"

"Vaguely," said La Ponte.

Corso dipped a finger in his beer and began to draw pictures on the marble counter. "Period: mid-seventeenth century. Scene: Venice. Central character: a printer by the name of Aristide Torchia, who had the idea of publishing the so-called *Book of the Nine Doors of the Kingdom of Shadows*, a kind of manual for summoning the devil. It wasn't a good time for that sort of thing: the Holy Office managed, without much trouble, to have Torchia handed over to them. He was charged with practicing satanic arts and all that goes with them, aggravated by the fact, they said, that he'd reproduced nine prints from the famous *Delomelanicon*, the occult classic that, tradition has it, was written by Lucifer himself."

Makarova had moved closer on the other side of the bar and was listening with interest, wiping her hands on her shirt. La Ponte, about to take another swallow of beer, stopped and asked, instinctively taking on the look of a greedy bookseller, "What happened to the book?"

"You can imagine: all the copies went onto a big bonfire." Corso frowned evilly. He seemed sorry to have missed it. "They also say that as they burned, you could hear the devil screaming."

Her elbows on Corso's beer diagrams between the beer handles, Makarova grunted skeptically. With her blond, manly looks and her cool, Nordic temperament, she didn't go in for these murky southern superstitions. La Ponte was more impressionable. Suddenly thirsty, he gulped down his beer.

"It must have been the printer they heard screaming."

"It must have been."

Corso went on. "Tortured with the thoroughness the Inquisition reserved for dealing with the evil arts, the printer finally confessed, between screams, that there remained one book, hidden somewhere. Then he shut his mouth and didn't open it again until they burned him alive. And then it was only to say *Aagh.*"

Makarova smiled contemptuously at the fate of Torchia the printer, or maybe at the executioners who hadn't been able to make him confess. La Ponte was frowning.

"You say that only one of the books was saved," he objected. "But before, you said there were three known copies."

Corso had taken off his glasses and was looking at them against the light to check how clean they were.

"And that's the problem," he said. "The books have appeared and disappeared through wars, thefts, and fires. It's not known which is the authentic one."

"Maybe they're all forgeries," Makarova suggested sensibly.

"Maybe. So I have to find out whether or not Varo Borja was taken for a ride. That's why I'm going to Sintra and Paris." He adjusted his glasses and looked at La Ponte. "While I'm there, I'll see about your manuscript as well."

The bookseller agreed thoughtfully, in the mirror eyeing the woman with the big breasts. "Compared to that, it seems ridiculous to make you waste your time on *The Three Musketeers*...."

"What are you talking about?" said Makarova, no longer neutral. She was really offended. "It's the best book I ever read!"

She slammed her hands down on the counter for emphasis, making the muscles on her bare forearms bulge. Boris Balkan would be happy to hear that, thought Corso. Besides the Dumas novel, Makarova's top-ten list of books, for which he was literary advisor, included *War and Peace*, *Watership Down*, and Patricia Highsmith's *Carol*.

"Don't worry," he told La Ponte, "I'll charge the expenses to Varo Borja. But I'd say your 'Anjou Wine' is authentic. Who would forge something like that?"

"People do all sorts of things," Makarova pointed out sagely.

La Ponte agreed with Corso—forging such a document would be absurd. The late Taillefer had guaranteed its authenticity to him. It was in Dumas's own hand. And Taillefer could be trusted.

"I used to take him old newspaper serials. He'd buy them all." He took a sip and then laughed to himself. "Good excuse to go and get a look at his wife's legs. She's a pretty spectacular blonde. Anyway, one day he opened a drawer and put 'The Anjou Wine' on the table. 'It's yours,' he said straight out, 'provided you get an expert opinion on it and put it on sale immediately.' "

A customer called, ordering a tonic water. Makarova told him to go to hell. She stayed where she was, her cigarette burning down in her mouth and her eyes half-closed because of the smoke. Waiting for the rest of the story.

"Is that all?" asked Corso.

La Ponte gestured vaguely. "Almost. I tried to dissuade him, because I knew he was crazy about that sort of thing. He would sell his soul for a rare book. But he'd made up his mind. 'If you don't do it, I'll give it to someone else,' he said. That touched a nerve, of course. My professional nerve, I mean."

"You don't need to explain," said Corso. "What other kind do you have?"

La Ponte turned to Makarova for support. But one glance at her slate-gray eyes and he gave up. They were about as warm as a Scandinavian fjord at three in the morning.

"It's nice to feel loved," he said bitterly.

The man wanting a tonic water must really have been thirsty, Corso thought, because he was getting insistent. Makarova, looking at the customer out of the corner of her eye and not moving a muscle, suggested that he find another bar before she gave him a black eye. The man thought it over. He seemed to get the message. He left.

"Enrique Taillefer was a strange man." La Ponte ran his hand again through his thinning hair, still watching the blonde in the mirror. "He wanted me to sell the manuscript and get publicity for the whole business." He lowered his voice so the blonde wouldn't hear. " 'Somebody's in for a surprise,' Taillefer told me mysteriously. He winked at me, as if he was going to play a joke on someone. Four days later, he was dead."

"Dead," repeated Makarova in her guttural way, savoring the word. She was more and more interested.

"Suicide," explained Corso.

She shrugged, as if to say there wasn't that much difference between suicide and murder. There was one doubtful manu-script and a definite corpse: quite enough for a conspiracy theory.

On hearing the word *suicide*, La Ponte nodded lugubriously. "So they say."

"You don't seem too sure."

"No, I'm not. It's all a bit odd." He frowned again, suddenly looking somber and forgetting the blonde in the mirror. "Smells fishy to me."

"Did Taillefer ever tell you how he got hold of the manu-script?"

"At the beginning I didn't ask. Then it was too late."

"Did you speak to his widow?"

La Ponte brightened. He grinned from ear to ear. "I'll save that story for another time." He sounded like someone who has just remembered he has a brilliant trick up his sleeve. "That'll be your payment. I can't afford even a tenth of what you'll get out of Varo Borja for his *Book of the Nine Lies*."

"I'll do the same for you when you find an *Audubon* and become a millionaire. I'll just collect my money later."

La Ponte looked hurt. For such a cynic, Corso thought, he seemed rather sensitive.

"I thought you were helping me as a friend," protested La Ponte. "You know. The Club of Nantucket Harpooneers. Thar she blows, and all that."

"Friendship," said Corso, looking around as if waiting for someone to explain the word to him. "Bars and cemeteries are full of good friends."

"Who's side are you on, damn it?"

"On his own side," sighed Makarova. "Corso's always on his own side."

La Ponte was disappointed to see the woman with the breasts leave with a smart young man who looked like a model. Corso was still watching the fat woman at the slot ma-chine, who'd run out of coins again. She was standing with a disconcerted, blank look, her hands at her sides. Her place at the machine was taken by a tall, dark man. He had a thick black mustache and a scar on his face. For a fleeting moment Corso thought he looked familiar, but the impression vanished before he could grasp it. To the fat woman's despair, the machine was now spewing out a noisy stream of coins.

Makarova offered Corso one last beer on the house. La Ponte had to pay for his own this time.

II. THE DEAD MAN'S HAND

There are inconsolable widows, and then there are widows to whom any adult male would be delighted to provide the appropriate consolation. Liana Taillefer was undoubtedly the second kind. Tall and blond, with pale skin, she moved languorously. She was the type of woman who takes an age to light a cigarette and looks straight into a man's eyes as she does so. She had the cool composure that was a result of knowing that she looked a little like Kim Novak, with a full, almost overgenerous figure, and that she was the sole beneficiary of the late Enrique Taillefer, Publisher, Ltd., who had a bank account for which the term *solvent* was a pale euphemism. It's amazing how much dough a person can make, if you'll excuse the feeble pun, from publishing cookbooks, such as *The Thousand Best Desserts of La Mancha* or all fifteen bestselling editions of that classic, *The Secrets of the Barbecue*.

The Taillefers lived in part of what had once been the palace of the Marqués de Los Alumbres, now converted into luxury apartments. In matters of décor, the owners seemed to have more money than taste. This could be the only excuse for placing a vulgar Lladro porcelain figure—a little girl with a duck, noted Lucas Corso dispassionately—in the same glass cabinet with a group of little Meissen shepherds, for which the late Enrique Taillefer, or his wife, must have paid some sharp antique dealer a handsome sum. There was a Biedermeier desk, of course, and a Steinway piano standing on a luxurious oriental rug. And a comfortable-looking, white leather sofa on which Liana Taillefer was sitting at that moment, crossing her extraordinarily shapely legs. She was dressed, as befits a widow, in a black skirt. It came to just above the knee when she sat, but hinted at voluptuous curves higher up, curves hidden in mystery and shadow, as Lucas Corso later put it. I would add that Corso's comment should not be ignored. He looked like one of those dubious men you can easily imagine living with an elderly mother who knits and brings him cocoa in bed on a Sunday morning; the kind of son you see in films, a solitary figure walking behind the coffin in the rain, with reddened eyes and moaning "Mama" inconsolably, like a helpless orphan. But Corso had never been helpless in his life. And when you got to know him better, you began to wonder if he had ever had a mother.

"I'm sorry to bother you at a time like this," said Corso.

He sat facing the widow, still in his coat, his canvas bag on his knees. He held himself straight on the edge of the seat. Liana Taillefer's large ice-blue eyes studied him from top to toe, determined to pigeonhole him in some known category of the male species. He was sure she'd find it difficult. He submitted to her scrutiny, trying not to create any particular impression. He was familiar with the procedure, and he knew that at that moment he didn't rate very high in the estimation of Enrique Taillefer's widow. This limited the inspection to a kind of contemptuous curiosity. She'd kept him waiting for ten minutes, after he'd had a skirmish with a maid who'd taken him for a salesman and tried to slam the door in his face. But now the widow was glancing at the plastic folder that Corso had taken out of his bag, and the situation changed. As for him, he tried to hold Liana Taillefer's gaze through his crooked glasses, avoiding the roaring reefs—to the south her legs and to the north her bust (*exuberant* was the word, he decided, having pondered the matter for some time), which was molded to devastating effect by her black angora sweater.

"It would be a great help," he added at last, "if you could tell me whether you knew about this document."

He handed her the folder, and as he did so accidentally brushed her hand with its long blood-red fingernails. Or maybe it was her hand that brushed his. Whichever, this slight contact showed that Corso's prospects were looking more favorable. He adopted a suitably embarrassed expression, just enough to show her that bothering beautiful widows wasn't his specialty. Her ice-blue eyes weren't on the folder now, they were watching Corso with a flicker of interest.

"Why would I know about it?" asked the widow. Her voice was deep, slightly husky. The echo of a heavy night. She hadn't looked inside the folder yet and was still watching Corso, as if she expected something else before examining the document and satisfying her curiosity. He adjusted his glasses on the bridge of his nose and assumed a serious expression. This was the formal introduction stage, so he kept his efficient "honest rabbit" smile for later.

"Until recently it belonged to your husband." He paused a moment. "May his soul rest in peace."

She nodded slowly, as if that explained it, and opened the folder. Corso was looking over her shoulder at the wall. There, between an adequate painting by Tàpies and another with a signature he couldn't make out, was a framed piece of child's needlepoint depicting little colored flowers, signed and dated *Liana Lasauca, school year 1970–71.* Corso would have found it touching if flowers, embroidered birds, and little girls in bobby socks and blond pigtails had been the sort of thing that made his heart melt. But they weren't. So he turned to another, smaller picture in a silver frame. It showed the late Enrique

Taillefer, publisher, with a gold wine-sampling ladle around his neck, wearing a leather apron that made him look like a Mason. He was smiling at the camera and preparing to cut into a roast suckling pig. He held a plate in one hand and one of his publishing successes in the other. He appeared placid, chubby, paunchy, and happy at the sight of the little animal laid out before him on the dish. Corso reflected that Taillefer's premature demise at least meant that he wouldn't have to worry about high cholesterol and gout. Corso also wondered, with cold technical curiosity, how Liana Taillefer had managed, while her husband was alive, when she needed an orgasm. With that thought he cast another quick glance at the widow's bust and legs and decided he'd been right. She was too much a woman to be satisfied with suckling pig.

"This is that Dumas thing," she said, and Corso sat up slightly, alert and clearheaded. Liana Taillefer was tapping one of her red nails on the plastic that protected the pages. "The famous chapter. Of course I know about it." As she leaned her head forward, her hair fell over her face. Behind the blond curtain she observed her visitor suspiciously. "Why do you have it?"

"Your husband sold it. I'm trying to find out if it's authentic."

The widow shrugged. "As far as I know, it's not a forgery." She gave a long sigh and handed back the folder. "You say he sold it? That's strange." She thought a moment. "These papers meant a lot to Enrique."

"Perhaps you can recall where he might have bought them."

"I couldn't say. I think somebody gave them to him."

"Did he collect original manuscripts?"

"As far as I know, this was the only one he ever had."

"Did he ever mention that he intended to sell it?"

"No. This is the first I've heard about it. Who bought it?"

"A bookseller who's a client of mine. He'll put it on the market once I give him a report on it."

Liana Taillefer decided to grant Corso a little more attention. His prospects took another little leap. He removed his glasses and cleaned them with his crumpled handkerchief. Without them he looked more vulnerable, and he knew it. When he squinted like a shortsighted rabbit, everybody felt they just had to help him cross the road.

"Is this your job?" she asked. "Authenticating manuscripts?"

He nodded vaguely. The widow was slightly blurred and, strangely, closer.

"Sometimes. I also look for rare books, prints, things like that. I get paid for it."

"How much?"

"It depends." He put his glasses back on, and her image was sharp again. "Sometimes a lot, sometimes not so much. The market has its ups and downs."

"You're a kind of detective, aren't you?" she said, amused. "A book detective."

This was the moment to smile. He did so, showing his incisors, with a modesty calculated to the millimeter. Adopt me, said his smile.

"Yes. I suppose you could call it that."

"And your client asked you to come and see me ..."

"That's right." He could now allow himself to look more confident, so he tapped the manuscript with his knuckles. "After all, this came from here. From your house."

She nodded slowly, looking at the folder. She seemed to be thinking something over. "It's strange," she said. "I can't imagine Enrique selling this Dumas manuscript. Although he was acting strangely those last few days ... What did you say the name of the bookseller was? The new owner."

"I didn't."

She looked him up and down, with calm surprise. It seemed she was unused to waiting for more than three seconds for any man to do as she said.

"Well, tell me then."

Corso waited a moment, just long enough for Liana Taillefer to start tapping her nails impatiently on the arm of the sofa.

"His name's La Ponte," he said at last. This was another one of his tricks: he made only small concessions but allowed others to feel they'd won. "Do you know him?"

"Of course I know him. He supplied my husband with books." She frowned. "He'd come around every so often to bring him those stupid serials. I suppose he has a receipt. I'd like a copy of it, if he doesn't mind."

Corso nodded vaguely and leaned toward her slightly. "Was your husband a great fan of Alexandre Dumas?"

"Of Dumas?" Liana Taillefer smiled. She had shaken back her hair, and now her eyes shone, mocking. "Come with me."

She stood up, taking her time, smoothing down her skirt, glancing around as if she had suddenly forgotten why she had got up. She was much taller than Corso, even though she was not wearing high heels. She led him into the adjoining study. Following her, he noticed her broad back, a swimmer's back, and her cinched-in waist. He guessed she must be about thirty. She would probably become one of those Nordic matrons on whose hips the sun never sets, made to give birth effortlessly to blond Eriks and Siegfrieds.

"I wish it had only been Dumas," she said, gesturing at the contents of the study. "Look at this."

Corso looked. The walls were covered with shelves bowing under the weight of thick volumes. Professional instinct made his mouth water. He took a few steps toward the shelves, adjusting his glasses. *The Countess de Charny*, A. Dumas, eight volumes, the Illustrated Novel collection, editor Vicente Blasco Ibanez. *The Two Dianas*, A. Dumas, three volumes. *The Musketeers*, A. Dumas, Miguel Guijarro publisher, engravings by Ortega, four volumes. *The Count of Monte Cristo*, A. Dumas, four volumes in the Juan Ros edition, engravings by A. Gil. Also forty volumes of *Rocambole*, by Ponson du Terrail. The complete edition of the *Pardellanes* by Zevaco. More Dumas, together with nine volumes of Victor Hugo and the same number by Paul Feval, with an edition of *The Hunchback* luxuriously bound in red morocco and edged with gold. And Dickens's *Pickwick Papers*, translated into Spanish by Benito Pérez Galdós, alongside several volumes by Barbey d'Aurevilly and *The Mysteries of Paris* by Eugene Sue. And yet more Dumas—*The Forty-Five, The Queen's Necklace, The Companions of Jehu*—and *Corsican Revenge* by Mérimée. Fifteen volumes of Sabatini, several by Ortega y Frías, Conan Doyle, Manuel Fernández y González, Mayne Reid, Patricio de la Escosura...

"Very impressive," commented Corso. "How many books are there here?"

"I don't know. About two thousand. Almost all of them first editions of serials, as they were bound after being published in installments. Some of them are illustrated editions. My husband was an avid collector, he'd pay whatever the asking price was."

"A true enthusiast, from what I can see."

"Enthusiast?" Liana Taillefer gave an indefinable smile. "It was a real passion."

"I thought gastronomy..."

"The cookbooks were just a way of making money. Enrique had the Midas touch: in his hands any cheap recipe book turned into a bestseller. But this was what he really loved. He liked to shut himself in here and leaf through these old serials. They were often printed on poor-quality paper, and he was obsessed with preserving them. Do you see that thermometer and humidity gauge? He could recite whole pages from his favorite books. He'd sometimes even say 'gadzooks,' 'ye gods,' things like that. He spent his last months writing."

"A historical novel?"

"A serial. Keeping to all the clichés of the genre, of course." She went to a shelf and took down a heavy manuscript with hand-stitched pages. The handwriting was large and round. "What do you think of the title?"

"*The Dead Man's Hand, or Anne of Austria's Page,*" read Corso. "Well, it's certainly . . ." He ran a finger over his eyebrow, searching for the right word. "Suggestive."

"And dull," she added, putting the manuscript back. "Full of anachronisms. Completely idiotic, I assure you. Believe me, I know what I'm talking about. At the end of each writing session he'd read it to me page by page, from beginning to end." She tapped bitterly on the title, handwritten in capitals. "God, I really hated that stupid queen and her page."

"Was he intending to publish it?"

"Yes, of course. Under a pseudonym. He probably would have chosen something like Tristan de Longueville or Paulo Florentini. It would have been so typical of him."

"What about hanging himself? Was that typical of him?"

Liana Taillefer stared intently at the book-lined walls and said nothing. An uncomfortable silence, Corso thought, even a little forced. She seemed absorbed in her thoughts, like an actress who pauses before going on with her speech in a convincing manner.

"I'll never know what happened," she answered at last, her composure once again perfect. "During his last week he was hostile and depressed. He hardly left this study. Then, one afternoon, he went out and slammed the door. He came back in the early hours. I was in bed and heard the door close. In the morning I was woken by the maid screaming. Enrique had hanged himself from the light fixture."

Now she was looking at Corso, to see the effect of her words. She didn't seem too upset, he thought, remembering the photograph with the apron and the suckling pig. He even saw her blink once, as if to hold back a tear, but her eyes were perfectly dry. Of course that didn't mean anything. Centuries of makeup that can be smudged by emotion have taught women to control their feelings. And Liana Taillefer's makeup—light shading to accentuate her eyes—was perfect.

"Did he leave a note?" asked Corso. "People who commit suicide often do."

"He decided to spare himself the effort. No explanation, not even a few words. Nothing. Because of his selfishness I've had to answer a lot of questions from an examining magistrate and several policemen. Very unpleasant, believe me."

"I understand."

"Yes. I'm sure you do."

Liana Taillefer made it obvious that their meeting was now at an end. She saw him to the door and held out her hand to him. With the folder under his arm and his bag on his shoulder, Corso shook hands with her and felt her firm grip. Inwardly he gave her a good mark for her performance. Not the happy widow, yet not devastated by grief; no cold "I'm glad that idiot's gone" or "Alone at last" or "You can come out of the wardrobe now, darling." If there was anyone in the wardrobe, it was none of Corso's business. Nor was Enrique Taillefer's suicide, however strange—and it was mighty strange, gadzooks, with all that business of the queen's page and the disappearing manuscript. But neither the suicide nor the beautiful widow were any concern of his. For now.

He looked at her. I'd love to know who's having you, he thought with cool technical curiosity. He drew a mental picture of the man: handsome, mature, cultured, wealthy. He was almost a hundred percent sure it must be a friend of her deceased husband. He wondered if the publisher's suicide had anything to do with it, then stopped himself in disgust. Professional quirk or not, he sometimes had the absurd habit of thinking like a policeman. He shivered at the thought. Who knows what depths of depravity, or stupidity, lie hidden in our soul?

"I must thank you for taking the time to see me," he said, choosing the most touching smile from his repertoire, the one that made him resemble a friendly rabbit.

It was met with a blank. She was looking at the Dumas manuscript.

"You don't have to thank me. I'm just naturally interested to know how all this will end."

"I'll let you know how it's going . . . Oh, and there's something else. Do you intend to keep your husband's collection, or are you thinking of selling it?"

She looked at him, disconcerted. Corso knew from experience that when a book collector died, the books often followed the body out the front door twenty-four hours later. He was surprised, in fact, that none of his predatory colleagues had dropped by yet. After all, as she had admitted herself, Liana Taillefer didn't share her husband's literary tastes.

"The truth is, I haven't had time to think about it. . . . Do you mean you'd be interested in those old serials?"

"I could be."

She hesitated a moment. Perhaps a few seconds longer than necessary. "It's all too recent," she said at last, with a suitable sigh. "Maybe in a few days' time."

Corso put his hand on the banister and started down the stairs. He took the first few steps slowly, feeling uneasy, as if he'd left something behind but couldn't remember what. He was certain he hadn't forgotten anything. When he reached the first landing, he looked up and saw that Liana Taillefer was still at the door, watching him. She appeared both worried and curious. Corso continued on down the stairs, and his frame of vision, like a slow-motion camera, slid down her body. He could no longer see the inquiring look in her ice-blue eyes; he saw instead her bust, hips, and finally her firm, pale legs set slightly apart, as strong as temple columns, and suggestive.

He was still reeling as he crossed the hall and went into the street. He could think of at least five unanswered questions and needed to put them in order of importance. He stopped at the curb, opposite the railings of the park of El Retiro, and looked casually to his left, waiting for a taxi. An enormous Jaguar was parked a few meters away. The chauffeur, in a dark gray, almost black, uniform, was leaning on the hood and reading a newspaper. At that instant, the man looked up and his eyes met Corso's. It lasted only a second, and then he went back to reading his paper. He was dark, with a mustache, and his cheek was scored from top to bottom by a pale scar. Corso thought the chauffeur looked familiar: he definitely reminded him of somebody. It could have been the tall man who played at the slot machine in Makarova's bar. But there was something else. That face stirred some vague, distant memory. Before Corso could give it any more thought, however, an empty taxi appeared. A man in a loden coat carrying an executive briefcase hailed it from the other side of the street, but the driver was looking in Corso's direction. Corso made the most of this and quickly stepped off the curb to snatch the taxi from under the other man's nose.

He asked the driver to turn down the radio, then settled himself in the backseat, looking out at the surrounding traffic but not taking it in. He always enjoyed the sense of peace he got inside a taxi. It was the closest he ever came to a truce with the outside world: everything beyond the window was suspended for the duration of the journey. He leaned his head on the back of the seat and savored the view.

It was time to think of serious matters. Such as *The Book of the Nine Doors* and his trip to Portugal, the first step in this job. But he couldn't concentrate. His meeting with Enrique Taillefer's widow had raised too many questions and left him strangely uneasy. There was something he couldn't quite put his finger on, like watching a landscape from the wrong angle. And there was something else: it took him several stops at traffic lights to realize that the chauffeur of the Jaguar kept reappearing in his mind's eye. This bothered him. He was sure that he'd never seen him before that time at Makarova's bar. But an irrational memory recurred. I know you, he thought. I'm sure I do. Once, a long time ago, I bumped into a man like you. And I know you're out there somewhere. On the dark side of my memory.

GROUCHY WAS NOWHERE TO be seen, but it no longer mattered. Bulow's Prussians were retreating from the heights of Chapelle St. Lambert, with Sumont and Subervie's light cavalry at their heels. There was no problem on the left flank: the red formations of the Scottish infantry had been overtaken and devastated by the charge of the French cuirassiers. In the center, the Jerome division had at last taken Hougoumont. And to the north of Mont St. Jean, the blue formations of the good Old Guard were gathering slowly but implacably, with Wellington withdrawing in delicious disorder to the little village of Waterloo. It only remained to deal the coup de grâce.

Lucas Corso observed the field. The solution was Ney, of course. The bravest of the brave. He placed him at the front, with Erlon and the Jerome division, or what remained of it, and made them advance at a charge along the Brussels road. When they made contact with the British troops, Corso leaned back slightly in his chair and held his breath, sure of the implications of his action: in a few seconds he had just sealed the fate of twenty-two thousand men. Savoring the feeling, he looked lovingly over the compact blue and red ranks, the pale green of the forest of Soignes, the dun-colored hills. God, it was a beautiful battle.

The blow struck them hard, poor devils. Erlon's corps was blown to pieces like the hut of the three little pigs, but the lines formed by Ney and Jerome's men held. The Old Guard was advancing, crushing everything in its path. The English formations disappeared one by one from the map. Wellington had no choice but to withdraw, and Corso used the French cavalry's reserves to block his path to Brussels. Then, slowly and deliberately, he dealt the final blow. Holding Ney between his thumb and forefinger, he made him advance three hexagons. He compared forces, consulting his tables: the British were outnumbered eight to three. Wellington was finished. But there was still one small opening left to chance. He consulted his conversion table and saw that all he needed was a 3. He felt a stab of anxiety as he threw the dice to decide what the small factor of chance would be. Even with the battle won, losing Ney in the final minute was only for real enthusiasts. In the end he got a factor of 5. He smiled broadly as he gave an affectionate little tap to the blue counter representing Napoleon. *I know how you feel, friend.* Wellington and his remaining five thousand wretches were all either dead or taken prisoner, and the emperor had just won the battle of Waterloo. *Allons enfants de la Patrie!* The history books could go to hell.

He yawned. On the table, next to the board that represented the battlefield on a scale of 1 to 5,000, among reference books, charts, a cup of coffee, and an ashtray full of cigarette butts, his wristwatch showed that it was three in the morning. To one side, on the liquor cabinet, from his red label the color of a hunting jacket, Johnny Walker looked mischievous as he took a step. *Rosy-cheeked little so-and-so,* thought Corso. Walker didn't give a damn that several thousand of his fellow countrymen had just bitten the dust in Flanders.

Corso turned his back on the Englishman and addressed an unopened bottle of Bols on a shelf between *Memoirs of Saint Helena* in two volumes and a French edition of *The Red and the Black* that he lay before him on the table. He tore the seal off the bottle and leafed casually through the Stendhal as he poured himself a glass of gin.

> *Rousseau's* Confessions *was the only book through which his imagination pictured the world. The collection of Grande Armée reports and the Memoirs of Saint Helena completed his bible. He would have died for those three books. He never believed in any others.*

He stood there sipping his gin and stretching his stiff limbs. He gave a last glance to the battlefield, where the sounds of the fighting were dying down after the slaughter. He emptied his glass, feeling like a drunken god playing with real lives as if they were little tin soldiers. He pictured Lord Arthur

41

Wellesley, Duke of Wellington, handing over his sword to Ney. Dead young soldiers lay in the mud, horses cantered by without riders, and an officer of the Scots Greys lay dying beneath a shattered cannon, holding in his bloody fingers a gold locket that contained the portrait of a woman and a lock of blond hair. On the other side of the shadows into which Corso was sinking he could hear the beat of the last waltz. And the little dancer watched him from her shelf, the sequin on her forehead reflecting the flames in the fireplace. She was ready to fall into the hands of the spirit of the tobacco pouch. Or of the shop-keeper on the corner.

Waterloo. The bones of his great-great-grandfather, the old grenadier, could rest in peace. He pictured him in any one of the blue formations on the board along the brown line of the Brussels road. His face blackened, his mustache singed by the explosions of gunpowder, the old grenadier advanced, hoarse and feverish from three days of fighting with his bayonet. He had the same absent expression Corso imagined that all men in all wars had. Exhausted, he raised his bearskin cap, riddled with holes, on the end of his rifle, with his comrades. Long live the emperor. Bonaparte's solitary, squat, cancerous ghost was avenged. May he rest in peace. Hip, hip, hurray.

He poured himself another glass of Bols and, facing the saber hanging on the wall, drank a toast to the faithful ghost of Grenadier Jean-Pax Corso, 1770–1851, Legion of Honor, knight of the Order of Saint Helena, staunch Bonapartist to the end of his days, and French consul in the Mediterranean town where his great-great-grandson was born a century later. The taste of gin in his mouth, Corso recited under his breath the only inheritance left him by his great-great-grandfather, trans-mitted across the century by the line of Corsos that would die with him:

> And the Emperor, at the head of
> his impatient army,

will ride amidst the clamour.
And armed, I will leave this land,
and once more follow
the Emperor to war.

He was laughing to himself as he picked up the phone and dialed La Ponte's number. In the quiet of the room you could hear the record spinning on the turntable. Books on the walls; through the dark window, rain-soaked roofs. The view wasn't great, except on winter afternoons when the sunset, filtering through the blasts of centrally heated air and pollution from the street, turned red and ochre, like a thick curtain catching fire. His desk, computer, and the board with the battle of Waterloo sat facing the view, at the window against which the rain was falling that night. There were no mementos, pictures, or photos on the wall. Only the saber of the Old Guard in its brass and leather sheath. Visitors were surprised to find no signs here of his personal life, none of the ties to the past that people instinctively preserve, other than his books and the saber. Just as there were objects missing from his house, so the world Lucas Corso came from was long since dead and gone. None of the somber faces that sometimes appeared in his memory would have recognized him had they come back to life. And maybe it was better that way. It was as if he had never owned anything, or left anything behind. As if he had always been completely self-contained, needing nothing but the clothes on his back, an erudite, urban itinerant carrying all his worldly possessions in his pockets. And yet the few people he allowed to see him on such crimson evenings, as he sat at his window, dazzled by the sunset, his eyes bleary with gin, say that his expression—that of a clumsy, helpless rabbit—seemed sincere.

La Ponte's sleepy voice answered.

"I've just crushed Wellington," announced Corso.

After a nonplussed silence, La Ponte said that he was very happy for him. Perfidious Albion—steak-and-kidney pie and gas meters in dingy hotel rooms. Kipling. Balaclava, Trafalgar, the Falklands, and all that. And he'd like to remind Corso—the line went silent while La Ponte fumbled for his watch—that it was three in the morning. Then he mumbled something incoherent, the only intelligible words being "damn you" and "bastard," in that order.

Corso chuckled as he hung up. Once he had called La Ponte collect from an auction in Buenos Aires, just to tell him a joke about a whore who was so ugly she died a virgin. Ha, ha, very funny. And I'll make you swallow the phone bill when you get back, you idiot. Then there was the time, years earlier, when he woke up in Nikon's arms. The first thing he did was phone La Ponte and tell him he'd met a beautiful woman and it was very much like being in love. Any time he wanted to, Corso could shut his eyes and see Nikon waking slowly, her hair flowing over the pillow. He described her to La Ponte over the phone, feeling a strange emotion, an inexplicable, unfamiliar tenderness while he spoke, and she listened, watching him silently. And he knew that at the other end of the line—I'm happy for you, Corso, it was about time, I'm really happy for you, my friend—La Ponte was sincerely sharing in his awakening, his triumph, his happiness. That morning, he loved La Ponte as much as he loved her. Or maybe it was the other way around.

But that was all a long time ago. Corso turned off the light. Outside it was still raining. In his bedroom he lit one last cigarette. He sat motionless on the edge of the bed in the dark, listening for an echo of her absent breathing. Then he put out his hand to stroke her hair, no longer spilling over the pillow. Nikon was his only regret. The rain was coming down harder now, and the droplets on the window broke the faint light outside into minute reflections, sprinkling the sheets with moving dots, black trails, tiny shadows plunging in no particular direction, like the shreds of a life.

"Lucas."

He said his own name out loud, as she used to. She was the only one who'd always called him that. The name was a symbol of the common homeland, now destroyed, that they had once shared. Corso focused his attention on the tip of his cigarette glowing red in the darkness. Once he'd thought he really loved Nikon. When he found her beautiful and intelligent, infallible as a papal encyclical, and passionate, like her black-and-white photographs: wide-eyed children, old people, dogs with faithful expressions. When he watched her defending the freedom of peoples and signing petitions for the release of imprisoned intellectuals, oppressed ethnic minorities, things like that. And seals. Once she'd even managed to get him to sign something about seals.

He got up from the bed slowly, so as not to wake the ghost sleeping by his side, listening for the sound of her breathing. Sometimes he almost heard it. "You're as dead as your books, Corso. You've never loved anyone." That was the first and last time she'd used his surname. The first and last time she'd refused him her body, before leaving him for good. In search of the child he'd never wanted.

He opened the window and felt the cold damp night as rain splashed against his face. He took one last puff of his cigarette and then dropped it into the shadows, a red dot fading into the darkness, the curve of its fall broken, or hidden.

That night, it was raining on other landscapes too. On the footprints Nikon left behind. On the fields of Waterloo, great-great-grandfather Corso and his comrades. On the red-and-black tomb of Julien Sorel, guillotined for believing that with Bonaparte's death the bronze statues lay dying on old forgotten paths. A stupid mistake. Lucas Corso knew better than anyone that an itinerant, clearheaded soldier could still choose his battlefield and get his wages, standing guard alongside ghosts of paper and leather, amidst the hangover from a thousand failures.

III. MEN OF WORDS AND MEN OF ACTION

"The dead do not speak."
"They speak if God wishes it," retorted Lagardère.
—P. Feval, THE HUNCHBACK

The secretary's heels clicked loudly on the polished wood floor. Lucas Corso followed her down the long corridor—pale cream walls, hidden lighting, ambient music—until they came to a heavy oak door. He obeyed her sign to wait there a moment. Then, when she moved aside with a perfunctory smile, he went into the office. Varo Borja was sitting in a black leather reclining chair, between half a ton of mahogany and a window with a magnificent panoramic view of Toledo: ancient ochre rooftops, the Gothic spire of the cathedral silhouetted against a clean blue sky, and in the background the large gray mass of the Alcazar palace.

"Do sit down, Corso. How are you?"

"Fine."

"You've had to wait."

It wasn't an apology but a statement of fact. Corso frowned. "Don't worry. Only forty-five minutes this time."

Varo Borja didn't even bother to smile as Corso sat down in the armchair reserved for visitors. The desk was completely clear except for a complicated, high-tech telephone and intercom system. The book dealer's face was reflected in the desk surface, together with the view from the window as a backdrop. Varo Borja was about fifty. He was bald, with a tan acquired on a sun bed, and he looked respectable, which was far from the truth. He had sharp, darting little eyes. He hid his excessive girth beneath tight-fitting, exuberantly patterned vests and custom-made jackets. He was some sort of marquis, and his checkered past included a police record, a scandal over fraud, and four years of prudently self-imposed exile in Brazil and Paraguay.

"I have something to show you."

He had an abrupt manner, bordering on rudeness, which he cultivated carefully. Corso watched him walk over to a small glass cabinet. Borja opened it with a tiny key on a gold chain pulled from his pocket. He had no public premises, apart from a stand reserved at the major international fairs, and his catalogue never included more than a few dozen titles. He would follow the trail of a rare book to any corner of the world, fight hard and dirty to obtain it, and then sell it, profiting from the vagaries of the market. On his payroll at any one time he had collectors, curators, engravers, printers, and suppliers like Lucas Corso.

"What do you think?"

Corso took the book as carefully as if he were being handed a newborn baby. It was an old volume bound in brown leather, decorated in gold, and in excellent condition.

"*La Hypnerotomachia di Poliphilo* by Colonna," he said. "You managed to get hold of it at last."

"Three days ago. Venice, 1545. *In casa di figlivoli di Aldo*. One hundred and seventy woodcuts. Do you think that Swiss you mentioned would still be interested?"

"I suppose so. Is the book complete?"

"Of course. All but four of the woodcuts in this edition are reprints from the 1499 edition."

"My client really wanted a first edition, but I'll try to convince him a second edition is good enough. Five years ago, at the Monaco auction, a copy slipped through his fingers."

"Well, you have the option on this one."

"Give me a couple of weeks to get in touch with him."

"I'd prefer to deal directly." Borja smiled like a shark after a swimmer. "Of course you'd still get your commission, at the usual rate."

"No way. The Swiss is *my* client."

Borja smiled sarcastically. "You don't trust anyone, do you? I can picture you as a baby, testing your mother's milk before you'd suck."

"And you'd sell your mother's milk, wouldn't you?"

Borja stared pointedly at Corso, who at that instant didn't look at all like a friendly rabbit. More like a wolf baring his fangs.

"You know what I like about you, Corso? The easy way you fall into the part of a mercenary, with all the demagogues and charlatans out there. You're like one of those lean and hungry men Julius Caesar was so afraid of.... Do you sleep well at night?"

"Like a log."

"I'm sure you don't. I'd wager a couple of Gothic manuscripts that you're the type who spends a long time staring into the darkness... Can I tell you something? I distrust thin men who are willing and enthusiastic. I only use well-paid mercenaries, rootless, straightforward types. I'm suspicious of anyone who's tied to a homeland, family, or cause."

The book dealer put the *Poliphilo* back in the cabinet and gave a dry, humorless laugh. "Sometimes I wonder if a man like you can have friends. Do you have any friends, Corso?"

"Go to hell." Corso said it with an impeccably cold tone. Borja smiled slowly and deliberately. He didn't seem offended.

"You're right. Your friendship doesn't interest me in the least. I buy your loyalty instead. It's more solid and lasting that way. Isn't that right? The professional pride of a man meeting his contract even though the king who employed him has fled, the battle is lost, and there is no hope of salvation. . . ."

His expression was teasing, provocative, as he waited for Corso's reaction. But Corso just gestured impatiently, tapping his watch. "You can write down the rest and mail it to me," he said. "I'm not paid to laugh at your little jokes."

Borja seemed to think this over. Then he nodded, though still mockingly. "Once again, you're right, Corso. Let's get back to business. . . ." He looked around. "Do you remember the *Treatise on the Art of Fencing* by Astarloa?"

"Yes. A very rare 1870 edition. I got a copy for you a couple of months ago."

"I've now been asked for *Académie de l'épée* by the same client. Maybe one you're acquainted with?"

"I'm not sure if you mean the client or the book. Your talk is so convoluted, you're clear as mud sometimes."

Borja shot him a hostile look. "We don't all possess your clear, concise prose, Corso. I was referring to the book."

"It's a seventeenth-century Elzevir. Large format, with engravings. Considered the most beautiful treatise on fencing. And the most valuable."

"The buyer is prepared to pay any price."

"Then I'll have to find it."

Borja sat down again in his armchair before the window with a panoramic view of the ancient city. He crossed his legs, looking pleased with himself, his thumbs hooked in his vest pockets. Business was obviously going well. Very few of his high-powered European colleagues could afford such a view. But Corso wasn't impressed. Men like Borja depended on men like him, and they both knew it.

He adjusted his crooked glasses and stared at the book dealer. "What do we do about the *Poliphilo*, then?"

Borja hesitated between antagonism and greed. He glanced at the cabinet and then at Corso.

"All right," he said halfheartedly, "you make the deal with the Swiss."

Corso nodded without showing any satisfaction at his small victory. The Swiss didn't exist, but that was his business. It wouldn't be hard to find a buyer for a book like that.

"Let's talk about the *Nine Doors*," he said. The dealer's face grew more animated.

"Yes. Will you take the job?"

Corso was biting a hangnail on his thumb. He gently spat it out onto the spotless desk.

"Let's suppose for a moment that your copy is a forgery. And that one of the others is the authentic one. Or that neither of them is. That all three are forgeries."

Borja, irritated, looked to see where Corso's tiny hangnail had landed. At last he gave up. "In that case," he said, "you'll take good note and follow my instructions."

"Which are?"

"All in good time."

"No. I think you should give me your instructions now." He saw the book dealer hesitate for a second. In a corner of his brain, where his hunter's instinct lay, something didn't feel quite right. An almost imperceptible jarring sound, like a badly tuned machine.

"We'll decide things," said Borja, "as we go along."

"What's there to decide?" Corso was beginning to feel irritated. "One of the books is in a private collection and the other is in a public foundation. Neither is for sale. That's as far as things can go. My part in this and your ambitions end there. As I said, whether they're forgeries or not, once I've done my job, you pay me and that's it."

Much too simple, said the book dealer's half-smile.

"That depends."

"That's what worries me . . . You have something up your sleeve, don't you?"

Borja raised his hand slightly, contemplating its reflection in the polished surface of his desk. Then he slowly lowered it, until the hand met its reflection. Corso watched the wide, hairy hand, the huge gold signet ring on the little finger. He was all too familiar with that hand. He'd seen it sign checks on non-existent accounts, add emphasis to complete lies, shake the hands of people who were being betrayed. Corso could still hear the jarring sound, warning him. Suddenly he felt strangely tired. He was no longer sure he wanted the job.

"I'm not sure I want this job," he said aloud.

Borja must have realized Corso meant it, because his manner changed. He sat motionless, his chin resting on his hands, the light from the window burnishing his perfectly tanned bald head. He seemed to be weighing things as he stared intently at Corso.

"Did I ever tell you why I became a book dealer?"

"No. And I really don't give a damn."

Borja laughed theatrically to show he was prepared to be magnanimous and take Corso's rudeness. Corso could safely vent his bad temper, for the moment.

"I pay you to listen to whatever I want to tell you."

"You haven't paid me yet, this time."

Borja took a checkbook from one of the drawers and put it on the desk, while Corso looked around. This was the moment to say "So long" or stay put and wait. It was also the moment to be offered a drink, but Borja wasn't that kind of host. Corso shrugged, feeling the flask of gin in his pocket. It was absurd. He knew perfectly well he wouldn't leave, whether or not he liked what Borja was about to propose. And Borja knew it. Borja wrote out a figure, signed and tore out the check, then pushed it toward Corso.

Without touching it, Corso glanced at it. "You've convinced me," he said with a sigh. "I'm listening."

The book dealer didn't even allow himself a look of triumph. Just a brief nod, cold and confident, as if he had just made some insignificant deal.

"I got into this business by chance," he began. "One day I found myself penniless, with my great-uncle's library as my sole inheritance ... About two thousand books, of which only about a hundred were of any value. But among them were a first-edition *Don Quixote*, a couple of eighteenth-century Psalters, and one of the only four known copies of *Champfleuri* by Geoffroy Tory.... What do you think?"

"You were lucky."

"You can say that again," agreed Borja in an even, confident tone. He didn't have the smugness of so many successful people when they talk about themselves. "In those days I knew nothing about collectors of rare books, but I grasped the essential fact: they're willing to pay a lot of money for the real thing.... I learned terms I'd never heard of before, like colophon, dented chisel, golden mean, fanfare binding. And while I was becoming interested in the business, I discovered something else: some books are for selling and others are for keeping. Becoming a book collector is like joining a religion: it's for life."

"Very moving. So now tell me what I and your *Nine Doors* have to do with your taking vows."

"You asked me what I'd do if you discovered that my copy was a forgery. Well, let me make this clear: it is a forgery."

"How do you know?"

"I am absolutely certain of it."

Corso grimaced, showing what he thought of absolute certainty in matters of rare books. "In Mateu's *Universal Bibliography* and in the Terral-Coy catalogue it's listed as authentic."

"Yes," said Borja. "Though there's a small error in Mateu: it states that there are eight illustrations, when there are nine of them.... But *formal* authenticity means little. According to the bibliographies, the Fargas and Ungern copies are also authentic."

"Maybe all three are."

Borja shook his head. "That's not possible. The records of

Torchia's trial leave no doubt: only one copy was saved." He smiled mysteriously. "I have other proof."

"Such as?"

"It doesn't concern you."

"Then why do you need me?"

Borja pushed back his chair and stood up.

"Come with me."

"I've already told you," Corso said, shaking his head, "I'm not remotely interested in this."

"You're lying. You're burning with curiosity. You'd do the job for free."

He took the check and put it in his vest pocket. Then he lead Corso up a spiral staircase to the floor above. Borja's office was at the back of his house. The house was a huge medieval building in the old part of the city, and he'd paid a fortune for it. He took Corso along a corridor leading to the hall and main entrance; they stopped at a door that opened with a modern security keypad. It was a large room with a black marble floor, a beamed ceiling, and ancient iron bars at the windows. There was a desk, leather armchairs, and a large stone fireplace. All the walls were covered with glass cabinets full of books and with prints in beautiful frames. Some of them by Holbein and Dürer, Corso noted.

"Nice room," he said. He'd never been here before. "But I thought you kept your books in the storeroom in the basement...."

Borja stopped at his side. "These are mine. They're not for sale. Some people collect chivalric or romantic novels. Some search for *Don Quixotes* or uncut volumes.... All the books you see here have the same central character: the devil."

"Can I have a look?"

"That's why I brought you here."

Corso took a few steps forward. The books had ancient bindings, from the leather-covered boards of the incunabula to the morocco leather decorated with plaques and rosettes. His scuffed shoes squeaked on the marble floor as he stopped in front of one of the cabinets and leaned over to examine its contents: *De spectris et apparitionibus* by Juan Rivio, *Summa diabolica* by Benedicto Casiano, *La haine de Satan* by Pierre Crespet, the *Steganography* of Abbot Tritemius, *De Consummatione saeculi* by St. Pontius ... They were all extremely rare and valuable books, most of which Corso knew only from bibliographical references.

"Have you ever seen anything more beautiful?" said Borja, watching Corso closely. "There's nothing like that sheen, the gold on leather, behind glass.... Not to mention the treasures these books contain: centuries of study, of wisdom. Answers to the secrets of the universe and the heart of man." He raised his arms slightly and let them drop, giving up the attempt to express in words his pride at owning them all. "I know people who would kill for a collection like this."

Corso nodded without taking his eyes off the books. "You, for instance," he said. "Although you wouldn't do it yourself. You'd get somebody to do the killing for you."

Borja laughed contemptuously. "That's one of the advantages of having money—you can hire henchmen to do your dirty work. And remain pure yourself."

Corso looked at the book dealer. "That's a matter of opinion," he said. He seemed to ponder the matter. "I despise people who don't get their hands dirty. The pure ones."

"I don't care what you despise, so let's get down to serious matters."

Borja took a few steps past the cabinets, each containing about a hundred volumes. *"Ars Diavoli..."* He opened the one nearest to him and ran his finger over the spines of the books, almost in a caress. "You'll never see such a collection anywhere else. These are the rarest, most choice books. It took me years to build up this collection, but I was still lacking the prize piece."

He took out one of the books, a folio bound in black leather, in the Venetian style, with no title on the outside but with five raised bands on the spine and a golden pentacle on the front cover. Corso took it and opened it carefully. The first printed page, the title page, was in Latin: DE UMBRARUM REGNI NOVEM PORTIS, The book of the nine doors of the kingdom of shadows. Then came the printer's mark, place, name, and date: *Venetiae, apud Aristidem Torchiam. M.DC.LX.VI. Cum superiorum privilegio veniaque.* With the privilege and permission of the superiors.

Borja was watching to see Corso's reaction.

"One can always tell a book lover," he said, "by the way he handles a book."

"I'm not a book lover."

"True. But sometimes you make one forget that you have the manners of a mercenary. When it comes to books, certain gestures can be reassuring. The way some people touch them is criminal."

Corso turned more pages. All the text was in Latin, printed in handsome type on thick, quality paper that had withstood the passage of time. There were nine splendid full-page engravings, showing scenes of a medieval appearance. He paused over one of them, at random. It was numbered with a Latin V, together with one Hebrew and one Greek letter or numeral. At the foot, one word which was incomplete or in code: "FR.ST.A." A man who looked like a merchant was counting out a sack of gold in front of a closed door, unaware of the skeleton behind him holding an hourglass in one hand and a pitchfork in the other.

"What do you think?" asked Borja.

"You told me it was a forgery, but this doesn't look like one. Have you examined it thoroughly?"

"I've gone over the whole thing, down to the last comma, with a magnifying glass. I've had plenty of time. I bought it six months ago, when the heirs of Gualterio Terral decided to sell his collection."

The book hunter turned more pages. The engravings were beautiful, of a simple, mysterious elegance. In another one, a young girl was about to be beheaded by an executioner in armor, his sword raised.

"I doubt that the heirs would have sold a forgery," said Corso when he'd finished examining it. "They have too much money, and they don't give a damn about books. The catalogue for the collection even had to be drawn up by Claymore's auctioneers.... And I knew old Terral. He would never have accepted a book that had been tampered with or forged."

"I agree," said Borja. "And he inherited *The Nine Doors* from his father-in-law, Don Lisardo Coy, a book collector with impeccable credentials."

"And he," said Corso as he placed the book on the desk and pulled out his notebook from his coat pocket, "bought it from an Italian, Domenico Chiara, whose family, according to the Weiss catalogue, had owned it since 1817...."

Borja nodded, pleased. "I see you've gone into the matter in some depth."

"Of course I have." Corso looked at him as if he'd just said something very stupid. "It's my job."

Borja made a placating gesture. "I don't doubt Terral and his heirs' good faith," he clarified. "Nor did I say that the book wasn't old."

"You said it was a forgery."

"Maybe forgery isn't the word."

"Well, what is it then? The book belongs to the right era." Corso picked it up again and flicked his thumb against the edge of the pages, listening. "Even the paper sounds right."

"There's something in it that doesn't sound right. And I don't mean the paper."

"Maybe the prints."

"What's wrong with them?"

"I would have expected copperplates. By 1666 nobody was using woodcuts."

"Don't forget that this was an unusual edition. The engravings are reproductions of other, older prints, supposedly discovered or seen by the printer."

"The *Delomelanicon*... Do you really believe that?"

"You don't care what I believe. But the book's nine original engravings aren't attributed to just anybody. Legend has it that Lucifer, after being defeated and thrown out of heaven, devised the magic formula to be used by his followers: the authoritative handbook of the shadows. A terrible book kept in secret, burned many times, sold for huge sums by the few privileged to own it... These illustrations are really satanic hieroglyphs. Interpreted with the aid of the text and the appropriate knowledge, they can be used to summon the prince of darkness."

Corso nodded with exaggerated gravity. "I can think of better ways to sell one's soul."

"Please don't joke, this is more serious than it seems.... Do you know what *Delomelanicon* means?"

"I think so. It comes from the Greek: *delo*, meaning to summon. And *melas:* black, dark."

Borja's laugh was high-pitched. He said in a tone of approval: "I forgot that you're an educated mercenary. You're right: to summon the shadows, or illuminate them... The prophet Daniel, Hippocrates, Flavius Josephus, Albertus Magnus, and Leon III all mention this wonderful book. People have been writing only for the last six thousand years, but the *Delomelanicon* is reputed to be three times that old. The first direct mention of it is in the Turis papyrus, written thirty-three centuries ago. Then, between 1 B.C. and the second year of our era, it is quoted several times in the *Corpus Hermeticum.* According to the *Asclemandres*, the book enables one to 'face the Light.' And in an incomplete inventory of the library at Alexandria, before it was destroyed for the third and last time in the year 646, there is a specific reference to the nine magic enigmas it contains.... We don't know if there was one copy or several, or if any copies survived the burning of the library.... Since then, its trail has disappeared and reappeared throughout history, through fires, wars, and disasters."

Corso looked doubtful. "That's always the case. All magic books have the same pedigree: from Thoth to Nicholas Flamel.... Once, a client of mine who was fascinated by alchemy asked me to find him the bibliography quoted by Fulcanelli and his followers. I couldn't convince him that half the books didn't exist."

"Well, this one did exist. It must have, for the Holy Office to list it in its Index. Don't you think?"

"It doesn't matter what I think. Lawyers who don't believe their clients are innocent still get them acquitted."

"That's the case here. I'm hiring you not because you believe but because you're good."

Corso turned more pages of the book. Another engraving, numbered I, showed a walled city on a hill. A strange unarmed horseman was riding toward the city, his finger to his lips requesting complicity or silence. The caption read: NEM. PERV.T QUI N.N LEG. CERT.RIT.

"It's in an abbreviated but decipherable code," explained Borja, watching him. *"Nemo pervenit qui non legitime certaverit."*

"Only he who has fought according to the rules will prevail?"

"That's about it. For the moment it's the only one of the nine captions that we can decipher with any certainty. An almost identical one appears in the works of Roger Bacon, a specialist in demonology, cryptography, and magic. Bacon claimed to own a *Delomelanicon* that had belonged to King Solomon, containing the key to terrible mysteries. The book was made of rolls of parchment with illustrations. It was burned in 1350 by personal order of Pope Innocent VI, who declared: 'It contains a method to summon devils.' In Venice three centuries later, Aristide Torchia decided to print it with the original illustrations."

"They're too good," objected Corso. "They can't be the originals: they'd be in an older style."

"I agree. Torchia must have updated them."

Another engraving, number III, showed a bridge with gate towers spanning a river. Corso looked up and saw that Borja was smiling mysteriously, like an alchemist confident of what is cooking in his crucible.

"There's one last connection," said the book dealer. "Giordano Bruno, martyr of rationalism, mathematician, and champion of the theory that the Earth rotates around the sun ..." He waved his hand contemptuously, as if all this was trivial. "But that was only part of his work. He wrote sixty-one books, and magic played an important role in them. Bruno makes specific reference to the *Delomelanicon*, even using the Greek words *delo* and *melas*, and he adds: 'On the path of men who want to know, there are nine secret doors.' He goes on to describe the methods for making the Light shine once more. '*Sic luceat Lux*,' he writes, which is actually the motto"—Borja showed Corso the printer's mark: a tree split by lighting, a snake, and a motto—"that Aristide Torchia used on the frontispiece of *The Nine Doors*.... What do you think of that?"

"It's all well and good. But it all comes to the same. You can make a text mean anything, especially if it's old and full of ambiguities."

"Or precautions. Giordano Bruno forgot the golden rule for survival: *Scire, tacere*. To know and keep silent. Apparently he knew the right things, but he talked too much. And there are more coincidences: Bruno was arrested in Venice, declared an obdurate heretic, and burned alive in Rome at Campo dei Fiori in February 1600. The same journey, the same places, and the same dates that marked Aristide Torchia's path to execution sixty-seven years later: he was arrested in Venice, tortured in Rome, and burned at Campo dei Fiori in February 1667. By then very few people were being burned at the stake, and yet he was."

"I'm impressed," said Corso, who wasn't in the least.

Borja tutted reprovingly.

"Sometimes I wonder if you believe in anything."

Corso seemed to consider that for a moment, then shrugged. "A long time ago, I did believe in something. But I was young and cruel then. Now I'm forty-five: I'm old and cruel."

"I am too. But there are things I still believe in. Things that make my heart beat faster."

"Like money?"

"Don't make fun of me. Money is the key that opens the door to man's dark secrets. And it pays for your services. And grants me the only thing in the world I respect: these books." He took a few steps along the cabinets full of books. "They are mirrors in the image of those who wrote them. They reflect their concerns, questions, desires, life, death . . . They're living beings: you have to know how to feed them, protect them . . ."

"And use them."

"Sometimes."

"But this one doesn't work."

"No."

"You've tried it."

It was a statement, not a question. Borja looked at Corso with hostility. "Don't be absurd. Let's just say I'm certain it's a forgery, and leave it at that. Which is why I need to compare it to the other copies."

"I still say it doesn't have to be a forgery. Books often differ even if they're part of the same edition. No two books are the same really. From birth they all have distinguishing details. And each book lives a different life: it can lose pages, or have them added or replaced, or acquire a new binding. . . . Over the years two books printed on the same press can end up looking entirely different. That might have happened to this one."

"Well, find out. Investigate *The Nine Doors* as if were a

crime. Follow trails, check each page, each engraving, the paper, the binding. . . . Work your way backward and find out where my copy comes from. Then do the same with the other two, in Sintra and in Paris."

"It would help if I knew how you learned that yours was a forgery."

"I can't tell you. Trust my intuition."

"Your intuition is going to cost you a lot of money."

"All you have to do is spend it."

He pulled the check from his pocket and gave it to Corso, who turned it over in his fingers, undecided.

"Why are you paying me in advance? You never did that before."

"You'll have a lot of expenses to cover. This is so you can get started." He handed him a thick bound file. "Everything I know about the book is in there. You may find it useful."

Corso was still looking at the check. "This is too much for an advance."

"You may encounter certain complications. . . ."

"You don't say." As he said this, he heard Borja clear his throat. They were getting to the crux of the matter at last.

"If you find out that the three copies are forgeries or are incomplete," Borja said, "then you'll have done your job and we'll settle up." He paused briefly and ran his hand over his tanned pate. He smiled awkwardly at Corso. "But one of the books may turn out to be authentic. In which case, you'll have more money at your disposal. Because I'll want it by whatever means, and without regard for expense."

"You're joking."

"Do I look as if I'm joking, Corso?"

"It's against the law."

"You've done illegal things before."

"Not this kind of thing."

"Nobody's ever paid you what I'll pay you."

"How can I be sure of that?"

"I'm letting you take the book with you. You'll need the original for your work. Isn't that enough of a guarantee?"

The jarring sound again, warning him. Corso was still holding *The Nine Doors*. He put the check between the pages like a bookmark and blew some imaginary dust off the book before returning it to Borja.

"Before, you said that with money you could pay people to do anything. Now you can test that out yourself. Go and see the owners of the books and do the dirty work yourself."

He turned and walked toward the door, wondering how many steps he'd take before the book dealer said anything. Three.

"This business isn't for men of words," said Borja. "It's for men of action."

His tone had changed. Gone was the arrogant composure and the disdain for the mercenary he was hiring. On the wall, an engraving of an angel by Dürer gently beat its wings behind the glass of a picture frame, while Corso's shoes turned on the black marble floor. Next to his cabinets full of books and the barred window with the cathedral in the background, next to everything that his money could buy, Varo Borja stood blinking, disconcerted. His expression was still arrogant; he even tapped the book cover with disdain. But Lucas Corso had learned to recognize defeat in a man's eyes. And fear.

His heart was beating with calm satisfaction as, without a word, he retraced his steps. As he approached Borja, he took the check poking out from between the pages of *The Nine Doors*. He folded it carefully and put it in his pocket. Then he took the file and the book.

"I'll be in touch," he said.

He realized that he'd thrown the dice. That he'd moved to the first square in a dangerous game of Snakes and Ladders and that it was too late to turn back. But he felt like playing. He went down the stairs followed by the echo of his own dry laughter. Varo Borja was wrong. There were things money couldn't buy.

THE STAIRS FROM THE main entrance led to an interior courtyard that had a well and two Venetian marble lions fenced off from the street by railings. An unpleasant dankness rose from the Tagus, and Corso stopped beneath the Moorish arch at the entrance to turn up his collar. He walked along the silent, narrow, cobbled streets until he came to a small square. There was a bar with metal tables, and chestnut trees with bare branches beneath the bell tower of a church. He took a seat in a patch of tepid sun on the terrace and tried to warm his stiff limbs. Two glasses of neat gin helped things along. Only then did he open the file on *The Nine Doors* and look through it properly for the first time.

There was a forty-two-page typed report giving the book's historical background, both for the supposed original version, the *Delomelanicon, or Invocation of Darkness*, and for Torchia's version, *Book of the Nine Doors of the Kingdom of Shadows*, printed in Venice in 1666. There were various appendices providing a bibliography, photocopies of citations in classical texts, and information about the other two known copies—their owners, any restoration work, purchase dates, present locations. There was also a transcription of the records of Aristide Torchia's trial, with the account of an eyewitness, one Gennaro Galeazzo, describing the unfortunate printer's last moments:

> *He mounted the scaffold without agreeing to be reconciled with God and maintained an obstinate silence. When the fire was lit, smoke began to suffocate him. He opened his eyes wide and uttered a terrible cry, commending himself to the Father. Many of those present crossed themselves, for in death he requested God's mercy. Others say that he shouted at the ground, in other words toward the depths of the earth.*

A car drove past on the other side of the square and turned down one of the corner streets leading to the cathedral. The engine paused for a moment beyond the corner, as if the driver had stopped before continuing down the street. Corso paid little attention, engrossed as he was in the book. The first page was the title page and the second was blank. The third, which began with a handsome capital N, contained a cryptic introduction, which read:

Nos p.tens L.f.r, juv.te Stn. Blz.b, Lvtn, Elm, atq Ast.rot. ali.q, h.die ha.ems ace.t pct fo.de.is c.m t. qui no.st; et h.ic pol.icem am.rem mul. flo.em virg.num de.us mon. hon v.lup et op. for.icab tr.d.o,.os.ta int. nos ma.et eb.iet i.li c.ra er. No.is of.ret se.el in ano sag. sig. s.b ped. cocul.ab sa Ecl.e et no.s r.gat i.sius er.t; p.ct v.v.t an v.q fe.ix in t.a hom. et ven D:
 Fa.t in inf int co.s daem.
 Satanas. Belzebub, Lcfr, Elimi, Leviathan, Astaroth
 Siq pos mag. diab. et daem. pri.cp dom.

After the introduction, whose "authorship" was obvious, came the text. Corso read the first lines:

D.mine mag.que L.fr, te D.um m. et.pr ag.sco. et pol.c.or t ser.ire. a.ob.re quam.d p. vvre; et rn.io al.rum d. et js.ch.st et a.s sn.ts tq.e s.ctas e. ec.les. apstl. et rom. et om. i sc.am. et o.nia ips. s.cramen. et o.nes .atio et r.g. q.ib fid. pos.nt int.rcd. p.o me; et t.bi po.lceor q. fac. qu.tqu.t m.lum pot., et atra. ad mala p. omn. Et ab.rncio chrsm. et b.ptm et omn...

He looked up at the church portico. The arches were carved with images of the Last Judgment worn by the elements. Beneath them, dividing the door in two, a niche sheltered an angry-looking Pantocrator. His raised right hand suggested punishment rather than mercy. In his left hand he held an open book, and Corso could not help drawing parallels. He looked around at the church tower and the surrounding buildings. The facades still bore bishops' coats of arms, and he reflected that this square too had once witnessed the bonfires of the Inquisition. After all, this was Toledo. A crucible for underground cults, initiation rites, false converts. And heretics.

He drank some more gin before going back to the book. The text, in an abbreviated Latin code, took up another hundred and fifty-seven pages, the final page being blank. Nine contained the famous engravings inspired, according to legend, by Lucifer himself. Each print had a Latin, Hebrew, and Greek numeral at the top, including a Latin phrase in the same abbreviated code. Corso ordered a third gin and went over them. They looked like the figures of the tarot, or old, medieval engravings: the king and the beggar, the hermit, the hangman, death, the executioner. In the last engraving a beautiful woman was riding a dragon. Too beautiful, he thought, for the religious morality of the time.

He found an identical illustration on a photocopy of a page from Mateu's *Universal Bibliography*. But it wasn't the same. Corso was holding the Terral-Coy copy, whereas the engraving on the photocopy came, as recorded by the scholarly Mateu in 1929, from another one of the books:

> *Torchia (Aristide).* De Umbrarum Regni Novem Portis. Venetiae, apud Aristidem Torchiam. MDCLXVI. *Folio. 160 pages incl. title page. 9 full-page woodcuts. Of exceptional rarity. Only 3 known copies. Fargas Library, Sintra, Port. (see illustration). Coy Library, Madrid, Sp. (engraving 9 missing). Morel Library, Paris, Fr.*

Engraving 9 missing. Corso checked and saw that this was wrong. Engraving 9 was there in the copy he held, the copy formerly from the Coy, later the Terral-Coy Library, and now the property of Varo Borja. It must have been a printing error, or a mistake by Mateu himself. In 1929, when the *Universal Bibliography* was published, printing techniques and distribution methods weren't as efficient. Many scholars mentioned books that they only knew of through third parties. Maybe the

314

por ti solo ser causada
siente agora el gran dolor
que me das en tu partida
agradesce el gran amor
que te puse con fauor
reparando tu venida.

S. l. ni a. *(hàcia 1525).* 4.° let. gót. 4 *hojas sin foliacion con la sign.* a.

HOMERO. La Vlyxea de Homero. Repartida en XIII. Libros. Tradvzida de Griego en Romance castellano por el Señor Gonçalo Perez. Venetia, en casa de Gabriel Giolito de Ferrariis, y svs hermanos, MDLIII. 12.° let. curs. 209 *hojas foliadas, inclusos los prels. y una al fin, en cuyo reverso se repiten las señas de la impresion.*

He visto la primera edicion, con el siguiente título: *De la Ulyxea de Homero. XIII. libros, traduzidos de Griego en Romance Castellano por Gonçalo Perez. Anuers, en casa de Iuan Stelsio,* 1550. 8.° let. cursiva. 4 hojas prels. y 293 fols.
Nic. Antonio menciona otra tambien de *Anuers,* 1553. 12.°

Poema en ciento treinta y cinco octavas. Hai al fin una disertacion en prosa, intitulada: *Prueba, que huuo Gigantes, y que oy los ay,* y por cierto para mí solo prueba que el autor era sumamente cándido ó tenía mui grandes tragaderas: sea esto dicho con perdon de los varios textos bíblicos y de Santos Padres que aduce en confirmacion de sus ideas gigantescas.

OVIDIO NASON. Metamorphoseos del excelente poeta Ovidio Nasson. Traduzidos en verso suelto y octaua rima: con sus allegorias al fin de cada libro. Por el Doctor Antonio Perez Sigler. Nuevamente agora enmŏdados, y añadido por el mismo autor vn Diccionario Poetico copiosissimo. Bvrgos, Iuan Baptista Varesio, 1609. 12.° let. curs. 21 *hojas prels. y* 584 *fols.*

Este tomito por ser tan grueso suele hallarse dividido en dos volúmenes. No estoi cierto si mi ejemplar está perfectamente completo con las 21 hojas de preliminares.

VIIII

N.NC SC.O TEN.BR. LVX

Sedano, en el tom. VII. del *Autores* llama á esta primera edicion; sin embargo me pone en duda el ver lleva la Aprobacion, la Censura, el Privilegio, la Fe de erratas y la Tasa fechadas en 1666. Por otra parte tambien puede ser cierto lo sentado por dicho Sedano, pues D. José Pellicer, al principio de su introduccion biográfico-literaria, observa que *salen ya á luz pública, despues de*

He found an identical illustration on a photocopy of a page from Mateu's Universal Bibliography.

engraving was missing from one of the other copies. Corso made a note in the margin of the photocopy. He needed to check it.

A clock somewhere struck three, and pigeons flew up from the tower and roofs. Corso shuddered gently, as if slowly coming to. He felt in his pocket and took out some money. He put it on the table and stood up. The gin made him feel pleasantly detached, blurring external sounds and images. He put the book and file in his canvas bag, slung it over his shoulder, then stood for a few seconds looking at the angry Pantocrator in the portico. He wasn't in a hurry and wanted to clear his head, so he decided to walk to the train station.

When he reached the cathedral, he took a shortcut through the cloisters. He passed the closed souvenir kiosk and stood for a moment looking at the empty scaffolding over the murals undergoing restoration. The place was deserted, and his steps echoed beneath the vault. He thought he heard something behind him. A priest late to confession.

He came out through an iron gate into a dark, narrow street, where passing cars had taken chunks out of the walls. As he turned to the right, a car came from somewhere to the left. There was a traffic sign, a triangle warning that the street narrowed, and when Corso came to it, the car accelerated unexpectedly. He could hear it behind him, coming too fast, he thought as he turned to look, but he only had time to half-turn, just enough to see a dark shape bearing down on him. His reflexes were dulled by the gin, but by chance his attention was still on the traffic sign. Instinct pushing him toward it, he sought the narrow area of protection between the metal post and the wall. He slid into the small gap like a bullfighter hiding behind the barrier from the bull. The car managed to strike only his hand as it passed him. The blow was sharp, and the pain made his knees buckle. Falling onto the cobbles, he saw the car disappear down the street with a screech of tires.

Corso walked on to the station, rubbing his bruised hand. But now he turned every so often to look behind him, and his bag, with *The Nine Doors* inside, was burning his shoulder. For three seconds he'd caught a fleeting glimpse, but it had been enough: this time the man was driving a black Mercedes, not a Jaguar. The one who'd nearly run Corso down was dark, had a mustache, and a scar on his face. The man from Makarova's bar. The same man he'd seen in a chauffeur's uniform, reading a newspaper outside Liana Taillefer's house.

IV. THE MAN WITH THE SCAR

I know not where he comes from.
But I know where he is going: he is going to Hell.
—A. Dumas, THE COUNT OF MONTE CRISTO

Night was falling when Corso got home. Inside his coat pocket his bruised hand throbbed painfully. He went to the bathroom, picked up his crumpled pajamas and a towel from the floor, and held the hand under a stream of cold water for five minutes. Then he opened a couple of cans and ate, standing in the kitchen.

It had been a strange and dangerous day. As he thought about it, he felt confused, though he was less worried than curious. For some time, he had treated the unexpected with the detached fatalism of one who waits for life to make the next move. His detachment, his neutrality, meant that he could never be the prime mover. Until that morning in the narrow street in Toledo, his role had been merely to carry out orders. Other people were the victims. Every time he lied or made a deal with someone, he stayed objective. He formed no relationships with the persons or things involved—they were simply tools of the trade. He remained on the side, a mercenary with no cause other than financial gain. The indifferent third man. Perhaps this attitude had always made him feel safe, just as, when he took off his glasses, people and objects became blurred, indistinct; he could ignore them by removing their sharp outline. Now, though, the pain from his injured hand, the sense of imminent danger, of violence aimed directly at him and him alone, implied frightening changes in his world. Lucas Corso, who had acted as victimizer so many times, wasn't used to being a victim. And he found it highly disconcerting.

In addition to the pain in his hand, his muscles were rigid with tension and his mouth was dry. He opened a bottle of Bols and searched for aspirin in his canvas bag. He always carried a good supply, together with books, pencils, pens, half-filled notepads, a Swiss Army knife, a passport, money, a bulging address book, and books belonging to him and to others. He could, at any time, disappear without a trace like a snail into its shell. With his bag he could make himself at home wherever chance, or his clients, led him—airports, train stations, dusty European libraries, hotel rooms that merged in his memory into a single room with fluid dimensions, where he would wake with a start, disoriented and confused in the darkness, searching for the light switch only to stumble upon the phone. Blank moments torn from his life and his consciousness. He was never very sure of himself, or of anything, for the first thirty seconds after he opened his eyes, his body waking before his mind or his memory.

He sat at his computer and put his notepads and several reference books on the desk to his left. On his right he put *The Nine Doors* and Varo Borja's folder. Then he leaned back in the chair, letting his cigarette burn down in his hand for five minutes, bringing it to his lips only once or twice. During that time all he did was sip the rest of his gin and stare at the blank computer screen and the pentacle on the book's cover. At last he seemed to wake up. He stubbed out the cigarette in the ashtray and, adjusting his crooked glasses, set to work. Varo Borja's file agreed with Crozet's *Encyclopedia of Printers and Rare and Curious Books*:

TORCHIA, *Aristide (1620–1667). Venetian printer, engraver, and bookbinder. Printer's mark: a snake and a tree split by lightning. Trained as an apprentice in Leyden (Holland), at the workshop of the Elzevirs.* On his return to Venice he completed a series of works on philosophical and esoteric themes in small formats *(12mo, 16mo), which were highly esteemed. Notable among these are* The Secrets of Wisdom *by Nicholas Tamisso (3 vols, 12mo, Venice 1650),* Key to Captive Thoughts *(1 vol, 132x75mm, Venice 1653),* The Three Books of the Art *by Paolo d'Este (6 vols, 8vo, Venice 1658),* Curious Explanation of Mysteries and Hieroglyphs *(1 vol, 8vo, Venice 1659), a reprint of* The Lost Word *by Bernardo Trevisano (1 vol, 8vo, Venice 1661), and* Book of The Nine Doors of the Kingdom of Shadows *(1 vol, folio, Venice 1666). Because of the printing of the latter, he fell into the hands of the Inquisition. His workshop was destroyed together with all the printed and yet to be printed texts it contained. Torchia was put to death. Condemned for magic and witchcraft, he was burned at the stake on 17 February 1667.*

Corso looked away from the computer and examined the first page of the book that had cost the Venetian printer his life. The title was DE UMBRARUM REGNI NOVEM PORTIS. Beneath it came the printer's mark, the device that acted as the printer's signature, which might be anything from a simple monogram to an elaborate illustration. In Aristide Torchia's case, as mentioned in Crozet, the mark was a tree with one branch snapped off by lightning and a snake coiled around the trunk, devouring its own tail. The picture was accompanied by the motto SIC LUCEAT LUX: Thus shines the Light. At the foot of the page were the location, name, and date: *Venetiae, apud Aristidem Torchiam.* Printed in Venice, at the establishment of Aristide Torchia. Underneath, separated by a decoration: MDCLXVI *Cum superiorum privilegio veniaque.* By authority and permission of the superiors.

Corso entered into the computer:

Copy has no bookplates or handwritten notes. Complete according to catalogue for Terral-Coy collection auction (Claymore, Madrid). Error in Mateu (states 8, not 9, engravings in this copy). Folio. 299x215mm. 2 blank flyleaves, 160 pages and 9 full-page prints, numbered I to VIIII. Pages: 1 title page with printer's mark. 157 pages of text. Last one blank, no colophon. Full-page engravings on recto page. Verso blank.

He examined the illustrations one by one. According to Borja, legend attributed the original drawings to the hand of Lucifer himself. Each print was accompanied by a Roman ordinal, its Hebrew and Greek equivalent, and a Latin phrase in abbreviated code. He entered:

I. NEM. PERV.T.QUI N.N LEG. CERT.RIT: A horseman rides toward a walled city. He has a finger to his lips, advising caution or silence.

II. CLAUS. PAT.T: A hermit in front of a locked door, holding 2 keys. A lantern on the ground. He is accompanied by a dog. At his side a sign resembling the Hebrew letter Teth.

III. VERB. D.SUM C.S.T ARCAN.: A vagabond, or pilgrim, heads toward a bridge over a river. At both ends of the bridge, gate towers with closed doors bar the way. An archer on a cloud aims at the path leading to the bridge.

IIII. (The Latin numeral appears in this form, not the more usual IV). FOR. N.N OMN. A.QUE: A jester stands in front of a stone labyrinth. The entrance is also closed. Three dice on the ground, showing the numbers 1, 2, and 3.

V. FR.ST.A.: A miser, or merchant, is counting out a sack of gold pieces. Behind him, Death holds an hourglass in one hand and a pitchfork in the other.

VI. DIT.SCO M.R.: A hangman, like the one in the tarot, hands tied behind his back, is hanging by his foot from the battlements of a castle, next to a closed postern. A hand in a gauntlet sticks out of a slot window holding a flaming sword.

DE VMBRARVM REGNI
NOVEM PORTIS

Sic   *Luceat*

Lux

Venetiae, apud Aristidem Torchiam

M. DC. LX. VI.

Cum superiorum privilegio veniaque

NEM. PERV.T QVI N.N LEG. CERT.RIT

CLAVS. PAT:T

VERB. D.SVM C.S.T ARCAN.

FOR. N.N OMN. A.QVE

FR. ST. A

DIT.SCO M.R.

DIS.S P.TI.R M.

VIC. I.T VIR.

N.NC SC.O TEN.BR. LVX

VII. DIS.S. P.TI.R MAG: A king and a beggar are playing chess on a board with only white squares. The moon can be seen through the window. Beneath a window next to a closed door, two dogs are fighting.

VIII. VIC. I.T VIR.: Next to the wall of a city a woman kneels on the ground, offering up her bare neck to the executioner. In the background there is a wheel of fortune with three human figures: one at the top, one going up, and one going down.

VIIII. (Also in this form, not the usual numeral IX). N.NC SC.O TEN.EBR. LUX: A naked woman riding a seven-headed dragon. She holds an open book, and a half-moon hides her sex. On a hill in the background there is a castle in flames. The door is closed, as in the other engravings.

He stopped typing, stretched his stiffened limbs, and yawned. The room was in darkness beyond the cone of light from his work lamp and his computer screen. Through the window came the pale glow of streetlights. He went to the window and looked out, not quite knowing what he expected to see. A car waiting at the curb, perhaps, its headlights off and a dark figure inside. But nothing attracted his attention except, for a moment, the siren of an ambulance fading among the dark masses of buildings. He looked at the clock on the nearby church tower: it was five minutes past midnight.

He sat down again at the computer and the book. He examined the first illustration—the printer's mark on the title page, the snake with its tail in its mouth, which Aristide Torchia had chosen as the symbol of his work. SIC LUCEAT LUX. Snakes and devils, invocations and hidden meanings. He lifted his glass to drink a sarcastic toast to Torchia's memory. The man must have been very brave, or very stupid. You paid a high price for that kind of thing in seventeenth-century Italy, even if it was printed *cum superiorum privilegio veniaque*.

But then Corso stopped and cursed out loud, looking into the dark corners of the room, for not having noticed before. "With the privilege and license of the superiors." That wasn't possible.

Without taking his eyes from the page, he sat back in his chair and lit another of his crushed cigarettes. Spirals of smoke rose in the lamplight, a translucent gray curtain behind which the lines of print rippled.

Cum superiorum privilegio veniaque didn't make sense. Or else it was brilliantly subtle. The reference to the imprimatur couldn't possibly mean a conventional authorization. The Catholic Church would never have allowed such a book in 1666, because its direct predecessor, the *Delomelanicon,* had been listed in the index of forbidden books for the previous hundred and fifty years. So Aristide Torchia wasn't referring to a permission to print granted by the Church censors. Nor to a civil authority, the government of the republic of Venice. He must have had other superiors.

THE TELEPHONE INTERRUPTED HIS thought. It was Flavio La Ponte. He wanted to tell Corso how he'd found, in with some books (he'd had to buy the whole lot, that was the deal), a collection of European tram tickets, 5,775 of them to be exact. All palindromic numbers, sorted by country in shoe boxes. He wasn't joking. The collector had just died, and the family wanted to get rid of them. Maybe Corso knew someone who'd be interested. Naturally. La Ponte knew that the tireless, and pathological, activity of collecting 5,775 palindromic tickets was completely pointless. Who would buy such a stupid collection? Yes, the Transport Museum in London, that was a good idea. The English and their perversions... Would Corso deal with the matter?

La Ponte was also worried about the Dumas chapter. He'd received two telephone calls, from a man and a woman who didn't identify themselves, asking about "The Anjou Wine." Which was strange, because La Ponte hadn't mentioned the chapter to anyone and wasn't intending to until he had Corso's report. Corso told him of his conversation with Liana Taillefer and that he had revealed to her the identity of the new owner.

"She knew you because you used to go and see her late husband. Oh, and by the way," he remembered, "she wants a copy of the receipt."

La Ponte laughed at the other end of the line. There was no damn receipt. Taillefer had sold it to him, and that was that. But if the lovely widow wanted to discuss the matter, he added, laughing lewdly, he'd be delighted. Corso mentioned the possibility that before he died Taillefer might have told someone about the manuscript. La Ponte didn't think so; Taillefer had been very insistent that the matter be kept secret until he himself gave a sign. In the end, he never gave a sign, unless hanging himself from the light fixture was one.

"It's as good a sign as any," said Corso.

La Ponte agreed, chuckling cynically. Then he asked about Corso's visit to Liana Taillefer. After a couple more lecherous comments, La Ponte said good-bye. Corso hadn't mentioned the incident in Toledo. They agreed to meet the following day.

After he hung up, Corso went back to *The Nine Doors*. But his mind was on other things. He was drawn back to the Dumas manuscript. Finally he went and got the folder with the white and blue pages. He rubbed his painful hand and called up the Dumas directory. The computer screen began to flicker. He stopped at a file called Bio:

Dumas Davy de la Pailleterie, Alexandre. Born 24.7.1802. Died 5.12.1870. Son of Thomas Alexandre Dumas, general of the Republic. Author of 257 volumes of novels, memoirs, and stories. 25 volumes of plays. Mulatto on his father's side. His black blood gave him certain exotic features. Appearance: tall, powerful neck, curly hair, fleshy lips, long legs, physically strong. Character: bon vivant, fickle, overpowering, liar, unreliable, popular. He had 27 known mistresses, 2 legitimate children and 4 illegitimate. He

made several fortunes and squandered them on parties, travel, ex-
pensive wines, and flowers. He lost all the money earned from
his writing by extravagant spending on mistresses, friends, and
hangers-on who besieged his castle home at Montecristo. When he
fled Paris, it was to escape his creditors, not for political reasons,
like his friend Victor Hugo. Friends: Hugo, Lamartine, Michelet,
Gérard de Nerval, Nodier, George Sand, Berlioz, Théofile Gautier,
Alfred de Vigny, and others. Enemies: Balzac, Badère, and others.

None of this really got him anywhere. He felt he was stumbling
around in the dark, surrounded by countless false or useless
clues. And yet there had to be a link somewhere. With his good
hand he typed Dumas.nov:

Novels by Alexandre Dumas that appeared in installments:
1831: Historical scenes (Revue des Deux Mondes). 1834: Jacques
I and Jacques II (Journal des Enfants). 1835: Elizabeth of Ba-
varia (Dumont). 1836: Murat (La Presse). 1837: Pascal Bruno
(La Presse), Story of a Tenor (Gazette Musicale). 1838: Count
Horatio (La Presse), Nero's Night (La Presse), The Arms Hall
(Dumont), Captain Paul (Le Siècle). 1839: Jacques Ortis (Du-
mont), The Life and Adventures of John Davys (Revue de Paris),
Captain Panphile (Dumont). 1840: The Fencing Master (Revue
de Paris). 1841: Le Chevalier d'Harmental (Le Siècle). 1843:
Sylvandire (La Presse), The Wedding Dress (La Mode), Albine
(Revue de Paris), Ascanio (Le Siècle), Fernande (Revue de
Paris), Amaury (La Presse). 1844: The Three Musketeers (Le
Siècle), Gabriel Lambert (La Chronique), The Regent's Daughter
(Le Commerce), The Corsican Brothers (Démocratie Pacifique),
The Count of Monte Cristo (Journal des Débats), Countess Ber-
tha (Hetzel), Story of a Nutcracker (Hetzel), Queen Margot (La
Presse). 1845: Nanon (La Patrie), Twenty Years After (Le Sie-
cle), Le Chevalier de la Maison Rouge (Démocratie Pacifique),
The Lady of Monsoreau (Le Constitutionnel), Madame de Conde
(La Patrie). 1846: The Viscountess of Cambes (La Patrie), The

*Half-Brothers (Le Commerce), Joseph Balsam (La Presse),
Pessac Abbey (La Patrie).* 1847: *The Forty-Five (Le Constitu-
tionnel), Le Vicomte de Bragelonne (Le Siècle).* 1848: *The
Queen's Necklace (La Presse).* 1849: *The Weddings of Father
Olifus (Le Constitutionnel).* 1850: *God's Will (Evènement), The
Black Tulip (Le Siècle), The Dove (Le Siècle), Angel Pitou (La
Presse).* 1851: *Olympe de Clèves (Le Siècle).* 1852: *God and the
Devil (Le Pays), The Comtesse de Charny (Cadot), Isaac La-
quedem (Le Constitutionnel).* 1853: *The Shepherd of Ashbourn
(Le Pays), Catherine Blum (Le Pays).* 1854: *The Life and Ad-
ventures of Catherine-Charlotte (Le Mousquetaire), The Brigand
(Le Mousquetaire), The Mohicans of Paris (Le Mousquetaire),
Captain Richard (Le Siècle), The Page of the Duke of Savoy (Le
Constituionnel).* 1856: *The Companions of Jehu (Journal pour
Tous).* 1857: *The Last Saxon King (Le Monte-Cristo), The Wolf
Leader (Le Siècle), The Wild Duck Shooter (Cadot), Black (Le
Constitutionnel).* 1858: *The She-Wolves of Machecoul (Journal
Pour Tous), Memoirs of a Policeman (Le Siècle), The Palace of
Ice (Le Monte-Cristo).* 1859: *The Frigate (Le Monte-Cristo),
Ammalat-Beg (Moniteur Universel), Story of a Dungeon and a
Little House (Revue Européenne), A Love Story (Le Monte-
Cristo).* 1860: *Memoirs of Horatio (Le Siècle), Father La Ruine
(Le Siècle), The Marchioness of Escoman (Le Constitutionnel),
The Doctor of Java (Le Siècle), Jane (Le Siècle).* 1861: *A Night
in Florence (Levy-Hetzel).* 1862: *The Volunteer of 92 (Le Monte-
Cristo).* 1863: *The Saint Felice (La Presse).* 1864: *The Two Di-
anas (Levy), Ivanhoe (Pub. du Siècle).* 1865: *Memoirs of a
Favorite (Avenir National), The Count of Moret (Les Nouvelles).*
1866: *A Case of Conscience (Le Soleil), Parisians and Provincials
(La Presse), The Count of Mazarra (Le Mousquetaire).* 1867:
*The Whites and the Blues (Le Mousquetaire), The Prussian
Terror (La Situation).* 1869: *Hector de Sainte-Hermine (Moniteur
Universel), The Mysterious Physician (Le Siècle), The Marquis's
Daughter (Le Siècle).*

He smiled, wondering how much the late Enrique Taillefer would have paid to obtain all those titles. His glasses were misted, so he took them off and carefully cleaned the lenses. The lines on the computer were now blurred, as were other strange images he couldn't identify. With his glasses back on, the words on the screen became sharp again, but the images were still floating around, indistinct, in his mind, and without a key to give them any meaning. And yet Corso felt he was on the right path. The screen began to flicker again:

Baudry, editor of Le Siècle. *Publishes* The Three Musketeers *between the 14th of March and the 11th of July 1844.*

He took a look at the other files. According to his information, Dumas had had fifty-two collaborators at different periods of his literary life. Relations with a large number of them had ended stormily. But Corso was only interested in one of the names:

Maquet, Auguste-Jules. 1813–1886. Collaborated with Alexandre Dumas on several plays and 19 novels, including the most famous ones (The Count of Monte Cristo, Le Chevalier de la Maison Rouge, The Black Tulip, The Queen's Necklace) *and, in particular, the cycle of* The Musketeers. *His collaboration with Dumas made him famous and wealthy. While Dumas died penniless, Maquet died a rich man at his castle in Saint-Mesme. None of his own works written without Dumas survives.*

He looked at his biographical notes. There were some paragraphs taken from Dumas's *Memoirs*:

We were the inventors, Hugo, Balzac, Soulie, De Musset, and myself, of popular literature. We managed, for better or worse, to make a reputation for ourselves with that kind of writing, even though it was popular. . . .

My imagination, confronted with reality, resembles a man who, visiting the ruins of an old building, must walk over the rubble, follow the passageways, bend down to go through doorways, so as to reconstruct an approximate picture of the original building when it was full of life, when joy filled it with laughter and song, or when it echoed with sobs of sorrow.

Exasperated, Corso looked away from the screen. He was losing the feeling, it was disappearing into the corners of his memory before he could identify it. He stood up and paced the dark room. Then he angled his lamp at a pile of books on the floor, against the wall. He picked up two thick volumes: a modern edition of the *Memoirs* of Alexandre Dumas père. He went back to his desk and began to leaf through them until three photographs caught his eye. In one of them, his African blood clearly visible in his curly hair and mulatto looks, Dumas sat smiling at Isabelle Constant, who, Corso gathered from the caption, was fifteen when she became the novelist's mistress. The second photograph showed an older Dumas, posing with his daughter Marie. Here, at the height of his fame, the father of the adventure serial sat, good-natured and placid, before the photographer. The third photograph, Corso decided, was definitely the most amusing and significant. Dumas aged sixty-five, gray-haired but still tall and strong, his frock coat open to reveal a contented paunch, was embracing Adah Menken, one of his last mistresses. According to the text, "after the seances and sessions of black magic of which she was such a devotee, she liked to be photographed, scantily clad, with the great men in her life." In the photograph, La Menken's legs, arms, and neck were all bare, which was scandalous for the time. The young woman, paying more attention to the camera than to the object of her embrace, was leaning her head on the old man's powerful right shoulder. As for him, his face showed the signs of a long life of dissipation, pleasure, and parties. His smile, between the bloated cheeks of a bon viveur, was satisfied, ironic. His expression for the photographer was teasing, crafty, seeking complicity. The fat old man with the shameless,

Dumas was embracing Adah Menken, one of his last mistresses.

passionate young girl who showed him off like a rare trophy: he, whose characters and stories had made so many women dream. It was as if old Dumas was asking for understanding, having given in to the girl's capricious wish to be photographed.

After all, she was young and pretty, her skin soft and her mouth passionate, this girl that life had kept for him on the last lap of his journey, only three years before his death. The old devil.

Corso shut the book and yawned. His watch, an old chronometer that he often forgot to wind up, had stopped at a quarter past midnight. He went and opened the window and breathed in the cold night air. The street was still deserted.

It was all very strange, he thought as he went back to his desk and turned off the computer. His eyes came to rest on the folder with the manuscript. He opened it mechanically and took another look at the fifteen pages covered with two different types of handwriting, eleven of the pages blue, four of them white. *Après de nouvelles presque désespérées du roi...* Upon almost desperate news from the king... In the pile of books on the floor he found a huge red tome, a facsimile edition— J. C. Lattes, 1988—containing the entire cycle of *The Musketeers* and *Monte Cristo* in the Le Vasseur edition with engravings, published shortly after Dumas's death. He found the chapter "The Anjou Wine" on page 144 and started to read, comparing it with the original manuscript. Except for a small error here and there, the texts were identical. In the book, the chapter was illustrated with two drawings by Maurice Leloir, engraved by Huyot. King Louis XIII arriving at the siege of La Rochelle with ten thousand men, four horsemen at the head of his escort, holding their muskets, wearing the wide-brimmed hat and jacket of de Treville's company. Three of them are without doubt Athos, Porthos, and Aramis. A moment later they will be meeting their friend d'Artagnan, still a simple cadet in Monsieur des Essarts's company of guards. The Gascon still doesn't know that the bottles of Anjou wine, a gift from his mortal enemy Milady, Richelieu's agent, are poisoned. She wants to avenge the insult done to her by d'Artagnan. He has passed himself off as the Comte de Wardes, slipped into her bed, and enjoyed a night of love that should have been the count's. To make matters worse, d'Artagnan has by chance discovered Milady's terrible secret, the fleur-de-lis on her shoulder, the shameful mark branded on her by the executioner's iron. With such preliminaries, and given Milady's disposition, the contents of the second illustration are easy to guess: as d'Artagnan and his companions watch in astonishment, the manservant Fourreau expires in terrible agony after drinking the wine intended for his master. Sensitive to the magic of a text he hadn't read in twenty years, Corso came to the passage where the musketeers and d'Artagnan are speaking about Milady:

"Well," said d'Artagnan to Athos. "So you see, dear friend. It is a fight to the death."

Athos nodded. "Yes, yes," he said. "I know. But do you think it's really her?"

"I am sure of it."

"Nevertheless, I confess I still have doubts."

"And the fleur-de-lis on her shoulder?"

"She is an Englishwoman who must have committed some crime in France, and who has been marked for her crime."

"Athos, that woman is your wife, I tell you," repeated d'Artagnan. "Do you not recall that both marks are identical?"

"Nevertheless I would have sworn that the woman was dead, I hanged her very well."

This time it was d'Artagnan who shook his head.

"Well? What are we to do?" said the young man.

"We certainly can't go on like this, with a sword hanging eternally over our heads," said Athos. "We must find a way out of this situation."

"But how?"

"Listen, try to have a meeting with her and explain everything. Tell her: 'Peace or war! My word as a gentleman that I will never say or do anything against you. For your part, give me your solemn word to do nothing against me. Otherwise I will go to the Chancellor, the King, the executioner, I will incite the Court against you, I will denounce you as a marked woman, I will have

you put on trial, and should you be acquitted, then upon my word as a gentleman, I will kill you myself, in any corner, as I would a rabid dog.'"

"*I am delighted with this plan,*" said d'Artagnan.

Memories brought other memories in their wake. Corso tried to hold a fleeting, familiar image that had crossed his mind. He managed to capture it just before it faded, and once again it was the man in the black suit, the chauffeur of the Jaguar outside Liana Taillefer's house, at the wheel of the Mercedes in Toledo.... The man with the scar. And it was Milady who had stirred that memory.

He thought it over, disconcerted. And suddenly the image became perfectly sharp. Milady, of course. Milady de Winter as d'Artagnan first sees her at the window of her carriage in the opening chapter of the novel, outside the inn at Meung. Milady in conversation with a stranger. Corso quickly turned the pages, searching for the passage. He found it easily:

A man of forty to forty-five years of age, with black, piercing eyes, a pale complexion, a strongly pronounced nose, and a perfectly trimmed, black mustache...

Rochefort. The Cardinal's sinister agent and d'Artagnan's enemy, who has him beaten in the first chapter, steals the letter of recommendation to Monsieur de Treville and is indirectly responsible for the Gascon's almost fighting duels with Athos, Porthos, and Aramis.... Following this somersault of his memory, Corso scratched his head, puzzled by the unusual association of ideas and characters. What link was there between Milady's companion and the driver who tried to run him down in Toledo? Then there was the scar. The paragraph didn't mention a scar, but he remembered clearly that Rochefort always had a mark on his face. He turned more pages until he found the confirmation of this in chapter 3, where d'Artagnan is recounting his adventure to Treville:

"Tell me," he replied, *"did this gentleman have a faint scar on his temple?"*

"Yes, the sort of mark that might have been made by a bullet grazing it...."

A faint scar on his temple. There was his confirmation, but as Corso remembered it, Rochefort's scar was bigger, and not on his temple but on his cheek, like that of the chauffeur dressed in black. Corso went over it all until at last he let out a laugh. The picture was now complete, and in full color: Lana Turner in *The Three Musketeers*, at her carriage window, beside a suitably sinister Rochefort, not pale as in Dumas's novel, but dark, with a plumed hat and a long scar—it was definite this time—cutting his right cheek from top to bottom. He remembered it as a film, not a novel, and his exasperation at this both amused and irritated him. Goddamn Hollywood.

Film scenes aside, he had at last managed to find some order to all of this, a common, if secret, thread, a tune composed of disparate, mysterious notes. Through the vague uneasiness that Corso had experienced since his visit to Taillefer's widow, he could now glimpse outlines, faces, an atmosphere and characters, halfway between reality and fiction, and all linked in strange, as yet unclear ways. Dumas and a seventeenth-century book. The devil and *The Three Musketeers*. Milady and the bonfires of the Inquisition... Although it was all more absurd than definite, more like a novel than real life.

He turned out the light and went to bed. But it took him some time to fall asleep, because one image wouldn't leave his mind. It floated in the darkness before his open eyes. A distant landscape, that of his reading as a boy, filled with shadows which reappeared now twenty years later, materialized as ghosts that were so close, he could almost feel them. The scar. Rochefort. The man from Meung. His Eminence's mercenary.

V. REMEMBER

He was sitting just as he had left him, in front of the fireplace.
—A. Christie, THE MURDER OF ROGER ACKROYD

This is the point at which I enter the stage for the second time. Corso came to me again, and he did so, I seem to remember, a few days before leaving for Portugal. As he told me later, by then he already suspected that the Dumas manuscript and Varo Borja's *Nine Doors* were only the tip of the iceberg. To understand it all he first needed to locate the other stories, all knotted together like the tie Enrique Taillefer used to hang himself. It wouldn't be easy, I told him, because in literature there are never any clear boundaries. Everything is dependent on everything else, and one thing is superimposed on top of another. It all ends up as a complicated intertextual game, like a hall of mirrors or those Russian dolls. Establishing a specific fact or the precise source involves risks that only some of my very stupid or very confident colleagues would dare take. It would be like saying that you can see the influence of *Quo Vadis*, but not Suetonius or Appollonius of Rhodes, on Robert Graves. As for me, all I know is that I know nothing. And when I want to know something, I look it up in books—their memory never fails.

"Count Rochefort is one of the most important secondary

characters in *The Three Musketeers*," I explained to Corso when he came to see me. "He is the cardinal's agent, a friend of Milady's, and the first enemy that d'Artagnan makes. I can pinpoint the exact date: the first Monday of April 1625, in Meung-sur-Loire.... I refer to the fictional Rochefort of course, although a similar character did exist. Gatien de Courtilz described him, in the supposed *Memoirs* of the real d'Artagnan, a man with the name of Rosnas. But the Rochefort with the scar didn't exist in real life. Dumas took the character from another book, the *Memoires de MLCDR (Monsieur le comte de Rochefort)*, possibly apocryphal and also attributed to Courtilz. Some say that that book could refer to Henri Louis d'Aloigny, Marquis de Rochefort, born around 1625, but that's stretching things."

I looked out at the lights of the evening traffic in the avenues beyond the window of the café where I meet with my literary friends. A few of them were sitting with us around a table covered with newspapers, cups, and smoking ashtrays— two writers, a painter down on his luck, a woman journalist on the rise, a stage actor, and four or five students, the kind who sit in a corner and don't open their mouths, watching you as if you were God. Corso sat among them, still in his coat. He leaned against the window, drank gin, and occasionally took notes.

"To be sure," I added, "the reader who goes through the sixty-seven chapters of *The Three Musketeers* waiting for the duel between Rochefort and d'Artagnan is in for a disappointment. Dumas settles the matter in three lines, and is rather underhand about it. Because when we next meet Rochefort in *Twenty Years After*, he and d'Artagnan have fought three times, and Rochefort bears as many scars as a result. Nevertheless no hatred remains between them. Instead they have the twisted respect for each other that is possible only between two old enemies. Once again fate has decreed that they fight on different sides, but now they are friendly, complicit, two gentlemen who have known each other for twenty years. . . . Rochefort falls out of favor with Mazarin, breaks out of the Bastille, and helps the Duke of Beaufort escape. He conspires in the Fronde rebellion and dies in the arms of d'Artagnan, who has stabbed him with his sword, failing to recognize him in all the confusion. 'You were my fate,' Rochefort more or less says to the Gascon. 'I recovered from three of your sword wounds, but I will not recover from the fourth.' And he dies. 'I have just killed an old friend,' d'Artagnan later tells Porthos. This is the only epitaph Richelieu's former agent is given."

My words provoked a lively discussion with several factions. The actor hadn't taken his eyes off the woman journalist all afternoon. He was an old heartthrob who'd played Monte Cristo in a television series. Encouraged by the painter and the two writers, he launched into a brilliant account of his recollections of the characters. In this way we moved from Dumas to Zevaco and Paul Féval, and ended by once again confirming Sabatini's indisputable influence on Salgari. I seem to recall that somebody timidly mentioned Jules Verne but was shouted down by all present. Verne's cold, soulless heroes had no place in a discussion of passionate tales of cloak and dagger.

As for the journalist, one of those fashionable young ladies with a column in a leading Sunday newspaper, her literary memory began with Milan Kundera. So she remained in a state of cautious expectation, agreeing with relief whenever a title, anecdote, or character (the Black Swan, Yañez, Nevers's sword wound) stirred some memory of a film glimpsed on TV. Meanwhile, Corso, with a hunter's calm patience, looked steadily at me over his glass of gin, waiting for a chance to return the conversation to the original subject. And he succeeded, making the most of an awkward silence that fell when the journalist said that, anyway, she found these adventure stories rather lightweight, I mean kind of superficial, don't you think?

Corso chewed the end of his pencil.

"And how do you see Rochefort's role in history, Mr. Balkan?" he asked.

They all looked at me, in particular the students, two of them girls. I don't know why, but in certain circles I'm considered a high priest of letters and every time I open my mouth, people expect to hear pearls of wisdom. A review of mine, in the appropriate literary magazine, can make or break a writer who's starting out. Absurd, certainly, but that's life. Think of the last Nobel prizewinner, the author of *I, Onan* and *In Search of Myself* and the ultrasuccessful *Oui, C'est Moi.* It was I who made him a household name fifteen years ago, with a page and a half in *Le Monde* on April Fools' Day. I'll never forgive myself, but that's how things work.

"At first, Rochefort is the enemy," I said. "He symbolizes the hidden forces, darkness.... He is the agent of the satanic conspiracy surrounding d'Artagnan and his friends, of the cardinal's plot growing in the shadows, threatening their lives...."

I saw one of the students smile, but I couldn't tell if her absorbed, slightly mocking expression was a result of my comments or of private thoughts that had nothing to do with the discussion. I was surprised because, as I've said, students tend to listen to me with the awe of an editor of the *Osservatore Romano* getting the exclusive rights to one of the Pope's encyclicals. So it made me look at her with interest. Although she'd already caught my eye at the beginning, when she joined us, because of her unsettling green eyes. She was wearing a blue duffel coat and carried a pile of books under her arm. Her chestnut hair was cut short, like a boy's. Now she sat at a slight distance, not quite part of the group. There are always a few young people at our table, literature students that I invite for a coffee. But this girl had never attended before. It was impossible to forget her eyes. In contrast to her tanned face, their color was so light, it was almost transparent. A slender, supple girl, one could tell she spent a lot of time outdoors. Under her jeans her long legs were no doubt also tanned. And I noticed another thing about her: she wore no rings, no watch, no earrings. Her ears weren't pierced.

"Rochefort is also the man glimpsed, never caught," I went on. "A mysterious mask with a scar. He stands for paradox and d'Artagnan's powerlessness. D'Artagnan is always in pursuit but never quite catches up with him. He tries to kill him but only manages to do so by mistake twenty years later. By then Rochefort is not an adversary but a friend."

"Your d'Artagnan's a bit jinxed," said one of my circle, the older of the two writers. He'd sold only five hundred copies of his last novel, but he earned a fortune writing mysteries under the perverse pseudonym of Emilia Forster. I looked at him gratefully, pleased by his opportune remark.

"Absolutely. The love of his life gets poisoned. Despite all his exploits and services to the crown of France, he spends twenty years as an obscure lieutenant in the musketeers. And in the last lines of *The Vicomte de Bragelonne,* when he is finally awarded the marshal's staff, which has taken him four volumes and four hundred and twenty-five chapters to achieve, he is killed by a Dutch bullet."

"Like the real d'Artagnan," said the actor, who had managed to place his hand on the fashionable woman columnist's thigh.

I took a sip of coffee before nodding. Corso was staring at me intently.

"There are three d'Artagnans," I explained. "Of the first, Charles de Batz Castlemore, we know that he died on the twenty-third of June 1673, from a shot in the throat during the siege of Maastricht, as reported in the *Gazette de France* at the time. Half his men fell with him. Apart from this posthumous detail, in life he was only slightly more fortunate than his fictional namesake."

"Was he a Gascon too?"

"Yes, from Lupiac. The village still exists, and he is

commemorated by a stone plaque there: 'D'Artagnan, whose real name was Charles de Batz, was born here around 1615. He died in the siege of Maastricht in 1673.' "

"It doesn't quite fit historically," said Corso, looking at his notes. "According to Dumas, d'Artagnan was eighteen at the start of the novel, around 1625. At that time the real d'Artagnan would have been only ten years old." He smiled like a clever, skeptical little rabbit. "Too young to handle a sword."

I agreed. "Yes. Dumas altered things so d'Artagnan could take part in the adventure of the diamond tags under Richelieu and Louis XIII. Charles de Batz must have arrived in Paris very young: he was listed among the guards of Monsieur Des Essarts's company in documents on the siege of Arras in 1640, and two years later in the Roussillon campaign. But he never served as a musketeer under Richelieu, because he joined the elite regiment only after Louis XIII's death. His real protector was Cardinal Jules Mazarin. There is indeed a gap of ten or fifteen years between the two d'Artagnans. But following the success of *The Three Musketeers*, Dumas extended the action to cover almost forty years of France's history. In later volumes he adjusted his story to coincide better with real events."

"Which events have been verified? I mean, historical events in which the real d'Artagnan was involved?"

"Quite a few. His name appears in Mazarin's letters and in the correspondence of the Ministry of War. Like the fictional hero, he was the cardinal's agent during the Fronde rebellion, with important responsibilities at the court of Louis XIV. He was even entrusted with the delicate matter of detaining and escorting the finance minister Fouquet. All these events were confirmed in the letters of Madame de Sévigné. He could even have met the painter Velázquez on the Isle of Pheasants when he accompanied Louis XIV on the king's journey to meet his bride-to-be, Maria Theresa of Austria. . . ."

"He was quite a man of the court then. Very different from Dumas's swashbuckling d'Artagnan."

I raised my hand in defense of Dumas's respect for the facts.

"Don't be fooled. Charles de Batz, or d'Artagnan, went on fighting to the end of his life. He served under Turenne in Flanders, and in 1657 was appointed lieutenant in the gray musketeers, which was equivalent to commander. Ten years later he became a captain in the musketeers and fought in Flanders, a post equivalent to cavalry general."

Corso was squinting behind his glasses.

"Excuse me." He leaned across the table toward me, pencil in hand. He'd been writing down a name or date. "In what year did this happen?"

"His promotion to general? 1667. Why did that draw your attention?"

He showed his incisors as he bit his lower lip. But only for an instant. "No reason." As he spoke, his face regained its impassivity. "That same year a certain person was burned at the stake in Rome. A strange coincidence. . . ." Now he was staring at me blankly. "Does the name Aristide Torchia mean anything to you?"

I tried to remember. I had no idea. "Not a thing," I answered. "Does he have anything to do with Dumas?"

He hesitated. "No," he said at last, although he didn't seem very convinced. "I don't think so. But please go on. You were talking about the real d'Artagnan in Flanders."

"He died at Maastricht, as I've said, at the head of his men. A heroic death. The English and the French were besieging the town. They needed to cross a dangerous pass, and d'Artagnan offered to go first out of courtesy to his allies. A musket bullet tore through his jugular."

"He never got to be marshal, then."

"No. Alexandre Dumas deserves sole credit for giving the fictional d'Artagnan what a miserly Louis XIV refused his flesh-and-blood predecessor. . . . There are a couple of interesting books on the subject. You can take down the titles if you want. One is by Charles Samaran, *D'Artagnan, capitaine des mousquetaires du roi, histoire véridique d'un héros de roman,* published in 1912. The other one is *Le vrai d'Artagnan,* written by the Duke of Montesquieu-Fezensac, a direct descendant of the real d'Artagnan. Published in 1965, I think."

None of this information was obviously related to the Dumas manuscript, but Corso noted it down as if his life depended on it. Occasionally he looked up from his notepad and glanced at me inquisitively through his crooked glasses. Or he put his head to one side as if he were no longer listening, absorbed in his own thoughts. At that time, I knew all the facts about "The Anjou Wine," even certain keys to the mystery of which Corso was unaware. But I had no idea of the complex implications that *The Nine Doors* would have for this story. Despite his logical turn of mind, Corso was already beginning to glimpse sinister links between the facts at his disposal and—how shall I put it—the literary source of those facts. This may all appear rather confused, but we must remember that this was how it seemed to Corso at the time. And although I am narrating the story after the resolution of its momentous events, the very nature of the loop—think of Escher's paintings, or the work of that old trickster, Bach—forces us to return continually to the beginning and limit ourselves to the narrow confines of Corso's knowledge. The rule is to know and keep silent. Even if there is foul play, without the rule there is no game.

"OK," said Corso once he'd written down the recommended titles. "That's the first d'Artagnan, the real one. And Dumas's fictional character is the third one. I'm assuming the connection between them is the book by Gatien de Courtilz you showed me the other day, the *Memoirs of M. d'Artagnan.*"

"Correct. We can call him the missing link, the least famous of the three. A Gascon who is an intermediary, a literary character and a real person in one. The very same that Dumas used to create his character ... The writer Gatien de Courtilz de Sandras was a contemporary of d'Artagnan. He recognized the novelistic potential of the character and set to work. A century and a half later, Dumas found out about the book during a trip to Marseilles. His landlord had a brother who ran the municipal library. Apparently the brother showed Dumas the book, edited in Cologne in 1700. Dumas saw that he could make use of the story and asked to borrow the book. He never returned it."

"What do we know about this predecessor of Dumas's, Gatien de Courtilz?"

"Quite a lot. Partly because he had a sizable police file. He was born in 1644 or 1647 and was a musketeer, a bugler in the Royal-Etranger, which was a type of foreign legion of the time, and captain of the cavalry regiment of Beaupré-Choiseul. At the end of the war against Holland, in which d'Artagnan was killed, Courtilz remained in Holland and traded his sword for a pen. He wrote biographies, historical monographs, more or less apocryphal memoirs, shocking tales of gossip and intrigue at the French court. This got him into trouble. *The Memoirs of M. d'Artagnan* was astonishingly successful: five editions in ten years. But the book displeased Louis XIV. He disliked the irreverent tone used to recount certain details regarding the royal family and its entourage. As a result Courtilz was arrested on his return to France and held in the Bastille at His Majesty's pleasure until shortly before his death."

The actor made the most of my pause to slip in, quite irrelevantly, a quotation from "The Sun Has Set in Flanders" by Marquina. "*Our captain,*" he recited, "*gravely wounded, led us, sparing no effort though in his final agony. Sirs, what a captain he was indeed that day....*" Or something like that. It was a shameless attempt to shine in front of the journalist, whose thigh he now held with a proprietary air. The others, in particular the novelist who wrote under the pseudonym of Emilia Forster, were looking at him with either envy or barely concealed resentment.

After a polite silence, Corso decided to hand control of the situation back to me.

"How much does Dumas's d'Artagnan owe to Courtilz?" he asked.

"A great deal. Although in *Twenty Years After* and in *Bragelonne* he used other sources, the basic story of *The Three Musketeers* is to be found in Courtilz. Dumas applied his genius to it and gave it breadth, but it contained a rough outline of all the elements of the story: d'Artagnan's father granting his blessing, the letter to Treville, the challenge to the musketeers, who incidentally were brothers in the first draft. Milady also appears. And the two d'Artagnans were like two peas in a pod. Courtilz's character was slightly more cynical, more miserly, and less trustworthy. But they're the same."

Corso leaned forward slightly. "Earlier you said that Rochefort stands for the evil plot surrounding d'Artagnan and his friends. But Rochefort is just a henchman."

"Indeed. In the pay of His Eminence Armand Jean du Plessis, Cardinal Richelieu . . ."

"The evil one," said Corso.

"The spirit of evil," commented the actor, determined to butt in.

Impressed by our foray into the subject of serials that afternoon, the students were taking notes or listening open-mouthed. The girl with the green eyes, however, remained impassive, slightly apart, as if she had only dropped in by chance.

"For Dumas," I went on, "at least in the first part of *The Musketeers* cycle, Richelieu provided the character essential to all romantic adventure and mystery stories: the powerful enemy lurking in the shadows, the embodiment of evil. For the history of France, Richelieu was a great man. But in *The Musketeers* he is rehabilitated only twenty years later. Shrewd Dumas fitted in with reality without diminishing the novel's interest. He'd found another villain: Mazarin. This correction, even as voiced by d'Artagnan and his companions when they praise the nobility of their former enemy, is morally questionable. For

Dumas it was a convenient act of contrition. Nevertheless in the first volume of the cycle, whether plotting Buckingham's murder, Anne of Austria's downfall, or giving carte blanche to the sinister Milady, Cardinal Richelieu is the embodiment of the perfect villain. His Eminence is to d'Artagnan what Prince Gonzaga is to Lagardère, or Professor Moriarty to Sherlock Holmes. A mysterious, demonic presence."

Corso seemed about to interrupt me, which I thought odd. I was getting to know him and typically he wouldn't interrupt until the other person had delivered all his information, until every last detail had been squeezed out.

"You've used the word *demonic* twice," he said, looking over his notes. "And both times referring to Richelieu. Was the cardinal a devotee of the occult?"

His words had a strange effect. The young girl turned to look curiously at Corso. He was looking at me, and I was watching the girl. He awaited my answer, unaware of this strange triangle.

"Richelieu was keenly interested in many things," I explained. "In addition to turning France into a great power, he had time to collect pictures, carpets, porcelain, and statues. He was also an important book collector. He bound his books in calfskin and red morocco leather—"

"And had weapons of silver and three red angles on his coat of arms." Corso gestured impatiently. All this information was trivial and he didn't need me to tell him about it. "There's a very well-known Richelieu catalogue."

"The catalogue is incomplete, because the collection was broken up. Parts of it are now kept in the national library of France, the Mazarin library, and the Sorbonne, while other books are in private hands. He owned Hebrew and Syrian manuscripts, notable works on mathematics, medicine, theology, law, and history.... And you were right. Scholars were most surprised to find many ancient texts on the occult, from cabbala to black magic."

Corso swallowed without taking his eyes off mine. He seemed tense—a bowstring about to snap.

"Any book in particular?"

I shook my head before I answered. His insistence intrigued me. The girl was listening attentively, but it was apparent that she was no longer directing her attention at me. I said, "My information on Richelieu as a character in a serial doesn't go that far."

"What about Dumas? Was he, too, interested in the occult?"

Here I was emphatic:

"No. Dumas was a bon vivant who did everything out in the open, to the great enjoyment and shock of all those around him. He was also somewhat superstitious. He believed in the evil eye, wore an amulet on his watch chain, and had his fortune told by Madame Desbarolles. But I don't see him practicing black magic in the back room. He wasn't even a Mason, as he confesses in *The Century of Louis XV*. He had debts, and he was hounded by his publishers and his creditors—he was too busy to waste his time on such things. Perhaps when researching one of his characters once, he studied the subject, but never in much depth. I believe he drew all the Masonic practices described in *Joseph Balsam* and *The Mohicans of Paris* directly from Clavel's *Picturesque History of Freemasonry*."

"What about Adah Menken?"

I looked at Corso with respect. This was an expert's question.

"That was different. Adah-Isaacs Menken, his last lover, was an American actress. During the Exhibition of 1867, while attending a performance of *The Pirates of the Savannah*, Dumas noticed a pretty young woman on stage who had to grab hold of a galloping horse. The girl embraced the novelist as he left the theater and told him bluntly that she had read all his books and was prepared to go to bed with him immediately. Old Dumas needed a great deal less than that to become infatuated with a woman, so he accepted her tribute. She claimed to have been the wife of a millionaire, a king's mistress, a general's wife.... Actually she was a Portuguese Jew born in America and the mistress of a strange man who was both a pimp and a boxer. Her relationship with Dumas caused a great deal of scandal, because Menken liked to be photographed scantily clad and frequented number 107 Rue Malesherbes, Dumas's last house in Paris. She died from peritonitis after falling from a horse at the age of thirty-one."

"Was she interested in black magic?"

"So they say. She liked ceremonies where she would dress in a tunic, burn incense, and make offerings to the Prince of Darkness.... Sometimes she claimed to be possessed by Satan, in various ways that today we might describe as pornographic. I'm sure old Dumas never believed a word of it, but he must have enjoyed the whole performance. It seems that when Menken was possessed by the devil, she was very hot in bed."

There was laughter around the table. I even allowed myself a slight smile, but the girl and Corso remained serious. She seemed to be thinking, her light-colored eyes intent on Corso while he nodded slowly, though he was now distracted and distant. He was looking out the window at the streets and seemed to be searching in the night, in the silent flow of car lights reflected in his glasses, for the lost word, the key to uniting all these different stories that floated like dead leaves on the dark waters of time.

I NOW MOVE ONCE more into the background, as the near-omniscient narrator of Lucas Corso's adventures. In this way, with the information Corso later confided to me, the tragic events that followed can be put into some sort of order. So we come to the moment when, returning home, he sees that the concierge has just swept the hallway and is about to leave. He passes him as the man is bringing the garbage cans up from the basement.

"They came to fix your TV this afternoon, Mr. Corso."

Corso had read enough books and seen enough films to know what that meant. So he couldn't help laughing, much to the concierge's astonishment.

"I haven't had a television for ages."

The concierge let out a stream of confused apologies but Corso barely paid attention. It was all beginning to seem wonderfully predictable. Since this was a question of books, he had to approach the problem as a lucid, critical reader, not as the hero of a dime novel, which was what somebody was trying to make of him. Not that he had any choice: he was by nature cool and skeptical. He wasn't the kind to break into a sweat and moan, "Oh no!"

"I hope I haven't done anything wrong, Mr. Corso."

"Not at all. The repairman was dark, wasn't he? With a mustache and a scar on his face?"

"Exactly."

"Don't worry. He's a friend of mine. A bit of a joker."

The concierge sighed with relief. "That's a weight off my mind, Mr. Corso."

Corso wasn't worried about *The Nine Doors* or the Dumas manuscript. When he wasn't carrying them with him in his canvas bag, he left them for safekeeping at Makarova's bar. That was the safest place for any of his things. So he climbed the stairs calmly, trying to picture the coming scene. By now he had become what some refer to as a second-level reader, and he would have been disappointed had he been met by too stereotypical a scene. He was relieved when he opened the door. There were no papers strewn on the floor, no opened drawers, not even armchairs slashed with knives. It was all tidy, just as he'd left it in the early afternoon.

He went to his desk. The boxes of floppy disks were in their place, the papers and documents in their trays just as he remembered them. The man with the scar, Rochefort or whoever the hell he was, was certainly efficient. But there are limits to everything. When he switched on the computer, Corso smiled triumphantly.

DAGMAR PC 555K (S1) ELECTRONIC PLC
LAST USED AT 19:35/THU/3/21
A> ECHO OFF
A>

Used at 19:35 that day, the screen stated. But Corso hadn't touched the computer in the last twenty-four hours. At 19:35 he was with us around the table at the café, while the man with the scar was lying his way into Corso's apartment.

Corso found something else, which he hadn't noticed at first, by the telephone. It hadn't been left there by chance, out of carelessness on the part of the mysterious visitor. In the ashtray, among the butts put out by Corso himself, he found a fresh one that wasn't his. It was a Havana cigar almost completely burnt down, but the band was intact. He held it up by the tip. He couldn't believe it. Then, gradually, as he understood, he laughed, showing his eyeteeth like a malicious, angry wolf.

The brand was Montecristo. Naturally.

FLAVIO LA PONTE HAD had a visitor too. A plumber, in his case.

"It's not funny, damn it," he said by way of a greeting. He waited for Makarova to serve the gin and then emptied the contents of a small cellophane packet onto the counter. The cigar end was identical, and the band was also intact.

"Edmond Dantès strikes again," said Corso.

La Ponte couldn't get into the spirit of the thing. "Well, he smokes expensive cigars, the bastard." His hand was trembling, and he spilled some gin down his curly blond beard. "I found it on my bedside table."

Corso teased him. "You should take things more calmly,

Flavio. You've got to be hard." He patted him on the shoulder. "Remember the Nantucket Harpooners' Club."

La Ponte shook his hand, frowning. "I was hard, until I turned eight. Back then I understood the virtue of survival. After that I got a bit softer."

Between gulps of gin Corso quoted Shakespeare. *A coward dies a thousand deaths*, and so on. But La Ponte wasn't about to be reassured by quotations. At least not by that type.

"I'm not scared, really," he said thoughtfully, looking down. "What worries me is losing things . . . like money. Or my incredible sexual powers. Or my life."

These were weighty arguments, and Corso had to admit that there could be uncomfortable developments. La Ponte added that there were other clues: strange clients wanting to purchase the Dumas manuscript at any price, mysterious phone calls in the night . . .

Corso sat up, interested. "You're getting calls in the middle of the night?"

"Yes, but they don't say anything. There's a moment or two of silence, and then they hang up."

While La Ponte was recounting his misfortunes, Corso felt the canvas bag he had retrieved moments earlier. Makarova had kept it under the counter all day, between boxes of bottles and barrels of beer.

"I don't know what to do," ended La Ponte tragically.

"Why don't you sell the manuscript and have done with it? Things are getting out of hand."

La Ponte shook his head and ordered another gin. A double.

"I promised Enrique Taillefer that the manuscript would go on public sale."

"Taillefer's dead. And anyway, you've never kept a promise in your life."

La Ponte agreed gloomily, as if he didn't want to be reminded. But then he suddenly brightened. A slightly dazed expression showed through his beard. If you tried hard, you could take it for a smile.

"By the way, guess who called."

"Milady."

"Almost. Liana Taillefer."

Corso looked at his friend wearily. Then he picked up his glass and emptied it in one long gulp. "You know what, Flavio?" he said, wiping his mouth with the back of his hand. "Sometimes it seems that I've read this book before."

La Ponte was frowning again.

"She wants 'The Anjou Wine' back," he explained. "Just as it is, without authentification or anything . . ." He took a drink, then smiled uncertainly at Corso. "Strange, isn't it, this sudden interest?"

"What did you tell her?"

La Ponte raised his eyebrows. "That it wasn't in my hands. That you have the manuscript and I've signed a contract with you."

"That's a lie. We haven't signed anything."

"Of course it's a lie. But this way I put everything on you if things get nasty. And it doesn't mean I can't consider any offers. I'm going to have dinner with the lovely widow one evening. To discuss business. I'm the daring harpooner."

"You're not a harpooner. You're a dirty, lying bastard."

"Yes. England made me, as that pious old goody-goody Graham Greene would have said. At school my nickname was Wasn't Me. . . . Did I ever tell you how I passed Math?" He raised his eyebrows again, tenderly nostalgic at the memory. "I'm a born liar."

"Well, be careful with Liana Taillefer."

"Why?" La Ponte was admiring himself in the bar mirror. He smiled lewdly. "I've had the hots for that woman ever since I started taking serials over to her husband. She's got a lot of class."

"Yes," admitted Corso, "a lot of middle class."

"What do you have against her?"

"There's something funny going on."

"That's fine by me, if it involves a beautiful blonde."

Corso tapped his finger against the knot of his tie. "Listen, idiot. In mysteries the friend always dies. Don't you see? This is a mystery and you're my friend." He winked at him for emphasis. "So you'll be bumped off."

Obstinately clinging to his dreams of the widow, La Ponte wouldn't be intimidated. "Oh, come on. I've never hit the jackpot before. Anyway I told you where I intend to take the bullet: in the shoulder."

"I'm serious. Taillefer's dead."

"He committed suicide."

"Who knows? More people could die."

"Well, you go and die, you bastard, ruining my fun."

The rest of the evening consisted of variations on the same theme. They left after five or six more drinks and agreed to speak on the phone once Corso got to Portugal. La Ponte, rather unsteady on his feet, left without paying, but he did give Corso Rochefort's cigar butt. "Now you have a pair," he told him.

VI. OF APOCRYPHA AND INTERPOLATIONS

*Chance? Permit me to laugh, by God. That is an explanation
that would satisfy only an imbecile.*
—M. Zevaco, LOS PARDELLANES

CENIZA BROS.
BOOKBINDING AND RESTORATION

The wooden sign, cracked,
faded with age and mildew, hung in a window thick with dust.
The Ceniza brothers' workshop was on the mezzanine floor of
an old four-story building, shored up at the back, on a shady
street in the old quarter of Madrid.

Lucas Corso rang the bell twice, but nobody answered. He
looked at his watch, leaned against the wall, and prepared himself for a wait. He knew the habits of Pedro and Pablo Ceniza
well. At that hour they would be a few streets away, at the
marble counter of La Taurina, draining half a liter of wine for
their breakfast and discussing books and bullfighting. Both
grumpy bachelors and fond of their drink, they were insep-
arable.

They arrived ten minutes later, side by side, their gray overalls floating like shrouds on their skinny frames. Stooped from
a lifetime spent hunched over their press and stamping tools,

stitching pages together and gilding leather, they were both under fifty, but you could easily have believed they were ten years older. Their cheeks were sunken, their hands and eyes worn out by their painstaking craft, and their skin was faded, as if the parchment they worked with had transmitted its pale, cold quality to them. The resemblance between the two brothers was extraordinary. They had the same large nose, identical ears stuck to their skulls, and sparse hair combed straight back. The only noticeable differences between them were that Pablo, the younger of the two, was taller and quieter and that Pedro was frequently racked by the hoarse rattling cough of a heavy smoker, his hands shaking as he lit one cigarette after another.

"It's been a long time, Mr. Corso. How nice to see you."

They led him up stairs that were worn with use, to a door that creaked as it opened, and switched on the light to reveal their motley workshop. An ancient printing press presided. Next to this was a zinc-topped table covered with tools, half-stitched or already backed gatherings, guillotines, dyed skins, bottles of glue, tooled designs, and other equipment. There were books everywhere: large piles of them, bound in morocco, shagreen, or vellum, packets of them ready for dispatch or only half ready, books without boards or with limp covers. Ancient tomes damaged by worms or mildew sat on benches and shelves, waiting to be restored. The room smelled of paper, glue, and new leather. Corso breathed it in with pleasure. Then he took the book out of his bag and laid it on the table.

"I'd like your opinion on this."

It wasn't the first time. Slowly, even cautiously, Pedro and Pablo Ceniza moved closer. As usual, the older of the two brothers spoke first. *"The Nine Doors."* He touched the book without moving it. His bony, nicotine-stained fingers seemed to be stroking living skin. "Beautiful. A very valuable book."

His eyes were gray, like a mouse. Gray overalls, gray hair, gray eyes, just like his surname, *ceniza* meaning ash. He looked at the book greedily.

"Have you ever seen it before?"

"Yes. Less than a year ago, when Claymore asked us to clean twenty books from the library of Mr. Gualterio Terral."

"What condition was it in when you got it?"

"Excellent. Mr. Terral knew how to look after his books. Almost all of them came to us in good condition, except for a Teixeira, which we had to do quite a bit of work on. The rest, including this one, needed only a little cleaning."

"It's a forgery," said Corso bluntly. "Or so I'm told."

The two brothers looked at each other.

"Forgeries...," muttered the older of the two. "People speak too lightly of forged books."

"Much too lightly," echoed his brother.

"Even you, Mr. Corso. And that comes as a surprise. It isn't worth forging a book, it's too much effort to be profitable: I mean a high-quality forgery, not a facsimile for fooling ignoramuses."

Corso made a gesture as if pleading for clemency. "I didn't say that the *entire* book was a forgery, only part of it. Pages from complete copies can be interpolated into books that have one or several pages missing."

"Of course, that's a basic trick of the trade. But adding a photocopy or facsimile doesn't give the same results as completing a book with pages according to..." He half-turned to his brother but still looked at Corso. "Tell him, Pablo."

"According to all the rules of our art," added the younger Ceniza.

Corso gave them a conspiratorial look. A rabbit sharing half a carrot. "That could be the case with this book," he said.

"Who says so?"

"The owner. Who is no ignoramus, by the way."

Pedro Ceniza shrugged his narrow shoulders and lit a cigarette with the previous one. As he took his first drag, he was shaken by a dry cough. But he continued smoking, unperturbed.

"Do you have access to an authentic copy, to compare them?"

"No, but I soon will. That's why I want your opinion first."

"It's a valuable book, and ours is not an exact science." He turned again to his brother. "Isn't that so, Pablo?"

"It's an art," insisted his brother.

"Yes. We wouldn't want to disappoint you, Mr. Corso."

"I'm sure you won't. You know what you're talking about. After all, you were able to forge a *Speculum Vitae* from the only known copy and have it listed as an original in one of the best catalogues in Europe."

They both smiled sourly at exactly the same time. Si and Am, thought Corso, a cunning pair of cats who've just been stroked.

"It was never proved to be our work," said Pedro Ceniza at last. He was rubbing his hands, looking at the book out of the corner of his eye.

"No, never," repeated his brother sadly. They seemed sorry not to have gone to prison in return for public recognition.

"True," admitted Corso. "Nor was there any proof in the case of the Chaucer, allegedly bound by Marius Michel, listed in the catalogue for the Manoukian collection. Or for that copy of Baron Bielke's *Polyglot Bible* with three missing pages you replaced so perfectly that even today experts don't dispute its authenticity...."

Pedro Ceniza lifted a yellowed hand with long nails. "I'd like to say a little about that, Mr. Corso. It's one thing to forge books for profit, quite another to do it out of love for one's art, creating something for the satisfaction provided by that very act of creation, or, as in most cases, of re-creation." The bookbinder blinked a few times, then smiled mischievously. His small, mouselike eyes shone as he looked at *The Nine Doors* again. "Although I don't recall having had a hand in the works you've just described as admirable, and I'm sure my brother doesn't either."

"I called them perfect."

"Did you? Well, never mind." Putting his cigarette in his

mouth and sucking in his cheeks, he took a long drag. "But whoever the person or persons responsible, you can be sure that he or they derived a great deal of enjoyment from it, a degree of personal satisfaction that money can't buy...."

"*Sine pecunia,*" added his brother.

Pedro Ceniza blew cigarette smoke through his nose and half-open mouth. He continued: "Let's take the *Speculum,* for instance, which the Sorbonne bought in the belief that it was authentic. The paper, typography, printing, and binding alone must have cost those you call forgers five times more than any money they might have made. People just don't understand.... What would be more satisfying to a painter with the talent of a Velázquez and the skill to imitate his works: making money or seeing one of his own paintings hanging in the Prado between *Las Meninas* and *Vulcan's Forge?*"

Corso agreed. For eight years, the Ceniza brothers' *Speculum* had been one of the most valuable books owned by the University of Paris. It was discovered to be a forgery not by experts but due to a chance indiscretion by a middleman.

"Do the police still bother you?"

"Rarely. You must remember that the business of the Sorbonne erupted in France between the buyer and the intermediaries. True, our name was linked to the affair, but nothing was ever proved." Pedro Ceniza smiled his crooked smile again, as if sorry that there had been no proof. "We have a good relationship with the police. They even come to see us sometimes when they need to identify a stolen book." He waved his cigarette in his brother's direction. "There's no one as good as Pablo when it comes to erasing traces of library stamps, or removing bookplates and marks of origin. But sometimes they want him to work his way backward through the process. You know how it is: live and let live."

"What do you think of *The Nine Doors?*"

The older Ceniza looked at his brother, then at the book. He shook his head. "Nothing drew our attention while we were working on it. The paper and ink are as they should be. Even at first glance, you notice that sort of thing."

"We notice them," corrected his brother.

"What's your opinion now?"

Pedro Ceniza took a last puff of his cigarette, which was now a tiny stub between his fingers. He dropped it on the floor between his feet, where it burned itself out. The linoleum was covered with cigarette burns.

"Seventeenth-century Venetian binding, in good condition ..." The brothers leaned over the book, but only the elder touched the pages with his pale, cold hands. They looked like a pair of taxidermists working out the best way to stuff a corpse with straw. "The leather is black morocco, with gold rosettes imitating flowers."

"Somewhat sober for Venice," added Pablo Ceniza.

His brother agreed, with another coughing fit.

"The artist kept it restrained. No doubt the subject matter ..." He looked at Corso. "Have you tested the core of the binding? Sixteenth and seventeenth-century books bound in leather or hide sometimes contain surprises. The board inside was made of separate sheets assembled with paste and pressed. Sometimes people used proofs of the same book, or earlier editions. Some discovered bindings are now more valuable than the texts they cover." He pointed to papers on the table. "There's an example there. Tell him about it, Pablo."

"Papal bulls of the Holy Crusade, dated 1483." The brother smiled equivocally. He might have been talking about pornographic material rather than a pile of old papers. "Bound with boards from sixteenth-century memorials of no value."

Pedro Ceniza meanwhile was examining *The Nine Doors*. "The binding seems to be in order," he said. "It all fits. Odd book, isn't it? The five raised bands on the spine, no title, and this strange pentacle on the cover. Torchia, Venice 1666. He might have bound it himself. A beautiful piece of work."

"What about the paper?"

"That's just like you, Mr. Corso. A good question." The bookbinder licked his lips as if trying to warm them. He listened carefully to the sound of the pages as he flicked them, just as Corso had done at Varo Borja's. "Excellent paper. Nothing like the cellulose they use nowadays. Do you know the average lifespan of a book printed today? Tell him, Pablo."

"Sixty years," said the brother bitterly, as if it were Corso's fault. "Sixty miserable years."

Pedro was searching among the tools on the table. At last he found a special high-magnification lens and held it up to the book.

"A century from now," he murmured as he lifted a page and examined it against the light, closing one eye, "almost all the contents of today's libraries will have disappeared. But these books, printed two hundred or even five hundred years ago, will remain intact. We have the books, and the world, that we deserve. . . . Isn't that so, Pablo?"

"Lousy books printed on lousy paper."

Pedro Ceniza nodded in agreement. He was examining the book now through the lens. "That's right. Cellulose paper turns yellow and brittle as a wafer, and cracks irreparably. It ages and dies."

"Not the case here," said Corso, pointing at the book.

The bookbinder held a page against the light.

"Rag-content paper, which is as it should be. Good paper handmade from rags, it'll withstand both the passage of time and human stupidity. . . . No, I tell a lie. It's linen. Authentic linen paper." He put down the lens and looked at his brother. "How strange, it's not Venetian paper. It's thick, spongy, fibrous. Could it be Spanish?"

"From Valencia," said his brother. "Jativa linen."

"That's right. One of the best in Europe at the time. The printer could have got hold of an imported batch. . . . He really did things properly."

"He was very conscientious," said Corso, "and it cost him his life."

"Risks of the trade." Pedro accepted the crushed cigarette Corso offered him. He lit it immediately, coughing. "As you know yourself, it's difficult to fool anyone about paper. The ream used would have had to be blank, from the same time, and even then there would be differences: the sheets go brown, the inks fade and change over time. . . . Of course, the added pages can be stained, or darkened by being washed in tea. Any restoration work, or addition of missing pages, should leave the book all of a piece. It's these small details that count. Don't they, Pablo? Always the damned details."

"What's your diagnosis?"

"So far, we have established that the binding is seventeenth century. That doesn't mean that the pages match this binding and not another. But let's assume they do. As for the paper, it seems similar to other batches whose origin has been authenticated."

"Right. The binding and paper are authentic. Let's look at the text and illustrations."

"Now, that's more complicated. We can approach the typography from two different angles. One: we can assume that the book is authentic. The owner, however, denies this, and according to you he has ways of knowing. So authenticity is possible but not very probable. Let's assume that it's a forgery and work out the possibilities. On the one hand, the entire text might be a forgery, a fabrication, printed on paper dating from the time and bound using boards from the time. This is unlikely. Or, to be more precise, not very convincing. The cost of such a book would be enormous. . . . On the other hand, and this is reasonable, the forgery might have been made shortly after the first edition of the book. I mean that it was reprinted with alterations, disguised to resemble the first edition, some ten or twenty years after this date of 1666 that appears in the frontispiece. But to what end?"

"It was a banned book," Pablo Ceniza pointed out.

"It's possible," agreed Corso. "Somebody who had access to the equipment—the plates and types—used by Aristide Torchia might have been able to print the book again."

The elder brother had picked up a pencil and was scribbling on the back of a printed sheet. "That would be one explanation," he said. "But there are other alternatives that seem more plausible. Imagine, for instance, that most of the book's pages are authentic but that some were missing, either torn out or lost, and that somebody replaced those missing pages using paper that dates from the time, good printing techniques, and a lot of patience. In that case, there are two further possibilities: one is that the added pages are reproductions of those from a complete copy. Another is that, in the absence of the original to reproduce or copy, the contents of the pages were invented." The bookbinder showed Corso what he had been writing. "It would be a true case of forgery, as illustrated by this diagram."

While Corso and Pablo were looking at the paper, Pedro again leafed through *The Nine Doors.*

"I am inclined to think," he added after a moment, once he had their attention again, "that if some pages were interpolated, it was done either around the time of the original edition, or now, in our time. We can discount the time between the two, because such a perfect reproduction of an ancient work has become possible only very recently."

Corso handed back the diagram and asked, "Imagine you were faced with a book that had pages missing. And you wanted to complete it using modern techniques. How would you go about it?"

The Ceniza brothers sighed deeply in unison, professionally relishing the prospect. They were now both staring intently at *The Nine Doors.*

"Let us suppose," Pedro said, "that this hundred-and-sixty-eight-page book has page 100 missing. Pages 100 and 99, since

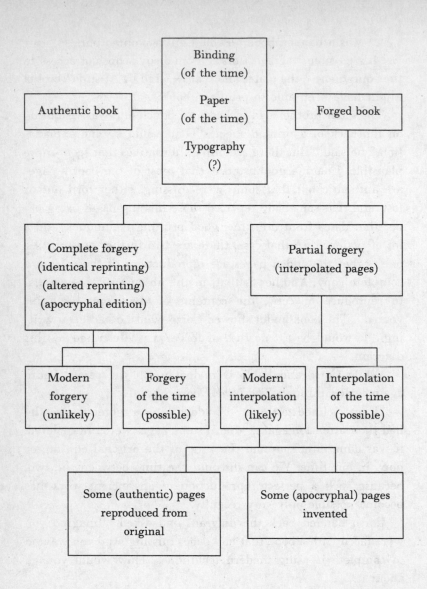

one sheet has two sides. And we want to replace it. The trick is to locate a twin."

"A twin?"

"As we say in the trade," said Pablo, "another complete copy."

"Or at least a copy where the two pages we need to duplicate are intact. It would also be advisable to compare the twin with our incomplete copy, to see if the depths of the type impressions in the paper are different or if the letters have worn differently. As you know yourself, types were moveable then and could easily wear down or be damaged. So with manual printing, the first and last copy of the same print run could vary greatly. They might have crooked or broken letters, hold the ink differently, things like that. Examining such variations allows you to add or remove imperfections on an interpolated page so that the page matches the rest of the book. We would then proceed with photomechanical reproduction and produce a plastic photolith. And from that we would obtain a polymer or a zinc."

"A plate in relief," said Corso, "made of resin or metal."

"Exactly. However perfect the reproduction technique, we would never get the relief, the mark on paper typical of old printing methods that used inked wood or metal. So the entire page has to be reproduced using a moldable material—resin or metal. Such a plate creates very similar effects to printing with the kind of movable lead types used in 1666. We put the plate on the press and print the page manually, as was done four centuries ago . . . using paper that dates from the same time, of course, or treated both before and after with artificial aging methods. The composition of the ink must be thoroughly researched. The page is treated with chemical agents so that it matches the other pages. And there you are, the crime is carried out."

"But suppose the original sheet doesn't exist. Suppose there's no model from which to copy the two missing pages."

The Ceniza brothers both smiled confidently.

"That," said Pedro, "makes it even more interesting."

"Research and imagination," added Pablo.

"And daring, of course, Mr. Corso. Suppose Pablo and I have that copy of *The Nine Doors* with pages missing. The other one hundred sixty-six pages provide us with a catalogue of all the letters and symbols used by the printer. We take samples until we have obtained an entire alphabet. We reproduce the alphabet on photographic paper, which is easier to handle, and then multiply each letter by the number of times it appears on the page. The ideal, the artistic flourish, would be to reproduce the types in molten lead, as ancient printers used to do. Unfortunately this is too complicated and expensive. We make do with modern techniques. We divide up the letters with a blade into loose types, and Pablo, who has a steadier hand, composes the two pages on a template, line by line, just as a compositor would have done in the seventeenth century. From that we produce another proof on paper and eliminate any joins or imperfections in the letters, or we add faults similar to those found in the letters of the original text. Then all we need do is make a negative. From the negative you get a reproduction in relief, and there you have your printing plate."

"What if the missing pages are illustrations?"

"It makes no difference. If we had access to the original engraving, of course, the technique for making a copy would be easier. In this case, the fact that the engravings are all woodcuts, which have lighter lines than copperplate or drypoint, means that we can produce an almost perfect piece of work."

"Suppose the original engraving no longer exists."

"That's not a problem either. If we know of it from references, we can imitate it. If not, we can invent it. After studying the technique used for the book's other engravings, of course. Any good draftsman could do it."

"What about printing it?"

"As you know, a woodcut is an engraving in relief. A cube of wood is cut with the grain and covered with a white background. The picture is drawn on top. Then the wood is carved and the ink applied on the crests, or ridges, so that it can be transferred onto paper. When reproducing woodcuts, there are two options. One is to make a copy of the drawing, preferably in resin. The alternative, if you have a good engraver, is to make another real woodcut, with the same techniques that were used to produce the original engravings, and to print directly from that. In my case, as I have a good engraver in my brother, I would hand print it from a woodcut. Wherever possible, art should imitate art."

"You get better results," added Pablo.

Corso looked at him conspiratorially.

"As with the Sorbonne's *Speculum*."

"Maybe. The creator or creators of that piece of work may have thought like us.... Don't you think, Pablo?"

"They must have been romantics," agreed his brother with a faint smile.

"Yes, they must." Corso pointed at the book. "So, what's your verdict?"

"I would say that it's original," answered Pedro Ceniza without hesitation. "Even we wouldn't be able to produce such perfect results. Look, the quality of the paper, stains on the pages, identical tones and variations in the ink, and the typography . . . It's possible that some forged pages may have been inserted, but I think it improbable. If it is a forgery, the only explanation is that the forgery must have been done around the same time. How many known copies are there? Three? I assume you have considered the possibility that all three are forgeries."

"Yes, I have. What about the woodcuts?"

"They're definitely very strange. All those symbols . . . But they do date from the time. The degree of impression on the plates is identical. The ink, the shades of the paper . . . Maybe the key lies not in how or when they were printed but in their contents. I'm sorry we haven't made much progress."

"You're wrong." Corso prepared to close the book. "We've made a lot of progress."

Pedro Ceniza stopped him. "There's one more thing . . . I'm sure you've noticed them yourself. The printer's marks."

Corso looked at him, confused. "I don't know what you mean."

"The tiny signatures at the foot of each illustration. Show him, Pablo."

The younger brother wiped his hands on his overalls, as if to wipe off sweat. Then, moving closer to *The Nine Doors*, he showed Corso some of the pages through a magnifying glass.

"Each engraving," he explained, "has the usual abbreviations: *Inv.* for *invenit*, with the signature of the original artist, and *Sculp.* for *sculpsit*, the engraver.... Look. In seven of the nine woodcuts, the abbreviation A. TORCH appears as both *sculp.* and *inv.* Obviously the printer himself drew and engraved seven of the illustrations. But in the other two, he is named only as *sculp.* That means that he only engraved them. Someone else created the drawings, someone else was the *inv.* Someone with the initials L.F."

Pedro Ceniza nodded in approval at his brother's explanation and lit yet another cigarette. "Not bad, eh?" He started to cough amid the smoke. He watched for Corso's reaction, a malicious glint in his astute, mouselike eyes. "That printer might have been the one burned at the stake, but he wasn't the only one involved."

"No," agreed his brother, "somebody helped light the fire at his feet."

THE SAME DAY, CORSO had a visit from Liana Taillefer. The widow arrived unannounced, at that hour which is neither afternoon nor evening, when Corso, dressed in a faded cotton shirt and old corduroys, was standing by the west-facing window, watching the sunset turn the city rooftops red and ochre. Maybe it wasn't a good moment; maybe much of what happened later might have been avoided had she turned up at a different time of day. We'll never know. What we do know is that Corso was looking out the window, his eyes growing mistier as he emptied his glass of gin. The doorbell rang, and Liana Taillefer—blond, impressively tall, in an English raincoat, tailored suit, and black stockings—appeared on the doorstep. Her hair was gathered into a bun beneath a tobacco-colored, wide-brimmed hat elegantly tilted to one side. The hat suited her very well. She was a beautiful woman. She knew it and expected everyone to notice.

"To what do I owe the honor?" asked Corso. It was a stupid question, but at that hour and with all the Bols in him, he couldn't be expected to shine in conversation. Liana Taillefer had already stepped into the room. She was standing at the desk where the folder with the Dumas manuscript lay next to his computer and box of diskettes.

"Are you still working on this?"

"Of course."

She lifted her gaze from "The Anjou Wine" and glanced around calmly at the books covering the walls and piled up all over the room. Corso knew she was looking for photographs, mementos, clues to the personality of the occupant. She arched an arrogant eyebrow, irritated at not finding any. At last she saw the saber of the Old Guard.

"Do you collect swords?"

This was a logical inference. Of an inductive nature. At least, Corso thought with relicf, Liana Taillefer's ability to smooth over embarrassing situations didn't match her appearance. Unless she was teasing him. He smiled warily, feeling cornered.

"I collect that one. It's called a saber."

She nodded, expressionless. Impossible to tell whether she was simple or a good actress.

"A family heirloom?"

"An acquisition," lied Corso. "I thought it would look nice on the wall. Books on their own can get a bit boring."

"How come you have no pictures or photographs?"

"There's no one I particularly want to remember." He thought of the photograph in the silver frame, the late Taillefer in an apron carving the suckling pig. "In your case it's different, of course."

She looked at him intently, perhaps trying to decide how rude his comment had been. There was steel in her blue eyes, steel so cold that it chilled you. She paced the room, stopping to look at some of his books, at the view from the window, then returned to the desk. She ran a blood-red fingernail over the folder with the Dumas manuscript. Maybe she was expecting Corso to say something, but he remained silent. He waited patiently. If she was after something—and it was pretty obvious that she was—he'd let her do all the work. He wasn't going to make it easier for her.

"May I sit down?"

The slightly husky voice. The echo of a heavy night, thought Corso again. He stood in the middle of the room, hands in his pockets, waiting. Liana Taillefer took off her hat and raincoat. She looked around with her interminable slowness and chose an old sofa. She went over to it and sat down slowly, her skirt riding up high. She crossed her legs with an effect that anyone, even Corso with half a gin less in him, would have found devastating.

"I've come on business."

That was plain. She must be after something, to put on such a display. Corso had as much self-esteem as the next person, but he was no fool.

"Fine," he said. "Have you had dinner with Flavio La Ponte yet?"

No reaction. For a few seconds she continued looking at him, unperturbed, with the same air of contemptuous confidence.

"Not yet," she answered at last, without anger. "I wanted to see you first."

"Well, here I am."

Liana Taillefer leaned back a little more against the sofa. One of her hands was resting on a split in the shabby leather upholstery, where the horsehair stuffing poked through.

"You work for money," she said.

"I do."

"You sell yourself to the highest bidder."

"Sometimes." Corso showed one of his eyeteeth. He was on his own territory, so he could allow himself his friendly rabbit expression. "Generally what I do is hire myself out. Like Humphrey Bogart in the movies. Or like a whore."

For a widow who'd spent her schooldays doing needlework, Liana Taillefer didn't seem shocked by his language.

"I want to offer you a job."

"How nice. Everybody's offering me jobs these days."

"I'll pay you well."

"Wonderful. They all want to pay me well too."

She pulled at some of the horsehair poking from the sofa arm and twisted it absentmindedly around her index finger.

"What are you charging your friend La Ponte?"

"Flavio? Nothing. You couldn't get a penny out of him."

"Why are you working for him, then?"

"As you put it yourself, he's my friend."

"Friend," she repeated thoughtfully. "It sounds strange to hear you say that word," she said. A slight smile, with curious disdain. "Do you have girlfriends as well?"

Corso looked at her legs unhurriedly, from ankles to thighs. Shamelessly.

"I have memories of some. The memory of you tonight might not be bad."

She took the crude remark without blinking. Maybe, Corso thought, she hadn't understood it.

"Name a price," she said coldly. "I want my husband's manuscript."

Things were looking good. Corso went and sat in an arm chair opposite Liana Taillefer. From there he could get a better view. She had taken off her shoes and was resting her feet on the rug.

"You didn't seem that interested last time."

"I've thought it over. That manuscript has . . ."

"Sentimental value?" mocked Corso.

"Something like that." Her voice now sounded defiant. "But not in the way you think."

"What would you be prepared to do to get it?"

"I've told you. Pay you."

Corso leered. "You offend me. I'm a professional."

"You're a professional mercenary, Mr. Corso. And mercenaries change sides. I've read books too, you know."

"I have as much money as I need."

"I'm not talking about money."

She was lying back on the sofa, and with one bare foot she stroked the instep of the other. Corso pictured her toenails painted red under the black stockings. As she moved, her skirt rode up, giving a glimpse of white flesh above the black garters, where all mysteries are reduced to one, which is as old as time itself. Corso looked up with difficulty. Her ice-blue eyes were still on him.

He took off his glasses before getting up and going to the sofa. Liana Taillefer followed him impassively with her eyes, even when he was right in front of her, so close that their knees touched. Then she put out her hand and placed her fingers with their red lacquered nails precisely on the zipper of his corduroy trousers. Her smile was contemptuous and self-assured as Corso at last leaned over her and lifted her skirt up to her waist.

IT WAS A MUTUAL assault rather than a sharing. A settling of scores there on the sofa. A crude, hard struggle between adults, with the appropriate moans at the right moment, a few muttered curses, and the woman's nails digging mercilessly into Corso's back. And it happened in barely any space, without their taking off their clothes. Her skirt was up over her strong, wide hips, which he gripped as the studs on her garter belt pressed into his groin. He never even saw her breasts, although he did manage to touch them a couple of times, dense, warm, abundant flesh beneath the jacket, silk shirt, and bra. In the heat of the fray, Liana Taillefer didn't have time to remove them. And now there they were, the two of them, still tangled in each other, among a mess of crumpled clothes, and breathless, like two exhausted wrestlers. Corso was wondering how to extricate himself.

"Who's Rochefort?" he asked.

She looked at him from a few inches away. The setting sun threw reddish glints across her face. The hairpins had fallen out of her bun, and her blond hair was spread untidily over the leather sofa. She looked relaxed for the first time.

"It doesn't matter," she answered, "now that I'm getting the manuscript back."

Corso kissed her disordered cleavage, bidding farewell to its contents. He had a feeling he wouldn't be kissing it again for some time.

"What manuscript?" he said, and saw her expression harden instantly. Her body went rigid under his.

"The Anjou Wine." For the first time there was a hint of anxiety in her voice. "You're going to return it to me, aren't you, Mr. Corso?"

Corso noted the return to a formal mode of address. He vaguely remembered having been on first-name terms during the skirmish.

"I never said that."

"I thought . . ."

"You thought wrong."

Her steely blue eyes flashed with anger. She sat up, furious, pushing him away abruptly with her hips.

"Bastard!"

Corso, who was about to laugh and make a couple of cynical jokes, felt himself pushed back violently. He fell to his knees. As he struggled to his feet, fastening his belt, he saw Liana

Taillefer stand up, pale and terrifying, unconcerned by her disheveled clothes, her magnificent thighs still exposed. She slapped him so hard, his left ear vibrated like a drum.

"Pig!"

Corso staggered from the blow. Stunned, he was like a boxer searching for something to stop him from falling into the ropes. Liana Taillefer crossed his field of vision, but he didn't pay her much attention because of the agonizing pain in his ear. He was staring stupidly at the saber from Waterloo when he heard the sound of breaking glass. He saw her again against the reddish light from the window. She had pulled her skirt down. In one hand she held the manuscript and in the other the neck of a broken bottle. Its edge was aimed at Corso's throat.

Instinctively he raised his arm and stepped back. The danger had brought him back to his senses and made the adrenaline pump. He pushed aside the hand with the bottle and punched her in the neck. It left her winded, stopping her dead. The following scene was somewhat calmer. Corso picked the manuscript and broken bottle off the floor. Liana Taillefer was once again sitting on the sofa, her tousled hair hanging over her face. She was holding a hand to her neck, breathing with difficulty between sobs of fury.

"They'll kill you for this, Corso," she said at last. The sun had now set beyond the city, and the corners of the room were filling with shadow. Ashamed, he switched on the light and held out her coat and hat before calling for a taxi. He avoided her eyes. Then, as he listened to her steps receding down the stairs, he stood for a moment by the window, watching the dark roofs in the brightness of the rising moon.

"They'll kill you for this, Corso."

He poured himself a large glass of gin. He couldn't rid himself of Liana Taillefer's expression once she realized she'd been tricked. Eyes as deadly as a dagger, a rictus of vengeful fury. And she meant it, she really had wanted to kill him. Once again

. . . keeping her at bay with the tip of his sword.

the memories stirred, gradually filling his mind. This time, though, he needed no effort to relive them. The image was sharp, and he knew exactly where it came from. The facsimile edition of *The Three Musketeers* was on his desk. He opened it and searched for the scene. Page 129. There, among overturned furniture, leaping from the bed, dagger in hand like a furious demon, Milady throws herself at d'Artagnan, who retreats, terrified, in his shirt, keeping her at bay with the tip of his sword.

VII. BOOK NUMBER ONE
AND BOOK NUMBER TWO

The truth is that the devil is very cunning.
The truth is that he is not always as ugly as they say.
—J. Cazotte, THE DEVIL IN LOVE

With only a few minutes to go before the departure of the express train to Lisbon, he saw the girl. Corso was on the platform, about to mount the steps to his carriage—COMPANHIA INTERNACIONAL DE CARRUAGEMS-CAMAS—when he bumped into her in a group of other passengers heading toward the first-class carriages. She was carrying a small rucksack and wearing the same blue duffel coat, but he didn't recognize her at first. He only felt that there was something familiar about her green eyes, so light they seemed transparent, and her very short hair. He continued to watch her for a moment, until she disappeared two carriages farther down. The whistle blew. As he climbed onto the train and the guard shut the door behind him, Corso remembered the scene: the girl sitting at one end of the table at the gathering of Boris Balkan and his circle in the café.

He walked along the corridor to his compartment. The station lights streamed past with increasing speed outside the windows, and the train clattered rhythmically. Moving around the cramped compartment with difficulty, he hung up his coat and jacket before sitting down on the bunk, his canvas bag beside him. In it, together with *The Nine Doors* and the folder with the Dumas manuscript, was a book by Les Cases, the *Memoirs of Saint Helena:*

Friday, 14 July 1816. The Emperor has been unwell all night...

He lit a cigarette. Occasionally, when lights from the window strobed across his face, he would glance out before returning to the tale of Napoleon's slow agony and the wiliness of his English jailer, Sir Hudson Lowe. He frowned as he read, and adjusted his glasses on the bridge of his nose. From time to time he stopped and stared for a moment at his own reflection in the window, and he made a face. Even now, he felt indignant at the way the victors had condemned the fallen titan to a miserable end, having him cling to a rock in the middle of the Atlantic. Strange, going over the historical events and his earlier feelings about them from his present, clearheaded perspective. How far away he seemed, that other Lucas Corso who reverently admired the Waterloo veteran's saber; the boy absorbing the family myths with aggressive enthusiasm, the precocious Bonapartist and avid reader of books with engravings of the glorious campaigns, names that echoed like drumrolls for a charge: Wagram, Jena, Smolensk, Marengo... The boy wide-eyed with wonder had long ceased to exist; a hazy ghost of him sometimes appeared in Corso's memory, between the pages of a book, in a smell or a sound, or through a dark window with the rain from another country beating against it, outside in the night.

The conductor passed the door, ringing his bell. Half an hour till the restaurant car closed. Corso shut the book. He put on his jacket, slung the canvas bag over his shoulder, and left the compartment. At the end of the corridor, from the door, a cold draft blew through the passageway leading to the next sleeper. He felt the thundering beneath his feet as he crossed into the section of first-class carriages. He let a couple of passengers go by and then looked into the nearest compartment, which was only half full. The girl was there, by the door, wearing a sweater and jeans, her bare feet resting on the seat opposite. As Corso passed, she looked up from her book and their eyes met. He was about to nod briefly in her direction, but when she showed no sign of recognition, he stopped himself. She must have sensed something, because she looked at him with curiosity. But by then he was continuing down the corridor.

He ate his dinner, rocked by the swaying of the train, and had time for a coffee and a gin before they closed for the evening. The moon, in shades of raw silk, was rising. Telephone poles rushed past in the darkened plain, fleeting frames for a sequence of stills from a badly adjusted movie projector.

He was on his way back to his compartment when he saw the girl in the corridor of the first-class carriage. She had opened the window, and the cold night air was blowing against her face. As he came up to her, he turned sideways so he could get past. She turned toward him.

"I know you," she said.

Close up, her green eyes seemed even lighter, like liquid crystal, and luminous against her suntanned skin. It was only March, and with her hair parted like a boy's, her tan made her look unusual, sporty, pleasantly ambiguous. She was tall, slim, and supple. And very young.

"Yes," said Corso, pausing a moment. "A few days ago, at the café."

She smiled. Another contrast, this time of white teeth against brown skin. Her mouth was big and well defined. A pretty girl, Flavio La Ponte would have said, stroking his curly beard.

"You were the one asking about d'Artagnan."

The cold air from the window blew her hair. She was still barefoot. Her white sneakers were on the floor by her empty seat. He instinctively glanced at the book lying there: *The Adventures of Sherlock Holmes.* A cheap paperback, he noticed. The Mexican edition, published by Porrua.

"You'll catch cold," he said.

Still smiling, the girl shook her head, but she turned the handle and shut the window. Corso, about to go on his way, paused to find a cigarette. He did it as he always did, taking one directly from his pocket and putting it in his mouth, when he realized she was watching him.

"Do you smoke?" he asked hesitantly, stopping his hand halfway.

"Sometimes."

He put the cigarette in his mouth and took out another one. It was dark tobacco, without a filter, and as crushed as all the packs he usually carried with him. The girl took it. She looked to see the brand. Then she leaned over for Corso to light it, after his own, with the last match in the box.

"It's strong," she said, breathing out her first mouthful of smoke, but then made none of the fuss he expected. She held the cigarette in an unusual way, between forefinger and thumb, with the ember outward. "Are you in this carriage?"

"No, in the next one."

"You're lucky to have a sleeper." She tapped her jeans pocket, indicating a nonexistent wallet. "I wish I could. Luckily the compartment's half empty."

"Are you a student?"

"Sort of."

The train thundered into a tunnel. The girl turned then, as if the darkness outside drew her attention. Tense and alert, she leaned against her own reflection in the window. She seemed to be expecting something in the noisy rush of air. Then, when the train emerged into the open and small lights again punctuated the night like brush strokes as the train passed, she smiled, distant.

"I like trains," she said.

"Me too."

The girl was still facing the window, touching it with the fingertips of one hand. "Imagine," she said. She was smiling nostalgically, obviously remembering something. "Leaving Paris in the evening to wake up on the lagoon in Venice, en route to Istanbul..."

Corso made a face. How old could she be? Eighteen, twenty at most.

"Playing poker," he suggested, "between Calais and Brindisi."

She looked at him more attentively.

"Not bad." She thought a moment. "How about a champagne breakfast between Vienna and Nice?"

"Interesting. Like spying on Basil Zaharoff."

"Or getting drunk with Nijinsky."

"Stealing Coco Chanel's pearls."

"Flirting with Paul Morand...Or Mr. Barnabooth."

They both laughed, Corso under his breath, she openly, resting her forehead on the cold glass. Her laugh was loud, frank, and boyish, matching her hair and her luminous green eyes.

"Trains aren't like that anymore," he said.

"I know."

The lights of a signal post passed like a flash of lightning. Then a dimly lit, deserted platform, with a sign made illegible by their speed. The moon was rising and now and then clarified the confused outline of trees and roofs. It seemed to be flying alongside the train in a mad, purposeless race.

"What's your name?"

"Corso. And yours?"

"Irene Adler."

He looked at her intently, and she held his gaze calmly.

"That's not a proper name."

"Neither is Corso."

"You're wrong. I am Corso. The man who runs."

"You don't look like a man who runs anywhere. You seem the quiet type."

He bowed his head slightly, looking at the girl's bare feet on the floor of the corridor. He could tell she was staring at him, examining him. It made him feel uncomfortable. That was unusual. She was too young, he told himself. And too attractive. He automatically adjusted his crooked glasses and moved to go on his way.

"Have a good journey."

"Thanks."

He took a few steps, knowing that she was watching him.

"Maybe we'll see each other around," she said, behind him.

"Maybe."

Impossible. That was another Corso returning home, uneasy, the Grande Armée about to melt in the snow. The fire of Moscow crackling in his wake. He couldn't leave like that, so he stopped and turned around. As he did so, he smiled like a hungry wolf.

"Irene Adler," he repeated, trying to remember. "*Study in Scarlet?*"

"No," she answered. "*A Scandal in Bohemia.*" Now she was smiling too, and her gaze shone emerald green in the dim corridor. "*The Woman*, my dear Watson."

Corso slapped his forehead as if he'd just remembered.

"Elementary," he said. And he was sure they'd meet again.

HE SPENT LESS THAN fifty minutes in Lisbon. Just enough time to get from Santa Apolonia Station to Rossio Station. An hour and a half later he stepped onto the platform in Sintra, beneath a sky full of low clouds that blurred the tops of the melancholy gray towers of the castle of Da Pena farther up the hill. There was no taxi in sight, so he walked to the small hotel that was opposite the National Palace with its two large chimneys. It was ten o'clock on a Wednesday morning, and the esplanade was empty of tourists and coaches. He had no trouble getting a room. It looked out onto the uneven landscape, where the roofs and towers of old houses peered above the thick greenery, their ruined gardens suffocating in ivy.

After a shower and a coffee he asked for the Quinta da Soledade, and the hotel receptionist told him the way, up the road. There weren't any taxis on the esplanade either, although there were a couple of horse-drawn carriages. Corso negotiated a price, and a few minutes later he was passing under the lacy baroque stonework of Regaleira Tower. The sound of the horse's hooves echoed from the dark walls, the drains and fountains running with water, the ivy-covered walls, railings, and tree trunks, the stone steps carpeted with moss, and the ancient tiles on the abandoned manor houses.

The Quinta da Soledade was a rectangular, eighteenth-century house, with four chimneys and an ochre plaster facade covered with water trails and stains. Corso got out of the carriage and stood looking at the place for a moment before opening the iron gate. Two mossy, gray-green stone statues on granite columns stood at either end of the wall. One was a bust of a woman. The other seemed to be identical, but the features were hidden by the ivy climbing up it, enfolding and merging with the sculpted face.

As he walked toward the house, dead leaves crackled beneath his steps. The path was lined with marble statues, almost all of them lying broken next to their empty pedestals. The garden was completely wild. Vegetation had taken over, climbing up benches and into alcoves. The wrought iron left rusty trails on the moss-covered stone. To his left, in a pond full of aquatic plants, a fountain with cracked tiles sheltered a chubby angel with empty eyes and mutilated hands. It slept with its head resting on a book, and a thread of water trickled from its mouth. Everything seemed suffused with infinite sadness, and Corso couldn't help being affected. Quinta da Soledade, he repeated. House of Solitude. The name suited it.

He went up the stone steps leading to the door and looked up. Beneath the gray sky no time was indicated on the Roman numerals of the ancient sundial on the wall. Above it ran the legend: OMNES VULNERANT, POSTUMA NECAT.

They all wound, he read. The last one kills.

"YOU'VE ARRIVED JUST IN time," said Fargas, "for the ceremony."

Corso held out his hand, slightly disconcerted. Victor Fargas was as tall and thin as an El Greco figure. He seemed to move around inside his loose, thick woolen sweater and baggy trousers like a tortoise in its shell. His mustache was trimmed with geometrical precision, and his old-fashioned, worn-out shoes gleamed. Corso noticed this much at first glance, before his attention was drawn to the huge, empty house, its bare walls, the paintings on the ceiling that were falling into shreds, eaten by mildew.

Fargas examined his visitor closely. "I assume you'll accept a brandy," he said at last. He set off down the corridor, limping slightly, without bothering to check whether Corso was following or not. They passed other rooms, which were empty or contained the remains of broken furniture thrown in a corner. Naked, dusty lightbulbs hung from the ceilings.

The only rooms that seemed to be in use were two interconnecting reception rooms. There was a sliding door between them with coats of arms etched into the glass. It was open, revealing more bare walls, their ancient wallpaper marked by long-gone pictures, and furniture, rusty nails, and fixtures for nonexistent lamps. Above this gloomy scene was a ceiling painted to resemble a vault of clouds with the sacrifice of Isaac in the center. The cracked figure of the old patriarch held a dagger, about to strike a blond young man. His hand was restrained by an angel with huge wings. Beneath the trompe l'oeil sky, dusty French windows, some of the panes replaced with cardboard, led to the terrace and, beyond that, to the garden.

"Home sweet home," said Fargas.

His irony was unconvincing. He seemed to have made the remark too often and was no longer sure of its effect. He spoke Spanish with a heavy, distinguished Portuguese accent. And he moved very slowly, perhaps because of his bad leg, like someone who has all the time in the world.

"Brandy," he said again, as if he didn't quite remember how they'd reached that point.

Corso nodded vaguely, but Fargas didn't notice. At one end of the vast room was an enormous fireplace with logs piled up in it. There were a pair of unmatched armchairs, a table and sideboard, an oil lamp, two big candlesticks, a violin in its case, and little else. But on the floor, lined up neatly on old, faded, threadbare rugs, as far away as possible from the windows and the leaden light coming through them, lay a great many books; five hundred or more, Corso estimated, maybe even a thousand. Many codices and incunabula among them. Wonderful old books bound in leather or parchment. Ancient tomes with studs in the covers, folios, Elzevirs, their bindings decorated with goffering, bosses, rosettes, locks, their spines and front edges covered with gilding and calligraphy done by medieval monks in the scriptoria of their monasteries. He also noticed a dozen or so rusty mousetraps in various corners.

Fargas, who had been searching through the sideboard, turned around with a glass and a bottle of Rémy Martin. He held it up to the light to look at the contents.

"Nectar of the gods," he said triumphantly. "Or the devil." He smiled only with his mouth, twisting his mustache like an old-fashioned movie star. His eyes remained fixed and expressionless, with bags beneath them as if from chronic insomnia. Corso noticed his delicate hands—a sign of good breeding—as he took the glass of brandy. The glass vibrated gently as Corso raised it to his lips.

"Nice glass," he said to make conversation.

Fargas agreed, and made a gesture halfway between resignation and self-mockery, suggesting a different reading of it all: the glass, the tiny amount of brandy in the bottle, the bare house, his own presence. An elegant, pale, worn ghost.

"I have only one more left," he confided in a calm, neutral tone. "That's why I take care of them."

Corso nodded. He glanced at the bare walls and again at the books.

"This must have been a beautiful house," he said.

Fargas shrugged. "Yes, it was. But old families are like civilizations. One day they just wither and die." He looked around without seeing. All the missing objects seemed to be reflected in his eyes. "At first one resorts to the barbarians to guard the *limes* of the Danube, but it makes the barbarians rich and they end up as one's creditors. . . . Then one day they rebel and invade, looting everything." He suddenly peered at his visitor suspiciously. "I hope you understand what I mean."

Corso nodded, smiling his best conspiratorial smile. "Perfectly," he said. "Hobnail boots crushing Saxony porcelain. Isn't that it? Servants in evening dress. Working-class parvenus who wipe their arses on illuminated manuscripts."

Fargas nodded approvingly. He was smiling. He limped over to the sideboard in search of the other glass. "I'll have a brandy too," he said.

They drank a toast in silence, looking at each other like two members of a secret fraternity who have just exchanged sign and countersign. Then, moving closer to the books, Fargas gestured at them with the hand holding the glass, as if Corso had just passed his initiation test and Fargas was inviting him to pass through an invisible barrier.

"There they are. Eight hundred and thirty-four volumes. Less than half of them are worth anything." He drank some more and ran his finger over his damp mustache, looking around. "It's a shame that you didn't know them in better days, lined up on their cedarwood shelves.... I managed to collect five thousand of them. These are the survivors."

Corso put his canvas bag on the floor and went over to the books. His fingers itched instinctively. It was a magnificent sight. He adjusted his glasses and immediately saw a 1588 first-edition Vasari in quarto, and a sixteenth-century *Tractatus* by Berengario de Carpi bound in parchment.

"I would never have dreamed that the Fargas collection, listed in all the bibliographies, was kept like this. Piled on the floor against the wall, in an empty house..."

"That's life, my friend. But I have to say, in my defense, that they are all in immaculate condition. I clean them and make sure they're aired. I check that insects or rodents don't get at them, and that they're protected against light, heat, and moisture. In fact I do nothing else all day."

"What happened to the rest?"

Fargas looked toward the window, asking himself the same question. He frowned. "You can imagine," he answered, and he looked a very unhappy man when he turned back to Corso. "Apart from the house, a few pieces of furniture, and my father's library, I inherited nothing but debts. Whenever I got any money, I invested it in books. When my savings dwindled, I got rid of everything else—pictures, furniture, china. I think you understand what it is to be a passionate collector of books. But I'm pathologically obsessed. I suffered atrociously just at the thought of breaking up my collection."

"I've known people like that."

"Really?" Fargas regarded him, interested. "I still doubt you can really imagine what it's like. I used to get up at night and wander about like a lost soul looking at my books. I'd talk to them and stroke their spines, swearing I'd always take care of them.... But none of it was any use. One day I made my decision: to sacrifice most of the books and keep only the most cherished, valuable ones. Neither you nor anyone will ever understand how that felt, letting the vultures pick over my collection."

"I can imagine," said Corso, who wouldn't have minded in the least joining in the feast.

"Can you? I don't think so. Not in a million years. Separating them took me two months. Sixty-one days of agony, and an attack of fever that almost killed me. At last, people took them away, and I thought I would go mad. I remember it as if it were yesterday, although it was twelve years ago."

"And now?"

Fargas held up the empty glass as if it were a symbol.

"For some time now I've had to resort to selling my books again. Not that I need very much. Once a week someone comes in to clean, and I get my food brought from the village. Almost all the money goes to pay the state taxes for the house."

He pronounced *state* as if he'd said vermin. Corso looked sympathetic, glancing again at the bare walls. "You could sell it."

"Yes," Fargas agreed indifferently. "There are things you can't understand."

Corso bent to pick up a folio bound in parchment and leafed through it with interest. *De Symmetria* by Dürer, Paris 1557, reprinting of the first Nuremberg edition in Latin. In good condition, with wide margins. Flavio La Ponte would have gone wild over it. Anybody would have gone wild over it.

"How often do you have to sell books?"

"Two or three a year is enough. After going over and over them, I choose one book to sell. That's the ceremony I was referring to when I answered the door. I have a buyer, a compatriot of yours. He comes here a couple of times a year."

"Do I know him?" asked Corso.

"I have no idea," answered Fargas, not supplying a name. "In fact I'm expecting him any day now. When you arrived, I was getting ready to choose a victim. . . ." He made a guillotine movement with one of his slender hands, still smiling wearily. "The one that must die in order for the others to stay together."

Corso looked up at the ceiling, drawing the inevitable parallel. Abraham, a deep crack across his face, was making visible efforts to free the hand in which he held the knife. The angel was holding on to it firmly with one hand and severely reprimanding the patriarch with the other. Beneath the blade, his head resting on a stone, Isaac waited, resigned to his fate. He was blond with pink cheeks, like an ancient Greek youth who never said no. Beyond him a sheep was tangled up in brambles, and Corso mentally voted for the sheep to be spared.

"I suppose you have no other choice," he said, looking at Fargas.

"If there was one, I would have found it." Fargas smiled bitterly. "But the lion demands his share, and the sharks smell the bait. Unfortunately there aren't any people left like the Comte d'Artois, who was king of France. Do you know the story? The old Marquis de Paulmy, who owned sixty thousand books, went bankrupt. To escape his creditors he sold his collection to the Comte d'Artois. But the Count stipulated that the old man should keep them until his death. In that way Paulmy used the money to buy more books and extend the collection, even though it was no longer his. . . ."

He had put his hands in his pockets and was limping up and down along the books, examining each one, like a shabby, gaunt Montgomery inspecting his troops at El Alamein.

"Sometimes I don't even touch them or open them." He stopped and leaned over to straighten a book in its row, on the old rug. "All I do is dust them and stare at them for hours. I know what lies inside each binding, down to the last detail. Look at this one: *De revolutionis celestium*, Nicholas Copernicus. Second edition, Basle, 1566. A mere trifle, don't you think? Like the *Vulgata Clementina* to your right, between the six volumes of the *Polyglot* by your compatriot Cisneros, and the Nuremberg *Cronicarum*. And look at the strange folio over there: *Praxis criminis persequendi* by Simon de Colines, 1541. Or that monastic binding with four raised bands and bosses that you see there. Do you know what's inside? *The Golden Legend* by Jacobo de la Voragine, Basle, 1493, printed by Nicolas Kesler."

Corso leafed through *The Golden Legend.* It was a magnificent edition, also with very wide margins. He put it back carefully. Then he stood up, wiping his glasses with his handkerchief. It would have made the coolest of men break out in a sweat.

"You must be crazy. If you sold all this, you wouldn't have any money problems."

"I know." Fargas was leaning over to adjust the position of the book imperceptibly. "But if I sold them all, I'd have no reason to go on living. So I wouldn't care if I had money problems or not."

Corso pointed at a row of books in very bad condition. There were several incunabula and manuscripts. Judging from the bindings, none dated from later than the seventeenth century.

"You have a great many old editions of chivalric novels."

"Yes. Inherited from my father. His obsession was acquiring the ninety-five books of Don Quixote's collection, in particular those mentioned in the priest's expurgation. He also left me that strange *Quixote* that you see there, next to the first edition of *Os Lusiadas.* It's a 1789 Ibarra in four volumes. In addition to the corresponding illustrations, it is enriched with others printed in England in the first half of the eighteenth century, six wash drawings and a facsimile of Cervantes's birth certificate printed on vellum. To each his own obsessions. In the case of my father, a diplomat who lived for many years in Spain, it was Cervantes. In some people it's a mania. They won't accept restoration work, even if it's invisible, or they won't buy a book numbered over fifty.... My passion, as you must have noticed, was uncut books. I scoured auctions and bookshops, ruler in hand, and I went weak in the knees if I found one that was

intact, that hadn't been plowed. Have you read Nodier's bur-
lesque tale about the book collector? The same happened to me.
I'd have happily shot any bookbinder who'd been too free with
the guillotine. I was in ecstasy if I discovered an edition with
margins two millimeters wider than those described in the canonical bibliographies."

"I would be too."

"Congratulations, then. Welcome to the brotherhood."

"Not so fast. My interest is financial rather than aesthetic in
nature."

"Never mind. I like you. I believe that when it comes to
books, conventional morality doesn't exist." He was at the other
end of the room but bent his head toward Corso confidingly.
"Do you know something? You Spaniards have a story about a
bookseller in Barcelona who committed murder. Well, I too
would be capable of killing for a book."

"I wouldn't recommend it. That's how it starts. Murder
doesn't seem like a big deal, but then you end up lying, voting
in elections, things like that."

"Even selling your own books."

"Even that."

Fargas shook his head sadly. He stood still a moment, frowning. Then he studied Corso closely for some time.

"Which brings us," he said at last, "to the business I was
engaged in when you rang at the door.... Every time I have
to address the problem, I feel like a priest renouncing his faith.
Are you surprised that I should think of this as a sacrilege?"

"Not at all. I suppose that's exactly what it is."

Fargas wrung his hands in torment. He looked around at
the bare room and the books on the floor, and back at Corso.
His smile seemed false, painted on.

"Yes. Sacrilege can only be justified in faith. Only a believer
can sense the terrible enormity of the deed. We'd feel no horror
at profaning a religion to which we were indifferent. It would
be like an atheist blaspheming. Absurd."

Corso agreed. "I know what you mean. It's Julian the Apostate crying, 'Thou hast conquered, O Galilean.'"

"I'm not familiar with that quotation."

"It may be apocryphal. One of the Marist brothers used to quote it when I was at school. He was warning us not to go off on a tangent. Julian ends up shot through with arrows on the battlefield, spitting blood at a heaven without God."

Fargas assented, as if it was all terribly close to him. There was something disturbing in the strange rictus of his mouth, in the fixed intensity of his eyes.

"That's how I feel now," he said. "I get up because I can't sleep. I stand here, resolved to commit another desecration." He moved so close to Corso as he spoke that Corso wanted to take a step back. "To sin against myself and against them . . . I touch one book, then change my mind, choose another one but end up putting it back in its place. . . . I must sacrifice one so that the others can live, snap off a branch so that the tree . . ." He held up his right hand. "I would rather cut off one of my fingers."

As he made the gesture, his hand trembled. Corso nodded. He knew how to listen. It was part of the job. He could even understand. But he wasn't prepared to join in. This didn't concern him. As Varo Borja would have said, he was a mercenary, and he was paying a visit. What Fargas needed was a confessor, or a psychiatrist.

"Nobody would pay a penny for an old book collector's finger," Corso said lightly.

The joke was lost in the immense void that filled Fargas's eyes. He was looking through Corso. In his dilated pupils and absent gaze there were only books.

"So which should I choose?" Fargas went on. Corso took a cigarette from his coat pocket and offered it to the old man, but Fargas didn't notice. Absorbed, obsessed, he was listening only to himself, was aware of nothing but his tortured mind. "After much thought I have chosen two candidates." He took two books from the floor and put them on the table. "Tell me what you think."

Corso bent over the books. He opened one of them at a page with an engraving, a woodcut of three men and a woman working in a mine. It was a second edition of *De re metallica* by Georgius Agricola, in Latin, printed by Froben and Episcopius in Basle only five years after its first edition in 1556. He gave a grunt of approval as he lit his cigarette.

"As you can see, making a choice isn't easy." Fargas was following Corso's movements intently. Anxiously he watched him turn the pages, barely brushing them with his fingertips. "I sell one book each time. And not just any one. The sacrifice has to ensure that the rest are safe for another six months. It's my tribute to the Minotaur." He tapped his temple. "We all have one at the center of the labyrinth.... Our reason creates him, and he imposes his own horror."

"Why don't you sell several less valuable books at one time? Then you'd raise the money you need and still keep the rarer ones. Or your favorites."

"Place some over others?" Fargas shuddered. "I simply couldn't do it. They all have the same immortal soul. To me they all have the same rights. I have my favorites, of course. How could I not? But I never make distinctions by a gesture, a word that might raise them above their less favored companions. Rather the opposite. Remember that God chose his own son to be sacrificed. For the redemption of mankind. And Abraham ..." He seemed to be referring to the painting on the ceiling, because he looked up and smiled sadly at the empty space, leaving the sentence unfinished.

Corso opened the second book, a folio with an Italian parchment binding from the 1700s. Inside was a magnificent Virgil. Giunta's Venetian edition, printed in 1544. This revived Fargas.

"Beautiful, isn't it?" He stepped in front of Corso and snatched it from him impatiently. "Look at the title page, at the architectural border. One hundred and thirteen woodcuts, all perfect except for page 345, which has a small, ancient restoration, almost imperceptible, in one of the bottom corners. As it happens, this is my favorite. Look: Aeneas in hell, next to the Sibyl. Have you ever seen anything like it? Look at these flames behind the triple wall, the cauldron of the damned, the bird devouring their entrails. . . ." The old book collector's pulse was almost visible, throbbing in his wrists and temples. His voice became deeper as he held the book up to his eyes so he could read more clearly. His expression was radiant. *"Moenia amnlata videt, triplici circundata muro, quae rapidus flamnis ambit torrentibus amnis."* He paused, ecstatic. "The engraver had a beautiful, violent, medieval view of Virgil's Hades."

"A magnificent book," confirmed Corso, dragging on his cigarette.

"It's more than that. Feel the paper. 'Esemplare buono e genuino con le figure assai ben impresse,' assure the old catalogues." After this feverish outburst, Fargas once more stared into empty space, absorbed, engrossed in the dark corners of his nightmare. "I think I'll sell this one."

Corso exhaled impatiently. "I don't understand. This is obviously one of your favorites. So is the Agricola. Your hands tremble as you touch them."

"My hands? What you mean is that my soul burns in the torments of hell. I thought I'd explained. The book to be sacrificed can never be one to which I am indifferent. What meaning would this painful act have otherwise? A sordid transaction determined by market forces, several cheap books instead of a single expensive one . . ." Scornful, he shook his head violently. He looked around grimly, searching for someone on whom to vent his anger. "These are the ones I love best. They shine above the rest for their beauty, for the love they have inspired. These are the ones I walk hand in hand with to the brink of the abyss. . . . Life may strip me of all I have. But it won't turn me into a miserable wretch."

He paced aimlessly about the room. The sad scene, his bad

leg, his shabby clothes all added to his weary, fragile appearance.

"That's why I remain in this house," he went on. "The ghosts of my lost books roam within its walls." He stopped in front of the fireplace and looked at the pile of logs in the hearth. "Sometimes I feel they come back to demand that I make amends. So, to placate them, I take up the violin that you see there and I play for hours, wandering through the house in darkness, like one of the damned. . . ." He turned to look at Corso, was silhouetted against the dirty window. "The wandering book collector." He walked slowly to the table and laid a hand on each book, as if he had delayed making his decision until that moment. Now he smiled inquiringly.

"Which one would you choose, if you were in my place?"

Corso fidgeted, uneasy. "Please, leave me out of this. I'm lucky enough not to be in your place."

"That's right. Very lucky. How clever of you to realize. A stupid man would envy me, I suppose. All this treasure in my house . . . But you haven't told me which one to sell. Which son to sacrifice." His face suddenly became distorted with anguish, as if the pain were in his body too. "May his blood taint me and mine," he added in a very low, intense voice, "unto the seventh generation."

He returned the Agricola to its place on the rug and stroked the parchment of the Virgil, muttering, "His blood." His eyes were moist and his hands shook uncontrollably. "I think I'll sell this one," he said.

Fargas might not be out of his mind yet, but he soon would be. Corso looked at the bare walls, the marks left by pictures on the stained wallpaper. The highly unlikely seventh generation didn't give a damn about any of this. Like Lucas Corso's own, the Fargas line would end here. And find peace at last. Corso's cigarette smoke rose up to the decrepit painting on the ceiling, straight up, like the smoke from a sacrifice in the calm of dawn. He looked out the window, at the garden overrun with weeds, searching for a way out, like the lamb tangled in the brambles. But there was nothing but books. The angel let go of the hand that held up the knife and went away, weeping. And left Abraham alone, the poor fool.

Corso finished his cigarette and threw it into the fireplace. He was tired and cold. He had heard too many words within these bare walls. He was glad there were no mirrors for him to see the expression on his face. He looked at his watch without noticing the time. With a fortune sitting there on the old rugs and carpets, Victor Fargas had more than paid their price in suffering. For Corso it was now time to talk business.

"What about *The Nine Doors?*"

"What about it?"

"That's what brought me here. I assume you got my letter."

"Your letter? Yes, of course. I remember. It's just that with all of this . . . Forgive me. *The Nine Doors.* Of course."

He looked around, bewildered, like a sleepwalker who has just been jolted awake. He suddenly seemed infinitely tired, after a long ordeal. He lifted a finger, requesting a minute to think, then limped over to a corner of the room. Some fifty books were lined up there on a faded French rug. Corso could just make out that the rug depicted Alexander's victory over Darius.

"Did you know," asked Fargas, pointing at the scene on the Gobelin, "that Alexander used his rival's treasure chest to store Homer's books?" He nodded, pleased, looking at the Macedonian's threadbare profile. "He was a fellow book collector. A good man."

Corso didn't give a damn about Alexander the Great's literary tastes. He knelt and read the titles printed on some of the spines and front edges. They were all ancient treatises on magic, alchemy, and demonology. *Les trois livres de l'Art, Destructor omnium rerum, Disertazioni sopra le apparizioni de' spiriti e diavoli, De origine, moribus et rebus gestis Satanae . . .*

"What do you think?" asked Fargas.

"Not bad."

The book collector laughed wearily. He got down on the rug beside Corso and went over the books mechanically, making sure that none of them had moved by a millimeter since he last checked them.

"Not bad at all. You're right. At least ten of them are extremely rare. I inherited all this part of the collection from my grandfather. He was a devotee of the hermetic arts and astrology, and he was a Mason. Look. This is a classic, the *Infernal Dictionary* by Collin de Plancy, a first edition dating from 1842. And this is the 1571 printing of the *Compendi dei secreti*, by Leonardo Fioravanti.... That strange duodecimo there is the second edition of the *Book of Wonders.*" He opened another book and showed Corso an engraving. "Look at Isis.... And do you know what this is?"

"Yes, of course. The *Oedipus Aegiptiacus* by Atanasius Kircher."

"Correct. The 1652 Rome edition." Fargas put the book back and picked up another one. Corso recognized the Venetian binding: the black leather with five raised bands and a pentacle but no title on the cover. "Here's the one you're looking for, *De Umbrarum Regni Novem Portis.* The nine doors of the kingdom of shadows."

Corso shivered in spite of himself. On the outside at least the book was identical to the one he had in his canvas bag. Fargas handed him the book, and Corso stood up as he leafed through it. They looked identical, or almost. The leather on the back of Fargas's copy was slightly worn, and there was an old mark left by a label that had been added and then removed. The rest was in the same immaculate condition as Varo Borja's copy, even engraving number VIIII, which was intact.

"It's complete and in good condition," said Fargas, correctly interpreting the look on Corso's face. "It's been out in the world for three and a half centuries, but when you open it, it looks as fresh as the day it came off the press. As if the printer made a pact with the devil."

"Maybe he did," said Corso.

"I wouldn't mind knowing the magic formula. My soul in exchange for keeping all this." The book collector made a sweeping gesture that took in the desolate room, the rows of books on the floor.

"You could try it," said Corso pointing at *The Nine Doors*. "They say the formula is in there."

"I never believed all that nonsense. Although maybe now would be a good time to start. Don't you think? You have a saying in Spain: If all is lost, we may as well jump in the river."

"Is the book in order? Have you noticed anything strange about it?"

"Nothing whatsoever. There are no pages missing. And the engravings are all there, nine of them, plus the title page. Just as it was when my grandfather bought it at the turn of the century. It matches the description in the catalogues, and it's identical to the other two copies, the Ungern in Paris and the Terral-Coy."

"It's no longer Terral-Coy. It's now in the Varo Borja collection in Toledo."

Corso saw that Fargas's expression had become suspicious, alert.

"Varo Borja, you say?" He was about to add something, but changed his mind. "His collection is remarkable. And very well known." He paced aimlessly, looking again at the books lined up on the rug. "Varo Borja . . . ," he repeated thoughtfully. "A specialist in demonology, isn't he? A very rich book collector. He's been after that *Nine Doors* you've got there for years. He's always been prepared to pay any price. . . . I didn't know that he'd managed to find a copy. And you work for him."

"Occasionally," admitted Corso.

Fargas nodded a couple of times, looking puzzled. "Strange that he should send you. After all . . ."

He broke off and let his sentence hang. He was looking at Corso's bag. "You brought the book with you? Could I see it?"

They went up to the table and Corso laid his copy next to Fargas's. As he did so, he could hear the old man's agitated breathing. His face looked ecstatic again.

"Look at them closely," he whispered, as if afraid of waking something that slept between their pages. "They're perfect, beautiful. And identical. Two of the only three copies that escaped the flames, brought together for the first time since they were parted three hundred and fifty years ago. . . ." His hands were trembling again. He rubbed his wrists to slow the blood coursing through them. "Look at the errata on page 72, and the split *s* here, in the fourth line of page 87. . . . The same paper, identical printing. Isn't it a wonder?"

"Yes." Corso cleared his throat. "I'd like to stay awhile. Have a thorough look at them."

Fargas gave him a piercing look. He seemed to hesitate.

"As you wish," he said at last. "But if you have the Terral-Coy copy, there's no doubt as to its authenticity." He looked at Corso with curiosity, trying to read his mind. "Varo Borja must know that."

"I suppose he must." Corso gave his best neutral smile. "But I'm getting paid to make sure." He kept smiling. They were coming to the difficult part. "By the way, speaking of money, I was told to make you an offer."

The book collector's curiosity turned to suspicion. "What kind of offer?"

"Financial. And substantial." Corso laid his hand on the second copy. "You could solve your money problems for some time."

"Would it be Varo Borja paying?"

"It could be."

Fargas stroked his chin. "He already has one of the books. Does he want all three of them?"

The man might have been a little insane, but he was no fool. Corso gestured vaguely, not wanting to commit himself. Perhaps. One of those things collectors get into their heads. But if Fargas sold the book, he would be able to keep the Virgil.

"You don't understand," said Fargas. But Corso understood only too well. He wasn't going to get anywhere with the old man.

"Forget it," he said. "It was just a thought."

"I don't sell at random. I choose the books. I thought I'd made that clear."

The veins on the back of his tensed hands were knotted. He was becoming irritated, so Corso spent the next few minutes in placatory mode. The offer was a secondary matter, a mere formality. What he really wanted, he said, was to make a comparative study of both books. At last, to his relief, Fargas nodded in agreement.

"I don't see any problem with that," he said, his mistrust receding. It was obvious that he liked Corso. If he hadn't, things would have gone quite differently. "Although I can't offer you many creature comforts here...."

He led him down a bare passage to another, smaller room, which had a dilapidated piano in one corner, a table with an old bronze candelabrum covered with wax drips, and a couple of rickety chairs.

"At least it's quiet here," said Fargas. "And all the window-panes are intact."

He snapped his fingers, as if he'd forgotten something. He disappeared for a moment and returned holding the rest of the bottle of brandy.

"So Varo Borja finally managed to get hold of it," he repeated. He smiled to himself, as if at some thought that obviously caused him great satisfaction. Then he put the bottle and glass on the floor, at a safe distance from the two copies of *The*

Nine Doors. Like an attentive host he looked around to make sure that everything was in order, then said ironically, before leaving, "Make yourself at home."

Corso poured the rest of the brandy into the glass. He took out his notes and set to work. He had drawn three boxes on a sheet of paper. Each box contained a number and name:

Copy one (Varo Borja), Toledo.
Copy two (Fargas), Sintra.
Copy three (Von Ungern), Paris.

Page after page, he jotted down any difference between book number one and book number two, however slight: a stain on a page, the ink slightly darker in one copy than in the other. When he came to the first engraving, NEM. PERVT.T QUI N.N LEG. CERT.RIT, the horseman advising the reader to keep silent, he took out a magnifying glass with a power of seven from his bag and examined both woodcuts, line by line. They were identical. He noticed that even the pressure of the engravings on the paper, like that of the typography, was the same. The lines and characters looked worn, broken, or crooked in exactly the same places in both copies. This meant that number one and number two had been printed one after the other, or almost, and on the same press. As the Ceniza brothers would have put it, Corso was looking at a pair of twins.

He went on making notes. An imperfection in line 6 of page 19 in book number two made him stop a moment, then he realized it was just an ink stain. He turned more pages. Both books had the same structure: two flyleaves and 160 pages stitched into twenty gatherings of eight. All nine illustrations in both books occupied a full page. They had been printed separately on the same type of paper, blank on the reverse, and inserted into the book during the binding process. They were positioned identically in both books:

I. *between pages 16 and 17*
II. *32–33*
III. *48–49*
IIII. *64–65*
V. *80–81*
VI. *96–97*
VII. *112–113*
VIII. *128–129*
VIIII. *144–145*

Either Varo Borja was raving, or this was a very strange job Corso had been sent on. There was no way that they were forgeries. At the most, they might both have come from an edition that was apocryphal but still dated from the seventeenth century. Number one and number two were the embodiment of honesty on printed paper.

He drank the rest of the brandy and examined illustration II with his magnifying glass. CLAUS. PAT. T., the bearded hermit holding two keys, the closed door, a lantern on the ground. He had the illustrations side by side and suddenly felt rather silly. It was like playing Find the Difference. He grimaced. Life as a game. And books as a reflection of life.

Then he saw it. It happened suddenly, just as something that has seemed meaningless, when viewed from the correct angle, all at once appears ordered and precise. Corso breathed out, as if he were about to laugh, astounded. All that emerged was a dry sound, like a laugh of disbelief but without the humor. It wasn't possible. One didn't joke with that kind of thing. He shook his head, confused. This wasn't a cheap book of puzzles bought at a railroad station. These books were three and a half centuries old. Their printer had lost his life over them. They had been included among the books banned by the Inquisition. And they were listed in all the serious bibliographies. "Illustration II. Caption in Latin. Old man holding two keys and a lantern, standing in front of a closed door..." But nobody had compared two of the three known copies, not until now. It wasn't easy bringing them together. Or necessary. Old man holding two keys. That was enough.

Corso got up and went to the window. He stood there awhile, looking through the panes misted by his own breath. Varo Borja was right after all. Aristide Torchia must have been laughing to himself on his pyre at Campo dei Fiori, before the flames took away his sense of humor forever. As a posthumous joke it was brilliant.

VIII. *POSTUMA NECAT*

"Is anybody there?"
"No."
"Too bad. He must be dead."
——M. Leblanc, ARSÈNE LUPIN

Lucas Corso knew better than anyone that one of the main problems of his profession was that bibliographies were compiled by scholars who never actually saw the books cited; scholars relied instead on secondhand accounts and information recorded by others. An error or incomplete description could circulate for generations without being noticed. Then by chance it came to light. This was the case with *The Nine Doors.* Apart from its obligatory mention in the canonical bibliographies, even the most precise references had included only summary descriptions of the nine engravings, without minor details. In the case of the book's second illustration, all the known texts referred to an old man who looked like a sage or a hermit, standing before a door and holding two keys. But nobody had ever bothered to specify in which hand he held the keys. Now Corso had the answer: in the engraving in book number one, the left, and in book number two, the right.

He still had to find out what number three was like. But this wasn't possible yet. Corso stayed at the Quinta da Soledade until dark. He worked solidly in the light of the candelabra, taking copious notes, checking both books over and over again. He examined each engraving until he had confirmed his theory More proof emerged. At last he sat looking at his booty in the form of notes on a sheet of paper, tables and diagrams with strange links between them. Five of the engravings were not identical in both books. In addition to the old man holding the key in different hands in engraving II, the labyrinth in IIII had an exit in one of the books but not in the other. In illustration V of book one, Death brandished an hourglass with the sand in the lower half, while in book two the sand was in the upper half. As for the chessboard in number VII, in Varo Borja's copy the squares were all white while in Fargas's copy they were black. And in engraving VIII, the executioner poised to behead the young woman in one of the books became an avenging angel in the other through the addition of a halo.

There were more differences. Close examination through the magnifying glass yielded unexpected results. The printer's marks hidden in the woodcuts contained another subtle clue. A.T., Aristide Torchia, was named as the sculptor in the engraving of the old man, but as the inventor only in the same engraving in book number two, while, as the Ceniza brothers had pointed out, the signature in book number one was L.F. The same difference occurred in four more illustrations. This could mean that all the woodcuts were carved by the printer himself but that the original drawings for his engravings were created by somebody else. So it wasn't a matter of a forgery dating from the same era as the books or of apocryphal reprintings. It was the printer, Torchia himself, "by authority and permission of the superiors," who had altered his own work in accordance with a preestablished plan. He had signed the engravings he changed to make sure it was clear that L.F. had created the others. Only one copy remains, he told his executioners. Whereas in fact he had left three copies, and a key that might possibly turn them into a single one. The rest of his secret he took with him to the grave.

Corso resorted to an ancient collating system: the comparative tables used by Umberto Eco in his study of the Hanau. Having set out in order on paper the illustrations that contained differences, he obtained the following table:

	I	II	III	IIII	V	VI	VII	VIII	VIIII
One		left hand		no exit	sand down		white board	no halo	
Two		right hand		exit	sand up		black board	halo	

As for the engraver's marks, the variations in the signatures A.T. (the printer, Torchia) and L.F. (unknown? Lucifer?) that corresponded to *sculptor* or *inventor* were set out as follows:

	I	II	III	IIII	V	VI	VII	VIII	VIIII
One	AT(s) AT(i)	AT(s) LF(i)	AT(s) AT(i)	AT(s) AT(i)	AT(s) LF(i)	AT(s) AT(i)	AT(s) AT(i)	AT(s) AT(i)	AT(s) AT(i)
Two	AT(s) AT(i)	AT(s) AT(i)	AT(s) AT(i)	AT(s) LF(i)	AT(s) AT(i)	AT(s) AT(i)	AT(s) LF(i)	AT(s) LF(i)	AT(s) AT(i)

A strange code. But Corso at last had something definite. He now knew that there was a key of some sort. He stood up slowly, as if afraid that all the links would vanish before his eyes. But he was calm, like a hunter who is sure that he will catch his prey at the end, however confusing the trail.

Hand. Exit. Sand. Board. Halo.

He glanced out the window. Beyond the dirty panes, silhouetting a branch, a remnant of reddish light refused to disappear into the night.

Books one and two. Differences in illustrations 2, 4, 5, 7, and 8.

He had to go to Paris. Book number three was there, together with the possible solution to the mystery. But he was now preoccupied with another matter, something he had to deal with urgently. Varo Borja had been categorical. Now that Corso was sure he wouldn't be able to obtain book number two by conventional methods, he had to devise a plan to acquire it by means that were not conventional. With the minimum risk to Fargas, and to Corso himself, of course. Something gentle and discreet. He took out his diary from his coat pocket and searched for the phone number he needed. It was the perfect job for Amilcar Pinto.

One of the candles had burned down and went out with a small spiral of smoke. Corso could hear the violin being played somewhere in the house. He laughed dryly again, and the flames of the candelabra made shadows dance on his face as he leaned over to light a cigarette. He straightened and listened. The music was a lament that floated through the dark empty rooms with their remnants of dusty, worm-eaten furniture, painted ceilings, stained walls covered with spiderwebs and shadows; with their echoes of footsteps and voices extinguished long ago. And outside, above the rusty railings, the two statues, one with its eyes open in the darkness, the other covered by a mask of ivy, listened motionless, as time stood still, to the music that Victor Fargas played on his violin to summon the ghosts of his lost books.

CORSO RETURNED TO THE village on foot, his hands in his coat pockets and his collar turned up. It took him twenty minutes on the deserted road. There was no moon, and he walked into large patches of darkness beneath the black canopy of trees. The almost total silence was broken only by the sound of his shoes crunching on the gravel at the side of the road, and by the channels of water coursing down the hill between rockrose and ivy, invisible in the darkness.

A car came from behind and overtook him. Corso saw his own shadow, saw its enlarged, ghostly outline glide undulating across the nearby tree trunks and farther dense woods. Only when he was again enveloped in shadow did he breathe out and feel his tense muscles relax. He wasn't one who expected ghosts around every corner. Instead he viewed things, however extraordinary they were, with the southern fatalism of an old soldier, a fatalism no doubt inherited from his great-great-grandfather Corso. However much you spurred your horse in the opposite direction, the inevitable was always lurking at the gate of the nearest Samarkand, picking its nails with a Venetian dagger or Scottish bayonet. Even so, since the incident in the street in Toledo, Corso felt understandably apprehensive every time he heard a car behind him.

Maybe because of this, when the lights of another car pulled up beside him, Corso turned sharply and moved his canvas bag to his other shoulder. He found his bunch of keys inside his coat pocket. It was not much of a weapon, but with it he could poke out the eye of an attacker. But there seemed no reason to worry. He saw a large, dark shape, like that of an old berlin carriage, and inside, lit by the faint glow from the dashboard, the profile of a man. His voice was friendly, well educated.

"Good evening..." The accent was indefinable, neither Portuguese nor Spanish. "Do you have a match?"

The request might be genuine, or just a pretext, Corso couldn't be sure. But, asked for a light, he didn't need to run or brandish his sharpest key. He let go of the keys, took out his matches, and lit one, shielding the flame with his hand.

"Thanks."

There was the scar, of course. It was an old one, long and vertical, from the temple to halfway down the left cheek. Corso got a close look as the man leaned forward to light his Montecristo cigar. Corso held the light long enough to glimpse the thick, black mustache and dark eyes watching him intently from the gloom. Then the match went out, and it was as if a black mask covered the stranger's face. The man became a shadow again, his outline barely distinguishable in the faint light from the dashboard.

"Who in the hell are you?"

Not a particularly brilliant question. In any case, it came too late. The question was drowned out by the sound of the engine accelerating. The twin red points of the car's taillights were already receding into the distance, leaving a fleeting trail against the dark ribbon of road. The red shone more intensely for an instant as the car turned a corner, then disappeared as if it had never been.

The book hunter stood motionless by the side of the road, trying to piece the picture together. Madrid, outside Liana Taillefer's house. Toledo, his visit to Varo Borja. And Sintra, after an afternoon at Victor Fargas's house. There were also Dumas's serials, a publisher hanged in his study, a printer burned at the stake with his strange manual ... And among all this, shadowing Corso: Rochefort, a fictional, seventeenth-century swordsman reincarnated as a uniformed chauffeur of luxury cars. Responsible for an attempted hit-and-run incident, and breaking and entering. A smoker of Montecristo cigars. A smoker without a lighter.

Corso swore gently under his breath. He'd have given a rare incunabulum, in good condition, to punch the face of whoever was writing this ridiculous script.

As soon as he got back to the hotel, he made several phone calls. First he dialed the Lisbon number in his notebook. He was lucky, Amilcar Pinto was at home. He ascertained as much in a conversation with Pinto's bad-tempered wife. Through the black Bakelite earpiece he could hear the sound of a television blaring in the background, the high-pitched crying of children, and adult voices arguing violently. Finally Pinto came to the phone. They agreed to meet in an hour and a half, the time it would take the Portuguese to travel the fifty kilometers to Sintra. Having arranged this, Corso looked at his watch and called Varo Borja. The book collector wasn't home. Corso left a message on the answering machine and dialed Flavio La Ponte's number in Madrid. La Ponte wasn't home either, so Corso hid his canvas bag on top of the wardrobe and went out for a drink.

The first thing he saw as he pushed open the door of the small hotel lounge was the girl. It couldn't be anyone else: her cropped hair giving her a boyish look, her skin as tanned as if it were August. She sat in an armchair, reading in the cone of light from a lamp, her legs stretched out and crossed on the chair opposite. She was barefoot, in jeans and a white cotton T-shirt, her sweater around her shoulders. Corso stopped, his hand on the doorknob, an absurd feeling hammering at his brain. This was too much of a coincidence.

Incredulous, he went up to the girl. He was almost by her side when she looked up from her book and fixed her green eyes on him with their deep, liquid clarity that he remembered so well from the train. He stopped, not knowing what to say. He had the strange sensation that he was going to fall into those eyes.

"You didn't tell me you were coming to Sintra," he said.

"Nor did you."

She smiled calmly as she said it, looking neither surprised nor embarrassed. She seemed sincerely pleased to see him.

"What are you doing here?" asked Corso.

She removed her feet from the chair and gestured for him to have a seat. But the book hunter remained standing.

"Traveling," said the girl, and she showed him her book. It wasn't the same one as on the train. *Melmoth the Wanderer* by Charles Maturin. "Reading. And bumping into people unexpectedly."

"Unexpectedly," repeated Corso like an echo.

He'd bumped into too many people for one evening, whether

unexpectedly or not. He found himself trying to establish a link between her presence at the hotel and Rochefort's appearance on the road. From the right angle, all these things would fit together, but he could not find that angle. He didn't even know where to start.

"Won't you sit down?"

He did so, vaguely anxious. The girl shut her book and regarded him curiously. "You don't look like a tourist," she said.

"I'm not."

"Are you working?"

"Yes."

"Any job in Sintra must be interesting."

That's all I need, thought Corso, adjusting his glasses. Being interrogated after everything I've been through, even if it's by an extremely young, beautiful girl. Maybe that was the problem. She was too young to be dangerous. Or maybe that was where the danger lay. He picked up the girl's book from the table and flicked through it. It was a modern English edition, some of the paragraphs underlined in pencil. He read one:

His eyes remained fixed in the diminishing light and growing darkness. That preternatural blackness that seems to be saying to God's most luminous and sublime creation: "Give me space. Stop shining."

"You like Gothic novels?"

"I like to read." She bowed her head slightly, and the light made a foreshortened outline of her bare neck. "And to hold books. I always carry several in my rucksack when I travel."

"Do you travel a lot?"

"Yes. I've been traveling for ages."

Corso winced at her answer. She said it very seriously, frowning slightly, like a child talking about serious matters.

"I thought you were a student."

"I am sometimes."

Corso put the *Melmoth* back on the table.

"You're a strange young lady. How old are you? Eighteen? Nineteen? Sometimes your expression changes, as if you were older."

"Maybe I am. One's expressions are influenced by what one has experienced and read. Look at you."

"What's the matter with me?"

"Have you ever seen yourself smile? You look like an old soldier."

He shifted slightly in his seat, embarrassed. "I don't know how an old soldier smiles."

"Well, I do." The girl's eyes darkened. She was searching in her memory. "Once I knew ten thousand men who were looking for the sea."

Corso lifted an eyebrow in mock-interest. "Really. Is that something you read or experienced?"

"Guess." She stopped and looked at him intently before adding, "You seem like a clever man, Mr. Corso."

She stood up, taking the book from the table and her white sneakers off the floor. Her eyes brightened, and Corso recognized the reflections in them. He saw something familiar in her gaze.

"Maybe we'll see each other around," she said as she left.

Corso had no doubt that they would. He wasn't sure whether he wanted to or not. Either way, the thought lasted only a moment. As she left, the girl passed Amilcar Pinto at the door.

He was a short, greasy little man. His skin was dark and shiny, as if it had just been varnished, and his thick, wiry mustache was roughly trimmed. He would have been an honest policeman, even a good policeman, if he didn't have to feed five children, a wife, and a retired father who secretly stole his cigarettes. His wife was a mulatto and twenty years ago had been very beautiful. Pinto brought her back from Mozambique at the time of independence, when Maputo was called Lourenço Marques and he himself was a decorated sergeant in the paratroops, a slight, brave man. During the course of some of the deals Pinto and Corso did from time to time, Corso had seen Pinto's wife—eyes ringed with fatigue, large, flaccid breasts, in old slippers, and her hair tied with a red scarf—in the hallway to their house that smelled of dirty kids and boiled vegetables.

The policeman came straight into the lounge, looking at the girl out of the corner of his eye as he passed her, and sank into the armchair opposite Corso. He was out of breath, as if he'd just walked all the way from Lisbon.

"Who's the girl?"

"Nobody important," answered Corso. "She's Spanish. A tourist."

Pinto nodded. He wiped his sweaty palms on his trouser legs. It was something he often did. He sweated abundantly, and his shirt collars always had a dark ring where they touched his skin.

"I have a bit of a problem," said Corso.

Pinto's grin widened. No problem is insoluble, his expression said. Not as long as you and I still get along. "I'm sure we'll figure something out," he answered.

It was Corso's turn to smile. He'd met Amilcar Pinto four years ago. Some stolen books had appeared on stands at the Ladra Book Fair—a bad business. Corso came to Lisbon to identify them, Pinto made a couple of arrests, and en route back to their owner a few very valuable books disappeared forever. To celebrate the beginning of a fruitful friendship, Corso and Pinto got drunk together in the *fados* bars of the Barrio Alto. The former paratroop sergeant reminisced about his time in the colonies, told how he'd nearly had his balls blown off at the battle of Gorongosa. The two men ended up singing "Grandola Vila Morena" at the top of their voices on Santa Luzia. Illuminated by the moon, the district of Alfama lay at their feet with the Tagus beyond it, wide and gleaming like a sheet of silver. The dark shapes of boats, moving very slowly, headed out toward the Belem tower and the Atlantic.

A waiter brought Pinto the coffee he had ordered. Corso said nothing until the waiter left.

"It's about a book."

The policeman bent over the little low table and put sugar in his coffee.

"It's always about a book," he said gravely.

"This one's special."

"Which one isn't?"

Corso smiled a sharp, metallic smile. "The owner doesn't want to sell."

"That's bad." Pinto drank some coffee, savoring it. "Commerce is a good thing. Goods moving, coming and going. It generates wealth, makes money for the middlemen..." He put the cup down and wiped his hands on his trousers. "Products have to circulate. It's the law of the market, of life. Not selling should be banned: it's almost a crime."

"I agree," said Corso. "We should do something about it."

Pinto leaned back in his chair. Calm and confident, he looked at Corso expectantly. Once, after an ambush in the *mato* in Mozambique, he had fled, carrying a dying officer ten kilometers through the jungle. At dawn he felt the lieutenant die, but didn't want to leave him behind. So he went on, the corpse over his shoulders, until he reached the base. The lieutenant was very young, and Pinto thought that the man's mother would like to have him buried back in Portugal. They gave him a medal for it. Now Pinto's children played about the house with his old tarnished medals.

"Maybe you know the man: Victor Fargas."

The policeman nodded. "The Fargases are a very old, very respectable family," he said. "In the past they had a lot of influence, but no more."

Corso handed him a sealed envelope. "This is all the information you need: owner, book, and location."

"I know the house." Pinto licked his upper lip, wetting his

mustache. "Very unwise, keeping valuable books there. Any unscrupulous individual might get in." He looked at Corso as if saddened by the irresponsibility of Victor Fargas. "I can think of one, a petty thief from Chiado who owes me a favor."

Corso shook some invisible dust from his clothes. It had nothing to do with him. Not in the operational stage, anyway.

"I don't want to be in the area when it happens."

"Don't worry. You'll get your book and Mr. Fargas will be disturbed as little as possible. A broken windowpane at the most. It'll be a clean job. About payment..."

Corso pointed at the unopened envelope that Pinto was holding. "That's an advance, a quarter of the total. The rest on delivery."

"Fine. When are you leaving?"

"First thing tomorrow morning. I'll get in touch with you from Paris." Pinto was about to get up, but Corso stopped him. "There's something else. I need an identification. Tall man, about six feet, with a mustache and a scar on his face. Black hair, dark eyes. Slim. He's not Spanish or Portuguese. He's been lurking around here tonight."

"Is he dangerous?"

"I don't know. He followed me from Madrid."

Pinto was taking notes on the back of the envelope. "Does this have anything to do with our business?"

"I'm assuming it does. But I don't have any more information."

"I'll do what I can. I have friends at the police station here in Sintra. And I'll take a look at the files at central headquarters in Lisbon."

He stood up and put the envelope in the inside pocket of his jacket. Corso caught a glimpse of a holstered revolver under his left arm.

"Why don't you stay for a drink?"

Pinto sighed and shook his head. "I'd like to, but three of

the kids have the measles. They catch it off each other, the little swine." He said this with a tired smile. All the heroes in Corso's world were tired.

They went to the hotel entrance where Pinto had parked his old Citroën 2CV. As they shook hands, Corso mentioned Fargas again.

"Make sure that Fargas is disturbed as little as possible. This is just a burglary."

Pinto turned on the engine and the lights. He looked at Corso reproachfully through the open window. He seemed offended. "Please. You don't need to tell me again. I know what I'm doing."

AFTER PINTO LEFT, CORSO went up to his room to sort out his notes. He worked late into the night, his bed covered with papers and *The Nine Doors* open on his pillow. He felt extremely tired and thought a hot shower might help him relax. He was on his way to the bathroom when the phone rang. It was Varo Borja, wanting to know how he had got on with Fargas. Corso gave him a general idea of how things were going, including the discrepancies he had found in five of the nine engravings.

"By the way," he added, "our friend Fargas won't sell."

There was silence at the other end of the line. Borja seemed to be thinking, although there was no way of telling whether it was about the engravings or Fargas's refusal to sell. When he spoke again, his tone was extremely cautious.

"That seemed likely," he said, and Corso still wasn't sure which thing he was referring to. "Is there any way of getting around the problem?"

"There might be."

Borja was silent again. Corso counted five seconds by his watch.

"I'll leave it in your hands."

They didn't say much else after that. Corso didn't mention his conversation with Pinto, and Borja didn't inquire into how Corso was going to solve the "problem," as he had euphemistically put it. He only asked if Corso needed more money, and Corso said no. They agreed to talk again when Corso reached Paris.

Corso then dialed La Ponte's number, but there was no answer. The blue pages of the Dumas manuscript were still in their folder. He gathered his notes and the black leather-bound book with the pentacle on the cover. He put them back in his canvas bag and slipped it under the bed, tying the strap to one of the legs. That way, if anybody got into the room and tried to take it, he'd have to wake Corso however soundly he was sleeping. Rather an awkward piece of luggage to carry around, he thought as he went to the bathroom to turn on the shower. And, for some reason, dangerous too.

He brushed his teeth. Then he undressed and dropped his clothes on the floor. The mirror was almost completely steamed over, but he could see his reflection, thin and hard like an emaciated wolf. Once again he felt a burst of anxiety from the distant past, swamping his mind in a painful wave. Like a string vibrating in his flesh and his memory. Nikon. He remembered her every time he undid his belt. She'd always insisted on undoing it for him, as if it was a ritual. He shut his eyes and saw her sitting on the edge of the bed in front of him, slipping his trousers and then his underpants down very slowly, savoring the moment with a conspiratorial, tender smile. Relax, Lucas Corso. Once she'd taken a photo of him secretly, while he was sleeping. He was facedown with a vertical crease on his brow and his cheek darkened by stubble. It made his face look thinner and emphasized the tense, bitter lines at the corners of his half-open mouth. He looked like an exhausted wolf, suspicious and tormented in the deserted snow plain of the pillow. He didn't like the photograph. He'd found it by chance, in the fixing tray in the bathroom that Nikon used as a darkroom. He'd torn it and the negative into little pieces. She'd never mentioned it.

When he stepped into the shower, the hot water scalded him. He let it run over his face, burning his eyelids. He put up with the pain, his jaw clenched and his muscles taut, suppressing the urge to howl with loneliness in the suffocating steam. For four years, one month, and twelve days, Nikon always got into the shower with him after they made love and soaped his back slowly, interminably. And often she put her arms around him, like a little girl in the rain. One day I'll leave without ever really knowing you. You'll remember my big, dark eyes. The reproachful silences. The moans of anxiety as I slept. The nightmares you couldn't save me from. You'll remember all this when I'm gone.

He rested his head against the dripping white tiles, in a steaming desert that seemed a kind of hell. Nobody had ever soaped his back before or since Nikon. Nobody. Ever.

After his shower he got into bed with the *Memoirs of Saint Helena* but managed to read only a couple of lines:

Returning to the subject of war, the Emperor continued: "The Spaniards en masse acted as a man of honor."

He frowned at Napoleon's praise, two centuries old. He remembered words he'd heard as a child, perhaps from one of his grandparents, or his father. "There's one thing we Spaniards do better than anyone else: appear in Goya's pictures." Men of honor, Bonaparte had said. Corso thought of Borja and his checkbook. Of La Ponte and widows' libraries plundered for a pittance. Of Nikon's ghost wandering in a lonely, white desert. Of himself, a hunter who worked for the highest bidder. These were different times.

He was still smiling, desperate and bitter, when he fell asleep.

WHEN HE WOKE, THE first thing he saw was the gray light of dawn through the window. Too early. Confused, he tried to find his watch on the bedside table when he realized that the phone was ringing. He dropped the receiver twice before managing to lodge it between his ear and the pillow.

"Hello?"

"This is your friend from last night. Remember? Irene Adler. I'm in the lobby. We have to talk. Now."

"What the hell . . ."

But she'd hung up. Cursing, Corso searched for his glasses. He threw back the sheets and pulled on his trousers, groggy and disconcerted. With sudden panic, he looked under the bed. The bag was still there, intact. He made an effort to focus on the things around him. Everything in the room was in order. It was outside that things were happening. He just had time to go to the bathroom and splash water on his face before she knocked at the door.

"Do you know what time it is?"

The girl was standing there in her blue duffel coat and with her rucksack on her back. Her eyes were even greener than Corso remembered.

"It's half past six in the morning," she said quietly. "And you have to get dressed right now."

"Have you gone crazy?"

"No." She came into the room without being asked and looked around critically. "We don't have much time."

"We?"

"You and I. Things have got rather complicated."

Corso snorted, angry. "It's too early for jokes."

"Don't be stupid." She wrinkled her nose with a grave expression. Despite her youth and boyishness, she looked different, older, and more self-assured. "I'm serious."

She put her rucksack on the unmade bed. Corso gave it back to her and showed her the door.

"Go to hell," he said.

She didn't move, just looked at him intently. "Listen." Her light eyes were very near, like liquid ice, so luminous against her tanned skin. "Do you know who Victor Fargas is?"

Corso caught sight of his own face in the mirror above the chest of drawers, beyond the girl's shoulder. He was open-mouthed, like an idiot.

"Of course I do."

It had taken him several seconds to answer, and he was still blinking, confused. She waited, not entirely satisfied with his response to her words. It was obvious that her mind was on other things.

"He's dead," she said.

She said it neutrally, as if she'd just told him that Fargas had coffee for breakfast or went to the dentist. Corso took a deep breath, trying to take in what she'd just said. "That's not possible. I was with him last night. He was fine."

"Well, he's not now. He's not fine at all."

"How do you know?"

"I just do."

Corso shook his head, suspicious, and went to get a cigarette. En route he saw the flask of Bols, so he took a swig. The gin hitting his empty stomach made him shudder. He waited, forcing himself not to look at the girl until he'd inhaled his first puff of smoke. He wasn't at all happy with the part he was being forced to play this morning. He needed time to think.

"The café in Madrid, the train, last night, and now this morning here in Sintra..." He counted on the fingers of his left hand, his cigarette in his mouth, his eyes half closed because of the smoke. "That's a lot of coincidences, don't you think?"

She shook her head impatiently. "I thought you were smarter than that. Who said anything about coincidences?"

"Why are you following me?"

"I like you."

Corso didn't feel like laughing. He twisted his mouth. "That's ridiculous."

She looked at him for a time, thoughtfully.

"I suppose it is," she said at last. "You don't exactly look breathtaking, always in that old coat and those glasses."

"What is it, then?"

"Find another answer. Anything would do. But now get dressed, will you? We have to go to Fargas's house."

"We?"

"You and I. Before the police get there."

THE DEAD LEAVES CRACKLED beneath their feet as they pushed the iron gate and walked up the path lined with broken statues and empty pedestals. The gray morning light cast no shadows, and above the stone staircase the sundial still showed no time. POSTUMA NECAT. The last one kills, Corso read again. The girl had followed his gaze.

"Absolutely true," she said coldly and pushed the door. It was locked.

"Let's try the back," suggested Corso.

They went around the house, past the tiled fountain with the chubby stone angel, eyes empty and hands cut off, water still trickling from its mouth into the pond. Surprisingly composed, the girl—Irene Adler or whatever her name was—went ahead of Corso in her blue duffel coat, the rucksack on her back. She walked, her long supple legs in jeans, her stubborn head tilted forward with the determined air of someone who knows exactly where she is going. Unlike Corso. He had overcome his doubt and let the girl lead him. He was leaving the questions for later. Clearheaded after a quick shower, carrying in his canvas bag all that was important to him, he could think of nothing now but Victor Fargas's *Nine Doors*, book number two.

They got in without difficulty through the French window that led from the garden into the drawing room. On the ceiling, dagger aloft, Abraham was still watching over the books lined up on the floor. The house seemed deserted.

"Where's Fargas?" asked Corso.

The girl shrugged. "I have no idea."

"You said he was dead."

"He is." After glancing at her surroundings, at the bare walls and the books, she picked up the violin from the sideboard and looked at it curiously. "What I don't know is where he is."

"You're lying."

She placed the violin under her chin and plucked at the strings before putting it back in its case, unhappy with the sound. Then she looked at Corso.

"Oh ye of little faith."

She was smiling again, absently. To Corso her composure, incongruously mature, seemed both deep and frivolous. This young lady behaved according to a strange code of conduct, motivated by things that were more complex than her age and appearance let one suppose.

Suddenly, these thoughts—the girl, the strange events, even the supposed corpse of Victor Fargas—all left Corso's mind. On the threadbare rug that depicted the battle of Arbelas, between books on satanic arts and the occult, there was a gap. *The Nine Doors* was no longer there.

"Shit," he said.

He muttered it again as he knelt beside the row of books. His expert glance, accustomed to finding a book instantly, went back and forth without success. Black morocco, five raised bands, no title on the exterior, a pentacle on the cover. *Umbrarum regni*, etc. He wasn't mistaken. A third of the mystery, exactly thirty-three point endless threes percent, had vanished.

"Shit."

It couldn't have been Pinto, he wouldn't have had time to

organize anything. The girl was watching him as if waiting for him to do something interesting. Corso stood up.

"Who are you?"

It was the second time in less than twelve hours that he'd asked the question, but to two different people. Things were getting complicated far too quickly. For her part, the girl held his gaze, not reacting to the question. After a time she looked away into empty space. Or possibly at the books lined up on the floor.

"It doesn't matter," she answered. "You'd be better off wondering where the book has gone."

"What book?"

She looked at him again but said nothing. He felt incredibly stupid.

"You know too much," he told the girl. "Even more than I do."

Again she shrugged. She was looking at Corso's watch.

"You don't have much time."

"I don't give a damn how much time I have."

"That's up to you. But there's a flight from Lisbon to Paris in five hours, from Portela Airport. We can just make it."

God. Corso shivered under his coat, horrified. She sounded like an efficient secretary, schedule book in hand, listing her boss's appointments for the day. He opened his mouth to complain. And so young with those disturbing eyes. Damned little witch.

"Why should I leave now?"

"Because the police might arrive."

"I don't have anything to hide."

The girl smiled indefinably, as if she had just heard a funny but very old joke. Then she put her rucksack on her back and waved good-bye.

"I'll bring you cigarettes in prison. Though they don't sell your brand here in Portugal."

She went out into the garden without a backward glance at the room. Corso was about to go after her and stop her. Then he saw something in the fireplace.

After a moment of disbelief, he went over to it. Very slowly, so that things might return to normal. But when he reached the fireplace and leaned on the mantelpiece, he saw that the damage was irreversible. In the brief interval between last night and this morning, a minute period of time compared to their centuries-old contents, the antiquarian bibliographies had gone out of date. There now remained not three known copies of *The Nine Doors*, but only two. The third, or what was left of it, was still smoldering among the embers.

He knelt, taking care not to touch anything. The binding, no doubt because of the leather covering, was less damaged than the pages inside. Two of the five raised bands on the spine were intact, and the pentacle was only half burned. But the pages had been almost entirely consumed by the flames. There were only a few charred edges, with fragments of print. Corso held his hand over the still-warm remains.

He took out a cigarette and put it in his mouth, but didn't light it. He remembered how the logs had been piled up in the fireplace the night before. Judging by the ashes—the burned logs lay underneath the ashes of the book, nobody had raked over the embers—the fire had gone out with the book on top. He remembered seeing enough logs piled there to last about four or five hours. And the warm ashes indicated that the fire had gone out about the same number of hours ago. This made a total of eight to ten hours. Somebody must have lit the fire between ten o'clock and midnight, and then put the book in. And whoever had done so hadn't hung around afterward to rake over the embers.

Corso wrapped in old newspaper what remains he could save from the fireplace. The page fragments were stiff and brittle, so it took him some time. As he did this, he noticed that the pages and cover had burned separately. Whoever had thrown them into the fire had torn them apart so that they would burn more efficiently.

Once he retrieved all the pieces, he paused to glance around the room. The Virgil and the Agricola were where Fargas had put them. The *De re metalica* lined up with the others on the rug—and the Virgil on the table, just as Fargas had left it when, with the tone of a priest performing a ritual sacrifice, he had uttered the words "I think I'll sell this one. . . ." There was a sheet of paper between its pages. Corso opened the book. It was a handwritten receipt, unfinished.

> *Victor Coutinho Fargas, Identity Card No. 3554712, address: Quinta da Soledade, Carretera de Colares, km. 4, Sintra. Received with thanks the sum of 800,000 escudos for the work in my possession, "Virgil. Opera nunc recens accuratissime castigata . . . Venezia, Giunta, 1544." (Essling 61. Sander 7671.) Folio, 10.587, 1c, 113 woodcuts. Complete and in good condition. The buyer . . .*

There was no name or signature. The receipt had never been completed. Corso put the paper back and shut the book. Then he went to the room where he'd spent the previous afternoon, to make sure he'd left no trace, no papers with his handwriting, or anything like that. He also removed his cigarette butts from the ashtray and put them in his pocket, wrapped in another piece of newspaper. He looked around for a little while longer. His steps echoed through the empty house. No sign of the owner.

As he again passed the books on the floor, he stopped, tempted. It would have been so easy—a couple of conveniently small Elzevirs attracted his attention. But Corso was a sensible man. It would only complicate matters if things got nasty. So, with a sigh, he bade farewell to the Fargas collection.

He went out through the French window into the garden to look for the girl, dragging his feet through the leaves. He found her sitting on a short flight of steps that led to the pond. He could hear the water trickling from the chubby angel's mouth onto the greenish surface covered with floating plants. She was staring, engrossed, at the pond. Only the sound of his steps interrupted her contemplation and made her turn her head.

Corso put his canvas bag on the bottom step and sat down next to her. He lit the cigarette he'd had in his mouth for some time. He inhaled, his head to one side, and threw away the match. He turned to the girl.

"Now tell me everything."

Still staring at the pond, she gently shook her head. Not abruptly or unpleasantly. On the contrary, the movement of her head, her chin, and the corners of her mouth was sweet and thoughtful, as if Corso's presence, the sad, neglected garden, and the sound of the water were all peculiarly moving. She looked incredibly young. Almost defenseless. And very tired.

"We have to go," she said so low that Corso scarcely heard her. "To Paris."

"First tell me what your link is with Fargas. With all of this."

She shook her head again, in silence. Corso blew out some smoke. The air was so damp that the smoke floated in front of him for a moment before gradually disappearing. He looked at the girl.

"Do you know Rochefort?"

"Rochefort?"

"Whatever his name is. He's dark, with a scar. He was lurking around here last night." As he spoke, Corso was aware of how silly it all was. He ended with an incredulous grimace, doubting his own memories. "I even spoke to him."

The girl again shook her head, still staring at the pond.

"I don't know him."

"What are you doing here, then?"

"I'm looking after you."

Corso stared at the tips of his shoes, rubbing his numb hands. The tinkle of the water in the pond was beginning to get on his nerves. He took a last drag on his cigarette. It was about to burn his lips and tasted bitter.

"You're mad, girl."

He threw away the butt, stared at the smoke fading before his eyes.

"Completely mad," he added.

She still said nothing. After a moment, Corso brought out his flask of gin and took a long swig, without offering her any. He looked at her again.

"Where's Fargas?"

She took a moment to answer, still absorbed, lost. At last she indicated with her chin. "Over there."

Corso followed the direction of her gaze. In the pond, beneath the thread of water from the mouth of the mutilated angel with empty eyes, he saw the vague outline of a man floating facedown among the water lilies and dead leaves.

IX. THE BOOKSELLER ON
THE RUE BONAPARTE

*"My friend," Athos said gravely, "remember that the
dead are the only ones whom one does not risk
meeting again on this earth."*
—A. Dumas, THE THREE MUSKETEERS

Lucas Corso ordered a second
gin and settled back comfortably in the wicker chair. It was
pleasant in the sun. He was sitting on the terrace of the Café
Atlas on the Rue de Buci, in a rectangle of light that framed
the tables. It was one of those cold, luminous mornings when
the left bank of the Seine crawls with people: disoriented
Japanese, Anglo-Saxons in sneakers with metro tickets marking
their place in a Hemingway novel, ladies with baskets full of
lettuces and baguettes, and slender gallery owners who've had
their noses fixed, all heading for a café during their lunch
break. An attractive young woman was looking in the window
of a luxury charcuterie, on the arm of a middle-aged, well-
dressed man who might have been an antique dealer or a scoun-
drel, or both. There was also a Harley Davidson with all its
shiny chrome, a bad-tempered fox terrier tied up at the door
of an expensive wine shop, a young man with braids playing
the flute outside a boutique. And at the table next to Corso's,
a couple of very elegant Africans kissing on the mouth in a
leisurely way, as if they had all the time in the world and as

if the arms race, AIDS, and the hole in the ozone layer were all insignificant on that sunny Parisian morning.

He saw her at the end of the Rue Mazarin, turning the corner toward the café where he waited. With her boyish looks, her duffel coat open over her jeans, her eyes like two points of light against her suntan, visible from a distance in the crowd, in the street overflowing with dazzling sunlight. Devilishly pretty, La Ponte would no doubt have said, clearing his throat and turning his best side—where his beard was a little thicker and curlier—to her. But Corso wasn't La Ponte, so he didn't say or think anything. He just gave a hostile glance at the waiter, who was putting a glass of gin on his table—"*Pas d'Bols, m'sieu*"—and handed him the exact amount on the bill—"*Service compris*, young man"—before looking back at the approaching girl. As far as love went, Nikon had left him a hole in the stomach the size of a clipful of bullets. That was enough love. Nor was Corso sure whether he had, now or ever, a good profile. And he was damned if he cared, anyway.

He took off his glasses and cleaned them with his handkerchief. The street was a series of vague outlines, of shapes with blurred faces. One stood out and became clearer as it drew nearer, although it never grew completely sharp: short hair, long legs, and white sneakers acquired definition as he focused on her with difficulty. She sat down in the empty chair.

"I found the shop. It's a couple of blocks away."

He put his glasses back on and looked at her without answering. They had traveled together from Lisbon, leaving Sintra for the airport posthaste, as old Dumas would have said. Twenty minutes before departure, Corso phoned Amilcar Pinto to tell him that Fargas's torment as a book collector was over and that the plan was canceled. Pinto would still be paid the sum agreed, for his trouble. Apart from being surprised—the call had woken him—Pinto reacted fairly well. All he said was, "I don't know what you're talking about, Corso, you and I didn't see each other last night in Sintra." But he promised he'd make some discreet inquiries into Fargas's death. After he heard about it officially, of course. For the time being, he knew nothing and didn't want to, and as for the autopsy, Corso should hope that the forensic report would give the cause of death as suicide. Just in case, Pinto would pass the description of the individual with the scar on to the relevant departments as a possible suspect. He'd keep in touch by phone. He urged Corso not to come back to Portugal for a while. "Oh, and one last thing," added Pinto as the departure of the Paris flight was being announced. Next time, before he thought of involving a friend in murder, Corso should think twice. Corso hurriedly protested his innocence as the phone swallowed his last escudo. Yeah, yeah, said Pinto, that's what they all say.

The girl was waiting in the departure lounge. Corso, still dazed and in no condition to tie up loose ends (there were loose ends all over the place), was surprised to see that she had been extremely efficient and managed to get them two plane tickets without any difficulty. "I just inherited some money" was her answer when, seeing that she had paid for both, he made an ironic remark about the limited funds she supposedly had. Afterward, during the two-hour flight from Lisbon to Paris, she refused to answer any of his questions. All in good time, she repeated, looking at him out of the corner of her eye, as if sneaking a glance, before she became absorbed in the trails of condensation left by the plane in the cold air. Then she fell asleep, or pretended to, resting her head on his shoulder. Corso could tell from her breathing that she was awake. It was a convenient way of avoiding questions that she wasn't prepared, or allowed, to answer.

Anyone else in his situation would have insisted on answers, would have shaken her out of her pretense. But Corso was a well-trained, patient wolf, with the instincts and reflexes of a hunter. After all, the girl was his only real lead in this unreal, novelistic, ridiculous situation. In addition, at this point in the script he had fully assumed the role of reader-protagonist that someone, whoever was tying the knots on the back of the rug, on the underside of the plot, seemed to be offering him with a wink that could be either contemptuous or conspiratorial, he couldn't tell which.

"Somebody's setting me up," Corso said out loud, nine thousand meters above the Bay of Biscay. He looked at the girl, but she didn't move. Annoyed by her silence, he moved his shoulder away. Her head lolled for a moment. Then she sighed and made herself comfortable again, this time leaning against the window.

"Of course they are," she said at last, sleepily, scornfully, her eyes still closed. "Any idiot could see that."

"What happened to Fargas?"

"You saw yourself," she said after a moment. "He drowned."

"Who did it?"

She turned her head slowly, from side to side, then looked out of the window. She slid her hand, slender, tan, with short unpainted nails, slowly across the armrest. She stopped at the edge, as if her fingers had come up against an invisible object.

"It doesn't matter."

Corso grimaced. He looked as if he was about to laugh, but instead showed his teeth.

"It does to me. It matters a lot."

The girl shrugged. They weren't concerned about the same things, she seemed to imply. They didn't have the same priorities.

Corso persisted. "What's your part in all this?"

"I already told you. To take care of you."

She turned and looked at him as directly as she had been evasive a moment ago. She slid her hand over the armrest again, as if to bridge the distance between her and him. She was altogether too near, so Corso moved away instinctively, embarrassed, uneasy. In the pit of his stomach, in Nikon's wake, obscure, disturbing things stirred. The emptiness and pain were returning. In the girl's eyes, silent eyes and without memory, he could see the reflection of ghosts from the past, he could feel them brush his skin.

"Who sent you?"

She lowered her lashes over her luminous eyes, and it was as if she had turned a page. There was nothing there anymore. The girl wrinkled her nose, irritated.

"You're boring me, Corso."

She turned to the window and looked at the view. The great expanse of blue flecked with tiny white threads was split in the distance by a yellow and ochre line. Land ho. France. Next stop, Paris. Or next chapter. To be continued in next week's issue. Ending, sword raised, a cliffhanger typical of all romantic serials. He thought of the Quinta da Soledade, the water trickling from the fountain, Fargas's body among the water lilies and dead leaves in the pond. He flushed and shifted uncomfortably in his seat. With good reason, he felt like a man on the run. Absurd. Rather than fleeing by choice, he was being forced to.

He looked at the girl and tried to size up his situation with the necessary objectivity. Maybe he wasn't running away but toward something instead. Or maybe the mystery he was trying to escape was hidden in his own suitcase. "The Anjou Wine." *The Nine Doors.* Irene Adler. The flight attendant, with a trained, fatuous smile, said something as she passed. Corso looked at her without seeing her, absorbed in his own thoughts. If only he knew whether the end of the story was already written, or whether he himself was writing it as he went along, chapter by chapter.

He didn't say another word to the girl. When they arrived at Orly, he ignored her, although he was aware of her walking behind him along the airport concourses. At passport control, after showing his identity card, he turned around to see what kind of document she had, but all he saw was a passport bound in black leather without any markings. It must have been

European, because she went through the gate for EC citizens. Outside, while Corso was climbing into a taxi, giving his usual address, the Louvre Concorde, she slipped into the seat beside him. They drove to the hotel in silence. She got out first and let him pay the fare. The driver didn't have any change, so Corso was slightly delayed. By the time he crossed the lobby, she had already checked in and was walking behind a porter who had her rucksack. She waved at Corso before she entered the elevator. . . .

"It's a very nice shop. Replinger, Booksellers, it says. Autographs and historical documents. And it's open."

She gestured to the waiter that she didn't want to order and inclined her head toward Corso across the table, in the café on the Rue de Buci. Like a mirror her liquid eyes reflected the street, which itself was a reflection in the café window.

"We could go there now."

They had met again at breakfast, as Corso was reading the papers at one of the windows overlooking the Place du Palais Royal. She had said good morning and sat down at the table. Had devoured toast and croissants with a healthy appetite. Then looked at Corso, with a rim of milky coffee on her upper lip, like a little girl. "Where do we start?"

So now there they were, two blocks from Achille Replinger's bookshop. The girl had offered to go and find it while Corso drank his first gin of the day. He had a feeling it wouldn't be the last.

"We could go there now," she said again.

Corso still hesitated. He'd seen her tanned skin in his dreams. He was holding her hand, crossing a deserted plain at dusk. Columns of smoke rose on the horizon, volcanoes about to erupt. Occasionally they passed a soldier with a grave face, his armor covered with dust, who stared at them in silence, the man as distant and cold as the sullen Trojans of Hades. The plain was darkening on the horizon, and the columns of smoke grew thicker. The impassive, ghostly faces of the dead warriors contained a warning. Corso wanted to get away. He pulled the girl along by the hand, anxious not to leave her behind, but the air was becoming thick and hot, stifling, dark. Their flight ended in an interminable fall, an agony in slow motion. The darkness burned like an oven. The only link with the outside was his hand holding on to to hers in an effort to continue. The last thing he felt was her hand, its grip fading, finally turn to ash. And in front of him, in the darkness enveloping the burning plain and his mind, white marks, traces as fleeting as lightning, picked out the ghostly contour of a skull. It wasn't pleasant to recall. To remove the taste of ash from his mouth and erase these horrors, Corso finished his glass of gin and looked at the girl. She was watching him, a disciplined collaborator waiting quietly for instructions. Serene, she simply accepted her strange part in the story. Her loyal expression was inexplicable.

She stood up at the same time as he did. He put the canvas bag over his shoulder, and they made their way slowly toward the river. The girl, walking on the inside, occasionally stopped in front of a shopwindow, calling his attention to a picture, an engraving, a book. She looked at everything with wide eyes and intense curiosity and seemed nostalgic as she smiled thoughtfully, as if searching for traces of herself in those old things. As if, in some corner of her memory, she shared a common past with the few survivors washed up by the tide after each of history's inexorable shipwrecks.

There were two bookshops, one on either side of the street, facing each other. Achille Replinger's had a very old, elegant front of varnished wood, with a sign that said LIVRES ANCIENS, AUTOGRAPHES ET DOCUMENTS HISTORIQUES. Corso told the girl to wait outside, and she didn't object. As he went to the door, he looked in the window and saw her reflection over his shoulder. She was on the other side of the street, watching him.

A bell rang as he pushed the door open. There was an oak

table, shelves full of old books, stands with folders of prints, and a dozen old wooden filing cabinets. These had letters in alphabetical order, carefully written in brass slots. On the wall was a framed autograph with the caption "Fragment of *Tartuffe*. Molière." Also, three good prints: Victor Hugo, Flaubert, and Dumas in the center.

Achille Replinger was standing by the table. He was thickset and had a reddish complexion. Porthos with a bushy gray mustache and double chin overlapping the collar of his shirt, which was worn with a knitted tie. He was expensively but carelessly dressed. His jacket strained to contain his girth, and his flannel trousers were creased and sagging.

"Corso . . . Lucas Corso," he said, holding Boris Balkan's letter of introduction in his thick, strong fingers and frowning. "Yes, he called me the other day. Something about Dumas."

Corso put his bag on the table and took out the folder with the fifteen manuscript pages of "The Anjou Wine." The book-seller spread them out in front of him, arching his brow.

"Interesting," he said softly. "Very interesting."

He wheezed as he spoke, breathing with difficulty like an asthmatic. He took his glasses from one of his jacket pockets and put them on after a brief glance at his visitor. He bent over the pages. When he looked up, he was smiling ecstatically.

"Extraordinary," he said. "I'll buy it from you here and now."

"It's not for sale."

Replinger seemed surprised. He pursed his lips, nearly pouting. "I thought . . ."

"I just need an expert opinion. You'll be paid for your time, of course."

Achille Replinger shook his head. He didn't care about the money. Confused, he stopped to look at Corso mistrustfully a couple of times over his glasses. He bent over the manuscript again.

"A pity," he said at last. He regarded Corso with curiosity, as if wondering how on earth such a thing had fallen into his hands. "How did you get hold of it?"

"I inherited it from an old aunt. Have you ever seen it before?"

Still suspicious, Replinger looked over Corso's shoulder, through the window at the street, as if someone out there might be able to give him some information about his visitor. Or maybe he was considering how to answer Corso's question. He pulled at his mustache, as if it were false and he were making sure it was still in place, and smiled evasively.

"Here in the *quartier* you can never be sure if you've seen something before.... This has always been a good area for people who deal in books and prints. People come here to buy and sell, and everything has passed several times through the same hands." He paused to catch his breath, then looked at Corso uneasily. "I don't think so.... No, I've never seen this manuscript before," he said. He looked out at the street again, flushed. "I'd be sure if I had."

"So it's authentic?" asked Corso.

"Well ... In fact, yes." Replinger wheezed as he stroked the blue pages. He seemed to be trying to stop himself from touching them. Finally he held one up between his thumb and forefinger. "Semirounded, medium-weight handwriting, no annotations or erasures ... Almost no punctuation marks, and unexpected capital letters. This is definitely Dumas at his peak, toward the middle of his life, when he wrote *The Musketeers*." He'd become more animated as he spoke. Now he fell silent and lifted a finger. Corso could see him smiling beneath his mustache. He seemed to have reached a decision. "Wait just one moment."

He went over to one of the filing cabinets marked D and took out some buff-colored folders.

"All this is by Alexandre Dumas père. The handwriting is identical."

There were about a dozen documents, some unsigned or else initialed A. D. Some had the full signature. Most were short notes to publishers, letters to friends, or invitations.

"This is one of his American autographs," explained Replinger. "Lincoln requested one, and Dumas sent him ten dollars and a hundred autographs. They were sold in Pittsburgh for charity." He showed Corso all the documents with restrained but obvious professional pride. "Look at this one. An invitation to dine with him on Montecristo, at the house he had built in Port-Marly. Sometimes he signed only his initials, and sometimes he used pseudonyms. But not all the autographs in circulation are authentic. At the newspaper *The Musketeer*, which he owned, there was a man called Viellot who could imitate his handwriting and signature. And during the last three years of his life, Dumas's hands trembled so much he had to dictate his work."

"Why blue paper?"

"He had it sent from Lille. It was made for him specially by a printer who was a great admirer. He almost always used this color, especially for the novels. Occasionally he used pale pink for his articles, or yellow for poetry. He used several different pens, depending on the kind of thing he was writing. And he couldn't stand blue ink."

Corso pointed to the four white pages of the manuscript, with notes and corrections. "What about these?"

Replinger frowned. "Maquet. His collaborator, Auguste Maquet. They are corrections made by Dumas to the original text." He stroked his mustache. Then he bent over and read aloud in a theatrical voice: *"Horrifying! Horrifying!" murmured Athos, as Porthos shattered the bottles and Aramis gave somewhat belated orders to send for a confessor....* Replinger broke off with a sigh. He nodded, satisfied, and then showed Corso the page. "Look: all Maquet wrote was: *And he expired before d'Artagnan's terrified companions.* Dumas crossed out that line and added others above it, fleshing out the passage with more dialogue."

"What can you tell me about Maquet?"

Replinger shrugged his powerful shoulders, hesitating.

"Not a great deal." Once again he sounded evasive. "He was ten years younger than Dumas. A mutual friend, Gérard de Nerval, recommended him. Maquet wrote historical novels without success. He showed Dumas the original version of one, *Buvat the Good, or the Conspiracy of Cellamare*. Dumas turned the story into *The Chevalier d'Harmental* and had it published under his name. In return Maquet was paid twelve hundred francs."

"Can you tell from the handwriting and the style of writing when 'The Anjou Wine' was written?"

"Of course I can. It's similar to other documents from 1844, the year of *The Three Musketeers.* ... These white and blue pages fit in with his way of working. Dumas and his associate would piece the story together. From Courtilz's *D'Artagnan* they took the names of their heroes, the journey to Paris, the intrigue with Milady, and the character of the innkeeper's wife— Dumas gave Madame Bonacieux the features of his mistress, Belle Krebsamer. Constance's kidnapping came from the *Memoirs* of De la Porte, a man in the confidence of Anne of Austria. And they obtained the famous story of the diamond tags from La Rochefoucauld and from a book by Roederer, *Political and Romantic Intrigues from the Court of France.* At that time, in addition to *The Three Musketeers,* they were also writing *Queen Margot* and *The Chevalier de la Maison Rouge.*"

Replinger paused again for breath. He was becoming more and more flushed and animated as he spoke. He mentioned the last few titles in a rush, stumbling a little over the words. He was afraid of boring Corso, but at the same time he wanted to give him all the information he could.

"There's an amusing anecdote about *The Chevalier de la Maison Rouge,*" he went on when he'd caught his breath.

"When the serial was announced with its original title, *The Knight of Rougeville*, Dumas received a letter of complaint from a marquis of the same name. This made him change the title, but soon afterward he received another letter. 'My dear Sir,' wrote the marquis. 'Please give your novel whatever title you wish. I am the last of my family and will blow my brains out in an hour.' And the Marquis de Rougeville did indeed commit suicide, over some woman."

He gasped for air. Large and pink-cheeked, he smiled apologetically and leaned one of his strong hands on the table next to the blue pages. He looked like an exhausted giant, thought Corso. Porthos in the cave at Locmaria.

"Boris Balkan didn't do you justice. You're an expert on Dumas. I'm not surprised you're friends."

"We respect each other. But I'm only doing my job." Replinger looked down, embarrassed. "I'm a conscientious Frenchman who works with annotated books and documents and handwritten dedications. Always by nineteenth-century French authors. I couldn't evaluate the things that come to me if I wasn't sure who wrote them and how. Do you understand?"

"Perfectly," answered Corso. "It's the difference between a professional and a vulgar salesman."

Replinger looked at him with gratitude. "You're in the profession. It's obvious."

"Yes," Corso grimaced. "The oldest profession."

Replinger's laugh ended in another asthmatic wheeze. Corso took advantage of the pause to turn the conversation to Maquet again.

"Tell me how they did it," he said.

"Their technique was complicated." Replinger gestured at the chairs and table, as if the scene had taken place there. "Dumas drew up a plan for each novel and discussed it with his collaborator, who then did the research and made an outline of the story, or a first draft. These were the white pages. Then Dumas would rewrite it on the blue paper. He worked in his shirtsleeves, and only in the morning or at night, hardly ever in the afternoon. He didn't drink coffee or spirits while writing, only seltzer water. Also he rarely smoked. He wrote page after page under pressure from his publishers, who were always demanding more. Maquet sent him the material in bulk by post, and Dumas would complain about the delays." Replinger took a sheet from the folder and put it on the table in front of Corso. "Here's proof, in one of the notes they exchanged during the writing of *Queen Margot.* As you can see, Dumas was complaining. "All is going perfectly, despite the six or seven pages of politics we'll have to endure so as to revive interest..... If we're not going faster, dear friend, it is your fault. I've been hard at work since nine o'clock yesterday." He paused to take a breath and pointed at "The Anjou Wine." "These four pages in Maquet's handwriting with annotations by Dumas were probably received by Dumas only moments before *Le Siècle* went to press. So he had to make do with rewriting a few of them and hurriedly correcting some of the other pages on the original itself."

He put the papers back in their folders and returned them to the filing cabinet, under D. Corso had time to cast a final glance at Dumas's note demanding more pages from his collaborator. In addition to the handwriting, which was similar in every way, the paper was identical—blue with faint squaring —to that of "The Anjou Wine" manuscript. One folio was cut in two—the bottom more uneven than the others. Maybe all the pages had been part of the same ream lying on the novelist's desk.

"Who really wrote *The Three Musketeers?*"

Replinger, busy shutting the filing cabinet, took some time to answer.

"I can't give you a definitive answer. Maquet was a resourceful man, he was well versed in history, he had read a lot . . . but he didn't have the master's touch."

"They fell out with each other in the end, didn't they?"

"Yes. A pity. Did you know they traveled to Spain together at the time of Isabel II's wedding? Dumas even published a serial, *From Madrid to Cadiz*, in the form of letters. As for Maquet, he later went to court to demand that he be declared the author of eighteen of Dumas's novels, but the judges ruled that his work had been only preparatory. Today he is considered a mediocre writer who used Dumas's fame to make money. Although there are some who believe that he was exploited—the great man's ghostwriter. . . ."

"What do you think?"

Replinger glanced furtively at Dumas's portrait above the door.

"I've already told you that I'm not an expert like my friend Mr. Balkan, just a trader, a bookseller." He seemed to reflect, weighing where his professional opinion ended and his personal taste began. "But I'd like to draw your attention to something. In France between 1870 and 1894, three million books and eight million serials were sold with the name of Alexandre Dumas on the title page. Novels written before, during, and after his collaboration with Maquet. I think that has some significance."

"Fame in his lifetime, at least," said Corso.

"Definitely. For half a century he was the voice of Europe. Boats were sent over from the Americas for the sole purpose of bringing back consignments of his novels. They were read just as much in Cairo, Moscow, Istanbul, and Chandernagor as in France. . . . Dumas lived life to the full, enjoying all his pleasures and his fame. He lived and had a good time, stood on the barricades, fought in duels, was taken to court, chartered boats, paid pensions out of his own pocket, loved, ate, drank, earned ten million and squandered twenty, and died gently in his sleep, like a child." Replinger pointed at the corrections to Maquet's pages. "It could be called many things: talent, genius. . . . But whatever it was, he didn't improvise, or steal from others." He thumped his chest like Porthos. "It's something you have in here. No other writer has known such glory in his lifetime. Dumas rose from nothing to have it all. As if he'd made a pact with God."

"Yes," said Corso. "Or with the devil."

HE CROSSED THE ROAD to the other bookshop. Outside, under an awning, stacks of books were piled up on trestle tables. The girl was still there, rummaging among the books and bunches of old pictures and postcards. She was standing against the light. The sun was on her shoulders, turning the hair on the back of her head and her temples golden. She didn't stop what she was doing when he arrived.

"Which one would you choose?" she asked. She was hesitating between a sepia postcard of Tristan and Isolde embracing and another of Daumier's *The Picture Hunter*. Undecided, she held them out in front of her.

"Take both," suggested Corso. In the corner of his eye he caught sight of a man who had stopped at the stall and was about to reach for a thick bundle of cards held together by a rubber band. Corso, with the reflex of a hunter, grabbed the packet. The man left, muttering. Corso looked through the cards and chose several with a Napoleonic theme: Empress Marie Louise, the Bonaparte family, the death of the Emperor, and his final victory—a Polish lancer and two hussars on horse-back in front of the cathedral at Reims, during the French campaign of 1814, waving flags snatched from the enemy. After hesitating a moment, he added one of Marshall Ney in dress uniform and another of an elderly Wellington, posing for pos-terity. Lucky old devil.

The girl's long tanned hands moved deftly through the cards and yellowed printed paper. She chose a few more postcards: Robespierre, Saint-Just, and an elegant portrait of Richelieu in his cardinal's habit and wearing the insignia of the Order of the Holy Spirit.

"How appropriate," remarked Corso acidly.

She didn't answer. She moved on toward a pile of books, and the sun slid across her shoulders, enveloping Corso in a golden haze. Dazzled, he closed his eyes. When he opened them again, the girl was showing him a thick volume in quarto.

"What do you think?"

He glanced at it: *The Three Musketeers*, with the original illustrations by Leloir, bound in cloth and leather, in good condition. Looking at her, he saw that she had a lopsided smile and was waiting, watching him intently.

"Nice edition," was all he said. "Are you intending to read it?"

"Of course. Don't tell me the ending."

Corso laughed halfheartedly.

"As if I could tell you the ending," he said, sorting the bundles of cards.

"I HAVE A PRESENT for you," said the girl.

They were walking along the Left Bank, past the stalls of the *bouquinistes* with their prints hanging in plastic and cellophane covers and their secondhand books lined up along the parapet. A *bateau-mouche* was heading slowly upriver, straining under the weight of what Corso estimated to be five thousand Japanese and as many Sony camcorders. Across the street, behind exclusive shopwindows covered with Visa and American Express stickers, snooty antique dealers scanned the horizon for a Kuwaiti, a black marketeer, or an African minister of state to whom they might sell Eugénie Grandet's Sèvres porcelain bidet. Their sales patter delivered in the most proper accent, of course.

"I don't like presents," muttered Corso sullenly. "Some guys once accepted a wooden horse. Handcrafted by the Achaeans, it said on the label. The fools."

"Weren't there any dissenters?"

"One, with his sons. But some beasts came out of the sea

and made a lovely sculpture of them. Hellenistic, I seem to remember. Rhodes school. In those days, the gods took sides."

"They always have." The girl was staring at the muddy river as if it were carrying away her memories. Corso saw her smile thoughtfully, absently. "I never knew an impartial god. Or devil." She turned to him suddenly—her earlier thoughts seemed to have been washed downstream. "Do you believe in the devil, Corso?"

He looked at her intently, but the river had also washed away the images that filled her eyes seconds before. All he could see there now was liquid green, and light.

"I believe in stupidity and ignorance." He smiled wearily at the girl. "And I think that the best cut of all is the one you get here. See?" He pointed at his groin. "In the femoral artery. While you're in somebody's arms."

"What are you so afraid of, Corso? That I'll put my arms around you? That the sky'll fall on you?"

"I'm afraid of wooden horses, cheap gin, and pretty girls. Especially when they give me presents. And when they go by the name of the woman who defeated Sherlock Holmes."

They continued walking and were now on the wooden planks of the Pont des Arts. The girl stopped and leaned on the metal rail, by a street artist selling tiny watercolors.

"I like this bridge," she said. "No cars. Only lovers and old ladies in hats. People with nothing to do. This bridge has absolutely no common sense."

Corso said nothing. He was watching the barges, masts down, pass between the pillars that supported the iron structure. Nikon's steps had once echoed alongside his on that bridge. He remembered that she too stopped at a stall that sold watercolors. Maybe it was the same one. She wrinkled her nose, because her light meter couldn't deal with the dazzling sunshine that came slanting across the spire and towers of Notre-Dame. They bought foie gras and a bottle of Burgundy. Later they had it for dinner in their hotel room, sitting on their bed watching one of those wordy discussions on TV with huge studio audiences that the French like so much. Earlier, on the bridge, Nikon had taken a photograph of him without his knowing. She confessed this, her mouth full of bread and foie gras, her lips moistened with Burgundy, as she stroked his side with her bare foot. I know you hate it, Lucas Corso, but you'll just have to put up with it. I got you in profile on the bridge watching the barges pass underneath, you almost look handsome this time, you bastard. Nikon was Ashkenazi, with large eyes. Her father had been number 77,843 in Treblinka, saved by the bell in the last round. Whenever Israeli soldiers appeared on TV, invading places in huge tanks, she jumped off the bed, naked, and kissed the screen, her eyes wet with tears, whispering "Shalom, shalom" in a caressing tone. The same tone she used when she called Corso by his first name, until the day she stopped. Nikon. He never got to see the photograph of him leaning on the Pont des Arts, watching the barges pass under the arches. In profile, almost looking handsome, you bastard.

When he looked up, Nikon had gone. Another woman was by his side. Tall, with tanned skin, a short boyish haircut, and eyes the color of freshly washed grapes, almost colorless. For a second he blinked, confused, until everything fell back into place. The present cut cleanly, like a scalpel. Corso, in profile, in black and white (Nikon always worked in black and white), fluttered down into the river and was swept downstream with the dead leaves and the rubbish discharged by the barges and the drains. Now, the woman who wasn't Nikon was holding a small, leather-bound book. She was holding it out to him.

"I hope you like it."

The Devil in Love, by Jacques Cazotte, the 1878 edition. When he opened it, Corso recognized the prints from the first edition in a facsimile appendix: Alvaro in the magic circle before the devil, who asks, *"Che vuoi?"*; Biondetta untangling her hair with her fingers; the handsome boy sitting at the harpsichord . . . He chose a page at random:

*. . . man emerged from a handful of earth and water. Why
should a woman not be made of dew, earthly vapors, and rays
of light, of the condensed residues of a rainbow? Where does
the possible lie? And where the impossible?*

He closed the book and looked up. His eyes met the smiling
eyes of the girl. Below, in the water, the sun sparkled in the
wake of a boat, and lights moved over her skin like the reflections from the facets of a diamond.

"Residues of a rainbow," quoted Corso. "What do you know
of any of that?"

She ran her hand through her hair and turned her face to
the sun, closing her eyes against the glare. Everything about
her was light: the reflection of the river, the brightness of the
morning, the two green slits between her dark eyelashes.

"I know what I was told a long time ago. The rainbow is
the bridge between heaven and earth. It will shatter at the end
of the world, once the devil has crossed it on horseback."

"Not bad. Did your grandmother tell you that?"

She shook her head. She looked at Corso again, absorbed
and serious.

"I heard it told to a friend, Bileto." As she said the name,
she stopped a moment and frowned tenderly, like a little girl
revealing a secret. "He likes horses and wine, and he's the most
optimistic person I know. He's still hoping to get back to
heaven."

THEY CROSSED TO THE other side of the bridge.
Strangely, Corso felt that the gargoyles of Notre-Dame were
watching him from a distance. They were forgeries, of course,
like so many other things. They and their infernal grimaces,
horns, and goatee beards hadn't been there when honest master
builders had looked up, sweaty and proud, and drunk a glass
of eau-de-vie. Or when Quasimodo brooded in the bell towers

over his unrequited love for the gypsy Esmeralda. But ever since Charles Laughton, as the hideous hunchback who resembled them, and Gina Lollobrigida in the remake—Technicolor, as Nikon would have specified—were executed in their shadow, it was impossible to think of Nôtre-Dame without the sinister neomedieval sentinels. Corso imagined the bird's-eye view: the Pont Neuf, and beyond it, narrow and dark in the luminous morning, the Pont des Arts over the gray-green band of river, with two tiny figures moving imperceptibly toward the right bank. Bridges and rainbows with black Caronte barges gliding slowly beneath the pillars and vaults of stone. The world is full of banks and rivers running between them, of men and women crossing bridges and fords, unaware of the consequences, not looking back or beneath their feet, and with no loose change for the boatman.

They emerged opposite the Louvre and stopped at a traffic light before crossing. Corso shifted the strap of his canvas bag on his shoulder and glanced absently to right and left. The traffic was heavy, and he happened to notice one of the passing cars. He froze, turned to stone like a gargoyle on the cathedral.

"What's the matter?" asked the girl when the lights turned green and she saw that Corso wasn't moving. "You look like you've seen a ghost!"

He had. Not one but two. They were in the back of a taxi already moving off in the distance, engaged in animated conversation, and they hadn't noticed Corso. The woman was blond and very attractive. He recognized her immediately despite her hat and the veil covering her eyes. Liana Taillefer. Next to her, an arm around her shoulders, showing his best side and stroking his curly beard vainly, was Flavio La Ponte.

X. NUMBER THREE

They suspected that he had no heart.
—R. Sabatini, SCARAMOUCHE

Corso had a rare knack: he could make a loyal ally of a stranger instantly, in return for a tip or even a smile. As we've seen, there was something about him—his half-calculated clumsiness, his customary, friendly rabbit expression, his air of absentminded helplessness which was nothing of the sort—that won people over. This happened to some of us. And it happened to Gruber, the concierge of the Louvre Concorde, with whom Corso had had dealings for fifteen years. Gruber was dry and imperturbable, with a crew cut and a permanent poker player's expression around the mouth. During the retreat of 1944, when he was sixteen years old and a Croat volunteer in the Horst Wessel Eighteenth Panzergrenadier division, a Russian bullet hit him in the spine. It left him with an Iron Cross Second Class and three fused vertebrae for life. This was why he was so stiff and upright behind the reception desk, as if he were wearing a steel corset.

"I need a favor, Gruber."

"Yes, sir."

He almost clicked his heels as he stood to attention. The impeccable burgundy jacket with the gold keys on the lapels

gave the old exile a military air, very much to the taste of the
Central Europeans who stayed at the hotel. After the fall of
Communism and the fragmenting of the Slav hordes, they arrived in Paris to glance at the Champs-Elysées out of the corners
of their eyes and dream of a Fourth Reich.

"La Ponte, Flavio. Nationality Spanish. Also Herrero, Liana,
though she may be going by the name of Taillefer or de
Taillefer. I want to know if they're at a hotel in the city."

He wrote the names on a card and handed it to Gruber,
together with five hundred francs. Corso always gave tips or
bribes with a shrug, as if to say, "I'll do the same for you
sometime." It made it such a friendly-conspiratorial exchange,
it was difficult to tell who was doing whom a favor. Gruber,
who murmured a polite *"Merci m'sieu"* to Spaniards on package
tours, to Italians in loud ties, and to Americans with airline
bags and baseball caps for a miserable ten-franc tip, took Corso's
banknote without a word or even a nod. He just slipped it in
his pocket with an elegant, semicircular movement of the hand
and a croupier's impassive gravity, reserved for the few, like
Corso, who still knew how to play the game. Gruber had
learned the job in the days when a guest had only to raise an
eyebrow for hotel employees to come running. The dear old
Europe of international hotels was now reduced to a few
cognoscenti.

"Are the lady and gentleman staying together?"

"I don't know." Corso frowned. He pictured La Ponte emerging from the bathroom in an embroidered dressing gown and
Taillefer's widow lying on the bed in a silk nightgown. "I'd
like to know that too."

Gruber bowed imperceptibly. "It'll take a few hours, Mr.
Corso."

"I know." He glanced down the corridor that led from the
lobby to the dining room. The girl was there, her duffel coat
under her arm and her hands in her pockets, examining a display of perfumes and silk scarves. "What about her?"

The concierge took a card from under the desk.

"Irene Adler," he read. "British passport, issued two months ago. Nineteen years old. Address: 223B Baker Street, London."

"Don't joke with me, Gruber."

"I'd never take such a liberty, Mr. Corso. That's what it says here."

There was the hint, the faintest suggestion of a smile on the face of the old SS Waffen. Corso had seen him smile only once: the day the Berlin Wall came down. He observed Gruber's white crew cut, stiff neck, hands arranged symmetrically, wrists resting exactly on the edge of the desk. Old Europe, or what was left of it. Gruber was too old to go back home and risk finding that nothing was as he remembered; not the bell tower in Zagreb, not the warm, blond peasant girls smelling of fresh bread, not the green plains with rivers and bridges that he had seen blown up twice—once in his youth, in the retreat from Tito's guerrillas, and then on TV, autumn 1991, in the faces of the Serbian Chetniks. Corso could picture Gruber in his room standing in front of a dusty portrait of the Emperor Franz Joseph, taking off the maroon jacket with little golden keys on the lapels as if it were his Austro-Hungarian army jacket. He probably played Radetsky's March on a record player, drank a toast with a glass of Montenegran liqueur, and masturbated to videos of the Empress Sissy.

The girl was no longer looking at the display but now at Corso. 223B Baker Street, he repeated to himself and felt the urge to guffaw. He wouldn't have been in the least surprised had a bellboy appeared with an invitation from Milady de Winter to take tea at If Castle or at the palace in Ruritania with Richelieu, Professor Moriarty, and Rupert de Hentzau. Since this was a literary matter, it would have seemed the most natural thing in the world.

He asked for a phone book and looked up Baroness Ungern's number. Then, ignoring the girl's stare, he went to the phone booth in the lobby and made an appointment for the following day. He also tried Varo Borja's number in Toledo, but there was no answer.

HE WAS WATCHING TELEVISION with the sound down: a film with Gregory Peck surrounded by seals, a fight in a hotel ballroom, two schooners side by side, waves crashing against the bow, heading north in full sail, toward true freedom which begins only ten miles off the nearest coast. At Corso's elbow a bottle of Bols, its level below the Plimsoll line, stood guard on the bedside table like an old, alcoholic grenadier on the eve of battle, between *The Nine Doors* and the folder with the Dumas manuscript.

Corso took off his glasses and rubbed his eyes, which were red from cigarette smoke and gin. On the bed, with the precision of an archaeologist, he had laid out the fragments of book number two rescued from the fireplace in Victor Fargas's house. There wasn't much left: the boards, protected by the covering of leather, were less damaged, but of the rest there remained no more than charred margins and a few barely legible paragraphs. He picked up one of the pieces, made yellow and brittle by the fire: ... *si non obig.nem me. ips.s fecere, f.r q.qe die, tib. do vitam m.m sicut t.m.* ... This came from one of the bottom corners. He examined it for a few moments, then searched for the same page in book number one. It was page 89, and the two paragraphs were identical. He did the same with as many paragraphs as he could, managing to identify sixteen. It was impossible to tell where another twenty-two of the fragments came from; they were too small or too damaged. Eleven more fragments were blank, and he identified only one, thanks to a crooked 7 that was the third and only legible digit in the page number, page 107.

The cigarette had burned down and was burning his lips. He stubbed it out in the ashtray, then took a swig of the Bols directly from the bottle. He was wearing an old cotton khaki shirt with big pockets, sleeves rolled up, and a crumpled tie. On the TV, the man from Boston standing by the helm was embracing a Russian princess. They both moved their lips soundlessly, happy and in love under a Technicolor sky. The only noise in the room was the gentle rattling of the window-panes caused by the traffic rumbling by, two floors below, head-ing for the Louvre.

Nikon loved that kind of thing. Corso remembered how she would be moved, like a sentimental little girl, by a couple kiss-ing against a cloudy sky to the sound of violins and "The End" across the screen. Sometimes, munching on potato chips at the cinema or in front of the television, she'd lean on Corso's shoul-der and cry quietly, gently, for a long time, her eyes fixed on the screen. It might be Paul Henreid singing the Marseillaise in Rick's café; Rutger Hauer dying, head bowed, in the final shots of *Blade Runner*; John Wayne and Maureen O'Hara in front of the fireplace at Innisfree; Custer and Arthur Kennedy on the eve of Little Big Horn; O'Toole as Jim deceived by Gentleman Brown; Henry Fonda on his way to the O. K. Corral; or Marcello Mastroianni up to his waist in a pond at a spa retrieving a woman's hat, waving to right and left, elegant, imperturbable, and in love with a pair of dark eyes. Nikon was happy crying over it all, and she was proud of her tears. It's because I'm alive, she'd say afterward, laughing, her eyes still wet. Because I'm part of the rest of the world and I'm glad I am. Films are for everyone, collective, generous, with children cheering when the cavalry arrives. They're even better on TV: two can watch and comment. But your books are selfish. Soli-tary. Some of them can't even be read, they fall to bits if you open them. A person who's interested only in books doesn't need other people, and that frightens me. Nikon was eating the last potato chip and watching him intently, her lips parted, searching his face for signs of an illness that would soon man-ifest itself. Sometimes you frighten me.

Happy endings. Corso pressed a button on the remote, and

the image disappeared from the screen. Now he was in Paris and Nikon was somewhere in Africa or the Balkans photographing children with tragic eyes. Once, in a bar, he thought he caught sight of her on the news, in the chaotic shots of a bombardment. She was surrounded by terrified fleeing refugees, her hair in a plait, cameras around her neck and one at her eye, backed by smoke and flames. Nikon. Of all the universal lies she accepted unquestioningly, the happy ending was the most absurd. The hero and heroine lived happily ever after, and the ending seemed indisputable, definitive. No questions asked about how long love or happiness lasts in that "forever" that can be divided into lifetimes, years, months. Even days. Until the very end, their inevitable end, Nikon refused to accept that the hero might have drowned two weeks later when his boat struck a reef in the Southern Hebrides. Or that the heroine was run over by a car three months later. Or that maybe everything turned out differently, in a thousand different ways: one of them had an affair, one of them became bitter or bored, one of them wanted to back out. Maybe nights full of tears, silence, and loneliness followed that screen kiss. Maybe cancer killed him before he was forty. Maybe she lived on and died in an old folks' home at the age of ninety. Maybe the handsome officer turned into a pathetic ruin, his wounds becoming hideous scars and his glorious battles forgotten by all. And maybe, old and defenseless, the hero and heroine suffered ordeals without the strength to fight or defend themselves, tossed this way and that by the storms of life, by stupidity, by cruelty, by the miserable human condition.

Sometimes you frighten me, Lucas Corso.

FIVE MINUTES BEFORE ELEVEN that night, he solved the mystery of the fire at Victor Fargas's house. Although it didn't make things any clearer. He looked at his watch as he stretched and yawned. Glancing again at the fragments spread out on the bedcover, he caught sight of his reflection in the mirror next to the old postcard, which was stuck into the wooden frame, of the hussars outside Reims cathedral. He was disheveled, unshaven, and his glasses sat crookedly on his nose. He started to laugh, one of his bad-tempered, wolflike, twisted laughs reserved for special occasions. And this was one. All the fragments of *The Nine Doors* that he had managed to identify came from pages with text. No trace remained of the nine engravings or the frontispiece. There were two possibilities: either they had burned in the fire or—more likely, considering the torn-off cover—somebody had taken them before throwing the rest of the book into the flames. Whoever it was must have thought himself, or herself, very clever. Or themselves. Maybe, after the unexpected sighting of La Ponte and Liana Taillefer at the traffic light, he should get used to the third person plural. The question was whether the clues Corso was following were his opponent's mistakes or tricks. In either case they were very elaborate.

Speaking of tricks. The doorbell rang, and Corso opened it to find the girl standing there. He had just had time to hide book number one and the Dumas manuscript carefully under the cover. She was barefoot and wearing her usual jeans and white T-shirt.

"Hello, Corso. I hope you're not intending to go out tonight."

She didn't come in but stood at the door with her thumbs in her pockets. She was frowning, as if expecting bad news.

"You can relax your guard," he reassured her.

She smiled, relieved. "I'm exhausted."

He turned his back on her and went to the bedside table. The bottle of gin was empty, so he started searching the liquor cabinet until he stood up triumphantly holding a miniature bottle of gin. He emptied it into a glass and took a sip. The girl was still at the door.

"They took the engravings. All nine of them." He waved his glass at the fragments of book number two. "They burned the rest so it wouldn't show. That's why all of it was not burned. They made sure some pieces were left intact so the book would be recorded as officially destroyed."

She cocked her head to one side, looking at him intently. "You're clever."

"Of course I am. That's why they involved me."

The girl took a few steps around the room. Corso saw her bare feet on the carpet, next to the bed. She was examining the charred bits of paper.

"Fargas didn't burn the book," he added. "He wasn't capable of something like that.... What did they do to him? Was it suicide, like Enrique Taillefer?"

She didn't answer right away. She picked up a piece of paper and looked at the words. "Find your own answers," she said. "That's why they involved you."

"What about you?"

She was reading silently, moving her lips as if she knew the words. When she put the fragment down on the bed, her smile was too old for her years.

"You already know why I'm here: I have to look after you. You need me."

"What I need is more gin."

He cursed to himself and finished his drink, trying to hide his impatience, or his confusion. Damn everything. Emerald green, luminous white—her eyes and that smile against her tanned skin, her bare, straight neck, warm and alive. Can you believe it, Corso. Even now, with all you have to deal with, you're thinking about her tanned arms, her fine wrists, her long fingers. He noticed also that her breasts, under her tight-fitting T-shirt, were magnificent. He hadn't been able to get a good look at them before. He imagined them tanned and heavy under the white cotton, imagined flesh of clarity and shadow. Once again he was struck by her height. She was as tall as he was. Maybe taller.

"Who are you?"

"The devil," she said. "The devil in love."

And she laughed. The book by Cazotte was on the sideboard, next to the *Memoirs of Saint Helena* and some papers. She looked at it but didn't touch it. Then she laid one finger on it and turned to Corso.

"Do you believe in the devil?"

"I'm paid to believe in him. On this job anyway."

She nodded slowly, as if she knew what he was going to say. She watched Corso with curiosity, her lips parted, waiting for a sign or gesture that only she would understand.

"Do you know why I like this book, Corso?"

"No. Tell me."

"Because the protagonist is sincere. His love isn't just a trick to damn a soul. Biondetta is tender and faithful. She admires in Álvaro the same things the devil admires in mankind: his courage, his independence. . . ." Her eyelashes lowered over her light irises for a moment. "His desire for knowledge and his lucidity."

"You seem very well informed. What do you know of all this?"

"Much more than you imagine."

"I don't imagine anything. Everything I know about the devil and his loves and hates comes from literature: *Paradise Lost*, *The Divine Comedy*, then *Faust* and *The Brothers Karamazov*." He made a vague, evasive gesture. "I know Lucifer only secondhand."

Now she was looking at him mockingly. "And which devil do you prefer? Dante's?"

"No. Much too terrifying. Too medieval for my taste."

"Mephistopheles?"

"Not him, either. He's too pleased with himself. Too much a trickster, like a crooked lawyer . . . Anyway, I never trust people who smile a lot."

"What about the one in *The Karamazovs*?"

Corso made a face. "Petty. A civil servant with dirty nails."

He paused. "I suppose the devil I prefer is Milton's fallen angel." He looked at her with interest. "That's what you were hoping I would say."

She smiled enigmatically, her thumbs still in her pockets. He'd never seen anyone wear jeans like that. It needed her long legs, of course. The legs of a young girl hitchhiking at the roadside, her rucksack at her feet and all the light in the world in those damned green eyes.

"How do you see Lucifer?" she asked.

"No idea." Corso grimaced, indifferent. "Taciturn and silent, I suppose. Boring." His expression became acid. "On a throne in a deserted hall. At the center of a cold, desolate, monotonous kingdom where nothing ever happens."

She looked at him in silence. "You surprise me, Corso," she said at last.

"I don't know why. Anyone can read Milton. Even me."

She moved slowly around the bed, in a semicircle, keeping the same distance from it, until she was standing between him and the lamp. Whether by design or not, her shadow fell across the fragments of *The Nine Doors* spread out on the bedcover.

"You've just mentioned the price that has to be paid." Her face was now in darkness, against the light. "Pride, freedom...Knowledge. Whether at the beginning or at the end, you have to pay for everything. Even for courage, don't you think? And don't you think a lot of courage is needed to face God?"

Her words were a soft murmur in the silence that filled the room, the silence that slipped under the door and through the gaps around the window. Even the noise of the traffic in the street outside seemed to fade. Corso looked at one silhouette, then the other. First the shadow stylized across the bedcover and the fragments of the book, then the body standing against the light. He wondered which was more real.

"With all those archangels," she, or her shadow, added. There was bitterness in her words, a contemptuous breath, a sigh of defeat. "Beautiful and perfect. As disciplined as Nazis."

At that moment she wasn't young. She seemed to be carrying the weariness of the ages: an obscure inheritance, the guilt of others, which he, surprised, couldn't identify. He thought that maybe neither the shadow across the bed nor the outline against the light was real.

"There's a painting in the Prado. Do you remember it, Corso? Men with knives standing before horsemen with their swords. I've always thought that the fallen angel looked like that when he rebelled. With the same lost expression as those poor bastards with only knives. The courage of desperation."

She moved slightly as she spoke, only a few inches, but as she did so, her shadow came nearer to Corso's, as if it had a will of its own.

"What do you know about any of that?" he asked.

"More than I want to."

Her shadow now almost touched his. He retreated instinctively, leaving a section of light between them, on the bed.

"Imagine him," she said in the same absorbed tone. "The most beautiful of the fallen angels plotting alone in his empty palace . . . He clings desperately to a routine he despises, but which at least allows him to hide his grief. To hide his failure." The girl laughed gently, joylessly, as if from a great distance. "He misses heaven."

The shadows had now come together and almost merged among the fragments of book snatched from the fireplace at the Quinta da Soledade. The girl and Corso, on the bed, with the nine doors of the kingdom of other shadows, or maybe the same shadows. Singed paper, incomplete clues, a mystery shrouded in several veils, by the printer, by time, and by fire. Enrique Taillefer swinging, his feet dangling in empty space, at the end of a silk cord. Victor Fargas floating facedown in the murky waters of the pond. Aristide Torchia burning at Campo dei Fiori, shouting the name of the father, not looking at heaven but at the ground beneath his feet. Old Dumas writing, sitting at the top of the world. While here in Paris, very near where Corso now was, another shadow, of a cardinal whose library contained too many books on the devil, held all the threads of the plot.

The girl, or her outline against the light, moved toward Corso. Only a single step, but enough for his shadow to disappear under hers.

"It was worse for those who followed him." It took Corso a moment to understand who she meant. "Those he dragged down with him: soldiers, messengers, servants by trade and by calling. Some mercenaries, like you . . . Many didn't even realize that they were choosing between submission and freedom, between God and mankind. Out of habit, with the absurd loyalty of faithful soldiers, they followed their leader in rebellion and defeat."

"Like Xenophon's ten thousand," teased Corso.

She was silent a moment, surprised by his accuracy.

"Maybe," she said at last. "Out in the world alone, they still hope that their leader will one day take them home."

Corso bent to look for a cigarette, and his shadow reappeared. Then he switched on the other lamp, on the bedside table, and the dark outline of the girl disappeared as her face was illuminated. Her light eyes were fixed on him. She seemed young again.

"Very moving," he said. "All those old soldiers searching for the sea."

She blinked, as if now, with her face in the light, she didn't understand what he was saying. There was no longer a shadow on the bed. The fragments of the book were merely pieces of charred paper. All he had to do was open the window, and a gust of air would blow them all over the room.

She smiled. Irene Adler, 223B Baker Street. The café in Madrid, the train, that morning in Sintra . . . The battle lost, the retreat of the defeated legions: she was very young to remember such things. She smiled like a little girl both mischievous and innocent, and there were traces of fatigue under her eyes. She was sleepy and warm.

Corso swallowed. A part of him went up to her and pulled her T-shirt up over her tanned skin, undid her jeans, and lay her on the bed, among the remains of the book that could summon the forces of darkness. And sank into her warm flesh, settling scores with God and Lucifer, with the inexorable flow of time, with his own ghosts, with life and death. But the rest of him just lit a cigarette and breathed out smoke in silence. She stared at him for a long time, waiting for something, a gesture, a word. Then she said good night and went to the door. But in the doorway, she turned and slowly raised her hand, palm inward, index and middle fingers joined and pointing upward. Her smile was both tender and conspiratorial, ingenuous and knowing. Like a lost angel pointing nostalgically at heaven.

BARONESS FRIEDA UNGERN HAD two sweet little dimples when she smiled. She looked as if she had smiled continuously for the past seventy years, and it had left a permanently benevolent expression around her eyes and mouth. Corso, a precocious reader, had known since childhood that there are many different types of witch: wicked stepmothers, bad fairies, beautiful, evil queens, and even nasty old witches with warts on their noses. But despite all he'd heard about the septuagenarian baroness, he didn't know to which category she belonged. She might have been one of those elderly ladies who live, as if cushioned by a dream, outside real life, where no unpleasantness ever intrudes upon their existence, but the depth of her quick, intelligent, suspicious eyes canceled that first impression. So did the right sleeve of her cardigan hanging empty, her arm amputated above the elbow. Otherwise she was small and plump and looked like a French teacher at a boarding school for young ladies. In the days when "young ladies" still existed, that is. Or so Corso thought as he looked at her gray hair tied into a bun on the nape of her neck and at her rather masculine shoes worn with white ankle socks.

"Mr. Corso. Pleased to meet you."

She held out her only hand—small, like the rest of her—with unusual energy and showed her dimples. She had a slight accent, more German than French. A certain Von Ungern, Corso remembered reading somewhere, had become notorious in Manchuria or Mongolia in the early twenties. A warlord of sorts, he had made a last stand against the Red Army at the head of a ragged army of White Russians, Cossacks, Chinese, deserters, and bandits. With armored trains, looting, killing, that sort of thing, concluding with a firing squad at dawn. Maybe he was a relation.

"He was my husband's great-uncle. His family was Russian and emigrated to France with a fair amount of money before the revolution." There was neither nostalgia nor pride in her tone. It had all happened in the past, to other people, to another family, she seemed to say. Strangers who disappeared before she even existed. "I was born in Germany. My family lost everything under the Nazis. I was married here in France after the war." She carefully removed a dead leaf from a plant by the window and smiled slightly. "I never could stand my in-laws' obsession with the past: their nostalgia for St. Petersburg, the Tsar's birthday. It was like a wake."

Corso looked at the desk covered with books, the packed shelves. He calculated that there must have been a thousand volumes in that room alone. The most rare and valuable ones seemed to be there, from modern editions to ancient, leather-bound tomes.

"And what about all this?"

"That's different. It's material for research, not for worship. I use it to do my work."

Times are bad, thought Corso, when witches, or whatever they are, talk about their in-laws and exchange their cauldron for a library, filing cabinets, and a place on the bestseller list.

Through the open door he could see more books in the other rooms and in the corridor. Books and plants. There were pots of them all over the place: the windowsills, the floor, the wooden shelves. It was a large, expensive apartment with a view of the river and, in another time, of the bonfires of the Inquisition. There were several reading tables occupied by young people who looked like students, and all the walls were covered with books. Ancient, gilded bindings shone from between the plants. The Ungern Foundation contained the largest collection in Europe of books on the occult. Corso glanced at the titles closest to him. *Daemonolatriae Libri* by Nicholas Remy. *Compendium Maleficarum* by Francesco Maria Guazzo. *De Daemonialitate et Incubus et Sucubus* by Ludovico Sinistrari. In addition to having one of the best catalogues of demonology, and a foundation named after her late husband the baron, Baroness Ungern enjoyed a solid reputation as a writer of books on magic and witchcraft. Her last book, *Isis, the Naked Virgin*, had been on the bestseller list for three years. The Vatican boosted sales by publicly condemning the work, which drew worrying parallels between a pagan deity and the mother of Christ. There were eight reprints in France, twelve in Spain, and seventeen in Catholic Italy.

"What are you working on at the moment?"

"It's called *The Devil, History and Legend.* An irreverent biography. It'll be ready by the beginning of next year."

Corso stopped at a row of books. His attention had been drawn by the *Disquisitionum Magicarum* by Martin del Rio, the three volumes of the Lovaina first edition, 1599–1600: a classic on demonic magic.

"Where did you get hold of this?"

Frieda Ungern must have been considering how much information to provide, because she took a moment to answer.

"At an auction in Madrid in '89. I had a great deal of trouble preventing your compatriot, Varo Borja, from acquiring it." She sighed, as if still recovering from the effort. "And money. I would never have managed it without help from Paco Montegrifo. Do you know him? A delightful man."

Corso smiled crookedly. Not only did he know Montegrifo, the head of the Spanish branch of Claymore's Auctioneers, he had worked with him on several unorthodox and highly profitable deals. Such as the sale, to a certain Swiss collector, of a *Cosmography* by Ptolemy, a Gothic manuscript dating from 1456, which had mysteriously disappeared from the University of Salamanca not long before. Montegrifo found himself in possession of the book and used Corso as an intermediary. The entire operation had been clean and discreet, and included a visit to the Ceniza brothers' workshop, where a compromising stamp had been removed. Corso delivered the book himself to Lausanne. All included in his thirty percent commission.

"Yes, I know him." He stroked the spines of the several volumes of the *Disquisitionum Magicarum* and wondered what Montegrifo charged the baroness for rigging the auction in her favor. "As for the Martin del Rio, I've only seen a copy once before, in the collection of the Jesuits in Bilbao. . . . Bound in a single piece of leather. But it's the same edition."

As he spoke, he moved his hand along the row of books, touching some. There were many interesting volumes, with quality bindings in vellum, shagreen, parchment. Many others were in mediocre or poor condition, and looked much used. Nearly all had markers in them, strips of white card covered with small, spiky handwriting in pencil. Material for her research. He stopped in front of a book that looked familiar: black, no title, five raised bands on the spine. Book number three.

"How long have you had this?"

Now, Corso was a man of steady nerves. Especially at this stage in the story. But he'd spent the night sorting through the ashes of number two and couldn't prevent the baroness from noticing something peculiar in his tone of voice. He saw that she was looking at him suspiciously despite the friendly dimples in her youthful old face.

"*The Nine Doors?* I'm not sure. A long time." Her only hand moved quickly and deftly. She took the book from the shelf effortlessly and, supporting the spine in her palm, opened it at the first page, decorated with several bookplates, some very old. The last one was an arabesque design with the name Von Ungern and the date written in ink. Seeing it, she nodded nostalgically. "A present from my husband. I married very young. He was twice my age. He bought the book in 1949."

That was the problem with modern-day witches, thought Corso: they didn't have any secrets. Everything was out in the open, you could read all about them in any *Who's Who* or gossip column. Baronesses or not, they'd become predictable, vulgar. Torquemada would have been bored to death by it all.

"Did your husband share your interest in this sort of thing?"

"Not in the slightest. He never read a single book. He just made all my wishes come true like the genie of the lamp." Her amputated arm seemed to shudder for a moment in the empty sleeve of her cardigan. "An expensive book or a perfect pearl necklace, it was all the same to him." She paused and smiled with gentle melancholy. "But he was an amusing man, capable of seducing his best friends' wives. And he made excellent champagne cocktails."

She was silent for a moment and looked around, as if her husband had left a glass behind.

"I collected all this myself," she added, waving at her library, "one by one, down to the last book. I even chose *The Nine Doors*, after discovering it in the catalogue of a bankrupt former Pétain supporter. All my husband did was sign the check."

"Why are you so interested in the devil?"

"I saw him once. I was fifteen and saw him as clearly as I'm seeing you. He had a hard collar, a hat, and a walking stick. He was very handsome. He looked like John Barrymore as Baron Gaigern in *Grand Hotel*. So, like a fool, I fell in love." She became thoughtful again, her only hand in her cardigan pocket, as if remembering something distant. "I suppose that's why I was never really troubled by my husband's infidelities."

Corso looked around, as if there might be someone else in the room, then leaned over confidentially.

"Three centuries ago, you would have burned at the stake for telling me this."

She made a guttural sound of amusement, stifling her laughter, and almost stood on tiptoe to whisper in the same tone: "Three centuries ago, I wouldn't have mentioned it to anyone. But I know a lot of people who would gladly burn me at the stake." She smiled again, showing her dimples. She was always smiling, Corso decided. But her bright, intelligent eyes remained alert, studying him. "Even now, in this day and age."

She handed him *The Nine Doors* and watched him as he leafed through the book slowly, although he could barely contain his impatience to check if there were any differences in the nine engravings. Sighing to himself with relief, he found them intact. In fact, Mateu's *Bibliography* was wrong: none of the three books had the final engraving missing. Book number three was in worse condition than Varo Borja's, and Victor Fargas's before it was thrown into the fire. The lower half had been exposed to damp and almost all the pages were stained. The binding also needed a thorough cleaning, but the book seemed complete.

"Would you like a drink?" asked the baroness. "I have tea and coffee."

No potions or magic herbs, Corso thought with disappointment. Not even a tisane.

"Coffee."

It was a sunny day, and the sky over the nearby towers of Notre-Dame was blue. Corso went over to a window and parted the net curtains so he could see the book in better light. Two floors down, between the bare trees on the banks of the Seine, the girl was sitting on a stone bench in her duffel coat and reading a book. He knew it was *The Three Musketeers*, because he'd seen it on the table when they met at breakfast. Afterward he walked along the Rue de Rivoli, knowing that the girl was following fifteen or twenty paces behind. He deliberately ignored her, and she kept her distance. Now he saw her look up. She must have seen him clearly from down there, but she made no sign of recognition. Expressionless and still, she continued to watch him until he moved away from the window. When he looked out again, she had gone back to her book, her head bowed.

There was a secretary, a middle-aged woman with thick glasses moving among the tables and books, but Frieda Ungern brought the coffee herself, two cups on a silver tray, which she carried with ease. One glance from her told him not to offer help, and they sat down at the desk, the tray among all the books, plant pots, papers, and note cards.

"What gave you the idea of setting up this foundation?"

"It was for tax purposes. Also, now people come here, and I can find collaborators...." She smiled sadly. "I'm the last of the witches, and I felt lonely."

"You don't look anything like a witch." Corso made the appropriate face, an ingenuous, friendly rabbit. "I read your *Isis.*"

Holding her coffee cup in one hand, she raised the stump of her other arm a little and at the same time tilted her head as if to rearrange her hair. Although incomplete, it was an unconsciously coquettish gesture, as old as the world itself and yet ageless.

"Did you like it?"

He looked her in the eyes as he raised his cup to his mouth. "Very much."

"Not everyone did. Do you know what *L'Osservatore Romano* said? It regretted the demise of the Index of the Holy Office. And you're right." She indicated *The Nine Doors* that Corso had put by her on the table. "In the past I would have been burned at the stake, like the poor wretch who wrote the gospel according to Satan."

"Do you really believe in the devil, Baroness?"

"Don't call me Baroness. It's ridiculous."

"What would you like me to call you?"

"I don't know. Mrs. Ungern. Or Frieda."

"Do you believe in the devil, Mrs. Ungern?"

"Sufficiently to dedicate my life, my collection, this foundation, many years of work, and the five hundred pages of my new book all to him." She looked at Corso with interest. He had taken off his glasses to clean them. His helpless smile completed the effect. "What about you?"

"Everybody's asking me that lately."

"Of course. You've been going around asking questions about a book that has to be read with a certain kind of faith."

"My faith is limited," Corso said, risking a hint of sincerity. This kind of frankness often proved profitable. "Really, I work for money."

The dimples appeared again. She must have been very pretty half a century ago, he thought. With both arms intact, casting spells or whatever they were, slender and mischievous. She still had something of that.

"Pity," remarked Frieda Ungern. "Others, who worked for nothing, had blind faith in the book's protagonist. Albertus Magnus, Raymund Lully, Roger Bacon, none of them ever disputed the devil's existence, only his nature."

Corso adjusted his glasses and gave a hint of a skeptical smile.

"Things were different a long time ago."

"You don't have to go that far back. 'The devil does exist, not only as a symbol of evil but as a physical reality.'" How do you like that? It was written by a pope, Paul VI. In 1974."

"He was a professional," said Corso equably. "He must have had his reasons."

"In fact all he was doing was confirming a point of doctrine: the existence of the devil was established by the fourth Council of Letran. In 1215..." She paused and looked at him doubtfully. "Are you interested in erudite facts? I can be unbearably scholarly if I try." The dimples appeared. "I always wanted to be at the top of the class. The smart aleck."

"I'm sure you were. Did you win all the prizes?"

"Of course. And the other girls hated me."

They both laughed. Corso sensed that Frieda Ungern was now on his side. So he took two cigarettes from his coat pocket and offered her one. She refused, glancing at him apprehensively. Corso ignored this and lit his cigarette.

"Two centuries later," continued the baroness as Corso bent over the lighted match, "Innocent VIII's papal bull *Sumnis Desiderantes Affectibus* confirmed that Western Europe was plagued by demons and witches. So two Dominican monks, Kramer and Sprenger, drew up the *Malleus Malleficarum*, a manual for inquisitors."

Corso raised his index finger. "Lyon, 1519. An octavo in the Gothic style, with no author's name. At least not the copy I know."

"Not bad." She looked at him, surprised. "Mine is a later one." She pointed at a shelf. "It's over there. "Published in 1668, also in Lyon. But the very first edition dated from 1486...." She shuddered, half closing her eyes. "Kramer and Sprenger were fanatical and stupid. Their *Malleus* was a load of nonsense. It might even seem funny, if thousands of poor wretches hadn't been tortured and burned in its name."

"Like Aristide Torchia."

"Yes, like him. Although he wasn't remotely innocent."

"What do you know about him?"

The baroness shook her head, drank the last of her coffee, and shook her head again. "The Torchias were a Venetian family of well-to-do merchants who imported vat paper from Spain and France. As a young man Aristide traveled to Holland and was an apprentice of the Elzevirs, who had corresponded with his father. He stayed there for a time and then went to Prague."

"I didn't know that."

"Well, there you are. Prague was Europe's capital of magic and the occult, just as Toledo had been four centuries earlier. . . . Can you see the links? Torchia chose to live in Saint Mary of the Snows, the district of magic, near Jungmannove Square, where there is a statue of Jan Hus. Do you remember Hus at the stake?"

" 'From my ashes a swan will rise that you will not be able to burn.' "

"Exactly. You're easy to talk to. I expect you know that. It must help you in your work." The baroness involuntarily inhaled some of Corso's cigarette smoke. She wrinkled her nose, but he remained unperturbed. "Now, where were we? Ah yes. Prague, act two. Torchia moves to a house in the Jewish quarter nearby, next to the synagogue. A district where the windows are lit up every night and the cabbalists are searching for the magic formula of the Golem. After a while he moves again, this time to the district of Mala Strana. . . ." She smiled at him conspiratorially. "What does all this sound like to you?"

"Like a pilgrimage. Or a field trip, as we'd say nowadays."

"That's what I think," the baroness agreed with satisfaction. Corso, now well and truly adopted, was moving quickly to the top of the class. "It must be more than coincidence that Aristide Torchia went to the three districts in which all the esoteric knowledge of the day was concentrated. And in a Prague whose streets still echoed with the steps of Agrippa and Paracelsus, where the last manuscripts of Chaldean magic and the Pythagorean keys, lost or dispersed after the murder of Metapontius, were to be found." She leaned toward him and lowered her voice: Miss Marple about to confide in her best friend that she found cyanide in the tea cakes. "In that Prague, Mr. Corso, in those dark studies, there were men who practiced the *carmina*, the art of magic words, and necromancy, the art of communicating with the dead." She paused, holding her breath, before whispering, "And goety..."

"The art of communicating with the devil."

"Yes." She leaned back in her armchair, deliciously shocked by it all. She was in her element. Her eyes shone, and she was speaking quickly, as if she had much to say and too little time. "At that time, Torchia lived in a place where the pages and engravings that had survived wars, fires, and persecution were hidden.... The remains of the magic book that opens the doors to knowledge and power: the *Delomelanicon*, the word that summons the darkness."

She said it in a conspiratorial, almost theatrical tone, but she was also smiling, as if she didn't quite take it seriously herself, or was suggesting that Corso maintain a healthy distance.

"Once he had completed his apprenticeship, Torchia returned to Venice," she went on. "Take note of this, because it's important: in spite of the risks he would run in Italy, the printer left the relative safety of Prague to return to his hometown. There he published a series of compromising books that led to his being burned at the stake. Isn't that strange?"

"Seems as if he had a mission to accomplish."

"Yes. But given by whom?" The baroness opened *The Nine Doors* at the title page. "By authority and permission of the superiors. Makes one think, doesn't it? It's very likely that Torchia became a member of a secret brotherhood in Prague and was entrusted with spreading a message. A kind of preaching."

"You said it yourself earlier: the gospel according to Satan."

"Maybe. The fact is that Torchia published *The Nine Doors* at the worst time. Between 1550 and 1666, humanist Neoplatonism and the hermetic and cabbalist movements were losing the battle amid rumors of demonism. Men like Giordano Bruno and John Dee were burned at the stake or died persecuted and destitute. With the triumph of the Counter-Reformation, the Inquisition grew unhindered. Created to fight heresy, it specialized in witches, wizards, and sorcery to justify its shadowy existence. And here they were offered a printer who had dealings with the devil. . . . Torchia made things easy for them, it must be said. Listen." She turned several pages of the book at random. "*Pot. m.vere im.go.*" She looked at Corso. "I've translated numerous passages. The code is quite simple. 'I will bring wax images to life,' it says. 'And unhinge the moon, and put flesh back on dead bodies.' What do you think of that?"

"Rather childish. It seems stupid to die for that."

"Maybe. One never knows. Do you like Shakespeare?"

"Sometimes."

"There are more things in heaven and earth, Horatio, than are dreamt of in your philosophy.' "

"Hamlet was a very insecure man."

"Not everyone is able, or deserves, to gain access to these occult things, Mr. Corso. As the old saying goes, one must know and keep silent."

"But Torchia didn't."

"As you know, according to the cabbala, God has a terrible and secret name."

"The tetragrammaton."

"That's right. The harmony and balance of the universe rests upon its four letters. . . . As the Archangel Gabriel warned Mohammed: 'God is hidden by seventy thousand veils of light and darkness. And were those veils to be lifted, even I would be annihilated.' But God isn't the only one to have such a name. The devil has one too. A terrible, evil combination of letters that summons him when spoken . . . and unleashes terrifying consequences."

"That's nothing new. It had a name long before Christianity and Judaism: Pandora's box."

She looked at him with satisfaction, as if awarding top marks.

"Very good, Mr. Corso. In fact, down through the centuries, we've always talked about the same things, but with different names. Isis and the Virgin Mary, Mitra and Jesus Christ, the twenty-fifth of December as Christmas or the festival of the winter solstice, the anniversary of the unconquered sun. Think of Saint Gregory. Even in the seventh century he was recommending that missionaries use the pagan festivals and adapt them to Christianity."

"Sound business sense. In essence it was a marketing operation: they were trying to attract somebody else's customers. . . . Could you tell me what you know about Pandora's boxes and such like. Including pacts with the devil."

"The art of locking devils inside bottles or books is very ancient. Gervase of Tilbury in the thirteenth century and Gerson in the fourteenth both mentioned it. As for pacts with the devil, the tradition goes back even further: from the Book of Enoch to Saint Jeronimus, through the cabbala and the Church Fathers. Not forgetting Bishop Theophilus, who was actually a 'lover of knowledge,' the historical Faust, and Roger Bacon. Or Pope Sylvester II, of whom it was said that he robbed the Saracens of a book that 'contained all one needs to know.' "

"So it was a question of obtaining knowledge."

"Of course. Nobody would take so much trouble, wandering to the very edge of the abyss, just to kill time. Scholarly demonology identifies Lucifer with knowledge. In Genesis, the devil in the form of a serpent succeeds in getting man to stop being a simpleton and gain awareness, free will, lucidity, knowledge, with all the pain and uncertainty that they entail."

The conversation of the evening before was too fresh so, inevitably, Corso thought of the girl. He picked up *The Nine Doors* and with the excuse of looking at it again in better light, he went to the window. She was no longer there. Surprised, he looked up and down the street, along the embankment and the stone benches under the trees, but couldn't see her. He was puzzled but didn't have time to think about it. Frieda Ungern was speaking again.

"Do you like guessing games? Puzzles with hidden keys? In

a way the book you're holding is exactly that. Like any intelligent being, the devil likes games, riddles. Obstacle courses where the weak and incapable fall by the wayside and only superior spirits—the initiates—win." Corso moved closer to the desk and put down the book, open at the frontispiece. The serpent with the tail in its mouth wound around the tree. "He who sees nothing but a serpent in the figure devouring its tail deserves to go no further."

"What is this book for?" asked Corso.

The baroness put a finger to her lips like the knight in the first engraving. She was smiling.

"Saint John of Patmos says that in the reign of the Second Beast, before the final, decisive battle of Armageddon, 'only he who has the mark, the name of the Beast or the number of his name, will be able to buy and sell.' Waiting for the hour to come, Luke (4:13) tells us at the end of his story about temptation that the devil, repudiated three times, 'has withdrawn until the appropriate time.' But the devil left several paths for the impatient, including the way to reach him, to make a pact with him."

"To sell him one's soul."

Frieda Ungern giggled confidentially. Miss Marple with her cronies, engaged in gossip about the devil. You'll never guess the latest about Satan. This, that, and the other. I don't know where to start, Peggy my dear.

"The devil learned his lesson," she said. "He was young and naive, and he made mistakes. Souls escaped at the last minute through the false door, saving themselves for the sake of love, God's mercy, and other specious promises. So he ended up including a nonnegotiable clause for the handing over of body and soul once the deadline had expired 'without reserve of any right to redemption, or future recourse to God's mercy.' The clause is in fact to be found in this book."

"What a lousy world," said Corso. "Even Lucifer has to resort to the small print."

"You must understand. Nowadays people will swindle you out of anything. Even their soul. His clients slip away and don't comply with their contractual obligations. The devil's fed up and he has every reason to be."

"What else is in the book? What do the nine engravings mean?"

"In principle they're puzzles that have to be solved. Used in conjunction with the text, they confer power. And provide the formula for constructing the magic name to make Satan appear."

"Does it work?"

"No. It's a forgery."

"Have you tried it yourself?"

Frieda Ungern looked shocked.

"Can you see me at my age, standing in a magic circle, invoking Beelzebub? Please. However much he looked like John Barrymore fifty years ago, a beau ages too. Can you imagine the disappointment at my age? I prefer to be faithful to the memories of my youth."

Corso looked at her in mock surprise. "But surely you and the devil . . . Your readers take you for a committed witch."

"Well, they're mistaken. What I look for in the devil is money, not emotion." She looked at the window. "I spent my husband's fortune building up this collection, so I have to live off my royalties."

"Which are considerable, I'm sure. You're the queen of the bookshops."

"But life is expensive, Mr. Corso. Very expensive, especially when one has to make deals with people like our friend Mr. Montegrifo to get the rare books one wants. Satan serves as a good source of income nowadays, but that's all. I'm seventy years old. I don't have time for gratuitous, silly fantasies, spinsters' dreams. . . . Do you understand?"

It was Corso's turn to smile. "Perfectly."

"When I say that this book is a forgery," continued the

baroness, "it's because I've studied it in depth. There's something in it that doesn't work. There are gaps in it, blanks. I mean this figuratively, because my copy is in fact complete. It belonged to Madame de Montespan, Louis XIV's mistress. She was a high priestess of Satanism and managed to have the ritual of the Black Mass included in the palace routine. There is a letter from Madame de Montespan to Madame De Peyrolles, her friend and confidante, in which she complains of the inefficacy of a book which, she states, 'has all that which the sages specify, and yet there is something incorrect in it, a play on words which never falls into the correct sequence.'"

"Who else owned it?"

"The Count of Saint Germain, who sold it to Cazotte."

"Jacques Cazotte?"

"Yes. The author of *The Devil in Love*, who was guillotined in 1792. Do you know the book?"

Corso nodded cautiously. The links were so obvious that they were impossible.

"I read it once."

Somewhere in the apartment a phone rang, and the secretary's steps could be heard along the corridor. The ringing stopped.

"As for *The Nine Doors*," the baroness continued, "the trail went cold here in Paris, at the time of the Terror after the revolution. There are a couple of subsequent references, but they're very vague. Gérard de Nerval mentions it in passing in one of his articles, assuring us that he saw it at a friend's house."

Corso blinked imperceptibly behind his glasses. "Dumas was a friend of his," he said, alert.

"Yes. But Nerval doesn't say at whose house. The fact is, nobody saw the book again until the Pétain collaborator's collection was auctioned, which is when I got hold of it. . . ."

Corso was no longer listening. According to the legend, Gérard de Nerval hanged himself with the cord from a bodice, Madame de Montespan's. Or was it Madame de Maintenon's?

Whoever it belonged to, Corso couldn't help drawing worrying parallels with the cord from Enrique Taillefer's dressing gown.

The secretary came to the door, interrupting his thoughts. Somebody wanted Corso on the telephone. He excused himself and walked past the tables of readers out into the corridor, full of yet more books and plants. On a walnut corner table there was an antique metal phone with the receiver off the hook.

"Hello."

"Corso? It's Irene Adler."

"So I gather." He looked behind him down the empty corridor. The secretary had disappeared. "I was surprised you weren't still keeping a lookout. Where are you calling from?"

"The bar on the corner. There's a man watching the house. That's why I came here."

For a moment Corso just breathed slowly. Then he bit off a hangnail. It was bound to happen sooner or later, he thought with twisted resignation. The man was part of the landscape, or the furniture. Then, although he knew it was pointless, he said:

"Describe him."

"Dark, with a mustache and a big scar on his face." The girl's voice was calm, without any trace of emotion or awareness of danger. "He's sitting in a gray BMW across the street."

"Has he seen you?"

"I don't know. But I can see him. He's been there an hour. He got out of the car twice: first to look at the names at the door, and then to buy a newspaper."

Corso spat the hangnail out of his mouth and sucked his thumb. It smarted. "Listen. I don't know what the man's up to. I don't even know if the two of you are part of the same setup. But I don't like him being near you. Not at all. So go back to the hotel."

"Don't be an idiot, Corso. I'll go where I have to." She added, "Regards to Treville," and hung up.

Corso made a gesture halfway between exasperation and sarcasm, because he was thinking the same thing and didn't like the coincidence. He stood for a moment looking at the receiver before hanging up. Of course, she was reading *The Three Musketeers*. She'd even had the book open when he saw her from the window. In chapter 3, having just arrived in Paris, and during an audience with Monsieur de Treville, commander of the king's musketeers d'Artagnan sees Rochefort from the window. He runs after him, bumps into Athos's shoulder, Porthos's shoulder belt, and Aramis's handkerchief. Regards to Treville. It was a clever joke, if it was spontaneous. But Corso didn't find it at all funny.

After he hung up, he stood thinking for a moment in the darkness of the corridor. Maybe that's exactly what they were expecting him to do: rush downstairs after Rochefort, sword in hand, taking the bait. The girl's call might even have been part of the plan. Or maybe—and this was really getting convoluted—it had been a warning about the plan, if there was one. That's if she was playing fair—Corso was too experienced to put his hand in the fire for anybody.

Bad times, he said to himself again. Absurd times. After so many books, films, and TV shows, after reading on so many different possible levels, it was difficult to tell if you were seeing the original or a copy; difficult to know whether the image was real, inverted, or both, in a hall of mirrors; difficult to know the authors' intentions. It was as easy to fall short of the truth as to overshoot it with one's interpretations. Here was one more reason to feel envious of his great-grandfather with the grenadier's mustache and with the smell of gunpowder floating over the muddy fields of Flanders. In those days a flag was still a flag, the Emperor was the Emperor, a rose was a rose was a rose. But now at least, here in Paris, something was clear to Corso: even as a second-level reader he was prepared to play the game only up to a certain point. He no longer had the youth, the innocence, or the desire to go and fight at a place chosen by his opponents, three duels arranged in ten minutes, in the grounds of the Carmelite convent or wherever the hell it might be. When the time came to say hello, he'd make sure he approached Rochefort with everything in his favor, if possible from behind, with a steel bar in his hand. He owed it to him since that narrow street in Toledo, not forgetting the interest accrued in Sintra. Corso would settle his debts calmly. Biding his time.

XI. THE BANKS OF THE SEINE

This mystery is considered insoluble for the very same reasons that should lead one to consider it soluble.
—E. A. Poe, THE MURDERS IN THE RUE MORGUE

The code is simple," said Frieda Ungern, "consisting of abbreviations similar to those used in ancient Latin manuscripts. This may be because Aristide Torchia took the major part of the text word for word from another manuscript, possibly the legendary *Delomelanicon*. In the first engraving, the meaning is obvious to anyone slightly familiar with esoteric language: NEM. PERV.T QUI N.N LEG. CERT.RIT is obviously NEMO PERVENIT QUI NON LEGITIME CERTAVERIT."

"Only he who has fought according to the rules will succeed."

They were on their third cup of coffee, and it was obvious, at least on a formal level, that Corso had been adopted. He saw the baroness nod, gratified.

"Very good. Can you interpret any part of this engraving?"

"No," Corso lied calmly. He had just noticed that in the baroness's copy there were three, not four, towers in the walled city toward which the horseman rode. "Except for the character's gesture, which seems eloquent."

"And so it is: he is turned to any follower, with a finger to his lips, advising silence.... It's the *tacere* of the philosophers of the occult. In the background the city walls surround the towers, the secret. Notice that the door is closed. It must be opened."

Tense and alert, Corso turned more pages until he came to the second engraving, the hermit in front of another door, holding the key in his *right* hand. The legend read CLAUS. PAT.T.

"CLAUSAE PATENT," the baroness deciphered. "They open that which is closed. The closed doors . . . The hermit symbolizes knowledge, study, wisdom. And look, at his side there's the same black dog that, according to legend, accompanied Agrippa. The faithful dog. From Plutarch to Bram Stoker and his *Dracula*, not forgetting Goethe's *Faust*, the black dog is the animal the devil most often chooses to embody him. As for the lantern, it belongs to the philosopher Diogenes who so despised worldly powers. All he requested of powerful Alexander was that he should not overshadow him, that he move because he was standing in front of the sun, the light."

"And this letter Teth?"

"I'm not sure." She tapped the engraving lightly. "The hermit in the tarot, very similar to this one, is sometimes accompanied by a serpent, or by the stick that symbolizes it. In occult philosophy, the serpent and the dragon are the guardians of the wonderful enclosure, garden, or fleece, and they sleep with their eyes open. They are the Mirror of the Art."

"*Ars diavoli*," said Corso casually, and the baroness half smiled, nodding mysteriously. But he knew, from Fulcanelli and other ancient texts, that the term "Mirror of the Art" came not from demonology but from alchemy. He wondered how much charlatanism lay beneath the baroness's display of erudition. He sighed to himself. He felt like a gold prospector standing up to his waist in the river, sieve in hand. After all, he thought, she had to find something to fill her five-hundred-page bestsellers.

But Frieda Ungern had moved on to the third engraving.

"The motto is VERB. D.SUM C.S.T. ARCAN. This stands for

VERBUM DIMISSUM CUSTODIAT ARCANUM. It can be translated as 'The lost word keeps the secret.' And the engraving is significant: a bridge, the union between the light and the dark banks. From classical mythology to Snakes and Ladders, its meaning is clear. Like the rainbow, it links earth with heaven or hell.... To cross this one, of course, one has to open the fortified gates."

"What about the archer hiding in the clouds?"

This time his voice shook as he asked the question. In books one and two, the quiver hanging from the archer's shoulder was empty. In book three, it contained an arrow. Frieda Ungern was resting her finger on it.

"The bow is the weapon of Apollo and Diana, the light of the supreme power. The wrath of the god, or God. It's the enemy lying in wait for anyone crossing the bridge." She leaned forward and said quietly and confidentially, "Here it represents a terrible warning. It's not advisable to trifle with this sort of thing."

Corso nodded and moved on to the fourth engraving. He could sense the fog lifting in his mind. Doors opening with a sinister creak. Now he was looking at the joker and his stone labyrinth, with the caption: FOR. N.N OMN. A.QUE. Frieda Ungern translated is as FORTUNA NON OMNIBUS AEQUE: Fate is not the same for all.

"The character is similar to the madman in the tarot," she explained. "God's madman in Islam. And, of course, he's also holding a stick or symbolic serpent.... He's the medieval fool, the joker in a pack of cards, the jester. He symbolizes destiny, chance, the end of everything, the expected or unexpected conclusion. Look at the dice. In the Middle Ages, jokers were privileged beings. They were permitted to do things forbidden to others. Their purpose was to remind their masters that they were mortal, that their end was as inevitable as other men's."

"Here he's stating the opposite," objected Corso. "Fate is not the same for all."

"Of course. He who rebels, exercises his freedom, and takes the risk can earn a different fate. That's what this book is about, hence the joker, paradigm of freedom. The only truly free man, and also the most wise. In occult philosophy the joker is identified with the mercury of the alchemists. Emissary of the gods, he guides souls through the kingdom of shadows. . . ."

"The labyrinth."

"Yes. There it is." She pointed at the engraving. "And, as you can see, the entry door is closed."

So is the exit, thought Corso with an involuntary shudder. He turned to the next engraving.

"This legend is simpler," he said. "FR.ST.A. It's the only one I dare take a guess at. I'd say there's a *u* and an *r* missing: FRUSTRA. Which means 'in vain.' "

"Very good. That's exactly what it says, and the picture matches the caption. The miser is counting his gold pieces, unaware of Death, who holds two clear symbols: an hourglass and a pitchfork."

"Why a pitchfork and not a scythe?"

"Because Death reaps, but the devil harvests."

They stopped at the sixth engraving, the man hanging from the battlements by his foot. Frieda Ungern pretended to yawn with boredom, as if it was too obvious.

"DIT.SCO M.R stands for DITESCO MORI, I am enriched by death, a sentence the devil can utter with his head held high. Don't you think?"

"I suppose so. It's his trade, after all." Corso ran a finger over the engraving. "What does the hanged man symbolize?"

"Firstly, arcanum twelve in the tarot. But there are other possible interpretations. I believe it symbolizes change through sacrifice. . . . Are you familiar with the saga of Odin?

> *Wounded, I hung from a scaffold*
> *swept by the winds,*
> *for nine long nights. . . .*

You can make the following associations," continued the baroness. "Lucifer, champion of freedom, suffers from love of mankind. And he provides mankind with knowledge through sacrifice, thus damning himself."

"What can you tell me about the seventh engraving?"

"DIS.S P.TI.R MAG. doesn't seem very clear at first. But my guess is that it's a traditional saying, one much liked by occult philosophers: DISCIPULUS POTIOR MAGISTRO."

"The disciple surpasses the master?"

"More or less. The king and the beggar play chess on a strange board where all the squares are the same color, while the black dog and the white dog, Good and Evil, viciously tear each other to pieces. The moon, representing both darkness and the mother, can be seen through the window. Think of the mythical belief that, after death, souls take refuge on the moon. You read my *Isis*, didn't you? Black is the symbolic color of darkness, Cimmerian shadows, sable in heraldry, earth, night, death.... The black of Isis corresponds with the color of the Virgin, who is robed in blue and dwells on the moon. When we die, we return to her, to the darkness from which we came. That darkness is ambiguous, as it is both protective and threatening. The dogs and the moon can be interpreted another way. The goddess of the hunt, Artemis, the Roman Diana, was known to take revenge on those who fell in love with her or tried to take advantage of her femininity.... I assume you know the story."

Corso, who was thinking about Irene Adler, nodded slowly. "Yes. She would let her dogs loose on such men after turning them into stags." He swallowed in spite of himself. The two dogs in the engraving, locked in mortal combat, now seemed ominous. Himself and Rochefort? "So they'd be torn to pieces."

The baroness glanced at him, expressionless. It was Corso who was providing the context, not she.

"The basic meaning of the eighth engraving," she continued, "is not difficult to grasp. VIC. I.T VIR. stands for a rather nice motto, VICTA IACET VIRTUS. Which means: Virtue lies defeated. The damsel about to have her throat slit, by the handsome young man in armor carrying the sword, represents virtue. Meanwhile, the wheel of fortune or fate turns inexorably in the background, moving slowly but always making a complete turn. The three figures on it symbolize the three stages which, in the Middle Ages, were referred to as *regno* (I reign), *regnavi* (I reigned), and *regnabo* (I will reign)."

"There's one more engraving."

"Yes. The last one, and also the most significant picture. N.NC SC.O TEN.BR. LUX without doubt stands for NUNC SCIO TENEBRIS LUX: Now I know that from darkness comes light. What we have here is in fact a scene from Saint John's Apocalypse. The final seal has been broken, the secret city is in flames. The time of the Whore of Babylon has come and, having pronounced the terrible name or the number of the Beast, she rides, triumphant, on the dragon with seven heads."

"Doesn't seem very profitable," said Corso, "going to all that trouble only to find this horror."

"That's not what it's about. All the allegories are kinds of compositions in code, rebuses. Just as on a puzzle page the word 'in' followed by the pictures of a fan and a tree make up the word 'infantry,' these engravings and their captions combined with the book's text enable one to determine a sequence, a ritual. The formula that provides the magic word. The *verbum dimissum* or whatever it might be."

"And then the devil will put in an appearance."

"In theory."

"In what language is this spell? Latin, Hebrew, or Greek?"

"I don't know."

"And where's the fault Madame de Montespan mentions?"

"As I said, I don't know that either. All I've been able to establish is that the celebrant must construct a magic territory in which to place the words obtained, having arranged them in sequence. I don't know that sequence, but the text on pages

242

158 and 159 of *The Nine Doors* may give an indication. Look."

She showed him the text in abbreviated Latin. A card covered with the her small, spiky handwriting marked the page.

"Have you managed to work out what it says?" asked Corso.

"Yes. At least, I think so." She handed him the card. "There you are."

Corso read:

It is the animal with the tail in its mouth that encircles the
  labyrinth
where you will go through eight doors before the dragon
which comes to the enigma of the word.
Each door has two keys:
one is air and the other matter,
but both are the same thing.
You will place matter on the serpent's skin
in the direction of the rising sun,
and on its belly the seal of Saturn.
You will break the seal nine times,
and when the reflection in the mirror shows the way,
you will find the lost word
which brings light from the darkness.

"What do you think?" asked the baroness.

"It's disturbing, I suppose. But I don't understand a word. Do you?"

"As I said, not much." She turned the pages of the book, preoccupied. "It provides a method, a formula. But there's something in it that isn't as it should be. And I ought to know what that is."

Corso lit another cigarette but said nothing. He already knew the answer to the question: the hermit's keys, the hourglass, the exit from the labyrinth, the chessboard, the halo . . . And other things. While Frieda Ungern was explaining the meaning of the pictures, he had discovered more differences, confirming his theory: each book differed from the other two.

The game of errors continued, and he urgently needed to get to work. But not with the baroness breathing down his neck.

"I'd like to take a good, long look at all of this," he said.

"Of course. I have plenty of time. I'd like to see how you work."

Corso cleared his throat, embarrassed. They'd reached the point he'd worried about: the unpleasantness.

"I work better on my own."

It sounded false. Frieda Ungern frowned.

"I'm afraid I don't understand." She glanced at Corso's canvas bag suspiciously. "Are you hinting that you want me to leave you alone?"

"If you wouldn't mind." Corso tried to hold her gaze as long as possible. "What I'm doing is confidential."

She blinked. Her frown became threatening, and Corso knew that everything could go out the window at any moment.

"You're free to do as you like, of course." Frieda Ungern's tone could have frozen all the plants in the room. "But this is my book and my house."

At that point anyone else would have apologized and beat a retreat, but not Corso. He remained seated, smoking, his eyes fixed on the baroness. At last, he smiled cautiously, like a rabbit playing blackjack about to ask for another card.

"I don't think I've explained myself fully." He smiled as he took a well-wrapped object from his canvas bag. "I just need to spend some time here with the book and my notes." He gently tapped the bag as he held out the package with his other hand. "As you can see, I've brought all I need."

The baroness undid the wrapping and looked at its contents in silence. It was a publication in German—Berlin, September 1943—a thick brochure entitled *Iden*, a monthly journal from Idus, a circle of devotees of magic and astrology which was very close to the leaders of Nazi Germany. Corso had put in a marker at a page that had a photograph. The photograph showed a young and very pretty Frieda Ungern smiling at the photographer. She had a man on each arm (for she had both arms then). One of the men was in civilian clothes and the caption named him as the Führer's personal astrologer. She was mentioned as his assistant, the distinguished Miss Frieda Wender. The man on the left had steel-rimmed glasses, a timid expression, and wore a black SS uniform. One didn't need to read the caption to recognize Reichsführer Heinrich Himmler.

When Frieda Ungern, née Wender, looked up and her eyes met Corso's, she no longer seemed a sweet little old lady. But it lasted only a moment. She nodded slowly and carefully tore out the page with the photo, ripping it into tiny pieces. And Corso reflected that witches and baronesses and little old ladies who worked surrounded by books and potted plants had their price, just like anyone else. *Victa iacet Virtus.* And he didn't see why it should be any other way.

ONCE HE WAS ALONE, he took the folder from his bag and set to work. He sat at a table by the window, *The Nine Doors* open at the frontispiece. Before starting, he parted the net curtains and glanced out. A gray BMW was parked across the street. The tenacious Rochefort at his post. Corso couldn't see the girl at the bar on the corner.

He turned his attention to the book: the type of paper, the pressure of the engravings, any flaws or misprints. Now he knew that the three copies were only outwardly identical: the same black leather binding with no lettering, five raised bands, a pentacle on the cover, the same number of pages and location of the engravings . . . With great patience, page by page, he completed the comparative tables he'd begun with book number one. On page 81, at the blank page on the reverse side of engraving number V, he found another of the baroness's cards. It was a translation of a paragraph on the page.

You will accept the pact of alliance that I offer you, surrendering myself to you. And you will promise me the love of women and the flower of maidens, the honor of nuns, the rank, pleasures, and riches of the powerful, princes, and ecclesiastics. I will fornicate every three days and the intoxication will be pleasing to me. Once a year I will pay homage to you in confirmation of this contract signed with my blood. I will tread upon the sacraments of the Church and I will address prayers to you. I will fear neither rope nor sword nor poison. I will pass among the plague-ridden and the lepers without sullying my flesh. But above all I will possess the Knowledge for which my first parents renounced paradise. By virtue of this pact you will erase me from the book of life and enter me in the black book of death. And beginning now I will live for twenty happy years on man's earth. But then I will go with you to your kingdom and curse God.

There was another note on the back of the card, relating to a paragraph deciphered on another page:

I will recognize your servants, my brothers, by the sign impressed on some part of their body, here or there, a scar or your mark....

Corso cursed emphatically under his breath, as if he were muttering a prayer. He looked around at the books on the walls, at their dark, worn spines, and he seemed to hear a strange, distant murmur coming from them. Each of the closed books was a door, and behind it stirred shadows, voices, sounds, heading toward him from a deep, dark place.

He got goose bumps. Just like a vulgar fan.

IT WAS NIGHT BY the time he left. He paused in the doorway a moment and glanced to the left and right, but saw nothing to worry him. The gray BMW had disappeared. A low mist was rising from the river, flowing over the stone parapet and sliding along the damp paving stones. The yellowish glow of the street lamps, illuminating successive stretches of the embankment, was reflected on the ground, lighting up the empty bench where the girl had been sitting.

He went to the bar. He searched for her face among the people standing at the bar or sitting at the narrow tables at the back, but couldn't find her. He sensed that a piece of the jigsaw was out of place, something that had been setting off alarm signals intermittently in his brain ever since her call to warn him of Rochefort's reappearance. Corso, whose instincts had become a great deal sharper recently, could smell danger in the deserted street, in the damp vapor rising from the river and trailing to the door of the bar where he was standing. He shook his shoulders to rid himself of the feeling. He bought a packet of Gauloises and gulped down two gins one after the other. They made his nostrils dilate, and everything fell slowly into place, like a picture coming into focus. The alarms faded in the distance, and echoes from the outside world were now comfortably softened. Holding a third gin, he went to sit down at an empty table by the slightly misted window. He looked out at the street, the quayside, and the mist sliding over the parapet and swirling up as the wheels of a car cut through it. He sat there for a quarter of an hour, looking for any unusual signs, his canvas bag on the floor by this feet. In it were most of the answers to the mystery posed by Varo Borja. The book collector hadn't wasted his money.

In the first place, Corso had now solved the problem of the differences between eight of the nine engravings. Book number three differed from the other two copies in engravings I, III, and VI. In engraving I, the walled city with the horseman riding toward it had only three towers, not four. In engraving III, there was an arrow in the archer's quiver, while in the Toledo and Sintra copies the quiver was empty. And in engraving VI, the hanged man hung by his right foot, but the figures in books one and two hung by their left. He could now fill in the comparative table he'd started in Sintra.

ENGRAVINGS

	I	II	III	IIII	V	VI	VII	VIII	VIIII
One	Four towers	Left hand	No arrow	No exit	Sand down	Left foot	White board	No halo	No diff.
Two	Four towers	Right hand	No arrow	Exit	Sand up	Left foot	Black board	Halo	No diff.
Three	Three towers	Right hand	Arrow	No exit	Sand up	Right foot	White board	No halo	No diff.

In other words, although the engravings appeared identical, one of the three was always different, with the exception of engraving VIIII. Moreover, the differences were distributed over the three books. But the apparently arbitrary distribution acquired meaning when one examined the differences alongside those between the printer's marks for the signatures of inventor

PRINTER'S MARKS FOR SIGNATURES

	I	II	III	IIII	V	VI	VII	VIII	VIIII
One	AT(s) AT(i)	AT(s) LF(i)	AT(s) AT(i)	AT(s) AT(i)	AT(s) LF(i)	AT(s) AT(i)	AT(s) AT(i)	AT(s) AT(i)	AT(s) AT(i)
Two	AT(s) AT(i)	AT(s) AT(i)	AT(s) AT(i)	AT(s) LF(i)	AT(s) AT(i)	AT(s) AT(i)	AT(s) LF(i)	AT(s) LF(i)	AT(s) AT(i)
Three	AT(s) LF(i)	AT(s) AT(i)	AT(s) LF(i)	AT(s) AT(i)	AT(s) AT(i)	AT(s) LF(i)	AT(s) AT(i)	AT(s) AT(i)	AT(s) AT(i)

(the original creator of the pictures) and sculptor (the artist who made the engravings), A. T. and L. F.

If he superimposed the two tables, he found a coincidence: in each of the engravings that differed from the other two, the initials of the inventor were also different. This meant that Aristide Torchia, as sculptor, had made all the woodcuts for the prints in the book. But he was identified as inventor of the original drawings in only nineteen of the twenty-seven engravings contained in the three books combined. The other eight, distributed over the three copies—two engravings in book one, three in book two, and three in book three—had been created by somebody else, somebody with the initials L. F. Phonetically very close to the name Lucifer.

Towers. Hand. Arrow. Exit from the labyrinth. Sand. Hanged man's foot. Board. Halo. This was where the errors lay. Eight differences, eight correct engravings, no doubt copied from the original, the obscure *Delomelanicon*, and nineteen altered, unusable engravings, distributed over the pages of the three copies, identical only in text and outward appearance. Therefore none of the three books was a forgery, but none of them was entirely authentic, either. Aristide Torchia had confessed the truth to his executioners, but not the whole truth. There did indeed remain only one book. As hidden and as safe from the flames as it was forbidden to the unworthy. The engravings were the key. One book hidden within three copies. For the disciple to surpass the master, he had to reconstruct the book using the codes, the rules of the Art.

Corso sipped his gin and looked out at the darkness over the Seine, beyond the streetlights that lit up part of the quayside and threw deep shadows beneath the bare trees. He didn't feel euphoric at his victory, nor even simply satisfied at finishing a difficult job. He knew the mood well: the cold, lucid calm when he finally got hold of a book he'd been chasing for a long time. When he managed to cut in front of a competitor, nail a book after a delicate negotiation, or dig up a gem in a pile of old papers and rubbish. He remembered Nikon in another time and

	I	II	III	IIII	V	VI	VII	VIII	VIIII
One	Four towers	Left hand	No arrow	No exit	Sand down	Left foot	White board	No halo	No diff.
Two	Four towers	Right hand	No arrow	Exit	Sand up	Left foot	Black board	Halo	No diff.
Three	Three towers	Right hand	Arrow	No exit	Sand up	Right foot	White board	No halo	No diff.

PRINTER'S MARKS FOR SIGNATURES

	I	II	III	IIII	V	VI	VII	VIII	VIIII
One	AT(s) LF(i)	AT(s) LF(i)	AT(s) AT(i)	AT(s) AT(i)	AT(s) LF(i)	AT(s) AT(i)	AT(s) AT(i)	AT(s) AT(i)	AT(s) AT(i)
Two	AT(s) AT(i)	AT(s) AT(i)	AT(s) AT(i)	AT(s) LF(i)	AT(s) AT(i)	AT(s) AT(i)	AT(s) LF(i)	AT(s) LF(i)	AT(s) AT(i)
Three	AT(s) LF(i)	AT(s) AT(i)	AT(s) LF(i)	AT(s) AT(i)	AT(s) AT(i)	AT(s) LF(i)	AT(s) AT(i)	AT(s) AT(s)	AT(s) AT(s)

place sticking labels on videotapes, sitting on the floor by the television, rocking gently in time to the music—Audrey Hepburn in love with a journalist in Rome—keeping her big dark eyes fixed on him, eyes that constantly expressed her wonder at life. By then, they already hinted at the hardness and reproach, premonitions of the loneliness closing in like an inexorable, fixed-interest debt. The hunter with his prey, Nikon had whispered, amazed at her discovery, because maybe she was seeing him like that for the first time. Corso recovering his breath, like a hostile wolf rejecting his prize after a long chase. A predator feeling no hunger or passion, no horror at the sight of blood or flesh. Having no aim other than the hunt itself. You're as dead as your prey, Lucas Corso. Like the dry, brittle paper that has become your flag. Dusty corpses that you don't love either, that don't even belong to you, and that you don't give a damn about.

For a moment he wondered what Nikon would think of him now, and his groin tingled and his mouth was dry, as he sat at the narrow table in the bar, watching the street and unable to leave because here, in the warmth and light, surrounded by cigarette smoke and the murmur of conversation, he felt temporarily safe from the dark premonition, from the danger without name or shape that he sensed approaching him through the deadening thickness of the gin in his blood, through the sinister low mist rising from the river. As on that English moor, in black and white. Nikon would have understood. Basil Rathbone, alert, listening to the hound of the Baskervilles howling in the distance.

AT LAST HE MADE up his mind. He finished his gin and left some coins on the table. Then he put the canvas bag over his shoulder and went out into the street, turning up his coat collar. As he crossed, he looked in both directions and, when he reached the stone bench where the girl had been reading, he turned and walked along the parapet on the left bank. The yellow lights of a barge on the river lit him from below as he passed a bridge, surrounding him with a halo of dirty mist.

The street and the riverside seemed deserted, with few cars passing. By the narrow passageway of the Rue Mazarin he hailed a taxi, but it didn't stop. He walked on to the Rue Guénégaud, intending to cross the Pont Neuf to the Louvre. The mist and dark buildings gave the scene a somber, timeless appearance. Sniffing the air like a wolf sensing danger, Corso felt unusually anxious. He moved the bag to his other shoulder to free his right hand and stopped to look around, perplexed. In that precise spot—chapter 11: the plot thickens, d'Artagnan saw Constance Bonacieux emerge from the Rue Dauphine, also on her way toward the Louvre and the same bridge. She was accompanied by a gentleman who turned out to be the Duke of Buckingham, whose nocturnal adventure almost earned him a thrust of d'Artagnan's sword through his body: *I loved her, Milord, and I was jealous....*

Maybe the feeling of danger was false, the perverse effect of the strange atmosphere and reading too many novels. But the girl's telephone call and the gray BMW at the door hadn't been figments of his imagination. A clock struck the hour in the distance and Corso breathed out. This was all absurd.

Then Rochefort jumped him. He seemed to emerge from the river, materializing from the shadows. In fact he had followed Corso along the riverside below the parapet, and then climbed a flight of stone steps to reach him. Corso found out about the steps when he found himself rolling down them. He'd never fallen down steps before, and he thought it would go on for longer, one step at a time or something, as in films. But it was over very quickly. A very professional first punch behind the ear, and the night became a blur. The outside world seemed distant, as if he'd drunk a whole bottle of gin. Thanks to this, he didn't feel much pain as he rolled down the steps, hitting the stone edges. He reached the bottom bruised but conscious. Possibly a little surprised not to hear the splash—a Conradian onomatopoeia, he thought incongruously—of his body hitting the water. From the ground, his head on damp paving stones and his legs on the bottom steps, he looked up, confused, and saw Rochefort's black outline descend the steps three at a time and jump on top of him.

You're buggered, Corso. This was all he had time to think. Then he did two things. First he tried to kick as Rochefort jumped over him. But his weak attempt hit only air. So all he had left was the old, familiar reflex of forming a ball and letting the gunfire fade into the dusk. With the damp from the river and his own private darkness—he'd lost his glasses in the scuffle—he winced. The guardsman dies but falls down the stairs too. So he formed a ball, curled up to protect the bag, which was still hanging from, or rather was tangled around, his shoulder. Maybe great-great-grandfather Corso from the other shore of Lethe would have appreciated his move. It was difficult to tell what Rochefort thought of it. Like Wellington, he rose to the occasion with traditional British efficiency: Corso heard a distant cry of pain, which he suspected came from his own mouth, as Rochefort dealt him a clean, precise kick in the back.

Nothing good was going to come of this, so he closed his eyes and waited, resigned, for someone to turn the page. He could feel Rochefort's breathing very near, could feel him leaning over him, searching inside the bag. Then Rochefort yanked violently at the strap. This caused Corso to open his eyes again, just enough to make out the flight of steps in his field of vision. But as his face was pressed down against the paving stones, the steps appeared horizontal, crooked, and blurred. So at first he couldn't tell whether the girl was going up or down. He just saw her move incredibly fast, from right to left, her long legs jumping from step to step. Her duffel coat, which she had just taken off, spread out in the air, or rather moved toward a corner of the screen surrounded by swirls of mist, like the cape of the Phantom of the Opera.

He blinked with interest, in an attempt to focus, and moved his head a little to keep the scene in the frame. Out of the corner of his eye he saw Rochefort, his image inverted, give a start as the girl jumped down the last few steps. She fell on top of him with a brief, sharp cry, harder and more piercing than broken glass. He heard a thick sound—a thump—and Rochefort disappeared from Corso's field of vision as suddenly as if he'd been on springs. Now all Corso could see was the empty steps. With difficulty he turned his head to the river and lay his other cheek on the paving stones. The image was still crooked: the ground on one side, the black sky on the other, the bridge below and the river above. But now at least it contained Rochefort and the girl. For a split second Corso saw her silhouetted against the hazy lights of the bridge. She was standing, her legs apart and her hands out in front of her, as if asking for a moment of calm to listen to some distant tune. Rochefort was facing her, with a knee and a hand on the ground, like a boxer who can't quite get up while the referee counts to ten. His scar was visible in the light from the bridge. Corso just had time to see his look of amazement before the girl again gave a piercing cry. She balanced on one leg and, raising the other in a semicircular movement that seemed quite effortless, kicked Rochefort sharply in the face.

XII. BUCKINGHAM
AND MILADY

The crime was committed with the help of a woman.
—E. de Queiroz, THE MYSTERY OF THE SINTRA ROAD

Corso sat on the bottom step, attempting to light a cigarette. Still too stunned, he hadn't recovered his spatial sense and couldn't get the match in the same plane as the tip of the cigarette. Also, one of the lenses in his glasses was cracked, and he had to squint with one eye to see with the other. When the flame reached his fingers, he dropped the match between his feet and kept the cigarette in his mouth. The girl, who had been collecting the contents of the bag strewn over the ground, came and handed the bag to him.

"Are you all right?"

Her tone was neutral, without concern or worry. She was probably annoyed at the stupid way that Corso had been taken by surprise in spite of her warning on the phone. He nodded, humiliated and confused. But he was comforted when he remembered the look on Rochefort's face just before the kick. The girl had struck precisely and cruelly, but she didn't follow up as Rochefort lay sprawled on his back. He didn't challenge her or try to retaliate, but turned over in pain and dragged himself away, while she, no longer interested in him, went to pick up the bag. Corso, had he been able, would have gone after the man and, without a second thought, throttled him until he'd extracted everything from him. But the girl might not have allowed that, and anyway he was too weak even to stand.

"Why did you let him go?" Corso asked.

They could make Rochefort out in the distance, a staggering figure that was now disappearing into the darkness around a bend of the riverbank, among moored barges that looked like ghost ships in the low mist. Corso pictured the man retreating, humiliated, his face swollen, wondering how on earth a woman could have done so much damage. Corso felt jubilant at this revenge.

"We should have questioned the bastard," he complained.

She'd retrieved her duffel coat and sat next to him, but didn't answer immediately. She seemed tired.

"He'll come after us again," she said. She glanced at Corso before looking out at the river. "Be more careful next time."

He took the damp cigarette from his mouth and started turning it over in his fingers, which made it fall apart.

"I would never have believed..."

"Men don't. Until they get their faces pushed in."

Then he saw that she was bleeding. It wasn't much: a trickle of blood from nose to lip.

"Your nose," he said stupidly.

"I know," she said, touching her face and looking at the blood on her fingers.

"How did he do that to you?"

"It was my fault." She wiped her fingers on her jeans. "When I fell on top of him. We bumped heads."

"Where did you learn to do that kind of thing?"

"What kind of thing?"

"I saw you, by the water." Corso moved his hands in a clumsy imitation of her movement. "Giving him what he deserved."

She smiled gently and stood up, brushing the back of her jeans.

"I once wrestled with an angel. He won, but I learned a few things."

With her bloody nose she looked impossibly young. She put the bag over her shoulder and held out her hand to help him. He was surprised by her firm grip. When he stood up, all his bones ached.

"I thought angels fought with lances and swords."

She was sniffing, holding her head back to stop the blood. She looked at him sideways, annoyed.

"You've looked at too many Dürer engravings, Corso. And see where that's got you."

THEY RETURNED TO THE hotel via the Pont Neuf and the passageway along the Louvre, without any more incidents. By the light of a street lamp he saw that the girl was still bleeding. He took his handkerchief from his pocket, but when he tried to help her, she took it from him and held it to her nose herself. She walked, absorbed in her own thoughts. Corso glanced at her long, bare neck and perfect profile, her matte skin in the hazy light from the lamps of the Louvre. He couldn't tell what she was thinking. She walked with the bag on her shoulder, her head slightly forward, which made her look determined, stubborn. Occasionally, when they turned a dark corner, her eyes darted, and she put the hand holding the handkerchief down by her side, walking tense and alert. Under the archways of the Rue de Rivoli, where there was more light, she seemed to relax. When her nose stopped bleeding, she returned his handkerchief stained with dry blood. Her mood improved. She didn't seem to find it so reprehensible that he let himself be caught like a fool. She put her hand on his shoulder a couple of times, as if they were two old friends returning from a walk. It was a spontaneous, natural gesture. But maybe she was also tired and needed support. Corso, his head clearing with the walk, found it pleasant at first. Then it began to trouble him. The feel of her hand on his shoulder awakened a strange feeling in him, not entirely disagreeable but unexpected. He felt tender, like the soft center of a candy.

GRUBER WAS ON DUTY that evening. He allowed himself a brief, inquisitive glance at the pair—Corso in his damp, dirty coat, his glasses cracked, the girl with her face stained with blood—but otherwise remained expressionless. He raised an eyebrow courteously and nodded, indicating that he was at Corso's disposal, but Corso gestured that he didn't need anything. Gruber handed him a sealed envelope and both room keys. They stepped into the elevator, and Corso was about to open the envelope when he saw that the girl's nose was bleeding again. He put the message in his pocket and gave her his handkerchief again. The elevator stopped at her floor. Corso said she should call a doctor, but the girl shook her head and got out of the elevator. After a moment of hesitation, he followed her. She had dripped some blood on the carpet. In the room, he made her sit on the bed, then went to the bathroom and soaked a towel in water.

"Hold this against your neck and lean your head back."

She obeyed without a word. All the energy she'd shown down by the river seemed to have evaporated. Maybe because of the nosebleed. He took off her coat and shoes and lay her on the bed, putting the pillow under her back. Like an exhausted little girl, she let him. Before turning off all the lights except for the one in the bathroom, Corso looked around. Other than a toothbrush, toothpaste, and shampoo above the washbasin, the only belongings he could see were her duffel coat, the rucksack open on the sofa, the postcards bought the day before with *The Three Musketeers*, a gray sweater, a couple of T-shirts, and a pair of white panties drying on the radiator. He looked at the girl, embarrassed. He wasn't sure whether he ought to sit on the edge of the bed or elsewhere. His feeling from the Rue de Rivoli was still there in his stomach. He couldn't leave. Not until she felt better. In the end he decided to remain standing. He had his hands in his coat pockets, and with one of them he could feel the empty flask of gin. He glanced greedily at the liquor cabinet, its hotel seal still unbroken. He was dying for a drink.

"You were great down there by the river," he said. "I haven't thanked you."

She smiled sleepily. But her eyes, with pupils dilated in the darkness, followed Corso's every move.

"What's going on?" he asked.

She looked back at him with irony, implying that his question was absurd.

"They obviously want something you have."

"The Dumas manuscript? Or *The Nine Doors?*"

The girl sighed. None of this is terribly important, she seemed to be saying.

"You're clever, Corso," she said at last. "By now you should have a theory."

"I have too many. What I don't have is any proof."

"A person doesn't always need proof."

"That's only in crime novels. All Sherlock Holmes or Poirot has to do is guess who the murderer is and how he committed the crime. He invents the rest and tells it as if he knew it was a fact. Then Watson or Hastings congratulates him admiringly and says, 'Well done. That's exactly how it happened.' And the murderer confesses. The idiot."

"I'd congratulate you."

This time there was no irony in her voice. She was watching him intently, waiting for him to say or do something.

He shifted uneasily. "I know," he said. The girl still held his gaze, as if she truly had nothing to hide. "But I wonder why."

He was about to add, "This is real life, not a crime novel," but didn't. At this point in the story, the line between fantasy and reality appeared rather tenuous. The flesh-and-blood Corso, having an ID, a known place of residence, and a physical presence, of which his aching bones—after the episode on the stone steps—were proof, was increasingly tempted to see himself as a real character in an imaginary world. But that wasn't good. From there it was only a small step to believing he was an imaginary character who thinks he's real in an imaginary world. Only a small step to going nuts. And he wondered whether someone, some twisted novelist or drunken writer of cheap screenplays, at that very moment saw him as an imaginary character in an imaginary world who thought he *wasn't* real. That really would be too much.

These thoughts made his mouth unbearably dry. He stood in front of the girl, his hands in his pockets, his tongue like sandpaper. If I were imaginary, he thought with relief, my hair would stand on end, I'd exclaim "Woe is me!" and my face would be beaded with sweat. And I wouldn't be this thirsty. I drink, therefore I am. So he went to the liquor cabinet, broke the seal, took a miniature bottle of gin, and drank it in two gulps. He was almost smiling when he stood up and shut the cabinet like someone closing a reliquary. Things gradually assumed their proper proportions.

The room was fairly dark. The dim light from the bathroom slanted across the bed where the girl was still lying. He looked at her bare feet, her legs, the T-shirt spattered with dry blood. Then his gaze lingered over her long, tanned, bare neck. The half-open mouth showing the tips of her white teeth in the gloom. Her eyes still watching him intently. He touched the key to his room inside his coat pocket. He ought to leave.

"Are you feeling better?"

She nodded. Corso looked at his watch, although he didn't really care about the time. He didn't remember having switched on the radio as they came into the room, but there was music playing somewhere. A melancholy song, in French. A waitress in a bar, in a port, in love with a sailor.

"Right. I've got to go."

The woman on the radio went on singing. The sailor, predictably, had gone for good, and the girl in the bar gazed at his empty chair and the wet ring left by his glass on the table. Corso went to the bedside table to get his handkerchief and used the cleanest part to wipe his undamaged lens. Then he saw that the girl's nose was bleeding.

"It's started again."

A trickle of blood was running down to her mouth. She put her hand to her face and smiled stoically, looking at her blood-stained fingers.

"It doesn't matter."

"You ought to see a doctor."

She half closed her eyes and shook her head. She looked helpless in the dim light of the room, dark spots of blood staining the pillow. Still holding his glasses, he sat down on the edge of the bed and leaned over to hold the handkerchief to her nose. As he did so, his shadow, outlined on the wall by the slanting light from the bathroom, seemed to hesitate a moment between light and darkness before disappearing into the corner.

Then the girl did something strange, unexpected. She ignored the handkerchief he was offering her and stretched out her bloody hand to him. She touched his face and drew four red lines with her fingers, from his forehead to his chin. Instead of moving her hand away after this singular caress, she kept it there, damp and warm, while he felt drops of blood running down the four lines on his face. Her luminous irises reflected the light from the half-open door, and he shuddered, seeing in each the image of his lost shadow.

Another song was playing on the radio, but neither of them

was listening. The girl smelled of heat and fever, a gentle pulse throbbing under the skin of her bare neck. The room was light and dark, and things became lost in the deep shadows. She whispered something unintelligible very low, and light glinted in her eyes as she slipped her hand around his neck, spreading the trail of warm blood. With the taste of blood on his tongue, he leaned toward her, toward her soft, half-open mouth. She gave a gentle moan which seemed to come from far away, slow and monotonous, centuries-old. For a brief moment, in the pulse of her flesh all Lucas Corso's previous deaths came to life, as if brought by the current of a dark, slow river whose waters were as thick as varnish. He regretted that she didn't have a name that he could carve in his memory with that moment.

It lasted only a second. Then, recovering his clearheadedness, he saw his other self sitting on the edge of the bed, still in his coat, mesmerized as she moved back slightly and undid her jeans, arching her back like a beautiful young animal. He watched her with a kind of internal, benevolent wink, with a familiar indulgence both weary and skeptical. More with curiosity than desire. As she slid her zipper open, the girl uncovered a dark triangle that contrasted with the white cotton panties that came down with her jeans. Her long, tanned legs, stretched out on the bed, took Corso's—both the Corsos'—breath away, just as they had kicked in Rochefort's teeth. Then she lifted her arms and took off her T-shirt. She did it naturally, neither flirtatious nor indifferent. She kept her calm, sweet eyes on him until her T-shirt covered her face. Then the contrast was even greater—more white cotton, this time sliding upward over tanned skin, her firm, warm flesh, her slender waist, her heavy, perfect breasts outlined against the light in the darkness, her neck, her half-open mouth, and once again her eyes, with all the light in them stolen from the sky. With Corso's shadow in them, like a soul locked in the bottom of a double crystal ball or emerald.

At that moment, he knew that he wouldn't be able to do it.

He sensed it with the lugubrious intuition that precedes certain events and marks them, even before they have taken place, with inevitable disaster. To be prosaic, Corso realized, as he threw the rest of his clothes on top of his coat at the foot of the bed, that his initial erection was now in visible retreat. Cut down in its prime. Or, as his Bonapartist great-great-grandfather would have said, "La Garde recule." Totally. Anxiously he hoped that, as he was standing against the light, his unfortunately flaccid state wouldn't be noticed. Very carefully he lay facedown next to her tanned, warm body waiting in the dark and used what the emperor, out on the muddy fields of Flanders, would have called an indirect-approach tactic—sizing up the terrain from the middle distance and making no contact in the critical zone. From a prudent distance he played for time in case Grouchy arrived with reinforcements; he caressed the girl and kissed her unhurriedly on the mouth and neck. But no luck. Grouchy was nowhere to be seen. The old fool was chasing Prussians miles from the battlefield. Corso's anxiety turned to panic as the girl moved nearer to him and slipped her firm, warm thigh between his thighs. She must have become aware of the extent of the disaster. He saw her smile, a slightly disconcerted smile, but encouraging, as if to say something like, "I know you can do it!" Then she kissed him with extreme tenderness and put out her hand, to help things along. And just when he felt her hand at the very epicenter of the drama, Corso went down completely. Like the Titanic. Straight to the bottom, no half measures. The orchestra playing on deck, women and children first. The next twenty minutes were agony, atonement for all his sins. Heroic attacks meeting the immovable barrier of the Scottish fusiliers. The infantry on the attack glimpsing only the slightest chance of victory. Improvised incursions by the light infantry, in the vain hope of taking the enemy by surprise. Skirmishes of hussars and heavy charges by cuirassiers. But all attempts met with the same results—Wellington was messing around in a remote Belgian village while his pipers were playing the march of the Scots Greys in Corso's face. The Old Guard, or what remained of it, was glancing desperately in all directions, teeth clenched and face against the sheets, twenty minutes by the watch, which, for his sins, he hadn't removed. Drops of sweat the size of fists ran from the roots of his hair down his neck. He looked with wide staring eyes over the girl's shoulder, desperately wishing for a gun to shoot himself.

SHE WAS ASLEEP. HE stretched out an arm, carefully so as not to wake her, and searched for a cigarette inside his coat. When it was lit, he propped himself up on an elbow and stared at her. She was on her back, naked, her head tilted back on the pillow spotted with dry blood, breathing gently through her half-open mouth. She still smelled of fever and warm flesh. In the glow from the bathroom, which traced her outline in light and shadow, Corso admired her perfect body. This, he told himself, is a masterpiece of genetic engineering. He wondered what mixture of blood, or mysteries, saliva, skin, flesh, semen, and chance had commingled to create her. All women, all females produced by the human species were there, summed up in her eighteen- or twenty-year-old body. He saw the pulse at her neck, the almost imperceptible beat of her heart, the gentle curve from her back to her waist, widening at the hips. He put out his hand and stroked the small curly triangle down where the skin was a little lighter, between her thighs where he'd been unable to bivouac in the classic manner. The girl had taken the situation with perfect good humor. She'd made light of it, and they'd drifted into a lighthearted, friendly game once she understood that on Corso's part and in that particular bout, there wasn't going to be any more action. This eased the tension. Lacking a gun—they shoot horses, don't they?—in his blind rage he had wanted to dash his head against the corner of the bedside table in an attempt to crack his skull. But he ended up discreetly punching the wall, almost breaking his hand. Surprised by that and the sudden tension of his body, she looked at him. The effort it took not to shout out in pain calmed him. He even managed to smile rather tensely and say that this usually happened to him only the first thirty times or so. She laughed, her arms around him, and kissed his eyes and mouth, amused and tender. You idiot, Corso. I don't mind at all. He did the only thing he could at that point—a meticulous play of fingers in the right place, with results that were, if not glorious, at least satisfactory. As she caught her breath, the girl stared at him for a long time in silence before kissing him slowly, conscientiously, until the pressure of her lips diminished and she fell asleep.

The burning tip of his cigarette lit up his fingers in the darkness. He kept the smoke in his lungs as long as he could, then exhaled, watching the patterns it made in the segment of light above the bed. He felt the girl's breathing falter for a moment, and he looked at her sharply. She was frowning and moaning quietly, like a child having a nightmare. Then, still asleep, she half turned toward him, her arm under her bare breasts and her hand under her face. Who the hell are you, he asked her soundlessly once again, bad-temperedly, although he next leaned over to kiss her. He stroked her short hair, the curve of her waist and hips now sharply silhouetted against the light. There was more beauty in that gentle line than in a melody, a sculpture, a poem, or a painting. He moved closer and smelled her neck, and at that instant his own pulse started to hammer more strongly, awakening his flesh. Keep calm now, he said to himself. Don't panic this time. Let's continue. He didn't know how long he could keep it up, so he hurriedly stubbed out his cigarette and pressed himself against the girl. His body seemed to respond in a satisfactory manner. Then he parted her legs and at last, bewildered, entered a moist, welcoming paradise of warm milk and honey. He felt the girl shift sleepily and put her arms around him, although she wasn't quite awake. He kissed her on the neck, the mouth. She was moaning gently, and he realized that she was moving her hips in time with him. And when he sank right to the root of the flesh and himself, making his way easily to a place lost in his memory, she opened her eyes and looked at him surprised and happy, green reflections through her long damp lashes. I love you, Corso. IloveyouIloveyouIloveyouIloveyou. I love you. Later he had to bite his tongue in order not to say something equally stupid. Amazed and incredulous, he watched from a distance and did not know himself. He was attentive to her, watching her beats, movements, anticipating her desires and discovering her secret springs, the intimate key to the soft yet tense body wound firmly around his own. They went on like that for about an hour. Afterward Corso asked her if there was any risk of pregnancy, and she told him not to worry, she had everything under control. Then he put it all away deep inside him, next to his heart.

HE WOKE AT DAYBREAK. The girl was sleeping pressed against him. For some time he didn't move in order not to wake her. He made himself stop thinking about what had happened or might happen. He closed his eyes and drifted, enjoying the peace of the moment. He could feel her breath on his skin. Irene Adler, 223B Baker Street. The devil in love. The outline in the mist confronting Rochefort. The blue duffel coat falling slowly, unfolding, onto the quayside. And Corso's shadow in her eyes. She slept, relaxed and tranquil, aware of nothing. He couldn't link the images in his mind logically. At that moment, logic had no appeal. He felt lazy and content. He put his hand between her warm thighs and kept it there, very still. Her naked body, at least, was real.

Later, he got out of bed carefully and went to the bathroom. In the mirror he saw that he still had traces of dried blood on his face, and also, as the result of his encounter with Rochefort and the stone steps, a bluish bruise on his left shoulder, and another across a couple of ribs, which hurt when he pressed it. He had a quick wash and went to look for a cigarette. As he was searching in his coat, he found the note Gruber had handed him.

He cursed under his breath for having forgotten it, but there was nothing he could do about that now. So he opened the envelope and went back to the light in the bathroom to read the note. It was brief and its contents—two names, a number, and an address—made him smile malevolently. He glanced at himself again in the mirror. His hair was matted, and he needed a shave. He put on his glasses as if arming himself, a mean wolf off to hunt. He picked up his clothes and canvas bag quietly, and gave the sleeping girl a last glance. Maybe it was going to be a beautiful day after all. Buckingham and Milady were about to choke on their breakfast.

THE HOTEL CRILLON WAS too expensive for Flavio La Ponte. Enrique Taillefer's widow must have been paying the bill. Corso reflected on this as he paid his taxi on the Place Concorde and crossed the marble lobby to the stairs and room 206. There was a DO NOT DISTURB sign on the door and no sound when he rapped loudly three times. *Three punctures were made in the heathen flesh, and the White Whale's barbs were then tempered.* The Brotherhood of Nantucket Harpooners was about to be dissolved. Corso didn't know if he was sorry or not. He and La Ponte had once imagined an alternative version of *Moby-Dick.* Ishmael writes the story, places the manuscript in the caulked coffin, and drowns with the rest of the crew of the *Pequod.* Queequeg is the only survivor, the wild harpooner with no intellectual pretensions. In time he learns to read. One day he reads his friend's novel and discovers that Ishmael's account and his own memories of what happened are completely different. So he writes his own version of the story. *Call me*

Queequeg the story begins, and he titles it *A Whale*. From the harpooner's point of view, Ishmael was a pedantic scholar who blew things out of proportion. Moby Dick wasn't to blame, he was a whale like any other. It was all a matter of an incompetent captain wanting to settle a personal score instead of filling barrels with oil. "What does it matter who tore his leg off?" writes Queequeg. Corso could remember the scene around the table in Makarova's bar. Makarova, with her masculine, Nordic reserve, listening carefully as La Ponte explained the use of the caulking on the carpenter's coffin while Zizi looked on jealously from the other side of the bar. In those days, if Corso dialed his own number, Nikon would answer—he always pictured her emerging from the darkroom, her hands wet with fixative. That's what happened the night they rewrote *Moby-Dick*. They all ended up at Corso's place, emptied more bottles, and watched a John Huston movie on the VCR. They drank a toast to old Melville when the *Rachel*, searching the seas for her lost sons, at last finds another orphan.

That's how it was. But now, standing outside room 206, Corso couldn't feel the anger of one about to confront another with his treachery. Maybe because, deep down, he believed that in politics, business, and sex, betrayal was only a question of timing. Ruling out politics, he didn't know whether his friend was in Paris for business or sex. Maybe it was both, because even Corso, in his cynicism, couldn't imagine La Ponte getting into trouble for money alone. He remembered Liana Taillefer during their brief skirmish at his apartment, beautiful and sensual, wide hips, smooth pale skin, a wholesome Kim Novak playing the femme fatale. He arched an eyebrow—friendship consisted of that kind of detail—he could well understand La Ponte's motives. Maybe this was why, when La Ponte opened the door, he found no hostility in Corso's expression. He was barefoot and in pajamas. He just had time to open his mouth before Corso gave him a punch that sent him staggering across the room.

In other circumstances Corso might have relished the scene. A luxury suite with a view of the obelisk in the Place Concorde, a thick pile carpet, and a huge bathroom. La Ponte on the floor, rubbing his jaw, trying to focus after the punch. A huge bed, with two breakfast trays. And Liana Taillefer sitting, blond and stunned, holding a half-eaten piece of toast, one voluminous white breast peeping out of the plunging neckline of her silk nightdress. With a nipple two inches wide, Corso noted dispassionately as he shut the door behind him. Better late than never.

"Good morning," he said.

He walked to the bed. Liana Taillefer, motionless, still holding her toast, stared as he sat next to her. Putting the canvas bag on the floor and glancing at the breakfast tray, he poured himself a cup of coffee. For half a minute nobody said a word. At last Corso took a sip and smiled at Liana Taillefer.

"I seem to remember that the last time we met, I was somewhat abrupt...." The stubble on his chin emphasized his features. His smile was as sharp as a razor blade.

She didn't answer. She put the toast on the tray and covered her generous figure with her nightgown. In her stare there was no fear, arrogance, or rancor. She seemed almost indifferent. After the scene at his apartment, Corso would have expected hatred in her eyes. "They'll kill you for this," etc.... And they nearly had. But Liana Taillefer's steely blue eyes had the same expression as a puddle of icy water, and this worried Corso more than an explosion of fury. He pictured her looking impassively at her husband's corpse hanging from the light fixture in his room. He remembered the photograph of the poor bastard in his leather apron holding a plate, about to dismember a roast suckling pig. This was some serial they'd all written for him.

"Bastard," muttered La Ponte from the floor, still dazed but managing to focus on Corso at last. He started to get up, hanging on to the furniture. Corso watched him with interest.

"You don't seem pleased to see me, Flavio."

"Pleased?" La Ponte was rubbing his beard and looking at the palm of his hand from time to time, as if worried that he would find a tooth there. "You've gone nuts. Completely nuts."

"Not yet. But you've been trying to drive me there, you and your henchmen." He pointed at Liana Taillefer. "Including the grieving widow."

La Ponte moved closer, but kept a cautious distance. "Would you mind explaining what on earth you're talking about?"

Corso raised his hand and began counting on fingers.

"I'm talking about the Dumas manuscript and *The Nine Doors*. About Victor Fargas drowned in Sintra. About Rochefort, who's my shadow. He attacked me a week ago in Toledo, and last night here in Paris." He pointed at Liana Taillefer again. "And about Milady. And about you, whatever your part is in all this."

La Ponte, watching Corso count, blinked five times, once for each finger. He rubbed his beard again, this time not from pain but with confusion. He started to say something but thought better of it. When at last he made up his mind to speak, he addressed Liana Taillefer.

"What have we got to do with all this?"

She shrugged contemptuously. She wasn't interested in explanations, wasn't going to cooperate. Still reclining against the pillows, with the breakfast tray beside her, she was tearing apart one of the pieces of toast with her red polished nails. Her only other movement was her breathing, which made her ample bosom move up and down inside her plunging nightgown. She stared at Corso like a cardplayer waiting for an opponent to show his hand, as unmoved as a sirloin steak.

La Ponte scratched his bald spot. He wasn't too dignified, standing in the middle of the room in crumpled striped pajamas, his cheek swollen from the punch. He looked at Corso, at Liana Taillefer, and back again.

"I'd like an explanation," he said.

"That's a coincidence. An explanation is what I came here to get from you."

With another anxious glance at Liana Taillefer, La Ponte gestured toward the bathroom. "Let's go in there." He was trying to sound dignified, but his swollen cheek made his speech slurred. "You and me."

She remained inscrutable, calm, looking at them with the bored expression of someone watching a quiz show on TV. Corso thought to himself that he'd have to do something about her, but at the moment he couldn't think what. He picked up his canvas bag and went into the bathroom with La Ponte. La Ponte shut the door behind them.

"Can you tell me why you hit me?"

He spoke quietly, so the widow wouldn't hear. Corso put his bag on the bidet, noticed the whiteness of the towels, and rummaged around on the bathroom shelf before turning to La Ponte.

"Because you're a liar and a traitor," he answered. "You didn't tell me you were mixed up in all this. You've let them trick me, follow me, attack me."

"I'm not mixed up in anything. And I'm the only one who's been attacked here." La Ponte was examining his face in the mirror. "God! Look what you've done to me! I'm disfigured."

"I'll disfigure you even more if you don't tell what this is all about."

La Ponte prodded his swollen cheek and looked at Corso sideways. "It's no secret. Liana and I have . . ." He searched for the appropriate words. "Hm. We've . . . Well, you saw yourself."

"You've become intimate."

"That's right."

"When?"

"The day you left for Portugal."

"Who approached whom?"

"I did. In effect."

"What do you mean, in effect?"

"More or less. I went to see her."

"Why?"

"To make an offer for her husband's collection."

"The idea just suddenly popped into your head, did it?"

"Well, no. She phoned me first. I told you about it at the time."

"That's true."

"She wanted the manuscript her late husband sold me."

"Did she give any reason?"

"Sentimental value."

"And you believed her."

"Yes."

"Or rather, you didn't care."

"Really . . ."

"I know. What you really wanted was to screw her."

"That too."

"And she fell into your arms."

"Like a stone."

"Of course. And you came to Paris on your honeymoon."

"Not exactly. She had things to do here."

"And she asked you to come with her."

"That's right."

"Quite casually? All expenses paid, so you could continue the romance."

"Something like that."

Corso frowned. "Love is a beautiful thing, Flavio. When you really are in love."

"Don't be such a cynic. She's extraordinary. You can't imagine . . ."

"Yes, I can."

"No, you can't."

"I said I can."

"I'd bet you'd like to. She's quite a woman."

"We're getting off the subject, Flavio. We were here, in Paris."

"Yes."

"What were you two planning to do about me?"

"We weren't planning to do anything. We were thinking of finding you today or tomorrow. To get the manuscript back."

"Just like that."

"Of course. How else?"

"You didn't think I might refuse?"

"Liana had her doubts."

"What about you?"

"I didn't think it would be a problem. We're friends, after all. And 'The Anjou Wine' is mine."

"I see. You were her second choice."

"I don't know what you mean. Liana's wonderful. And she adores me."

"Yes. She seems very much in love."

"Do you think so?"

"You're a fool, Flavio. They've pulled the wool over your eyes as well as mine."

Corso had a sudden intuition, as piercing as a fire alarm. He pushed La Ponte aside and ran into the bedroom to find Liana Taillefer out of bed, half dressed and packing a suitcase. He saw her icy eyes—the eyes of Milady de Winter—and realized that while he was shooting his mouth off like an idiot, she'd been waiting for something, a sound or a signal. Waiting like a spider in its web.

"Good-bye, Mr. Corso."

He heard the words, her deep, husky voice. But he didn't know what she meant, other than that she was about to leave. He took another step toward her, not knowing what he would do when he reached her, before realizing that there was someone else in the room. A shadow behind him, to his left, by the door. He turned to face the danger. He knew he'd made another mistake, but it was too late. He heard Liana Taillefer laughing, like a wicked blond vamp in a movie, and felt the blow—his second in less than twelve hours—in the same spot as before, behind the ear. He just had time to see Rochefort fading, blurring.

He was out cold before he hit the floor.

XIII. THE PLOT THICKENS

*At this moment you're trembling because of the situation
and the prospect of the hunt. Where would the tremor
be if I were as precise as a railway timetable?*
—A. Conan Doyle, THE VALLEY OF FEAR

First he heard a voice in the distance, an unintelligible murmur. He made an effort, sensing that he was being spoken to. Something about his appearance. Corso had no idea what he looked like at that moment and couldn't have cared less. He was comfortable wherever he was, lying on his back. He didn't want to open his eyes and make his head hurt even more.

Somebody was gently slapping his face, so he reluctantly opened one eye. La Ponte was leaning over him, looking worried. He was still in pajamas.

"Get your hands off me," Corso said grumpily.

La Ponte sighed with relief. "I thought you were dead," he said.

Corso opened the other eye and started to sit up. He immediately felt his brain moving inside his skull like jelly on a plate.

"They really gave it to you," La Ponte informed him unnecessarily as he helped him up. Corso leaned on his shoulder and looked around the room. Liana Taillefer and Rochefort were gone.

"Did you see who hit me?"

"Of course I did. A tall, dark guy with a scar on his face."

"Have you ever seen him before?"

"No." La Ponte frowned indignantly. "Seemed like she knew him well enough, though.... She must have let him in while we were arguing in the bathroom. He had a split lip, too, it was all swollen. He'd had a couple of stitches." He felt his own cheek. The swelling was going down. He gave a spiteful little laugh. "Seems like everyone around here is getting what he deserves."

Corso, searching unsuccessfully for his glasses, gave him a resentful look. "What I don't understand," he said, "is why they didn't clobber you too."

"They wanted too. But I told them it wasn't necessary. They could just go about their business. I was an accidental tourist."

"You could have done something."

"Me? You must be joking. That punch you gave me was quite enough. I held up my hands like this.... Peace signs. I just sat on the toilet seat nice and quiet until they left."

"My hero."

"Better safe than sorry. Look at this." He handed Corso a folded piece of paper. "They left this behind, under an ashtray with a Montecristo cigar end in it."

Corso had trouble focusing on the handwriting. The note was written in ink, in an attractive copperplate hand with complicated flourishes on the capitals:

It is by my order and for the benefit of the State that the bearer of this note has done what he has done.

> *3rd of December 1627*
> *Richelieu*

Despite the situation, he almost burst out laughing. It was the safe-conduct granted at the siege of La Rochelle when Milady demanded d'Artagnan's head, later stolen at gunpoint by Athos *(Bite if you can, viper)* and used to justify the woman's execution to Richelieu at the end of the novel.... In short, too much for a single chapter. Corso staggered to the bathroom, turned on the faucet, and put his head under the stream of cold water. Then he looked at himself: puffy eyes, unshaven, and dripping with water. Not a pretty sight. And his head was buzzing like a wasps' nest. What a way to start the day.

La Ponte appeared in the mirror beside him, handing him a towel and his glasses.

"By the way," he said, "they took your bag."

"Son of a bitch."

"Hey, I don't know why you're taking it out on me. All I did was get laid."

ANXIOUS, CORSO CROSSED THE hotel lobby, trying to think quickly. But with every passing minute it became more unlikely that he would catch the fugitives. All was lost except for a single link in the chain, book number three. They still had to get hold of it, and that offered, at least, the possibility of getting to them, provided he moved quickly. While La Ponte paid for the room, Corso went to the phone and dialed Frieda Ungern's number. But the line was busy. He called the Louvre Concorde and asked for Irene Adler's room. He wasn't sure how things stood on that front, but he calmed down a little when he heard the girl's voice. He let her know the situation in a few words and asked her to meet him at the Ungern Foundation. He hung up as La Ponte was coming toward him, very depressed, putting his credit card back in his wallet.

"The bitch. She left without paying the bill."

"Serves you right."

"I'll kill her, with my own hands, I swear."

The hotel was extremely expensive and La Ponte was outraged at her treachery. He had a clearer idea now what was going on, and was gloomy as Ahab bent on revenge. They climbed into a taxi, and Corso gave the driver Baroness

Ungern's address. En route he told La Ponte the rest of the story—the train, the girl, Sintra, Paris, the three copies of *The Nine Doors*, Fargas's death, the incident by the river...La Ponte listened and nodded, incredulous at first and then stunned.

"I've been living with a viper," he moaned, shuddering.

Corso was in a bad mood. He remarked that vipers very rarely bit cretins. La Ponte thought about that. He didn't seem offended.

"She's a determined woman," he said. "And what a body!"

In spite of his resentment at the recent dent in his finances, his eyes shone lecherously as he stroked his beard.

"What a body," he repeated with a silly little smile.

Corso was staring out the window. "That's exactly what the Duke of Buckingham said."

"Who's the Duke of Buckingham?"

"In *The Three Musketeers*. After the episode with the diamond tags, Richelieu entrusts Milady with the duke's murder. But the duke imprisons her when she returns to London. There she seduces her jailer, Felton, an idiot like you but in a more puritanical, fanatical guise. She persuades him to help her escape, and while they're at it, to murder the duke."

"I don't remember that episode. So what happened to Felton?"

"He stabs the duke. He's executed later. I don't know whether for the murder or just for being stupid."

"At least he didn't have to pay the hotel bill."

They were driving along the Quai de Conti, near where Corso had had his next-to-last encounter with Rochefort. Just then La Ponte remembered something.

"Doesn't Milady have a mark on her shoulder?"

Corso nodded. They were passing the stone steps he'd fallen down the night before. "Yes," he answered. "Branded by the executioner with a red-hot iron. The mark of criminals. She already has it when she's married to Athos. D'Artagnan discovers it when he sleeps with her, and the discovery almost gets him killed."

"It's odd. Liana has a mark too, you know."

"On her shoulder?"

"No, on her hip. A small tattoo. Very pretty, in the shape of a fleur-de-lis."

"I don't believe it."

"I swear."

Corso didn't remember seeing a tattoo. But he'd hardly had time to notice that kind of thing during the brief encounter with Liana Taillefer at his apartment. It seemed like years ago. One way or another, things were getting out of control. This was more than a matter of quaint coincidences. It was a premeditated plan, too complex and dangerous for the performances of Liana Taillefer and her henchman to be dismissed as mere parody. Here was a plot with all the classic ingredients of the genre, and somebody—aptly, an Eminence Grise—must be pulling the strings. He felt Richelieu's note in his pocket. It was too much. And yet, the key to the mystery had to lie in its very strangeness and novelistic nature. He remembered something he'd read once, in Edgar Allan Poe or Conan Doyle: "This mystery seems insoluble for the very reasons that make it soluble: the excessive, outré nature of the circumstances."

"I'm still not sure whether this is one big hoax or an elaborate plot," he said aloud.

La Ponte had found a hole in the plastic seat and was nervously tugging at it. "Whatever it is, I don't like it." He whispered even though there was a pane of safety glass between them and the driver. "I hope you know what you're doing."

"That's the problem. I'm not sure."

"Why don't we go to the police?"

"And say what? That Milady and Rochefort, Cardinal Richelieu's agents, have stolen from us a chapter of *The Three Musketeers* and a book for summoning Lucifer? That the devil has fallen in love with me and been incarnated as a twenty-year-old girl who now acts as my bodyguard? What would you do if you were Inspector Maigret and I came and told you all that."

"I'd assume you were drunk."

"There you are."

"What about Varo Borja?"

"That's another thing." Corso groaned anxiously. "I don't even want to think about it. When he finds out that I've lost his book. . . ."

The taxi was making its way slowly through the morning traffic. Corso looked at his watch impatiently. At last they reached the bar where he'd sat the night before. There were people hanging around on the pavement and NO ENTRY signs on the corner. As he got out of the taxi, Corso saw a police van and a fire engine. He clenched his teeth and swore loudly, making La Ponte start. Book number three had got away too.

THE GIRL CAME TOWARD them through the crowd, the small rucksack on her back and her hands in her coat pockets. There were still faint traces of smoke rising from the roofs.

"The fire started at three A.M.," she said, taking no notice of La Ponte, as if he didn't exist. "The firemen are still inside."

"What about Baroness Ungern?"

She made a vague gesture, not exactly indifferent, but resigned, fatalistic. As if it had been preordained. "Her charred remains were found in the study. That's where the fire started. The neighbors say it must have been an accident. A cigarette not properly put out."

"The baroness didn't smoke," said Corso.

"She did last night."

Corso glanced over the heads of the crowd gathered at the police cordon. He couldn't see much—the top of a ladder leaning against the building, intermittent flashes from the ambulance at the door, and the tops of numerous helmets, policemen's and firemen's. The air smelled of burned wood and plastic. Among the onlookers, a couple of American tourists were photographing each other posing next to the policemen by the cordon. A siren sounded and then stopped. Somebody in the crowd said they were bringing out the corpse, but it was impossible to see anything. Not that there would be much to see anyway, thought Corso.

He met the girl's gaze fixed on him. There was no sign of the night before. Her expression was attentive, practical, that of a soldier approaching the battlefield.

"What happened?" she asked.

"I was hoping you'd tell me."

"I don't mean this." She seemed to notice La Ponte for the first time. "Who's he?"

Corso told her. After a moment's hesitation, wondering whether La Ponte would catch on, he said, "The girl I told you about. Irene Adler."

La Ponte didn't catch on. He gave a disconcerted look and put out his hand. She didn't notice, or pretended not to. She was facing Corso.

"You don't have your bag," she said.

"No. Rochefort got it at last. He went off with Liana Taillefer."

"Who's Liana Taillefer?"

Corso gave her a hard look, but she returned it calmly.

"You don't know the grieving widow?"

"No."

She was unruffled, showing no anxiety or surprise. In spite of himself, Corso believed her.

"It doesn't matter," he said at last. "The fact is, they've gone."

"Where?"

"I have no idea." He grimaced with desperation and suspicion, showing his teeth. "I thought you'd know something."

"I don't know anything about Rochefort. Or that woman."

Her indifference said that it was none of her business. This confused Corso even more. He'd expected some emotion from her. Among other things, she had set herself up as his protector. He thought she'd at least reproach him, something like, Serves you right for thinking you're so clever. But she said nothing. She looked around, as if searching for a familiar face in the crowd. He had no idea whether she was thinking about what had just happened or whether her mind was on other things.

"What can we do?" he asked no one in particular. He was bewildered. The attacks aside, he'd seen the three copies of *The Nine Doors* and the Dumas manuscript disappear one after the other. He had three corpses in his wake, if he counted Enrique Taillefer, and he'd spent a huge amount of money that was Varo Borja's, not his. . . . Varus, Varus, give me back my legions. Damn his luck. At that instant he wished he was thirty-five years younger so he could sit down on the curb and burst into tears.

"We could go and have a coffee," La Ponte suggested, jokingly, as if to say, "Come on, guys, things aren't that bad," and Corso realized that the poor dope had no idea of the enormous mess they were in. Still, coffee didn't seem such a bad idea. Under the circumstances he couldn't think of anything better.

"LET'S SEE IF I'VE understood." Some coffee ran down La Ponte's beard as he dunked his croissant in his cup. "In 1666 Aristide Torchia hid a special book. A kind of safety copy distributed over three copies. Is that it? With differences in eight of the nine engravings. And the three original copies have to be brought together for the spell to work." He took a bite of croissant and wiped his mouth on his napkin. "How am I doing?"

The three of them were sitting at a terrace opposite Saint Germain des Prés. La Ponte was making up for his interrupted breakfast at the Crillon. The girl, still aloof, was sipping an

orangeade through a straw and listening in silence. She had
The Three Musketeers open in front of her on the table and
was reading distractedly, turning a page from time to time, then
looking up and listening again. As for Corso, events had knotted
his stomach and he couldn't swallow a thing.

"Pretty good," he told La Ponte. He was leaning back in his
chair, hands in his pockets, and staring blankly at the church
tower. "Although it's possible that the complete work, the one
burned by the Holy Office, also consisted of three books with
illustrations altered so that only those who were truly expert
on the subject, the initiated, would be able to combine the three
copies correctly." He arched his eyebrows, frowning wearily.
"But now we'll never know."

"Who says there were only three? Maybe he printed four,
or nine different versions."

"In that case all this would be pointless. There are only three
known copies."

"So somebody wants to piece together the original book. And
is collecting the authentic engravings . . ." La Ponte spoke with
his mouth full. He ate his breakfast with a hearty appetite.
"But he doesn't give a damn about the market value. Once he
has the engravings, he destroys the rest. And murders the
owner. Victor Fargas in Sintra. Baroness Ungern here in Paris.
And Varo Borja in Toledo . . ." He broke off and looked at Corso
with disappointment. "This theory doesn't work. Varo Borja's
still alive."

"I have his copy. Had. And they certainly tried to take
care of me, setting me up first last night and then this
morning."

La Ponte didn't seem convinced. "If they set you up, why
didn't Rochefort kill you?"

"I don't know." Corso shrugged. He'd asked himself the
same question. "He had the chance twice but didn't do it. . . .
As for Varo Borja's still being alive, I don't know what to say.
He hasn't answered my calls."

"That makes him another potential corpse. Or a suspect."

"Varo Borja is a suspect by definition, and he has the means to have organized the whole thing." He pointed at the girl. She was reading and appeared not to be following the conversation. "I'm sure she could shed some light on all this, if she wanted to."

"And she doesn't?"

"No."

"So turn her in. When people are getting murdered, there's a name for it: accomplice."

"How can I turn her in? I'm up to my neck in this, Flavio. And so are you."

The girl stopped reading. She said nothing, just sipped her drink. Her eyes went from Corso to La Ponte, reflecting each in turn. Finally they rested on Corso.

"Do you really trust her?" asked La Ponte.

"Depends what for. Last night she fought off Rochefort and did a pretty good job of it."

La Ponte frowned, perplexed, and stared at the girl. He must have been trying to imagine her as a bodyguard. He must also have been wondering how far things had gone between Corso and her. Corso saw him stroke his beard and cast an expert eye over the parts of her body that were visible beneath the duffel coat. Even if La Ponte did suspect her, there was no doubt how far he would go himself if the girl gave him the chance. Even at times like these, the ex-chairman of the Brotherhood of Nantucket Harpooners was willing to return to the womb. Any womb.

"She's too pretty." La Ponte shook his head. "And too young. Too young for you, that is."

Corso smiled. "You'd be surprised how old she seems sometimes."

La Ponte tutted dubiously. "Gifts like that don't just fall from heaven."

The girl had followed the conversation in silence. Now they

saw her smile for the first time that day, as if she'd just heard a funny joke.

"You talk too much, Flavio Whatever-your-name-is," she said to La Ponte, who blinked nervously. She grinned like a naughty child. "And whatever there is between Corso and me is none of your business."

It was the first time she'd said anything to La Ponte. Embarrassed, he turned to his friend for support. But Corso just smiled.

"I think I'm in the way here." La Ponte made as if to stand up but he didn't. He stayed like that until Corso tapped him on the arm. A dry, friendly tap.

"Don't be stupid. She's on our side."

La Ponte relaxed slightly, but he still wasn't entirely convinced. "Well, let her prove it. Let her tell us what she knows."

Corso turned to the girl and looked at her half-open mouth, her warm, comfortable neck. Wondering if she still smelled of heat and fever, he became lost in the memory for a moment. Her limpid green eyes, full of the morning light, as always met his gaze, unflinching, lazy, and calm. Her smile, sardonic a second before, now changed. Once again it was like an imperceptible breath, an unspoken, conspiratorial word.

"We were talking about Varo Borja," said Corso. "Do you know him?"

She stopped smiling and again was a tired, indifferent soldier. Corso thought he saw a glint of contempt in her expression. He rested his hand on the marble-topped table.

"He may have been using me," he added. "And put you on my trail." But it seemed absurd. He couldn't picture the millionaire book collector resorting to a young girl to set a trap for him. "Or maybe Rochefort and Milady are working for him."

She went back to reading *The Three Musketeers* and didn't answer. But the mention of Milady reminded La Ponte of his wounded pride. He finished his coffee and raised a finger.

"That's the part I don't understand," he said. "The link with Dumas . . . What's my 'Anjou Wine' got to do with any of this?"

" 'The Anjou Wine' is yours only by accident." Corso had taken off his glasses and was peering at them against the light, wondering if the cracked lens would hold up with all the activity. "It's what I find most puzzling. But there are several intriguing coincidences. Cardinal Richelieu, the villain in the novel, is interested in books on the occult. Pacts with the devil give power, and Richelieu is the most powerful man in France. And to complete the cast, it turns out that the cardinal has two faithful agents who carry out his orders—the Count of Rochefort and Milady de Winter. She is blond, evil, and has been branded by the executioner with a fleur-de-lis. Rochefort is dark and has a scar on his face. . . . Do you see what I'm saying? They both have some sort of mark. According to Revelations, the servants of the devil can be recognized by the mark of the Beast."

The girl took another sip of her orangeade but didn't look up from her book. La Ponte shuddered, as if a ghost had just walked over his grave. He clearly felt it was one thing to get involved with a statuesque blonde and quite another to take part in a witches' sabbath. He fidgeted.

"Shit. I hope it's not contagious."

Corso looked at him unsympathetically. "There are too many coincidences, aren't there? Well, there's more." Breathing on his lenses, he wiped them on a napkin. "In *The Three Musketeers* it turns out that Milady has been married to Athos, d'Artagnan's friend. When Athos discovers that his wife bears the executioner's mark, he decides to carry out the sentence himself. He hangs her and leaves her for dead, but she survives, etc." He put his glasses back on. "Somebody must be having a lot of fun with all this."

"I can sympathize with Athos hanging his wife," said La Ponte, no doubt thinking of the hotel bill. "I'd like to get my hands on her and do the same myself."

"Or as Liana Taillefer did to her husband. I'm sorry to hurt your pride, Flavio, but she was never interested in you, not in the slightest. She just wanted the manuscript her late husband sold you."

"The bitch," muttered La Ponte bitterly. "I bet she did him in. Helped by our friend with the mustache and the scar."

"What I still don't understand," Corso went on, "is the link between *The Three Musketeers* and *The Nine Doors*. All I can think of is that Alexandre Dumas was on top of the world. He had success and the kind of power he wanted—fame, wealth, and women. Everything went swimmingly for him, as if he was privileged or had made some special pact. And when he died, his son, the other Dumas, wrote a strange epitaph for him: 'He died as he lived—unaware.'"

La Ponte sniffed. "Are you suggesting that Dumas sold his soul to the devil?"

"I'm not suggesting anything. I'm just trying to work out the serial that somebody's writing at my expense. It obviously all started when Enrique Taillefer decided to sell the Dumas manuscript. The mystery began there. His presumed suicide, my visit to his widow, my first encounter with Rochefort... And the job Varo Borja gave me."

"What's so special about the manuscript? Why is it important and to whom?"

"I have no idea." Corso glanced at the girl. "Unless she can tell us something."

She shrugged, not looking up from her book. "This is your story, Corso," she said. "I understand you're getting paid for it."

"You're involved too."

"Up to a certain point." She made a vague, noncommittal gesture and turned the page. "Only up to a certain point."

Annoyed, La Ponte leaned over toward Corso. "Have you tried giving her a couple of slaps?"

"Shut up, Flavio."

"Yes, shut up," echoed the girl.

"This is ridiculous," complained La Ponte. "Who does she think she is, talking like that? And instead of giving her the third degree, you leave her alone. This isn't like you, Corso. However cute she is, I don't think..." He searched for the words. "How did she get so uppity?"

"She once wrestled with an angel," explained Corso. "And last night I saw her kick Rochefort's teeth in, remember? The same guy who clobbered me this morning while you sat safely out of the way on the bidet."

"On the toilet."

"Makes no difference. You, in your pajamas, looking like Prince Danilo in *Imperial Violets*. I didn't know you wore pajamas when you slept with your conquests."

"What do you care?" La Ponte glanced at the girl, embarrassed, annoyed. "I get cold at night, if you must know. Anyway," he said, changing the subject, "we were talking about 'The Anjou Wine.' How's the report going?"

"We know that it's authentic, and in two different hands—Dumas's and his collaborator's, Auguste Maquet."

"What have you found out about him?"

"Maquet? There's not much to find out. He ended up on bad terms with Dumas with all sorts of lawsuits and claims for money. There is one strange thing—Dumas spent everything during his lifetime, he died without a penny. But Maquet was wealthy in his old age and even owned a castle. Things went well for each in his own way."

"What about the half-written chapter?"

"Maquet wrote the original story, a simple first draft, and Dumas added to it, giving it style and quality. You're familiar with the subject: Milady trying to poison d'Artagnan."

La Ponte peered anxiously into his empty coffee cup. "To conclude..."

"Well, I'd say that someone who believes he's Richelieu's

reincarnation has managed to collect all the original engravings from the *Delomelanicon*. Also the Dumas chapter. Somehow those things hold the key to what's going on. This person may be trying to summon Lucifer as we speak. Meanwhile, you no longer have your manuscript and Varo Borja doesn't have his book. I've really screwed up."

He took Richelieu's note out of his pocket and read it again. La Ponte seemed to agree with him. "The loss of the manuscript isn't serious," he said. "I paid Taillefer for it, but not that much." He gave a cunning little laugh. "At least with Liana I got paid in kind. But you really are in a mess."

Corso looked at the girl, who was still reading in silence. "Maybe she could tell us what kind of mess I'm in."

He frowned, then rapped the table with his knuckles like a cardplayer throwing in the towel. But she didn't respond to that either.

La Ponte grunted reprovingly. "I still don't understand why you trust her."

"He's already told you," the girl answered at last. She put the straw from her drink in between the pages of her book as a marker. "I look after him."

Corso nodded, amused, although there wasn't much in his situation to be amused about. "She's my guardian angel," he said.

"Really? Well, she should take better care of you. Where was she when Rochefort stole your bag?"

"You were there."

"That's different. I'm just a cowardly bookseller. Peace-loving. The exact opposite of a man of action. If I entered a coward competition, I'm sure I'd be disqualified for being too cowardly."

Corso wasn't listening because he'd just made a discovery. The shadow of the church tower was being thrown on the ground near them. The wide, dark shape had been gradually moving away from the sun. He noticed that the cross on the top was at the girl's feet, very near but not actually touching her. The shadow of the cross maintained a prudent distance.

HE PHONED LISBON FROM a post office to find out how the investigation into Victor Fargas's death was going. The news wasn't encouraging. Pinto had seen the forensic report: death by forced immersion in the pond. The police in Sintra believed that robbery was the motive. Perpetrator or perpetrators unknown. The good news was that for the time being nobody had linked Corso with the murder. Pinto added that he had put out the description of the man with the scar, just in case. Corso told him to forget about Rochefort, the bird had flown.

It didn't seem that the situation could get any worse. But at midday it got more complicated. As soon as Corso entered the hotel lobby with La Ponte and the girl, he knew something was wrong. Gruber was at the reception desk, and beneath his usual imperturbable expression there was a warning. As they approached, Corso saw the concierge turn casually to the pigeonhole with Corso's key and give his lapel a slight tug, a gesture recognized throughout the world.

"Keep going," Corso told the others.

He almost had to drag away the perplexed La Ponte. The girl walked ahead of them down the narrow corridor that led to the restaurant-bar, which looked out onto the Place du Palais Royal. Looking back at Gruber, Corso saw him place his hand on the telephone.

When they were outside on the street, La Ponte glanced nervously behind him. "What's the matter?"

"Police," explained Corso. "In my room."

"How do you know?"

The girl didn't ask any questions. She just looked at Corso, waiting for instructions. He took out the envelope that Gruber had handed him the night before, removed the note informing him of La Ponte's and Liana Taillefer's whereabouts, and replaced it with a five-hundred-franc bill. He did it slowly, so the others wouldn't notice that his hands were trembling. He sealed the envelope, crossed out his own name, and wrote Gruber's on it, then handed it to the girl.

"Give this to one of the waiters in the restaurant." The palms of his hands were sweating. He wiped them on the insides of his pockets. He pointed at a phone booth across the square. "Meet me over there."

"What about me?" asked La Ponte.

In spite of the seriousness of the situation, Corso almost laughed. "You can do what you like. Although I think you might have just gone underground, Flavio."

He crossed the square through the traffic, heading for the phone booth without waiting to see whether La Ponte was following. When he closed the door and inserted the card in the slot, he saw La Ponte a few meters away, looking around, anxious and defenseless.

Corso dialed the hotel number and asked for Reception.

"What's going on, Gruber?"

"Two policemen came, Mr. Corso," said the former SS officer in a low voice. "They're still up in your room."

"Did they give any explanation?"

"No. They wanted to know the date you checked in and asked if we knew what your movements had been up till two A.M. I said I didn't and passed them on to my colleague, who was on night duty. They also wanted a description, not knowing what you look like. I told them I would get in touch with them when you returned. I'm about to do so now."

"What will you tell them?"

"The truth, of course. That you came into the lobby for a moment and went straight out again. That you were accompanied by a bearded man. As for the young lady, they didn't ask about her, so I see no reason to mention her."

"Thanks, Gruber." He paused and added with a smile. "I'm innocent."

"Of course you are, Mr. Corso. All the guests at this hotel are innocent." There was a sound of paper being torn. "Ah. I've just been handed your envelope."

"Be seeing you, Gruber. Keep my room for a couple of days. I'm hoping to come back for my things. If there's any problem, charge it to my credit card. And thanks again."

"At your service."

Corso hung up. The girl was back, standing next to La Ponte. Corso went to them. "The police have my name. Somebody gave it to them."

"Don't look at me," said La Ponte. "This whole thing has been beyond me for some time."

Corso thought bitterly that it was beyond him too. He was in a boat, in a rough sea, with no one at the helm.

"Can you think of anything?" he asked the girl. She was the only strand of the mystery that was still in his hands. His last hope.

She looked over Corso's shoulder at the traffic and the nearby railings of the Palais Royal. She had taken off her rucksack and put it down by her feet. She was frowning, silent as usual, absorbed in her thoughts. She looked obstinate, like a little boy refusing to do what he's told.

Corso smiled like a tired wolf. "I don't know what to do," he said.

He saw her nod slowly, possibly as a conclusion to some line of reasoning. Or maybe she was just agreeing that, indeed, he didn't know what to do.

"You're your own worst enemy," she said at last, distantly. She looked tired too, as she had the night before when they returned to the hotel. "Your imagination." She tapped her forehead. "You can't see the forest for the trees."

La Ponte grunted. "Let's leave the botany for later, shall we?" He was becoming increasingly worried about the possibility of gendarmes appearing. "We should get out of here. I can hire a car. If we hurry, we can be across the border by tomorrow. Which is April first, by the way."

"Shut up, Flavio." Corso was looking into the girl's eyes, searching for an answer. All he saw were reflections—the light of the square, the passing traffic, his own image, misshapen and grotesque. The defeated soldier. But defeat was no longer heroic. It hadn't been for a long time.

The girl's expression changed. She stared at La Ponte now, as if for the first time he was worth looking at.

"Say that again," she said.

La Ponte stuttered, surprised. "You mean, about hiring a car?" His mouth was open. "It's obvious. On planes they have passenger lists. And on the train they can look at your passport...."

"I didn't mean that. Tell us what date it is tomorrow."

"The first of April. Monday." La Ponte fiddled with his tie, confused. "My birthday."

But she was no longer paying attention. She was bending over her rucksack, searching for something inside it. When she straightened up, she held *The Three Musketeers.*

"You haven't paid enough attention to your reading," she said to Corso, handing it to him. "Chapter one, first line."

Corso, surprised, took the book and glanced at it. "The Three Gifts of Monsieur d'Artagnan the Elder." As soon as he read the first line, he knew where they had to go to find Milady.

XIV. THE CELLARS OF MEUNG

It was a dismal night.
—P. du Terrail, ROCAMBOLE

It was a dismal night. The Loire, turbulent, was rising, threatening to flood the old dikes in the small town of Meung. The storm had been raging since late afternoon. Occasionally a flash of lightning illuminated the black mass of the castle, and bright zigzags cracked like whips on the deserted wet pavements of the medieval town. Across the river, in the distance, amid the wind, rain, and leaves torn from the trees, as if the gale had drawn a line between the recent past and a distant present, the headlights of cars could be seen moving silently along the highway from Tours to Orleans.

At the Auberge Saint-Jacques, the only hotel in Meung, a window was lit. It gave onto a small terrace which could be reached from the street. Inside the room, a tall, attractive blonde, her hair tied back, was dressing in front of the mirror. She had just zipped up her skirt, covering the small tattoo of a fleur-de-lis on her hip. She stood up straight, her hands behind her back to fasten the bra supporting her white, voluminous bust, which shook gently as she moved. Then she put on a silk blouse. As she buttoned it, she smiled to herself in the mirror, no doubt finding herself beautiful. She must have been preparing for a date, because nobody dresses at eleven at night unless they're going to meet someone. Although maybe her smile, with its hint of cruelty, was due to the new leather folder that lay on the bed, containing the pages of the manuscript of "The Anjou Wine" by Alexandre Dumas, père.

A flash of lightning lit up the small terrace outside. There, under the dripping eaves, Lucas Corso finished his damp cigarette and threw it on the ground. He turned up his collar against the wind and rain. During the next bolt of lightning, as intense as a giant camera flash, he saw Flavio La Ponte's deathly-pale face, drawn in light and dark, his hair and beard dripping wet. La Ponte resembled a tormented monk, or maybe Athos, taciturn as desperation, somber as punishment. There were no more flashes for a time, but Corso could distinguish, in the third shadow crouching beside them beneath the eaves, the slender shape of Irene Adler wrapped in her duffel coat. When at last another flash of lightning tore diagonally across the night sky, and thunder rolled across the slate roofs, her bright green eyes were suddenly lit up beneath the hood of her coat.

The journey to Meung had been short and tense. An interval of appalling visibility, in a car hired by La Ponte: the highway from Paris to Orleans, then sixteen kilometers toward Tours. La Ponte sat in the passenger seat and by the flame of a cigarette lighter studied the Michelin map they'd bought at a gas station. La Ponte was fuddled. Not far to go now, I think we're on the right road. Yes, I'm sure we are. The girl was in the back, silent. She watched Corso intently, and he met her eyes in the mirror every time they were passed by the dazzling lights of an oncoming car. La Ponte got it wrong, of course. They missed the turn and went in the direction of Blois. When they realized their mistake, they had to go back, driving in the wrong direction on the highway to get off it. Corso gripped the steering wheel, praying that the storm was keeping all the gendarmes indoors. Beaugency. La Ponte insisted they cross the river and turn left, but luckily they ignored him. They retraced their steps, this time on the Nationale 152—the same route d'Artagnan took in chapter one—amid gusts of wind and rain, the black, roaring expanse of the Loire to their right, the windshield wipers working furiously, and hundreds of little black dots, the shadows of raindrops, dancing in front of Corso's eyes as they passed other cars. At last they were driving through deserted streets, an old district of medieval rooftops, facades with thick beams in the shape of crosses: Meung-sur-Loire. Journey's end.

"She's about to leave," whispered La Ponte. He was soaked through, and his voice trembled from the cold. "Why don't we go in now?"

Corso leaned over to take another look. Liana Taillefer had put on a tight-fitting sweater over her blouse, emphasizing her spectacular figure, and from the closet she took a long, dark cape fit for a masked ball. She hesitated a moment, looked around, then put the cape over her shoulders and picked up the folder with the manuscript from the bed. At that instant she noticed the open window and went to close it.

Corso put out his hand to stop her. There was a flash of lightning almost above his head, and his dripping face was lit up. He was framed in the window, his hand held out as if accusingly at the woman who stood paralyzed with surprise. Milady screamed in wild terror, as if she had just seen the devil himself.

Corso jumped over the ledge and hit her so hard with the back of his hand that she stopped screaming and fell on the bed, scattering the pages of "The Anjou Wine." The change in temperature made his glasses steam up, so he took them off quickly, threw them on the bedside table, and flung himself at Liana Taillefer, who was trying to get up and reach the door. He grabbed her first by her leg and then pinned her to the bed by the waist while she struggled and kicked. She was strong, and he wondered where the hell La Ponte and the girl were. While he waited for them to help, he tried to hold the woman down by the wrists, keeping his face away from her clawing nails. Entwined, they rolled on the bedcover, and Corso ended up with his leg between hers and his face buried in her breasts. Up so close, feeling them through her fine wool sweater, he thought again how incredibly resilient they were. He felt an unmistakable erection and cursed in exasperation while he struggled with this Milady with the physique of a champion swimmer. Where are you when I need you, he thought bitterly. Then La Ponte arrived, shaking himself like a wet dog, seeking revenge for his wounded pride and, above all, for the hotel bill burning a hole in his wallet. The battle was beginning to resemble a lynching.

"I presume you're not going to rape her," said the girl.

She was sitting on the window ledge, still wearing her hood, watching the scene. Liana Taillefer had stopped struggling and was now motionless. Corso was on top of her, and La Ponte was holding her down by one arm and one leg.

"Pigs," she said loudly and clearly.

"Whore," grunted La Ponte, out of breath from the struggle.

After this brief exchange they all calmed down. Certain that she could not escape, they let her sit up. She flashed venomous looks at both Corso and La Ponte as she rubbed her wrists. Corso stood between her and the door. The girl was still at the window, now closed. She had lowered her hood and was regarding Liana Taillefer with curiosity. La Ponte, after toweling his hair and beard on the bedcover, started to gather the pages of the manuscript scattered about the room.

"We need to have a little talk," said Corso. "Like reasonable people."

Liana Taillefer glared at him. "We have nothing to talk about."

"That's where you're wrong, beautiful lady. Now that we've got you, I don't mind going to the police. Either you talk to us or you'll have to explain things to them. Your choice."

She frowned. She looked around like a hunted animal searching for any way out of a trap.

"Careful," said La Ponte. "She's up to something."

Her eyes shot glances as sharp as needles. Corso twisted his mouth theatrically. "Liana Taillefer," he said. "Or maybe we should call you Anne de Breuil, Comtesse de la Fère. You also go by the names of Charlotte Backson, Baroness Sheffield, and Lady de Winter. You betray your husbands and your lovers. A murderess and poisoner, as well as Richelieu's agent. Better known by your alias"—he paused dramatically—"Milady."

He stopped, because he'd just tripped on the strap of his bag, which was protruding from under the bed. He pulled it out, not taking his eyes off Liana Taillefer or the door. She obviously intended to escape at the first opportunity. He checked the contents of the bag, and his sigh of relief made all of them, including Liana Taillefer, look at him with surprise. Varo Borja's copy of *The Nine Doors* was there, intact.

"Bingo," he said, holding it up. La Ponte looked triumphant, as if Queequeg had just harpooned the whale. But the girl showed no emotion, an indifferent spectator. Corso returned the book to the bag. The wind whistled at the window, where the girl still stood. At intervals she was silhouetted by a flash of lightning, which was followed by a rumble of thunder, dull and muffled, that made the rain-spattered glass vibrate.

"Fitting weather," he said. "As you can see, Milady, we didn't want to miss our appointment.... We've come prepared to do justice."

"In a group and at night, like cowards," she answered, spitting out the words. "Just as they did to the other Milady. The only one missing is the executioner of Lille."

"All in good time," said La Ponte.

The woman was gradually recovering her confidence. Her own mention of the executioner didn't seem to have cowed her. She stared back at La Ponte defiantly. "I see that you've all got into your respective parts," she added.

"You shouldn't be surprised," answered Corso. "You and your accomplices have made sure of that." His face twisted into a wolflike smile that held neither humor nor pity. "We've all had such fun."

The woman tensed her lips. She slid one of her blood-red nails across the bedcover. Corso followed it with his eyes, fascinated, as if it were a blade, and he shuddered at the thought of how close it had come to his face during their struggle.

"You have no right to do this," she said. "You're intruders."

"You're wrong. We're part of the game, just as you are."

"But you don't know the rules."

"Wrong again, Milady. The proof is, we're here." Corso took his glasses from the bedside table, put them on, and pushed them up with his finger. "That's what was so tricky—accepting the nature of the game. Accepting the fiction by entering the story and following the logic of the text, not of the outside world . . . After that, it's easy. In the real world, many things happen by chance, but in fiction nearly everything is logical."

Liana Taillefer's red fingernail stopped moving. "In novels?"

"Especially in novels. If the protagonist follows the internal logic of the criminal, he'll arrive at the criminal. That's why hero and villain, detective and murderer always meet in the end." He smiled, pleased with his reasoning. "What do you think?"

"Brilliant," said Liana Taillefer sarcastically while La Ponte stared at Corso with openmouthed admiration. "Brother William Baskerville, I presume," she sneered.

"Don't be superficial, Milady. You're forgetting Edgar Allan Poe. And Dumas himself . . . I thought you were better read."

"As you can see, you're wasting your talent on me," she said. "I'm not the right audience."

"I know. That's exactly why I've come here—for you to take us to him." He looked at his watch. "In a little over an hour, it'll be the first Monday in April."

"I'd like to know how you guessed that too."

"I didn't guess." He turned to the girl who was at the window. "She put the book under my nose. And in an investigation like this, a book is more helpful than the outside world. It's a self-contained world, with no annoying interruptions. Like Sherlock Holmes's laboratory."

"Stop showing off, Corso," said the girl, annoyed. "You've impressed her enough."

The woman arched an eyebrow and looked at the girl, as if seeing her for the first time. "Who's she?"

"Don't tell me you don't know. You haven't seen her before?"

"No. They mentioned a young woman, but not where she came from."

"Who mentioned her?"

"A friend."

"Tall, dark, with a mustache and a scar on his face? And a split lip? Our good friend Rochefort! I'd really like to know where he is. Not far away, I hope. The two of you chose worthy characters, didn't you?"

At this, Liana Taillefer dug her blood-red nails into the bed-cover as if it were Corso's flesh, and her eyes glinted with fury. "Are the other characters in the novel any better?" There was disdain and an arrogance in the way Milady threw back her head and stared at them one after another. "Athos, a drunk. Porthos, an idiot. Aramis, a hypocritical conspirator . . ."

"That's one way of looking at it," said Corso.

"Shut up. What do you know?" She paused, jutting out her chin, her eyes fixed on Corso as if it was his turn now. "And as for d'Artagnan, he's the worst of the lot. A swordsman? He has only four duels in *The Three Musketeers*. He wins one because Jussac is getting to his feet, another because Bernajoux, in a blind attack, impales himself on d'Artagnan's sword. In his attack on the Englishmen all he does is disarm the baron. And it takes three thrusts to bring down the Comte de Wardes. As far as generosity goes——" she jerked her chin in La Ponte's direction—"d'Artagnan is even more of a miser than your friend here. He buys his friends a drink for the first time in England, after the Monk affair. Thirty years later."

And on the other side of the river, the executioner raising his sword . . .

"I see you're an expert, although I should have guessed you would be. All those serials you claimed to hate so much... Congratulations. You played to perfection the part of the widow sick of her husband's extravagances."

"I wasn't pretending. Most of his stuff was mediocre—useless old paper. Like Enrique himself. My husband was a fool. He never knew how to read between the lines, or appreciate quality. He was one of those idiots who go around collecting postcards of monuments and understand nothing."

"Unlike you."

"Of course. Do you know which were the first two books I

ever read? *Little Women* and *The Three Musketeers*. Each book, in a different way, made a deep impression."

"How moving."

"Don't be stupid. You asked questions and I'm giving you answers. There are unsophisticated readers, like poor Enrique, and readers who go into things in more depth, looking beyond stereotypes: the brave d'Artagnan, chivalrous Athos, kind-hearted Porthos, faithful Aramis . . . It makes me laugh!" And her laughter actually did ring out, as dramatic and sinister as Milady's. "Nobody has any idea. Do you know what my most enduring image is, the one I've always admired most? Of the woman fighting alone, faithful to an idea of herself and to the man she's chosen as her master, relying only on herself, ignominiously murdered by four heroes who are no more than cardboard cutouts. And what about her long-lost son, an orphan, who appears twenty years later!" She bowed her head, somber, and there was so much hatred in her eyes that Corso almost took a step back. "I can picture the engraving as if it were in front of me now—the river at night, the four scoundrels kneeling in prayer but without mercy. And on the other side of the river, the executioner raising his sword above the woman's bare neck . . ."

A flash of lightning suddenly cast its brutal light across her distorted face—the delicate white flesh of her neck, her eyes full of the tragic scene she described as vividly as if she had experienced it herself. Then the windowpanes shook as the thunder rumbled.

"Bastards," she whispered, absorbed, and Corso didn't know whether she meant him and his companions, or d'Artagnan and his friends.

The girl rummaged in her rucksack and pulled out *The Three Musketeers*. Like a neutral spectator she searched for a page. When she found it, she threw the book on the bed without a word. It was the engraving described by Liana Taillefer.

"Victa iacet Virtus," murmured Corso, shivering at the scene's similarity to the eighth illustration in *The Nine Doors.*

The woman calmed down at the sight of the engraving. She arched an eyebrow, cold and imperious once again.

"It's true," she admitted. "You can't tell me that d'Artagnan symbolizes virtue. He's just an opportunist. And don't mention his skills as a seducer. In the entire novel he conquers only three women, and two of them through deceit. His great love is a little *bourgeoise* with big feet, lady-in-waiting to the queen. The other is an English maid of whom he ignominiously takes advantage." Liana Taillefer's laughter rang out like an insult. "And what about his love life in *Twenty Years After?* Living with the landlady of a guesthouse to save himself the rent... What fine conquests! Maids, landladies, and servants!"

"But d'Artagnan does seduce Milady," Corso pointed out mischievously.

A flash of anger again cracked the ice in Liana Taillefer's eyes. If looks could kill, Corso would have died at her feet that instant.

"He doesn't seduce her," answered the woman. "The bastard crawls into her bed by deceit, passing himself off as another man." Her manner was cold again. "You and he would have made a good pair."

La Ponte was listening attentively. One could almost hear his brain working. He frowned. "You don't mean to say that you two..."

He turned to the girl for help. He was always the last to find out what was going on. But she remained impassive, watching as if none of this had anything to do with her.

"I'm an idiot," concluded La Ponte. He went to the window and started banging his head against the frame.

Liana Taillefer gave him a contemptuous look, then said to Corso, "Did you have to bring him?"

La Ponte was repeating, "I'm an idiot," banging his head hard.

"He thought he was Athos," Corso explained.

"Aramis, rather. Fatuous and conceited. Did you know he admires his shadow on the wall while he's making love?"

"I don't believe it."

"I assure you he does."

La Ponte forgot about the window. "We've gone off the subject," he said, red in the face.

"True," said Corso. "We were talking about virtue, Milady. You were giving us lessons on the subject with regard to d'Artagnan and his friends."

"And why not? Why should a bunch of show-offs who use women, accept money from them, and think only of getting ahead and making their fortune be more virtuous than Milady, who is intelligent and courageous, who chooses to work for Richelieu and serve him faithfully, and risk her life for him?"

"And commit murder for him."

"You said it yourself a moment ago—the internal logic of the narrative."

"Internal? It depends on your point of view. Your husband's murder happened outside the novel, not in it. His death was real."

"You're mad, Corso. Nobody murdered Enrique. He hanged himself."

"And I suppose Victor Fargas drowned himself? And Baroness Ungern got carried away with the microwave last night, did she?"

Liana Taillefer turned to La Ponte and the girl, waiting for someone to confirm what she'd just heard. She looked disconcerted for the first time since they'd come in through the window.

"What are you talking about?"

"About the nine correct engravings," said Corso, "from *The Nine Doors of the Kingdom of Shadows.*"

The sound of a clock striking could be heard outside the closed window, through the wind and rain. Almost simultaneously a clock inside the building, downstairs, struck eleven times.

"I see there are more madmen in this affair," said Liana Taillefer. She was watching the door. There had been a noise behind it as the final chime struck. A glint of triumph flashed in her eyes.

"Careful," whispered La Ponte with a start. Corso knew what was going to happen. Out of the corner of his eye he saw the girl stand up straight, tense and alert, and he felt a rush of adrenaline.

They all looked at the door handle. It was turning very slowly, as in the movies.

"GOOD EVENING," SAID ROCHEFORT.

He was wearing a raincoat buttoned to the neck, shiny with rain. His dark eyes shone intensely beneath his felt hat. The pale zigzag of the scar stood out against his dark face. The bushy black mustache accentuated his southern looks. He stood motionless at the door for some fifteen seconds, his hands in his coat pockets, a puddle forming around his shoes. Nobody said a word.

"I'm glad you're here," said Liana Taillefer at last. Rochefort nodded briefly but didn't answer. Still sitting on the bed, she pointed at Corso. "They were becoming impertinent."

"Not too much, I hope," said Rochefort. His voice, as Corso remembered it from the Sintra road, was pleasant, educated, and had no definite accent. He didn't move from the doorway, his eyes fixed on Corso, as if La Ponte and the girl didn't exist. His lower lip still looked swollen, with traces of Mercurochrome, two stitches holding the recent wound together. Souvenir from the banks of the river Seine, thought Corso malevolently. He looked with interest to see the girl's reaction. But after her initial surprise, she had resumed the role of detached spectator.

Not taking his eyes off Corso, Rochefort asked Milady, "How did they get here?"

Milady gestured vaguely. "They're smart." A quick look at La Ponte. "One of them, anyway."

Rochefort nodded. His eyes half-closed, he seemed to be analyzing the situation. "This complicates things," he said. He took off his hat and threw it on the bed.

Liana Taillefer smoothed down her skirt and stood up with a sigh of agreement. Corso half turned toward her, tense and hesitant. Then Rochefort took his hand out of his coat pocket, and Corso deduced that the man was left-handed. The discovery didn't do him much good—the left hand held a snub-nosed revolver, small and dark blue, almost black. Meanwhile, Liana Taillefer went over to La Ponte and took the Dumas manuscript from his hands.

"Now call me a whore again." She was so close, she could have spat in his face. "If you have the guts."

La Ponte didn't. He was a born survivor. His intrepid-harpooner act was reserved for moments of alcohol-induced euphoria. "I was just passing through," he said placatingly, wanting to wash his hands of the whole business.

"What would I do without you, Flavio?" said Corso, resigned.

La Ponte looked injured. "You're being unfair," he said, and went and stood by the girl, which must have seemed to him the safest place in the room. "From a certain point of view, this is your adventure, Corso. And what's death to a guy like you? Nothing. A formality. Anyway, you're getting paid a fortune. And life is basically unpleasant." Looking down the barrel of Rochefort's revolver, he put his arm around the girl's shoulder and gave a melancholy sigh. "I hope nothing happens to you. But if it does, it'll be harder for us: we have to go on living."

"Traitor."

La Ponte looked saddened. "My friend, I'll ignore that last remark. You're overwrought."

"Of course I'm overwrought, you sewer rat."

"I'll ignore that too."

"Son of a bitch."

"I get the message, old buddy. Friendship is made up of little touches like that."

"Nice to see you've kept your team spirit," said Milady caustically.

Corso was thinking fast, even though there was nothing he could do. No amount of thinking could get the gun out of Rochefort's hand, although it wasn't pointing at anyone in particular. Rochefort seemed rather halfhearted, as if just showing the gun was all that was needed to get the desired effect. But however intense Corso's desire to settle a few scores with the man with the scar, he didn't possess the technical skill to do so. With La Ponte not in the running, the girl was his only hope of shifting the balance of power. But unless she was an extremely accomplished actress, he couldn't hope for anything on that flank. Irene Adler had shaken herself free of La Ponte's arm and sat down on the window ledge, from where she observed them all with inexplicable indifference. She seemed determined to stay out of it.

Liana Taillefer went over to Rochefort, holding the Dumas manuscript, delighted to have retrieved it so quickly. Corso found it strange that she showed no similar interest in *The Nine Doors*, which still lay inside the canvas bag at the foot of the bed.

"What do we do now?" he heard her whisper to Rochefort.

To Corso's surprise, Rochefort looked unsure. He moved the revolver from side to side, as if he not knowing where to point it. Exchanging a long and meaningful look with Milady, he took his right hand out of his pocket and passed it over his face, hesitant. "We can't leave them here," he said.

"We can't take them with us either," she said.

He nodded slowly. Judging by his renewed grip on the revolver, his indecision vanished. Corso felt his abdominal muscles tense as Rochefort aimed the gun at him. He tried to make some sort of syntactically coherent protest, but all he managed was an indistinct, guttural sound.

"You're not going to kill him, are you?" asked La Ponte.

"Flavio," Corso managed to say in spite of the dryness in his mouth. "If I get out of this, I swear I'll smash your face in. Completely."

"I was just trying to help."

"Better help your mother get off the streets."

"OK, OK, I'll shut up."

"Yes, shut up," said Rochefort. Keeping the revolver on Corso, he locked the door behind him and put the key in his coat pocket. What is there to lose, thought Corso, his pulse throbbing at his temples and wrists. The drums of Waterloo rolled somewhere in his memory, when, in the final moment of clarity before desperation set in, he found himself working out the distance between him and the gun and how long it would take him to cross it. He wondered when the first shot would be fired and where it would hit him. The chances of not being hit were minimal, but if he waited five seconds longer, he might have no chance at all. So the bugle sounded. The last charge with Ney at the head, the bravest of the brave, before the emperor's weary eyes. Against Rochefort instead of the Scots Guards, but a bullet was still a bullet. This is ridiculous, he told himself just before he went into action. And he wondered if the bullet in his chest would be real or imaginary, wondered if he'd find himself floating in the void or in the Valhalla for fictional heroes. If only the luminous eyes he felt staring intently at his back—the emperor? The devil in love?—would be waiting for him in the darkness to guide him to the other side.

Then Rochefort did something odd. He raised his free hand, as if to say, "Give me time," and started to put the revolver back in his pocket. The movement lasted only a moment, and he aimed the gun at Corso once again, but without conviction. And Corso, his pulse racing, his muscles taut, about to leap blindly forward, held back, bewildered, realizing it wasn't time for him to die.

Stunned, he watched Rochefort cross the room, press the button for an outside line, then dial a long number. From where he stood, he could hear the sound of the phone ringing on the line and then a click.

"I've got Corso here," said Rochefort. He waited, still lazily pointing the gun at a vague point in space. He said yes twice. Then he listened, motionless, and muttered OK before finally hanging up.

"He wants to see him," he said to Milady. They both turned to look at Corso. Milady was annoyed, Rochefort anxious.

"This is ridiculous," she complained.

"He wants to see him," Rochefort said again.

Milady shrugged, took a step, and angrily turned a few pages of "The Anjou Wine."

"As for us . . ." La Ponte began.

"You're staying here," said Rochefort, pointing the gun at him. He licked the wound on his lip. "The girl too."

In spite of his split lip he didn't seem to bear her any grudge. Corso even thought he saw a gleam of curiosity as Rochefort looked at her. Rochefort then handed Liana Taillefer the revolver. "Make sure they don't get out."

"Why don't you stay here?"

"He wants me to take him. It's safer."

Milady nodded sullenly. She'd obviously imagined herself playing a different part that evening. But like her fictional namesake, she was a disciplined hired assassin. In exchange for the weapon she gave Rochefort the Dumas manuscript. She scrutinized Corso. "I hope he doesn't give you any trouble."

Rochefort smiled confidently. He took a large switchblade from his pocket and stared at it thoughtfully, as if he'd only just remembered it was there. His white teeth were bright against his dark, scarred face. "I don't think he will," he answered, putting back the knife unopened and gesturing to Corso in a way that was both friendly and sinister. He took his hat from the bed, turned the key in the lock, and motioned toward the corridor with an exaggerated bow, as if he were holding a large plumed hat.

"His Eminence awaits, sir," he said, and gave a short, dry laugh that perfectly befitted a skilled henchman.

Before leaving the room, Corso looked at the girl. Milady was pointing the gun at her and La Ponte, but the girl had turned her back and was paying no attention. She was leaning against the window, looking out at the wind and rain, silhouetted against a night sky illuminated by flashes of lightning.

THEY WENT OUT INTO the storm. Rochefort held the folder with the Dumas manuscript under his raincoat to protect it from the rain. He led Corso through narrow streets to the old part of town. Blasts of rain shook the branches of the trees and splashed noisily in the puddles and on the paving stones. Large drops poured through Corso's hair and down his face. He turned up his collar. The town was in darkness, and there was not a soul to be seen. Only the brightness of the storm lit up the streets now and then, showing the medieval roofs, Rochefort's dark profile beneath his dripping hat, the shadows of the two men on the wet ground. The electrical discharges, like thunder from hell, struck the turbulent current of the Loire with a sound like the cracking of whips.

"Wonderful evening," said Rochefort, inclining his head to Corso to make himself heard above the roar.

He seemed to know his way. He walked confidently, turning occasionally to make sure his companion was still there. He didn't need to, because at that moment Corso would have followed him to the very gates of hell. And Corso didn't rule out the possibility that this in fact might be their ultimate destination. With each successive flash of lightning he saw a medieval archway, a bridge over an ancient moat, a sign saying

BOULANGERIE-PATISSERIE, a deserted square, a conical tower, and finally an iron gate with the sign CHÂTEAU DE MEUNG-SUR-LOIRE. XIIIÈME-XIIIIÈME SIÈCLE.

A window was lit up in the distance, beyond the gate, but Rochefort went right, and Corso followed. They walked along a stretch of ivy-clad wall until they reached a half-hidden door in the wall. Rochefort took out a huge, ancient iron key and put it in the lock.

"Joan of Arc came through this door," he told Corso as he turned the key. One final flash of lightning revealed steps descending into darkness. In the momentary brightness Corso also saw Rochefort's smile, his dark eyes shining beneath the hat, the livid scar on his cheek. At least the man was a worthy opponent, he thought. Nobody could complain about the staging; it was impeccable. In spite of himself he was beginning to feel a kind of twisted sympathy for this Rochefort—whoever he was—playing the villain so conscientiously. Alexandre Dumas would have approved.

Rochefort now held a small flashlight that lit up the long, narrow staircase disappearing into the cellar.

"You first," he said.

Their steps echoed around the turns of the passageway. Corso was soon shivering inside his wet coat. Cold, musty air, smelling of the damp of centuries, rose to meet them. The beam of light showed worn steps, water stains on the vaulted ceiling. The staircase ended in a narrow corridor with rusty railings. For a moment Rochefort shone the flashlight on a circular pit to their left.

"These are the ancient dungeons of Bishop Thibault D'Aussigny," he told Corso. "From there they threw the corpses into the Loire. François Villon was a prisoner here." And he muttered the following line melodramatically: *Ayez pitié, ayez pitié de moi* . . . Definitely a well-educated villain. Self-assured and with a hint of didacticism. Corso couldn't decide whether this made the situation better or worse. But a thought had been going through his head since they entered the passageway: If all is lost, we may as well jump in the river. But he didn't find his joke funny.

The passageway now rose beneath the dripping arches. The bright eyes of a rat glittered at the end of the gallery, and the animal disappeared with a cry. The passageway widened into a circular room whose ceiling, supported by pointed ribs, rested on a thick central column.

"The crypt," said Rochefort, moving the flashlight beam around. He was becoming talkative. "Twelfth century. The women and children hid here when the castle was attacked."

Very interesting. But Corso wasn't in the mood to appreciate the information provided by his outlandish guide. He was tense and alert, waiting for the right moment. They now climbed a spiral staircase, the storm still flashing and booming beyond the castle walls, filtered through the slot windows.

"Only a few meters more and we're there," said Rochefort from behind and below. He sounded quite conciliatory. The flashlight shone between Corso's legs. "Now that this business is nearly over," he added, "I must tell you something. In spite of everything, you did well. The proof is that you got this far.... I hope you aren't too sore about what happened by the Seine and at the Hotel Crillon. Occupational hazards."

He didn't say which occupation, but it didn't matter. Corso turned casually and stopped, as if to answer or ask him a question. The movement wasn't in the least suspicious, so Rochefort didn't object and wasn't at all ready when Corso, in the same motion, fell on him, his arms and legs braced against the wall so he wouldn't be dragged down the stairs. Rochefort's position was different—the steps were narrow, the wall smooth and without handholds, and in addition he had been caught off guard. The flashlight, miraculously intact, illuminated the scene for several moments as it rolled down the staircase: Rochefort with his eyes wide and a stunned look on his face, flailing wildly, trying desperately to grab something, falling down the spiral staircase, his hat rolling until it stopped on one of the steps ... Then, six or seven meters farther down, a muffled sound, something like *thump* or maybe *thud.* Corso, still gripping the walls with his arms and legs so he wouldn't accompany his opponent on his uncomfortable journey, now sprang into action. His heart pounded uncontrollably as he ran down the stairs, taking three steps at a time. He picked up the flashlight on his way. At the bottom lay Rochefort rolled into a ball, moving weakly, in pain.

"Occupational hazard," said Corso, shining the flashlight on his own face so that, from the floor, Rochefort could see his friendly smile. Then he kicked him in the head and heard it slam hard against the bottom step. He raised his foot to kick again, just to make sure, but one look told him it wasn't necessary: Rochefort was lying with his mouth open and blood was trickling from his ear. Corso leaned over to see if the man was breathing and saw that he was. Then he opened his raincoat and rifled through his pockets. He took the switchblade, a wallet full of money, a French ID, and the folder with the Dumas manuscript, which he put under his coat, between his belt and shirt. Then he pointed the flashlight beam at the staircase and went back up, to the top this time, where there was a landing with a door that had thick iron hinges and hexagonal nailheads. A crack of light filtered from beneath it. He stood motionless for some thirty seconds, trying to catch his breath and calm the beating of his heart. The solution to the mystery lay on the other side of the door, and he prepared to face it with his teeth clenched, the flashlight in one hand and Rochefort's knife, which opened with a menacing click, in the other.

Knife in hand, hair soaked and disheveled, and eyes shining with homicidal determination—that's how I saw Corso enter the library.

XV. CORSO AND RICHELIEU

And I, who had created a short novel around him,
had been completely mistaken.
—Souvestre et Allain, FANTOMAS

The time has come to reveal the narrator. Faithful to the tradition that the reader of a mystery novel must possess the same information as the protagonist, I have presented the events only from Lucas Corso's perspective, except on two occasions: chapters 1 and 5 of this story, when I had no choice but to appear myself. In both these cases, and as now for the third and final time, I used the first person for the sake of coherence. It would have been absurd to refer to myself as "he," a publicity stunt that may have yielded dividends for Julius Caesar in his campaign in Gaul but would have been judged, in my case, and quite rightly, as unpardonable pedantry. There is another, more perverse reason: telling the story as if I were Dr. Sheppard addressing Poirot struck me as, if not ingenious (everybody does that sort of thing now), then an amusing device. After all, people write for amusement, or excitement, or out of self-love, or to have others love them. I write for some of the same reasons. To quote Eugene Sue, villains who are all of a piece, if you'll permit me the expression, are very rare phenomena. Assuming—and it may be too much to assume—that I am a villain.

The fact is that I, the undersigned, Boris Balkan, was there in the library, awaiting our guest. Corso entered suddenly, knife in hand and an avenging gleam in his eye. I noticed that he had no escort, which worried me slightly, although I retained my mask of imperturbability. Otherwise I had set the stage well: the library in darkness, a candelabrum burning on the desk before me, a copy of *The Three Musketeers* in my hands ... I even wore a red velvet jacket that was—it must have seemed like pure coincidence to Corso but was in fact nothing of the sort—strongly reminiscent of a cardinal's purple.

My big advantage was that I was expecting Corso, with or without an escort, but he wasn't expecting me. I made the most of his surprise. The knife he held was worrying, together with the menacing look in his eyes, so I decided to speak to forestall any move from him.

"Congratulations," I said, closing the book as if his arrival had interrupted my reading. "You've managed to play the game right to the end."

He stood staring at me from the other end of the room, and I have to say that I found his look of disbelief highly amusing.

"Game?" he managed to say hoarsely.

"Yes, game. Suspense, uncertainty, a high level of skill ... The possibility of acting freely yet according to rules, as an end in itself. With a sense of tension and pleasure at the difference from ordinary life...." These were not my own words, but Corso wouldn't know that. "Do you think that's an adequate definition? As the second book of Samuel says: 'Let the young men now arise, and play before us.' Children are the perfect players and readers: they do everything with the utmost seriousness. In essence, games are the only universally serious activity. They leave no room for skepticism, wouldn't you agree? However incredulous or doubting you might be, if you want to play, you have no choice but to follow the rules. Only the person who respects the rules, or at least knows and applies them, can win. Reading a book is the same: you have to accept the plot and the characters to enjoy the story." I paused, trusting that my flow of words had had a sufficiently calming effect. "By the way, you didn't get here on your own. Where is he?"

"Rochefort?" Corso was grimacing in a very unpleasant way. "He had an accident."

"You call him Rochefort, do you? How amusing and appropriate. I see you've followed the rules. I don't know why it should surprise me."

Corso treated me to a rather unnerving smile. "He certainly looked surprised the last time I saw him."

"That sounds rather alarming." I smiled coolly, although I actually was alarmed. "I hope nothing serious happened."

"He fell down the stairs."

"What?"

"You heard me. But don't worry. Your henchman was still breathing when I left him."

"Thank God." I managed to smile again and hide my unease. This went beyond what I had planned. "So you've done a touch of cheating, have you? Well," I said, spreading my hands magnanimously, "no need to worry about it."

"I'm not. You're the one who should be worried."

I pretended not to hear this. "The important thing is that you've arrived," I went on, although I'd lost the thread momentarily. "As far as cheating goes, you have illustrious predecessors. Theseus escaped from the labyrinth thanks to Ariadne's thread, Jason stole the golden fleece with Medea's help.... The Kaurabas used subterfuge to win at dice in the Mahabharata, and the Achaeans checkmated the Trojans by moving a wooden horse. Your conscience is clear."

"Thanks, but my conscience is my business."

From his pocket he took Milady's letter folded in four, and he threw it on the table. I immediately recognized my own handwriting, with the slightly affected capitals. *It is by my order and for the benefit of the State that the bearer of this note, etc.*

"I hope, at least, that the game was enjoyable," I said, holding the paper in the candle flame.

"At times."

"I'm glad." I dropped the letter in the ashtray, and we both watched it burn. "In matters of literature, the intelligent reader may even enjoy the strategy used to turn him into the victim. I believe that enjoyment is an excellent reason for playing. Or for reading a story, or writing one."

I stood up, holding *The Three Musketeers,* and paced around the room, glancing discreetly at the clock on the wall. There were still twenty long minutes to go before twelve. The gilding shone on the spines of the ancient books lined up on their shelves. I looked at them a moment, as if forgetting Corso, then turned to him.

"There they are." I made a sweeping gesture to include the whole library. "They are silent and yet talk among themselves. They communicate through their authors, just as the egg uses the hen to produce another egg."

I put *The Three Musketeers* back on its shelf. Dumas was in good company: between *Los Pardellanes* by Zevaco and *The Knight with the Yellow Doublet* by Lucas de René. As there was time to spare, I opened *The Knight* at the first page and began to read aloud:

As Saint Germain l'Auxerrois struck twelve, three horsemen descended the Rue des Astruces, each wrapped in a cape, seemingly as sure as the stride of their horses....

"The first lines," I said. "Always those extraordinary first lines. Do you remember our conversation about Scaramouche? *He was born with the gift of laughter....* Some opening sentences leave their mark a whole lifetime, don't you agree? *Of arms and the man I sing.* Have you never played this game with someone you trust? *A modest young man headed in midsummer,* or that other one, *For a long time I used to go to bed early.* And of course, *On the 15th of May 1796, General Bonaparte entered Milan.*"

Corso frowned.

"You're forgetting the one that brought me here: *On the first Monday of April 1625, the market town of Meung, the birthplace of the author of* Roman de la Rose, *was in a state of commotion.*"

"Indeed, chapter one," I said. "You have done very well."

"That's what Rochefort said before he fell down the stairs."

There was silence, broken only by the clock striking a quarter to twelve. Corso pointed at the clock face. "Fifteen minutes to go, Balkan."

"Yes," I said. The man was devilishly intuitive. "Fifteen minutes till the first Monday in April."

I put *The Knight with the Yellow Doublet* back on the shelf and continued pacing. Corso stood watching me, holding the knife.

"You could put that away," I ventured.

He hesitated a moment before shutting the blade and putting it away in his pocket, still watching me. I smiled approvingly and again indicated the library.

"One is never alone with a book nearby, don't you agree?" I said, to be conversational. "Every page reminds us of a day that has passed and makes us relive the emotions that filled it. Happy hours underlined in red pencil, dark ones in black . . . Where was I, then? What prince called me his friend, what beggar called me his brother?" I hesitated, searching for another phrase to round off the idea.

"What son of a bitch called you his buddy?" suggested Corso.

I looked at him reprovingly. The wet blanket insisted on bringing down the tone. "No need to be unpleasant."

"I'll do what I please. Your Eminence."

"I detect sarcasm," I said, offended. "From that I deduce that you have given in to prejudice, Mr. Corso. It was Dumas who made Richelieu a villain when he wasn't one, and falsified reality for literary expediency. I thought I'd explained that at our last meeting at the café in Madrid."

"A dirty trick," said Corso, not specifying whether he meant Dumas or me.

I raised a finger, ready to state my case. "A legitimate device," I objected, "inspired by the shrewdness and genius of the greatest novelist who ever lived. And yet..." I smiled bitterly. "Sainte-Beuve respected him but didn't accept him as a man of letters. His friend, Victor Hugo, praised his capacity for dramatic action, but nothing more. Prolific, long-winded, they said. With little style. They accused him of not delving into the anxieties of human beings, of lacking subtlety.... Lacking subtlety!" I touched the volumes of *The Three Musketeers* lined up on the shelf. "I agree with our good father Stevenson— there is no paean to friendship as long, eventful, or beautiful. In *Twenty Years After*, when the protagonists reappear, they are distanced at first. They are now men of mature years, selfish, with all the pettiness that life imposes. They even belong to opposing camps. Aramis and d'Artagnan lie and dissemble, Porthos fears being asked for money.... When they agree to meet at the Place Royale, they come armed and almost fight. And in England, when Athos's imprudence puts them all in danger, d'Artagnan refuses to shake his hand. In *The Vicomte de Bragelonne*, with the mystery of the iron mask, Aramis and Porthos stand against their old comrades. This happens because they're alive, because they're human, full of contradictions. But always, at the moment of truth, friendship wins out. A great thing, friendship! Do you have friends, Corso?"

"That's a good question."

"For me, Porthos in the cave at Locmaria has always embodied friendship: the giant struggling beneath a rock to save his friends... Do you remember his last words?"

"It's too heavy?"

"Exactly!"

I confess I felt almost moved. Like the young man in a cloud of pipe smoke described by Captain Marlow, Corso was one of us. But he was also a bitter, stubborn man determined not to feel.

"You're Liana Taillefer's lover," he said.

"Yes," I admitted, reluctantly leaving thoughts of good Porthos aside. "Isn't she a splendid woman? With her own particular obsessions...Beautiful and loyal, like Milady in the novel. It's strange. There are characters in literature who have a life of their own, familiar to millions of people who haven't even read the books in which they appear. In English literature there are three: Sherlock Holmes, Romeo, and Robinson Crusoe. In Spanish, two: Don Quixote and Don Juan. And in French literature there is one: d'Artagnan. But you see that I..."

"Let's not go off on a tangent again, Balkan."

"I'm not. I was about to add the name of Milady to d'Artagnan's. An extraordinary woman. Like Liana, in her own way. Her husband never measured up to her."

"Do you mean Athos?"

"No, I mean poor old Enrique Taillefer."

"Was that why you murdered him?"

My amazement must have looked sincere. It *was* sincere. "Enrique murdered? Don't be ridiculous. He hanged himself. He committed suicide. I should imagine that, with his way of looking at the world, he thought it a heroic gesture. Very regrettable."

"I don't believe you."

"Suit yourself. But his death was the starting point for this entire story and, indirectly, the reason you are here."

"Explain it to me then. Nice and slowly."

He had certainly earned it. As I said earlier, Corso was one of us, although he didn't know it. And anyway—I looked at the clock—it was almost twelve.

"Do you have 'The Anjou Wine' with you?"

He looked at me alertly, trying to guess my intentions. Then I saw him give in. Reluctantly, he took the folder from under his coat, then hid it again.

"Excellent," I said. "And now follow me."

He must have been expecting a secret passage leading from the library, some sort of diabolical trap. I saw him put his hand in his pocket for the knife.

"You won't be needing that," I assured him.

He didn't look convinced but said nothing. I held the candelabrum high, and we walked down the Louis XIII—style corridor. A magnificent tapestry hung on one of the walls: Ulysses, bow in hand, recently returned to Ithaca, Penelope and the dog rejoicing, the suitors drinking wine in the background, unaware of what awaits them.

"This is an ancient castle, full of history," I said. "It has been plundered by the English, by the Huguenots, by revolutionaries. Even the Germans set up a command post here during the war. It was very dilapidated when the present owner —a British millionaire, a charming man and a gentleman— acquired it. He restored and furnished it with extraordinary good taste. He even agreed to open it to the public."

"So what are you doing here outside of visiting hours?"

As I passed a leaded window, I glanced out. The storm was dying down at last, the glow of lightning fading beyond the Loire, to the north.

"An exception is made once a year," I explained. "After all, Meung is a special place. A novel like *The Three Musketeers* doesn't open just anywhere."

The wooden floors creaked beneath our feet. A suit of armor, genuine sixteenth-century, stood in a bend in the corridor. The light from the candelabrum was reflected in the smooth, polished surfaces of the cuirass. Corso glanced at it as he walked past, as if there might be someone hidden inside.

"I'll tell you a story. It began ten years ago," I said, "at an auction in Paris, of a lot of uncatalogued documents. I was writing a book on the nineteenth-century popular novel in France, and the dusty packages fell into my hands quite by chance. When I went through them, I saw they were from the old archives of *Le Siècle*. Almost all consisted of printing proofs of little value, but one package of blue and white sheets attracted my attention. It was the original text, handwritten by Dumas and Maquet, of *The Three Musketeers*. All sixty-seven chapters, just as they were sent to the printer. Someone, possibly Baudry, the editor of the newspaper, had kept them after composing the galley proofs and then forgot all about them...."

I slowed and stopped in the middle of the corridor. Corso was very still, and the light from the candelabrum I held lit up his face from below, making shadows dance in his eye sockets. He listened intently to my story, seemed to be unaware of anything else. Solving the mystery that had brought him was the only thing that mattered to him. But he still kept his hand on the knife in his pocket.

"My discovery," I went on, pretending not to notice, "was of extraordinary importance. We knew of a few fragments of the original draft from Dumas and Maquet's notes and papers, but we were unaware of the existence of the complete manuscript. At first I thought to make my finding public, in the form of an annotated facsimile edition. But then I encountered a serious moral dilemma."

The light and shadow on Corso's face moved, and a dark line crossed his mouth. He was smiling. "I don't believe it. A moral dilemma, after all this."

I moved the candelabrum to make invisible the skeptical smile on his face, unsuccessfully.

"I'm quite serious," I protested as we moved on. "On examining the manuscript, I concluded that the real creator of the story was Auguste Maquet. He had done all the research and outlined the story in broad strokes. Dumas, with his enormous talent, his genius, had then brought the raw material to life and turned it into a masterpiece. Although obvious to me, this might not have been so obvious to detractors of the author and his work." I gestured with my free hand, as if to sweep them all aside. "I had no intention of throwing stones at my hero. Particularly now, in these times of mediocrity and lack of imagination . . . Times in which people no longer admire marvels, as theater audiences and the readers of serials used to. They hissed at the villains and cheered on the heroes with no inhibitions." I shook my head sadly. "That applause unfortunately can no longer be heard. It's become the exclusive domain of innocents and children."

Corso was listening with an insolent, mocking expression. He might have agreed with me, but he was the grudge-bearing type and refused to allow my explanation to grant me any sort of moral alibi.

"In short," he said, "you decided to destroy the manuscript."

I smiled smugly. He was trying to be too clever.

"Don't be ridiculous. I decided to do something better: to make a dream come true."

We had stopped in front of the closed door to the reception room. Through it the muffled sound of music and voices could be heard. I put the candelabrum down on a console table while Corso watched me, again suspicious. He was probably wondering what new trick was hidden there. He didn't understand, I realized, that we really had reached the solution to the mystery.

"Please allow me to introduce you," I said, opening the door, "to the members of the Club Dumas."

ALMOST EVERYONE WAS THERE. Through the French windows opening onto the castle terrace, late arrivals entered a room full of people, cigarette smoke, and the murmur of conversation above a background of gentle music. On the central table covered with a white linen cloth, there was a cold buffet: bottles of Anjou wine, sausages and hams from Amiens, oysters from La Rochelle, boxes of Montecristo cigars. Groups of guests, about fifty men and women, were drinking and conversing in several languages. Among them were well-known faces from the press, cinema, and television. I saw Corso touch his glasses.

"Surprised?" I asked, looking to see his reaction.

He nodded, disconcerted, surly. Several guests came to greet me, so I shook hands, exchanged amenities and jokes. The atmosphere was cordial. Corso looked like someone who had fallen out of bed and woken up. Highly amused, I introduced him to some of the guests and watched with perverse satisfaction as he greeted them, confused and unsure of the terrain he was crossing. His customary composure was in shreds, and this was my small revenge. After all, it was he who first came to me with "The Anjou Wine" under his arm, determined to complicate things.

"Allow me to introduce Mr. Corso. . . . Bruno Lostia, an antique dealer from Milan. Permit me. This is Thomas Harvey, of Harvey's Jewelers: New York, London, Paris, Rome. And Count von Schlossberg, owner of the most famous collection of paintings in Europe. As you can see, we have a little of everything here: a Venezuelan Nobel laureate, an Argentine ex-president, the crown prince of Morocco . . . Did you know that his father is an avid reader of Alexandre Dumas? Look who's arrived. You know him, don't you? Professor of semiotics in Bologna . . . The blond lady talking to him is Petra Neustadt, the most influential literary critic in Central Europe. In the group next to the duchess of Alba there's the financier Rudolf Villefoz and the English writer Harold Burgess. Amaya Euskal, of the Alpha Press group, with the most powerful publisher in the USA, Johan Cross, of O&O Papers, New York. And I assume you remember Achille Replinger, the book dealer from Paris."

This was the last straw. I savored Corso's shaken expression, almost pitying him. Replinger was holding an empty glass and smiling pleasantly beneath his musketeer's mustache, just as he had smiled when he identified the Dumas manuscript at his shop on the Rue Bonaparte. He greeted me with a huge bear hug and then warmly patted Corso on the back before going off in search of another drink, puffing away like a jovial, rosy-cheeked Porthos.

"Damn this," muttered Corso, drawing me aside. "What's going on here?"

"I told you it's a long story."

"Well, finish telling it, will you?"

We had moved close to the table. I poured us a couple of glasses of wine, but he shook his head. "Gin," he muttered. "Don't you have any gin?"

I indicated the liquor cabinet at the other end of the room. We walked over to it, stopping three or four times on the way to exchange more greetings: a well-known film director, a Lebanese millionaire, a Spanish minister of the interior . . . Corso grabbed a bottle of Beefeater and filled a glass to the brim, swallowing half of it in one gulp. He shuddered, and his eyes shone behind his glasses (one lens broken, the other intact). He held the bottle to his chest, as if afraid to lose it.

"You were going to tell me," he said.

I suggested we go out on the terrace beyond the French windows, where we could talk without interruption. Corso filled his glass again before following me. The storm had died down. Stars shone above us.

"I'm all ears," he announced after another large gulp.

I leaned on the balustrade still damp from the rain and took a sip from my glass of Anjou wine.

"Owning the manuscript of *The Three Musketeers* gave me the idea," I said. "Why not form a literary society, a sort of club for devoted admirers of the novels of Alexandre Dumas and the classic adventure serial? Through my work I already had contact with several ideal candidates for membership. . . ." I gestured toward the brightly lit salon. In the tall French windows the guests could be seen coming and going, chatting animatedly. It was proof of my success, and I didn't conceal my authorial pride. "A society dedicated to studying novels of that kind, rediscovering writers and forgotten works, promoting their republication and sale under an imprint with which you may be familiar: *Dumas & Co.*"

"I know it," said Corso. "They're based in Paris and have just published the entire works of Ponson du Terrail. Last year it was *Fantomas*. I didn't know you had a part in it."

I smiled. "That's the rule: no names, no starring roles . . . As you can see, the matter is scholarly and slightly childish at the same time. A nostalgic literary game that rediscovers long-lost novels and returns us to our innocence, to how we used to be. As we mature, we admire Flaubert or prefer Stendhal, or Faulkner, Lampedusa, García Marquez, Durrell, Kafka. We become different from each other, opponents even. But we all share a conspiratorial wink when we talk about certain magical authors and books. Those that made us discover literature without weighing us down with dogma or teaching us rules. This is our true common heritage: stories faithful not to what people see but to what people dream."

I let the words hang and paused, awaiting their effect. But Corso just raised his glass to look at it against the light. His homeland was in there.

"That was before," he answered. "Now neither children nor young people nor anyone has a spiritual heritage. They all watch TV."

I shook my head. I had written something on this very subject for the literary supplement of the *ABC* newspaper a couple of weeks before. "I don't agree. Even then they're treading, unknowingly, in old footsteps. Films on television, for instance, maintain the link. Those old movies. Even Indiana Jones is the direct descendant of all that."

Corso grimaced in the direction of the French windows. "It's possible. But you were telling me about these people. I'd like to know how you . . . recruited them."

"It's no secret," I answered. "I've been running this select society, the Club Dumas, for ten years now. It holds its annual meeting here in Meung. As you can see, the members arrive punctually from all corners of the globe. Every last one of them is a reader—"

"Of serials? Don't make me laugh."

"I don't have the slightest intention of making you laugh, Corso. Why are you looking at me like that? You know yourself that a novel, or a film made for pure consumption, can turn into an exquisite work, from *The Pickwick Papers* to *Casablanca* and *Goldfinger*. Audiences turn to these archetype-packed stories to enjoy, whether consciously or unconsciously, the device of repeated plots with small variations. *Dispositio* rather than *elocutio*... That's why the serial, even the most trite television serial, can become a cult both for a naive audience and for a more sophisticated one. There are people who find excitement in Sherlock Holmes's risking his life, while others go for the pipe, the magnifying glass, and the 'Elementary, my dear Watson,' which, by the way, Conan Doyle never actually wrote. The plot devices, the variations and repetition, are so ancient that they're mentioned in Aristotle's *Poetics*. And what is a television serial if not an updated version of a classic tragedy, a great romantic drama, or a Dumas novel? That's why an intelligent reader can obtain great enjoyment from all this, an exception to the rule. For exceptions to the rule are based on rules."

I thought Corso would be interested in what I was saying, but he shook his head, a gladiator refusing to accept the challenge offered by his opponent.

"Cut the literature lecture and get back to your Club Dumas, will you?" he said impatiently. "To that loose chapter that's been floating around ... Where's the rest?"

"In there," I answered, looking at the salon. "I based the organization of the society on the sixty-seven chapters of the manuscript—a maximum of sixty-seven members, each having a chapter as a registered share. Allocation is strictly based on a list of applicants, and changes in membership require the approval of the executive board, which I chair. Each applicant is discussed in depth before his admission is approved."

"How are shares transferred?"

"On no account are the shares transferred. If a member dies or wishes to leave the society, his chapter must be returned. The board then allocates it to another applicant. A member may never freely dispose of it."

"Is that what Enrique Taillefer tried to do?"

"In a way. He was an ideal applicant, and a model member of the Club Dumas until he broke the rules."

Corso finished his gin. He put the glass down on the mossy balustrade and said nothing for a moment, staring intently at the lights of the reception room. He shook his head.

"That's no reason to murder someone," he said quietly, as if to himself. "I can't believe that all these people..." He looked at me stubbornly. "They're all well known, respectable. They'd never get mixed up in something like this."

I suppressed my impatience. "You're blowing things out of all proportion.... Enrique and I were friends for some time. We shared a fascination for this kind of fiction, although his taste in literature wasn't on a level with his enthusiasm. The fact is, his success as a publisher of bestselling cookbooks meant he could spend time and money on his hobby. And to be fair, if anybody deserved to be a member of the club, it was Enrique. That's why I recommended his admission. As I said, we shared, if not in our tastes, at least in our enthusiasm."

"You shared more than that, I seem to remember."

Corso's sarcastic smile had returned, and I found it highly irritating. "I could tell you that that's none of your business," I retorted. "But I want to explain. Liana has always been very special, as well as very beautiful. She was a precocious reader. Do you know that at sixteen she had a fleur-de-lis tattooed on her hip? Not on the shoulder, like her idol, Milady de Winter, so that her family and the nuns at her boarding school wouldn't find out. What do you think of that?"

"Very moving."

"You don't seem very moved. But I assure you she's an admirable person. The fact is that, well . . . we became intimate. You'll recall that earlier I mentioned the heritage that is the lost paradise of childhood. Well Liana's heritage is *The Three Musketeers*. She was fascinated by the world depicted in its pages. She decided to marry Enrique after meeting him by chance at a party where they spent the evening exchanging quotes from the novel. He was already a very wealthy publisher."

"It was love at first sight," said Corso.

"I don't know why you say it like that. They married for the most sincere reasons. The thing is that, in the long run, even for someone as good-natured as his wife, Enrique could be tiresome. . . . We were good friends, and I often visited them. Liana . . ." I put my glass on the balustrade next to his empty one. "Anyway. You can imagine the rest."

"Yes, I can. Very clearly."

"I wasn't talking about that. She became an excellent collaborator. So much so that, four years ago, I sponsored her entry to the society. She owns chapter 37, 'Milady's Secret.' She chose it herself."

"Why did you set her on me?"

"Let's take this one step at a time. Not long ago, Enrique became a problem. Instead of limiting himself to the very profitable business of cookbooks, he decided to write a serial. But the novel was awful. That is a fact. Absolutely awful, believe me. He brazenly plagiarized all the plots of the genre. It was called—"

"The Dead Man's Hand."

"Exactly. Even the title wasn't his. And what's worse, unbelievably, he wanted Dumas & Co. to publish it. I refused, of course. His monstrous creation would never have been approved by the board. Anyway, Enrique had more than enough money to publish it himself, and I told him so."

"I assume he took it badly. I saw his library."

"Badly? That is something of an understatement. The argument took place in his study. I can still picture him, small and chubby, standing very straight, on tiptoe, staring at me with wild eyes. He looked as if he might burst a blood vessel. All very unpleasant. He said he'd decided to devote his whole life to writing. And who was I to judge it. That was up to posterity. I was a biased critic, an insufferable pedant, and on top of everything I was playing around with his wife. This absolutely stunned me—I didn't realize he knew. But apparently Liana talks in her sleep, and between cursing d'Artagnan and his friends (whom, by the way, she hates as if she had known them personally) she'd revealed the whole affair to her husband.... You can imagine my predicament."

"Very difficult for you."

"Extremely. Although the worst was yet to come. Enrique stormed. He said that if he was mediocre, Dumas wasn't much of a writer either. Where would Dumas have been without Auguste Maquet, whom he wretchedly exploited? The proof lay in the white and blue pages of 'The Anjou Wine,' which Enrique kept in his safe.... The argument became even more heated. He called me an adulterer—rather an old-fashioned insult—and I called him a moron, adding a few snide comments about his latest cookbook successes. I ended up comparing him to the baker in *Cyrano*.... 'I'll get my revenge,' he said, sounding rather like the Count of Monte Cristo. 'I'll publicize the fact that your beloved Dumas was a big cheat who appropriated other people's work. I'll make the manuscript public, and everyone will see how the old fraud produced his serials. I don't give a damn about the rules of the society. That chapter's mine, and I'll sell it to whoever I like. And you can go to hell.' "

"He got nasty."

"You don't know how furious a spurned author can become. My remonstrations were to no avail. He threw me out. Later I learned from Liana that he'd called that bookseller, La Ponte, to offer him the manuscript. He must have thought himself very clever and devious, like Edmond Dantès. He wanted to create a scandal without being directly implicated; he wanted to keep his reputation intact. That's how you became involved. You can understand my surprise when you came to see me with 'The Anjou Wine.' "

"You certainly didn't show it."

"I had my reasons. With Enrique dead, Liana and I had assumed that the manuscript was lost."

I saw Corso search his coat for one of his crumpled cigarettes. He put it in his mouth but didn't light it. He paced the terrace. "Your story's ridiculous," he said at last. "No Edmond Dantès would commit suicide before savoring his revenge."

I nodded, although he had his back to me and couldn't see my gesture.

"Well, more than that happened," I admitted. "The day after our conversation, Enrique came to my house in a final attempt to persuade me. I'd had enough. And I won't put up with blackmail. So, not quite realizing what I was doing, I dealt him the death blow. His serial was not only very bad, it felt familiar. I went to my library, searched for an old edition of *The Popular Illustrated Novel*, a little-known late-nineteenth-century publication, and opened it at the first page of a story written by a certain Amaury de Verona and titled 'Angeline de Gravaillac, or Unsullied Virtue.' Well, you can imagine the sort of thing. As I read the first paragraph aloud, Enrique went pale, as if the ghost of Angeline had risen from the grave. Which it more or less had. Assuming nobody would remember the story, he had plagiarized it, copied it almost word for word, except for one chapter he took whole from Fernandez y Gonzalez, in fact the best part of the story. I was sorry I didn't have my camera to take a picture of Enrique. He put his hand to his forehead as if to exclaim, 'Curses!' but couldn't actually get the word out. He just made a kind of gurgling sound, as if he was suffocating.

Then he turned, went home, and hanged himself from the light fixture."

Corso was listening. The forgotten cigarette was still in his mouth, unlit.

"Then things became complicated," I went on, sure that he was now starting to believe me. "You already had the manuscript, and your friend La Ponte wasn't willing, at first, to part with it. I couldn't go around playing Arsène Lupin, I have a reputation to protect. That's why I gave Liana the task of retrieving the chapter. The date of the annual meeting was approaching, and we had to find a new member to replace Enrique. I admit, Liana did make a few mistakes. First, she went to see you...." I cleared my throat, embarrassed. I didn't want to go into details. "Then she tried to enlist La Ponte, to have him get 'The Anjou Wine' back. But I didn't know how tenacious you could be.... The problem is that Liana had always dreamed of an adventure like her heroine's, full of deception, amorous trysts, and persecution. And this episode, based on the stuff of her dreams, gave such an opportunity. So she went after you enthusiastically. 'I'll bring you the manuscript bound in the skin of that Corso,' she promised. I told her not to get carried away. I realize now that the mistake was mine: I encouraged her in her fantasy, releasing the Milady that had been inside her ever since she first read *The Three Musketeers*."

"I wish she'd read something else. Like *Gone with the Wind*. She could have identified with Scarlett O'Hara and pestered Clark Gable instead of me."

"Yes, she went a bit over the top. It's a pity you took it so seriously."

Corso rubbed a spot behind his ear. I could imagine what he was thinking: the one who really took it seriously was the man with the scar.

"Who's Rochefort?"

"His name is Laszlo Nicolavic. He's a character actor who specializes in villains. He played Rochefort in the series Andreas

Frey made for British television a couple of years ago. He's played Gonzaga in *Lagardère*, Levasseur in *Captain Blood*, La Tour d'Azyr in *Scaramouche*, Rupert de Hentzau in *The Prisoner of Zenda*. He's fascinated by the genre, and has applied to join the Club Dumas. Liana was quite taken with him and insisted he work with her."

"Laszlo certainly took his part seriously."

"I'm afraid he did. I suspect he's trying to gain points so his admission is approved quickly. I also suspect that he serves as her occasional lover." I smiled like a man of the world, hoping it was convincing. "Liana is young, beautiful, and passionate. Let's say I stimulate her intellectual side and that Laszlo takes care of her impetuous nature's more down-to-earth needs."

"What else?"

"That's almost all. Nicolavic, or Rochefort, took charge of getting the Dumas manuscript from you. That's why he followed you from Madrid to Toledo and Sintra, while Liana headed for Paris, taking La Ponte with her as a backup in case their original plan failed and you didn't see reason. You know the rest: you didn't let them snatch the manuscript from you, Milady and Rochefort got slightly carried away, and that brought you here." I paused, reflecting on the events. "Do you know something? I wonder whether instead of Laszlo Nicolavic I shouldn't recommend you as a member of the club."

He didn't even ask whether I really meant it or was only being sarcastic. He removed his battered glasses and cleaned them mechanically, absorbed in his thoughts. "Is that all?" he said at last.

"Of course." I pointed to the reception room. "There's your proof."

He put his glasses on and took a deep breath. I didn't at all like the look on his face.

"What about the *Delomelanicon*? What about Richelieu's connection with *The Nine Doors of the Kingdom of Shadows*?" He came closer, tapping me on the chest until I had to take a step back. "Do you take me for a fool? You're not going to tell me that you knew nothing about the link between Dumas and that book, his pact with the devil and all the rest of it—Victor Fargas's murder in Sintra and the fire at Baroness Ungern's apartment in Paris. Did you give my name to the police yourself? And what about the book hidden in the three copies? Or the nine prints engraved by Lucifer, reprinted by Aristide Torchia on his return from Prague 'by authority and permission of the superiors,' and the whole damn business. . . ."

He said it all in a torrent, his chin jutting aggressively, his eyes piercing into me. I took another step back, open-mouthed.

"You've gone mad!" I protested indignantly. "Can you tell me what you're talking about?"

He took out a box of matches and lit his cigarette, cupping a hand around the flame. Through the glare reflected in his glasses, he kept his eyes fixed on me. Then he told me his version of events.

WHEN HE FINISHED, WE both stood in silence. We were leaning on the damp balustrade, next to each other, watching the lights of the reception room. Corso's story had lasted for the duration of the cigarette, and he now stubbed it out on the ground.

"I suppose," I said, "I should now confess, say, 'Yes, it's all true,' and hold out my hands for you to handcuff them. Is that what you're expecting?"

He hesitated. His recital of the story didn't seem to have given him confidence in his conclusions.

"But there is a link," he muttered.

I looked at his narrow shadow on the marble flagstones of the terrace floor, dark against the rectangles of light cast from the reception room and stretching beyond the steps into the darkness of the garden.

"I'm afraid," I said, "that your imagination has been playing tricks on you."

He shook his head slowly. "I didn't imagine that Victor Fargas was drowned in the pond, or that Baroness Ungern was burned with her books. Those things happened. They were real. The two stories are mixed up."

"You've just said it yourself—there are two stories. Maybe all that links them is your own intertextual reading."

"Spare me the technical jargon. The Dumas chapter triggered everything." He looked at me resentfully. "Your goddamn club and all your little games."

"Don't lay the blame on me. Games are perfectly valid. If this were a work of fiction and not a real story, you as the reader would be principally responsible."

"Don't be absurd."

"I'm not. From what you've just told me I deduce that, playing with facts and literary references, you constructed a theory and drew fantastic conclusions. But facts are objective, and you can't overlay them with your personal ideas. The story of 'The Anjou Wine' and the story about this mysterious book, *The Nine Doors*, are completely unrelated."

"You all led me to believe..."

"We, and by we I mean Liana Taillefer, Laszlo Nicolavic, and myself, did nothing of the sort. It was you who filled in the blanks on your own, as if what happened were a novel based on trickery, with Lucas Corso the reader too clever for his own good. Nobody ever told you that things were actually as you thought. No, the responsibility is entirely yours, my friend. The real villain in the piece is your excessive intertextual reading and linking of literary references."

"What else could I do? To take action, I needed some strategy, I couldn't just sit there waiting. In any strategy, one builds a picture of one's opponent, and the picture influences one's next move.... Wellington did such-and-such, thinking that

Napoleon was thinking of doing such-and-such. And Napoleon . . ."

"Napoleon made the mistake of confusing Blucher with Grouchy. Military strategy is as risky as literary strategy. Listen, Corso, there are no innocent readers anymore. Each overlays the text with his own perverse view. A reader is the total of all he's read, in addition to all the films and television he's seen. To the information supplied by the author he'll always add his own. And that's where the danger lies: an excess of references caused you to create the wrong opponent, or an imaginary opponent."

"The information was false."

"No. The information a book provides is an objective given. It may be presented by a malevolent author who wishes to mislead, but it is never false. It is the reader who makes a false reading."

Corso seemed to be thinking carefully. He shifted to face the garden in darkness. "Then there must be another author," he said quietly.

He stood motionless. After a time he took the folder with "The Anjou Wine" from under his coat and put it to one side, on the moss-covered stone.

"This story has two authors," he insisted.

"That's possible," I said, taking the Dumas manuscript. "And maybe one is more malevolent than the other. My story was the serial. You'll have to look for the crime novel elsewhere."

XVI. A DEVICE WORTHY
OF A GOTHIC NOVEL

"Here is the vexing part of the matter," said Porthos.
"In the old days one didn't have to explain anything.
One just fought because one fought."
—A. Dumas, THE VICOMTE DE BRAGELONNE

Leaning his head back against
the driver's seat, Lucas Corso looked at the view. He had pulled
off onto the shoulder at the final bend of the road before it
dipped into the town. Surrounded by ancient walls, the old
quarter floated in mist from the river, suspended in the air like
a ghostly blue island. It was a hazy world without light or
shadow. A cold, hesitant dawn over Castille, with the first glim-
mer of light showing roofs, chimneys, and bell towers to the
east.

He wanted to look at the time, but water had got into his
watch during the storm in Meung. The glass was misted and
the dial illegible. Corso saw his exhausted eyes in the rearview
mirror. Meung-sur-Loire, on the eve of the first Monday in
April. They were now far away, and it was Tuesday. It had
been a long return journey, and all the characters had faded
into the distance: Balkan, the Club Dumas, Rochefort, Milady,
La Ponte. Only the echoes of a story after the turning of the
last page. The author striking the final key on the QWERTY
keyboard, bottom row, second from the right. So with one ar-

bitrary action there was no more than pages of type, strange, inert paper. Lives suddenly alien.

On that dawn so like awakening from a dream, Corso sat, dirty and unshaven, with reddened eyes. By his side, his old canvas bag containing the last extant copy of *The Nine Doors*. And the girl. That was all that remained on the shore after the tide went out. She moaned softly, and he turned to look at her. She was sleeping in the seat next to him, under her duffel coat, her head on his right shoulder. Breathing gently, her lips parted, occasionally shaken by small shivers that made her start. Then she'd moan again, quietly. A small vertical crease between her eyebrows made her look like an upset little girl. One hand protruded from under her coat. It was turned palm up, the fingers half open, as if she had just let something slip from them, or as if she was waiting.

Corso thought again about Meung, and about the journey. And Boris Balkan two nights earlier, standing next to him on the terrace still wet from the rain. Holding the pages of "The Anjou Wine," Richelieu had smiled like an old opponent, both admiring and sympathetic. "You're unusual, my friend." He had offered these final words as a consolation or farewell; they were the only words with any meaning. The rest—an invitation to join the other guests—were uttered as a formality. Not that Balkan wanted to get rid of him—actually, he had seemed disappointed when Corso left. But Balkan knew that Corso would refuse to come inside. Corso in fact stayed on the terrace for some time, alone, leaning on the balustrade, listening to the echo of his own defeat. He slowly came to and looked around, remembering where he was. He walked away from the brightly lit windows and returned unhurriedly to the hotel, wandering through dark streets. He didn't come across Rochefort again, and at the Auberge Saint-Jacques he was told that Milady too had left. They both departed from his life and returned to the nebulous region from which they had come, fictional characters once more, as cryptic as chess pieces. La Ponte and the girl he found without difficulty. He hadn't worried about La Ponte but felt relief when he saw that she was still there. He'd thought —feared—that he would lose her along with the other characters in the story. He took her quickly by the hand, before she too vanished in the dust of the library of the castle of Meung, and led her to the car as La Ponte watched. Corso saw him receding in the rearview mirror. La Ponte looked lost, shouting, appealing to their long, much-abused friendship, not understanding what was going on. Like a discredited, useless harpooner, not to be trusted, abandoned with some bread and three days' supply of water, left to drift. "*Try to reach Batavia, Mr. Bligh.*" But then, at the end of the street, Corso stopped the car and sat with his hands on the wheel, looking at the road ahead, the girl staring, curious, at his profile. La Ponte wasn't a real character either. With a sigh, Corso put the car in reverse and went back to collect him. For the next day and night, until they left him at a traffic light on a street in Madrid, La Ponte said not one word. He didn't even protest when Corso told him the Dumas manuscript was gone. There wasn't much he could say.

Corso glanced at the canvas bag at the sleeping girl's feet. The defeat was painful, of course, like a knife wound in his memory. He knew he'd played according to the rules—*legitime certaverit*—but had gone in the wrong direction. At the very moment of victory, however partial and incomplete it was, all pleasure at winning had been snatched from him. The victory had been imaginary. It was like defeating imaginary ghosts, or punching the wind, or shouting at silence. Maybe that's why Corso was now staring suspiciously at the city suspended in the mist, waiting, before entering it, to make sure that its foundations were firmly rooted in the ground.

He could hear the girl's gentle, rhythmic breathing at his shoulder. He stared at her bare neck between the folds of the duffel coat. He moved his hand until he could feel the heat of her warm flesh throbbing in his fingers. As always, her skin smelled of youth and fever. In his imagination and in his memory he could easily follow the long, curving lines of her slender body, down to her bare feet by her sneakers and the bag. Irene Adler. He still didn't know what to call her. But he could remember her naked body in the shadows, the curve of her hips traced by the light, her parted lips. Impossibly beautiful and silent, absorbed in her own youth and at the same time as serene as tranquil waters, with the wisdom of ages. And in the luminous eyes watching him intently from the shadows, the reflection, the dark image of Corso himself amid all the light snatched from the sky.

She was watching him now, her emerald green eyes framed by long lashes. She had woken and was moving sleepily, rubbing against him. Then she sat up, alert. She looked at him.

"Hello, Corso." Her duffel coat slid to her feet. Her white T-shirt clung to her perfect torso, as supple as a beautiful young animal's. "What are we doing here?"

"Waiting." He gestured at the town, which seemed to be floating in the mist from the river. "For it to become real."

She looked, not understanding at first. Then she smiled slowly.

"Maybe it never will," she said.

"Then we'll stay here. It's not such a bad place, up here, with the strange, unreal world at our feet." He turned to the girl. "*I'll give you everything, if you prostrate yourself and adore me.* Isn't that the kind of offer you're going to make me?"

The girl's smile was full of tenderness. She bowed her head, thoughtful, then looked up and held Corso's gaze.

"No, I'm poor," she said.

"I know." It was true. Corso didn't have to read it in the clarity of her eyes. "Your luggage, and the train compartment . . . It's strange. I always thought you all had unlimited wealth, out there, at the end of the rainbow." His smile was as sharp as the knife he still had in his pocket. "Peter Schlemiel's bag of gold."

"Well, you're wrong." Now she was pursing her lips obstinately. "I'm all I have."

This was true too, and Corso had known it from the start. She had never lied. Both innocent and wise, she was faithful and in love, chasing after a shadow.

"I see." He made a gesture in the air, as if wielding an imaginary pen. "Aren't you going to give me a document to sign?"

"A document?"

"Yes. It used to be called a pact. Now it would be a contract with lots of small print, wouldn't it? 'In the event of litigation, the parties are to submit to the jurisdiction of the courts of...' That's a funny thing. I wonder which court covers this."

"Don't be silly."

"Why did you choose me?"

"I'm free," she sighed sadly, as if she'd paid the price for her right to say it. "I can choose. Anyone can."

Corso searched in his coat for his crumpled pack of cigarettes. There was only one left. He took it out and stared, undecided whether to put it in his mouth or not. He put it back in the pack. Maybe he'd need a smoke later. He was sure he would.

"You knew from the beginning," he said, "that there were two completely unrelated stories. That's why you never cared about the Dumas strand. Milady, Rochefort, Richelieu—they were nothing but film extras to you. Now I understand why you were so passive. You must have been horribly bored. You just flicked the pages of your *Musketeers*, watching me make all the wrong moves...."

She was looking through the windshield at the town veiled in blue mist. She started to raise her hand but let it drop, as if what she was about to say was pointless. "All I could do was go with you," she answered. "Everyone has to walk certain paths alone. Haven't you heard of free will?" She smiled sadly. "Some of us have paid a very high price for it."

"But you didn't always stay on the sidelines. That night, by the Seine . . . Why did you help me against Rochefort?"

She touched the canvas bag with her bare foot. "He was after the Dumas manuscript. But *The Nine Doors* was in there too. I just wanted to avoid any stupid interference." She shrugged. "And I didn't want him to hit you."

"What about Sintra? You warned me about the Fargas business."

"Of course. The book was tied up with it."

"And then the key to the meeting in Meung . . ."

"I didn't know about it. I just worked it out from the novel."

Corso made a face. "I thought you were all omniscient."

"Well, you were wrong." Now she was annoyed. "And I don't know why you keep talking to me as if I were one of many. I've been alone for a long time."

Centuries, Corso was sure. Centuries of solitude. He didn't doubt that. He had embraced her naked body, drowned in the clarity of her eyes, been inside her, tasted her skin, felt the gentle throbbing of her neck against his lips. He'd heard her moan quietly, like a frightened child or like a lonely fallen angel in search of warmth. He'd watched her sleep with her fists clenched, tormented by nightmares of gleaming, blond archangels, implacable in their armor, as dogmatic as the God who made them march in time.

Now, thanks to her, although too late, he understood Nikon and her ghosts and the desperate way she clung to life. Nikon's fear, her black-and-white photographs, her vain attempt to exorcise memories transmitted through the genes that survived Auschwitz, the number tattooed on her father's skin, the Black Order that had been as old as the spirit and the curse of man. Because God and the devil could be one and the same thing, and everybody understood it in his own way.

But just as with Nikon, Corso was cruel. Love was too heavy a burden for him, and he didn't have Porthos's noble heart.

"Was that your mission?" he asked the girl. "Protecting *The Nine Doors?* I don't think you'll get a medal for it."

"That's unfair, Corso."

Almost the same words. Once again, Nikon left to drift, small and fragile. Who did she cling to now, to escape her nightmares?

He looked at the girl. Maybe Nikon's memory was his penance. But he was no longer prepared to accept it with resignation. He glimpsed his face in the rearview mirror: it was contracted into a lost, bitter expression.

"Is it? We lost two of the three books. And what about the pointless deaths of Fargas and the baroness?" They mattered little to him, but he was bitter. "You could have prevented them."

She shook her head, very serious, her eyes fixed on his. "Some things can't be avoided, Corso. Some castles have to burn, and some men must hang. There are dogs destined to tear each other to pieces, virtuous people destined to be beheaded, doors destined to be opened for others to enter." She frowned and bowed her head. "My mission, as you call it, was to make sure you reached the end of the journey safely."

"Well, it's been a long journey, only to end back at the starting point." Corso indicated the town suspended in the mist. "And now I have to go down there."

"You don't *have* to. Nobody's forcing you. You could just forget about it and leave."

"Without finding out the answer?"

"Without undergoing the test. You have the answer within you."

"That's a pretty sentence. Put it on my headstone when I'm burning in hell."

She gave him a gentle, friendly tap on the knee. "Don't be an idiot, Corso. Things are as one wants them to be more often than people think. Even the devil can adopt different guises. Or qualities."

"Remorse, for instance."

"Yes. But also knowledge and beauty." She again looked anxiously at the town. "Or power and wealth."

"But the end result is the same: damnation." He repeated his gesture of signing an imaginary contract. "You have to pay with the innocence of your soul."

She sighed again. "You paid long ago, Corso. You're still paying. It's a strange habit, postponing it all till the end. Like the final act of a tragedy . . . Everyone drags his own damnation with him from the beginning. As for the devil, he is no more than God's pain; the wrath of a dictator caught in his own trap. The story told by the winners."

"When did it happen?"

"A longer time ago than you can conceive. It was very hard. I fought for a hundred days and a hundred nights without hope or refuge." An almost imperceptible smile played on her lips. "That's the only thing I'm proud of—having fought to the end. I retreated but didn't turn my back, surrounded by others also fallen from on high. I was hoarse with shouting out my fury, my fear and exhaustion. After the battle, I walked across a plain as desolate and lonely as eternity is cold. . . . I still sometimes come across a trace of the battle, or an old comrade who passes by without daring to look up."

"Why me, then? Why didn't you look for someone on the side of the winners? I win battles only on a scale of five thousand to one."

The girl turned to look into the distance. The sun was rising, and the first horizontal ray of light cut the morning air with a fine, reddish line that directly intersected her gaze. When she looked back at Corso, he felt vertigo as he peered into all the light reflected in her green eyes.

"Because lucidity never wins. And seducing an idiot has never been worth the trouble."

Then she leaned over and kissed him very slowly, with

infinite tenderness. As if she had had to wait an eternity to do so.

THE MIST SLOWLY BEGAN to clear. It was as if the town, suspended in midair, had decided to sink its foundations back into the earth. The dawn shone on the gray-and-ochre mass of the Alcazar palace, the cathedral bell tower, and the stone bridge with its pillars in the dark waters of the river, resembling a sinister hand stretched between the two banks.

Corso started the engine. He let the car slide gently down the deserted road. As they descended, the light of the rising sun was left behind, held above them. The town gradually moved closer, and they slowly entered the world of cold hues and immense solitude that persisted in the remnants of blue mist.

He hesitated before he crossed the bridge, stopping the car beneath the stone arch that led onto it; hands on the steering wheel, head slightly bowed, and chin jutting out—the profile of an alert hunter. He took off his glasses and cleaned them, though they didn't need it. He took his time, looking intently at the bridge, which without his glasses was a vague path with disturbingly imprecise outlines. He didn't look at the girl but knew that she was watching him. He put on his glasses, adjusting them on the bridge of his nose, and the landscape recovered its sharp lines but was no more reassuring for that. The far bank looked dark. The current flowing between the pillars resembled the black waters of time, of Lethe. In the last patches of the night that refused to die, his sense of danger was tangible, acute, like a steel needle. Corso could feel the pulse beating in his wrist when he grasped the stick shift. You can still turn back, he told himself. In that way, none of what happened has ever happened, and none of what will take place will ever take place. As for the practical value of *Nunc scio,* "Now I know," coined by God or by the devil, that was highly dubious. He frowned. They were nothing but words. He knew that in a few minutes he would be on the other side of the bridge and river. *Verbum dimissum custodiat arcanum.* He gazed up at the sky, looking for an archer with or without arrows in his quiver, before putting the car into gear and slowly moving on.

IT WAS COLD OUTSIDE the car, so he turned up his collar. He could feel the girl's intent gaze upon him as he crossed the street without looking back, holding *The Nine Doors* under his arm. She hadn't offered to go with him, and for some obscure reason he knew that it was better this way. The house occupied almost an entire block, and its gray stone bulk presided over a narrow square, among medieval buildings whose closed windows and doors made them look like motionless film extras, blind and mute. The gray facade had four gargoyles on the eaves: a billy goat, a crocodile, a gorgon, and a serpent. There was a star of David on the Moorish arch above the wrought-iron gate that led to the interior courtyard with two Venetian marble lions and a well. It was all familiar to Corso, but he had never been so apprehensive on entering the house. He remembered an old quotation: "Perhaps men who have been caressed by many women cross the valley of shadows with less remorse, or less fear...." It went something like that. Maybe he hadn't been caressed enough, because his mouth was dry, and he would have sold his soul for half a bottle of Bols. And *The Nine Doors* felt as if it contained nine lead plates instead of prints.

He pushed open the gate, but the silence remained unbroken. Not even his shoes caused the slightest echo as he crossed the courtyard, its paving stones worn down by ancient footsteps and centuries of rain. An archway led to the steep, narrow staircase. At the top he could see the dark, heavy door decorated with thick nails. It was closed: the last door. For an instant Corso winked sarcastically at empty space, to himself, baring his teeth. He was both involuntary author and butt of his own joke, or of his own error. An error carefully planned by an unscrupulous hand, and full of serpentine, illusory invitations to participate that had led him to certain conclusions, only for them to be refuted. In the end he'd had his conclusions confirmed by the text itself, as if it had been a damned novel, which it wasn't. Or what if it was? The fact is, the last thing he saw in the polished metal plate nailed to the door was his own, very real face. A distorted image that combined the name on the plate with his own shape, the light behind him in the archway over the stairs that led down to the courtyard and the street. His last stop on a strange journey to the other side of the shadows.

He rang. Once, twice, three times. No answer. The brass button was dead; there had been no sound inside when he pressed it. In his pocket he felt the crumpled pack containing his last cigarette. Again he decided against lighting it. He rang the bell a fourth time. And a fifth. He clenched his fist and knocked hard, twice. Then the door opened. Not with a sinister creak, but smoothly, on greased hinges. And without any dramatic effects, quite casually, Varo Borja stood in the doorway.

"Hello, Corso."

Borja didn't seem surprised to see him. There were beads of sweat all over his bald head, and he was unshaven. His shirtsleeves were rolled up and his vest undone. He looked tired, with dark rings under his eyes from a sleepless night. But his eyes shone feverishly. He didn't ask what Corso was doing there at such an hour, and he seemed barely to notice the book under Corso's arm. He stood there without moving, as if he had just been interrupted during some meticulous job, or dream, and just wanted to get back to it.

Here was the man responsible. Corso knew it, seeing his own stupidity materialize before him. Of course. Varo Borja— millionaire, international book dealer, famous collector, and methodical murderer. With an almost scientific curiosity, Corso scrutinized the face before him. He tried now to isolate the features, the clues that should have alerted him so much earlier. Signs overlooked; angles of madness, horror, or shadow in those familiar, vulgar features. But he couldn't see anything. Only a feverish, distant expression devoid of curiosity or passion, lost in images far removed from the man now at his door. Though Corso was holding the cursed book. It had been he, Varo Borja, in the shadow of that same book, following Corso's footsteps like an evil snake, who had killed Victor Fargas and Baroness Ungern. Not only to reunite the twenty-seven engravings and combine the nine correct ones but also to cover all traces and make sure that nobody else would solve the riddle set by Torchia, the printer. For the entire plot, Corso had been a tool to confirm a theory that proved correct—that the real book was distributed over three copies. He was also the victim of any repercussions involving the police. Now, paying twisted homage to his own instincts, Corso remembered how he felt looking up at the paintings on the ceiling of the Quinta da Soledade. Abraham's sacrifice with no alternative victim: he was the scapegoat. And Borja, of course, was the dealer who went to see Victor Fargas to purchase one of his treasures every six months. That day, while Corso was visiting Fargas, Borja was in Sintra finalizing the details of his plan, waiting for confirmation of his theory that all three copies were needed to solve Torchia's riddle. Fargas's half-written receipt was intended for him. That's why Corso hadn't been able to get hold of Borja when he phoned his house in Toledo. Then later that same evening, before going to his final appointment with Fargas, Borja had called Corso at the hotel, pretending he was making an international call. Corso had not only confirmed Borja's suspicions about the book but also given him the key to the mystery, thus condemning Fargas and the baroness. With bitter certainty Corso could see the pieces of the puzzle falling into place. When you set aside all the false clues that pointed to the Club Dumas, Varo Borja was the key to every inexplicable event in that other, diabolic, strand of the plot. It was enough to make you laugh out loud. If the whole damn business had been at all funny, that is.

"I've brought the book," Corso said, showing Borja *The Nine Doors*.

Borja nodded vaguely and took the book, barely glancing at it. He had his head slightly turned to the side, as if listening for a sound behind him, inside the house. After a moment he noticed Corso again and blinked, surprised that he was still there.

"You've given me the book. What else do you want?"

"To be paid for the job."

Borja stared at him uncomprehendingly. It was obvious that his thoughts were miles away. At last he shrugged, as if to say that it had nothing to do with him. He went back into the house, leaving it up to Corso whether to shut the door, stay where he was, or leave the way he'd come.

Corso followed him through another door into a room off the corridor and vestibule. The shutters were closed so no light could enter, and the furniture had been pushed to the far end, leaving the black marble floor empty. Some of the glass bookcases were open. The room was lit by dozens of candles that had almost burned down. Wax was dripping everywhere: on the mantelpiece above the empty fireplace, on the floor, on the furniture and objects in the room. The candles gave off a tremulous, reddish light that danced at the least draft or movement. The room smelled like a church, or a crypt.

Still taking no notice of Corso, Borja stopped in the middle of the room. There, at his feet, a circle approximately three feet in diameter was marked out in chalk, containing a square divided into nine boxes. The circle was surrounded by Roman numerals and strange objects: a piece of string, a water clock, a rusty knife, a dragon-shaped silver bracelet, a gold ring, a metal brazier full of burning charcoal, a glass vial, a small mound of earth, a stone. But Corso winced when he saw the other things strewn on the floor. Many of the books he'd admired, books lined up on shelves a few days earlier, now lay ruined, dirty, with pages torn out. The pages were covered with drawings and underlinings and full of strange marks. Candles burned on top of several of the books, and thick drops of wax dripped onto their covers or open pages. Some candles, guttering, had signed the paper. Among this wreckage Corso recognized the engravings from the copies of *The Nine Doors* belonging to Victor Fargas and Baroness Ungern. They were mixed up with the others on the floor and also covered with wax drips and mysterious annotations.

He bent to look more closely at the remains, not quite able to believe the magnitude of the disaster. One engraving from *The Nine Doors*, number VI, the man hanging by his right foot instead of his left, had been half burned away by the flickering flame of a candle. Two copies of engraving VII, one with a white chessboard and the other with a black one, lay beside a 1512 *Theatrum diabolicum* torn from its binding. Another engraving, I, protruded from the pages of a *De magna imperfectaque opera* by Valerio Lorena, an extremely rare incunabulum that Borja had shown Corso not long ago, barely allowing him to touch it. It was now on the floor, battered and torn.

"Don't touch anything," he heard Varo Borja say. Borja was standing before the circle, leafing through his copy of *The Nine Doors*, engrossed. He seemed to see not the pages themselves but something beyond them, something inside the square and circle on the floor, or even farther away: in the depths of the earth.

Corso looked at him as if seeing him for the first time. He stood up slowly. As he did so, the flames around him flickered.

"It makes no difference if I touch anything," he said, gesturing at the books and papers that lay scattered over the floor. "After what you've done."

"You don't know anything, Corso. You think you do, but you

don't. You're ignorant and very stupid. The kind who believes chaos is random and ignores the existence of a hidden order."

"Don't talk rubbish. You've destroyed everything, and you had no right to. Nobody has."

"You're wrong. In the first place they're *my* books. And what's more important, their purpose is to be used. They had practical rather than artistic or aesthetic value. As one travels along the path, one must make sure that no one else can follow. These books have now served their purpose."

"Madman. You deceived me from the start."

Borja didn't seem to be listening. He stood motionless, holding the remaining copy of *The Nine Doors,* scrutinizing engraving I.

"Deceived?" He kept his eyes fixed on the book as he spoke, which underlined his contempt for Corso. "You do yourself too much honor. I hired you without telling you my reasons or my intentions. A servant does not participate in the decisions of whoever is paying him. You were to steal the items I wanted and at the same time incur the technical consequences of certain unavoidable actions. I should imagine that as we speak, the police in both Portugal and France are closing in on you."

"What about you?"

"I'm far removed from all of that, and quite safe. In a little while nothing will matter."

Then, to Corso's horror, he tore the page with the engraving from *The Nine Doors.*

"What are you doing?"

Varo Borja was calmly tearing out more pages.

"I'm burning my boats, my bridges behind me. And moving into terra incognita." One by one, he tore the engravings from the book, until he had all nine. He looked at them closely. "It's a pity you can't follow me where I'm going. As the fourth engraving states, fate is not the same for all."

"Where do you believe you're going?"

Borja dropped the mutilated book on the floor with the others. He was looking at the nine engravings and at the circle, checking strange correspondences between them.

"To meet someone" was his enigmatic answer. "To search for the stone that the Great Architect rejected, the philosopher's stone, the basis of the philosophical work. The stone of power. The devil likes metamorphoses, Corso. From Faust's black dog to the false angel of light who tried to break down Saint Anthony's resistance. But most of all, stupidity bores him, and he hates monotony. . . . If I had the time and inclination, I'd invite you to take a look at some of the books at your feet. Several of them mention an ancient tradition: the advent of the Antichrist will occur in the Iberian peninsula, in a city with three superimposed cultures, on the banks of a river as deep as an ax cut, the Tagus."

"Is that what you're trying to do?"

"It's what I'm about to achieve. Brother Torchia showed me the way: *Tenebris Lux.*"

He was bending over the circle on the floor, laying some of the engravings on it and removing others, which he threw away from him, crumpled or torn. The candles illuminated his face from below, making him look ghostly, with deep shadows for eyes.

"I hope it all fits together," he muttered. His mouth was a line of shadow. "The ancient masters of the black art who taught the printer Torchia the most terrible and valuable mysteries knew the path leading to the kingdom of night. 'It is the animal with its tail in its mouth that encircles the place.' Do you understand? The *ourobouros* of the Greek alchemists: the serpent on the frontispiece, the magic circle, the source of wisdom. The circle in which everything is written."

"I want my money."

"Have you never been curious about these things?" Borja went on, not hearing, peering out from shadowed eyes. "To investigate, for instance, the devil-serpent-dragon constant which has reappeared suspiciously in all the texts on the subject since antiquity."

He picked up a glass object next to the circle, a goblet with handles in the shape of two linked serpents, and he raised it to his mouth and took a few sips. It held a dark liquid, Corso noticed, almost black, like very strong tea.

"Serpens aut draco qui caudam devoravit." Varo Borja smiled into empty space, wiping his mouth. The drink left a dark smear on the back of his hand and his left cheek. "They guard the treasures: the tree of knowledge in the Garden of Eden, the apples of the Hesperides, the golden fleece..." As he talked, he looked absent, insane, a man describing a dream from the inside. "They're the serpents or dragons that the ancient Egyptians painted in a circle, with their tail in their mouth to indicate that they came from a single thing and were self-sufficient. Sleepless guardians, proud and wise. Hermetic dragons that kill the unworthy and allow themselves to be seduced only by one who has fought according to the rules. Guardians of the lost word: the magic formula that opens eyes and makes one the equal of God."

Corso stuck out his jaw. He was standing, still and thin in his coat. The shadows of the candles danced between his half-closed eyelids and made his unshaven cheeks look sunken. He had his hands in his pockets, one touching the pack with its remaining cigarette, the other around the closed switchblade, next to his flask of gin.

"I said, give me my money. I want to get out of here."

There was a threat in his voice, but Corso couldn't tell if Borja had heard it. He saw him come to unwillingly, slowly.

"Money?" Borja regarded him with renewed contempt. "What are you talking about, Corso? Don't you understand what's about to happen? You have before you the mystery that men throughout the centuries have dreamed of. Do you know how many have been burned, tortured, and torn to pieces just for a glimpse of what you are about to witness? You can't come with me, of course. You will just stay still and watch. But even the most vile mercenary can share in his master's triumph."

"Pay me. Then you can go to the devil."

Borja didn't even look at him. He was moving around the circle and touching some of the objects that had been laid next to the numbers.

"How appropriate that you should send me to the devil. So typical of your down-to-earth style. I'd even honor you with a smile if I wasn't so busy. Although your remark was ignorant and imprecise: it will be the devil who comes to me." He paused and turned his head, as if he could already hear distant footsteps. "And I feel him coming."

He muttered, his speech interspersed with strange guttural exclamations, or with words that at times seemed addressed to Corso and at times to a third dark presence near them, in the shadows.

" 'You will go through eight doors before the dragon. . . .' Do you see? Eight doors come before the beast who guards the word, number nine, possessing the final secret. . . . The dragon sleeps with its eye open, and it is the Mirror of Knowledge. Eight engravings plus one. Or one plus eight. Which coincides with the number that Saint John of Patmos attributed to the Beast: 666."

Corso saw him kneel and write out numbers in chalk on the marble floor:

$$666$$
$$6 + 6 + 6 = 18$$
$$1-8$$
$$1 + 8 = 9$$

Then Borja stood, triumphant. For a moment the candles lit up his eyes. He must have swallowed some kind of drug with the dark liquid. His pupils were so dilated that almost none of the iris was visible, and the whites had taken on a reddish tinge from the light in the room.

"Nine engravings, or nine doors." Shadow once again covered his face like a mask. "They can't be opened by just anyone.... 'Each door has two keys.' Each engraving provides a number, a magic element, and a key word, if it's all studied in the light of reason, the cabbala, the occult, the true philosophy.... Of Latin and its combination with Greek and Hebrew." He showed Corso a piece of paper covered with signs and strange links. "You can take a look, if you like. You'll never understand it."

Aleph	Eis	I	ONMA	Air
Beth	Duo	II	CIS	Earth
Gimel	Treis	III	EM	Water
Daleth	Tessares	IIII	EM	Gold
He	Pente	V	OEXE	String
Vau	Es	VI	CIS	Silver
Zayin	Epta	VII	CIS	Stone
Cheth	Octo	VIII	EM	Iron
Teth	Ennea	VIIII	ODED	Fire

There were beads of sweat on his forehead and around his mouth, as if the flame of the candles were also burning inside his body. He began to walk around the circle slowly and carefully. He stopped a couple of times and bent over to adjust the position of an object: the rusty knife, the silver bracelet.

"You will place the elements on the serpent's skin," he recited without looking at Corso. He was following the circle with his finger but not quite touching it. "The nine elements are to be placed around it 'in the direction of the rising sun': from right to left."

Corso took a step toward him. "Once more. Give me my money."

Borja took no notice. He had his back to Corso and was pointing at the square drawn inside the circle.

" 'The serpent will swallow the seal of Saturn. . . .' The seal of Saturn is the most ancient and simple of the magic squares: the first nine numbers placed inside nine boxes, set out so that each row, whether down, across, or diagonally, adds up to the same number."

He bent and wrote nine numbers inside the box in chalk:

4	9	2
3	5	7
8	1	6

Corso took another step. As he did so he trod on a piece of paper covered with numbers:

$$4+9+2=15 \qquad 4+3+8=15 \qquad 4+5+6=15$$
$$3+5+7=15 \qquad 9+5+1=15 \qquad 2+5+8=15$$
$$8+1+6=15 \qquad 2+7+6=15$$

A candle went out with a hiss, having burned down on the charred frontispiece of *De occulta philosophia* by Cornelius Agripa. Borja's attention was still on the circle and the square. He stared at them intently, his arms folded on his chest, his head bowed. He looked like a player before a strange board, pondering his next move.

"There's one thing," he said, now no longer addressing Corso but talking to himself. Hearing his own voice apparently helped him to think. "Something that the ancients didn't foresee, at least not expressly . . . Added together in any direction, from up to down, down to up, left to right, or right to left, you get fifteen. But applying the codes of the cabbalists, fifteen also becomes a one and a five, which, added together, make six. . . . Six surrounds each side of the magical square with the serpent, the dragon, or the Beast, whatever you want to call it."

Corso didn't have to work it out for himself. It was on another piece of paper on the floor:

```
        6    6    6
   6  | 4 | 9 | 2 |  6
      |---|---|---|
   6  | 3 | 5 | 7 |  6
      |---|---|---|
   6  | 8 | 1 | 6 |  6
        6    6    6
```

Borja knelt before the circle, his head bowed. The sweat on his face gleamed in the candlelight. He was holding another piece of paper and reading out the strange words written on it.

" 'You will open the seal nine times,' says Torchia's text. That means the key words obtained must be placed in the box that corresponds to its number. In that way we get the following sequence."

1	2	3	4	5	6	7	8	9
ONMAD	CIS	EM	EM	OEXE	CIS	CIS	EM	ODED

"Written on the serpent, or the dragon." He rubbed out the numbers in the boxes and inserted the corresponding words in their place. "This is how it looks, to God's shame."

EM	ODED	CIS
EM	OEXE	CIS
EM	ONMAD	CIS

"It has all been carried out," muttered Borja as he wrote the final letters. His hand was trembling, and a drop of sweat slid from his forehead down his nose and onto the chalk-covered floor. "According to Torchia's text, it is sufficient for 'the mirror to reflect the path' to pronounce the lost word that brings light from the darkness.... These phrases are in Latin. They mean nothing on their own. But inside they contain the exact essence of the *Verbum dimissum,* the formula that makes Satan, our forebear, our mirror, and our accomplice, appear."

He was kneeling in the center of the circle now, surrounded by all the signs, objects, and words written in the square. His hands were shaking so violently that he clasped them together, clawlike, his fingers covered with chalk, ink, and wax. Proud and sure of himself, he started to laugh under his breath, a mad chuckle. But Corso was sure Borja wasn't insane. He looked around, aware that he was running out of time, and started to cross the distance between him and the book dealer. But he couldn't make up his mind to cross the line and stand with him inside the circle.

Borja looked at him malevolently, guessing his fear.

"Come, Corso. Don't you want to read it with me? Are you scared, or have you forgotten your Latin?" Light and shadow alternated with increasing speed on his face, as if the room were starting to spin. But the room was still. "Don't you want to know what these words contain? On the back of that engraving that pokes from between the pages of the Valerio

Lorena you'll find the translation in Spanish. Place them before the mirror, as the masters of the art ordered. At least then you will know what Fargas and Baroness Ungern died for."

Corso looked at the book, an incunabulum with a very old and worn parchment binding. Then he bent over cautiously, as if the pages contained a dangerous trap, and pulled out the engraving from between them. It was engraving I of book number three, Baroness Ungern's copy, with three towers instead of four. On the reverse Varo Borja had written nine words:

OGERTNE	EM	ISA
OREBIL	EM	ISA
OREDNOC	EM	ISA

"Courage, Corso," said the book dealer, his voice sour and disagreeable. "You have nothing to lose. . . . Hold the words to the mirror."

There was, indeed, a mirror close at hand on the floor, amid the melted wax from the guttering candles. It was silver, old, and stained, with a baroque worked handle. It lay faceup, and Corso's image appeared in it, tiny and distorted, as if at the end of a long tunnel of trembling red light. The image and its double, the hero and his infinite weariness, Bonaparte chained in agony to his rock on Saint Helena. Nothing to lose, Borja had said. A cold, desolate world, where the solitary skeletons of Waterloo grenadiers stood guard along dark, forgotten paths. He saw himself before the final door, holding the key like the hermit in engraving II, the letter Teth coiled around his shoulder like a serpent.

He stepped on the mirror and crushed it with his heel, slowly, without violence. The mirror shattered with a cracking sound. The fragments now multiplied Corso's image in countless tunnels of shadow at the end of which countless replicas of himself stood motionless, too small and indistinct to concern him.

"Black is the school of the night," he heard Borja say. Borja was still kneeling at the center of the circle, his back to Corso, leaving him to his fate. Corso leaned over one of the candles and held a corner of engraving I, with the nine inverted words on the reverse, to the flame. He watched the castle towers, the horse, the horseman turned to the viewer advising silence, burn between his fingers. At last he dropped what was left of it, which turned to ash a second later and floated on the hot air of the candles lit around the room. Then he entered the circle and moved toward Borja.

"I want my money. Now."

Lost ever deeper in darkness, Borja took no notice. Anxiously, as if the position of the objects on the floor suddenly appeared incorrect, he crouched and altered the position of some of them. After a brief hesitation, he began intoning a sinister prayer:

"Admai, Aday, Eloy, Agla . . ."

Corso grabbed him by the shoulder and shook him. Borja showed no emotion or fear. Nor did he try to defend himself. He continued to recite, as if he was in a trance, a martyr praying unaware of the roar of the lions or the executioner's sword.

"For the last time. Give me my money."

It was no good. All Corso saw before him were Borja's empty eyes looking through him, wells of darkness, blank, intent on the chasms of the kingdom of shadows.

"Zatel, Gebel, Elimi . . ."

He was summoning devils, Corso realized in disbelief. Standing inside the circle, aware of nothing, aware of neither Corso's presence nor his threats, the man was invoking devils by their first names.

"Gamael, Bilet . . ."

Borja stopped only when Corso struck him for the first time, a blow with the back of the hand that knocked his head to one side. His eyes rolled and then fixed on a point in space.

"Zaquel, Astarot . . ."

By the time Borja received the second blow, blood was already trickling from a corner of his mouth. With revulsion Corso pulled his hand away, stained with red. He'd felt he was striking something damp, viscous. He took a couple of breaths and counted ten beats of his heart before clenching his teeth, then his fists, and striking again. Blood now flowed from the book dealer's twisted mouth. He was still muttering his prayer, a disturbing, delirious smile of absurd joy on his swollen lips. Corso grabbed him by his collar and dragged him brutally outside the circle before hitting him again. Only then did Borja cry out like an animal, in pain and anguish, struggling free with unexpected energy and dragging himself back into the circle. Corso pushed him from it three times, and three times Borja returned to it, obstinately. By then blood was smeared all over the signs and letters written on the seal of Saturn.

"Sic dedo me . . ."

Something was wrong. In the trembling candlelight, Corso saw him hesitate, perplexed, and check the arrangement of the objects in the magic circle. The last few drops were draining from the water clock. Borja had little time left. He repeated his last words with greater emphasis, touching three of the nine boxes:

"Sic dedo me . . ."

An acrid taste in his mouth, Corso looked around hopelessly, wiping his bloodstained hands on his coat. Yet more candles had burned down and went out with a hiss. Spirals of smoke rose from their charred wicks in the reddish gloom. Like serpents, he thought bitterly. He went to the desk that had been pushed into a corner with the rest of the furniture, and searched through the drawers. There was no money. Not even a checkbook. Nothing.

"Sic exeo me . . ."

The book dealer continued to intone his litany. Corso glanced at him, at the magic circle one last time. Kneeling within it, bowing his distorted, fervent face toward the floor,

Varo Borja was opening the last of the nine doors with a smile of insane joy; his bleeding mouth, a black, demonic line across his face, like a cut from a knife made of night and shadow.

"Son of a bitch," said Corso. And with that he took his contract to be terminated.

HE MADE FOR THE gray light at the foot of the steps, beneath the arch leading to the courtyard. There, by the well and the marble lions, before the gate that led to the street, he stopped and breathed deeply, savoring the fresh, clean morning air. He searched in his coat for the crumpled pack with one remaining cigarette. He put it in his mouth but didn't light it. He stood there a moment while the first ray of the sun, which he'd left behind on entering the city, reached him, red and slanting. It slipped between the gray stone facades of the square, projecting the shadow of the wrought-iron gate on his face, and making him half-close his sleepless, weary eyes. Then the light grew, spreading slowly to fill the entire patio. The Venetian lions bowed their marble manes as if receiving a caress. The same glow, first red, then luminous as a suspension of gold dust, enveloped Corso. And at that instant, at the top of the stairs, beyond the last door of the kingdom of the shadows, where the calm light of dawn would never reach, there was a cry. A piercing, inhuman scream, full of horror and despair, in which he could barely recognize the voice of Varo Borja.

Not turning around, Corso pushed the gate and went out into the street. With each step he seemed to move a great distance away from what he was leaving behind, as if, in only a few seconds, he had retraced his steps on a journey that had taken him too long.

He stopped in the middle of the square, dazzled, enveloped in blinding sunlight. The girl was still in the car, and Corso shivered with deep, selfish delight when he saw that she hadn't disappeared with the remnants of the night. She smiled tenderly, looking impossibly young and beautiful, with her hair cut short like a boy's, her tanned skin, her tranquil eyes fixed on him, waiting. And all the golden, perfect light reflected in the liquid green of her eyes—the light driving back the dark angles of the ancient city, the shadow of the bell towers, and the pointed arches of the square—seemed to radiate from her smile as Corso went to meet her. He looked down at the ground as he walked, resigned, ready to bid his own shadow farewell. But there was no shadow at his feet.

Behind him, in the house guarded by four gargoyles beneath the eaves, Borja was no longer screaming. Or perhaps he was screaming from a dark place too far away to be heard from the street. *Nunc scio:* now I know. Corso wondered if the Ceniza brothers had used resin or wood to forge the illustration, lost through the whim of a child or the barbarity of a collector, in book number one. Although, as he thought of their pale, skilled hands, he inclined to think that they had carved it in wood, basing it on Mateu's *Bibliography.* That's why things didn't tally for Varo Borja: in the three copies, the final engraving was a forgery. *Ceniza sculpsit.* For love of their art.

He was laughing under his breath, like a cruel wolf, as he leaned over to light his last cigarette. Books play that kind of trick, he thought. And everyone gets the devil he deserves.

THE INFORMATION
by Martin Amis

Fame, envy, lust, violence, intrigues literary and criminal—they're all here in this deliriously entertaining, blackly hilarious novel, in which a failed writer, Richard Tull, is out to mess up his overly successful friend, Gwyn Barry.

"Satirical and tender, funny and disturbing . . . wonderful."
—Michiko Kakutani, *The New York Times*

Fiction/Literature/0-679-73573-9

POSSESSION
by A. S. Byatt

An exhilarating novel of wit and romance, at once an intellectual mystery and a triumphant love story, *Possession* is the tale of a pair of young scholars, who, through a treasure trove of letters, journals, and poems, trace the mysterious lives of two Victorian poets.

"Gorgeously written . . . dazzling . . . a tour de force."
—*The New York Times Book Review*

Winner of the Booker Prize

Fiction/Literature/0-679-73590-9

THE FIRST MAN
by Albert Camus

A moving journey through the lost landscape of youth that also discloses the wellsprings of Camus's aesthetic powers and moral vision, *The First Man* is the brilliant consummation of the life and work of one of the twentieth century's greatest novelists, published more than thirty years after his death.

"A masterpiece. . . . One of the most extraordinary evocations of childhood that exists in any language." —*Boston Globe*

Winner of the Nobel Prize

Fiction/Literature/0-679-76816-5

THE UNCONSOLED
by Kazuo Ishiguro

The Unconsoled is at once a gripping psychological mystery, a wicked satire of the cult of art, and a poignant character study of a man whose public life has accelerated beyond control, by the author of *The Remains of the Day*.

"Ishiguro is an original and remarkable genius. . . . *The Unconsoled* is a work of art."
—*The New York Times Book Review*
Fiction/Literature/0-679-73587-9

THE CROSSING
by Cormac McCarthy

A novel with the unstoppable momentum of a classic Western and the elegiac power of a lost American myth, *The Crossing* is luminous and appalling, a book that touches, stops, and starts the heart and mind at once.

"A miracle in prose, an American original."
—*The New York Times Book Review*
Fiction/Literature/0-679-76084-9

THE ENGLISH PATIENT
by Michael Ondaatje

During the final moments of World War II, four damaged people come together in a deserted Italian villa. As their stories unfold, a complex tapestry of image and emotion is woven, leaving them inextricably connected by the brutal circumstances of war.

"A rare and spellbinding web of dreams." —*Time*

Winner of the Booker Prize
Fiction/Literature/0-679-74520-3